PULLING

STRINGS

By

Nick DeWolf

Also by Nick DeWolf:

Frightfully Ever After

Find More At:

www.facebook.com/NickDeWolfAuthor
www.twitter.com/Nick_DeWolf

For Mollie
Who said it was good
But could be better

I hope it is.

CHAPTER ONE

AUSTIN, TEXAS

Two days ago, in Austin, Texas, workers went into a factory but didn't come out. The morning shift never left. The afternoon shift went in and didn't leave. When family members called the corporate offices, frantically looking for their loved ones, corporate buzzed the managers. Then the factory floor. They even tried the break room.

No answer.

Eventually, a regional VP humped his butt to the factory. A crowd had gathered. Those witnesses said he didn't storm over, but meandered, looking back over and over. They said he got halfway there, then froze. He staggered, then crept to the door, opened it, called inside, and went in.

A minute later, the screaming started.

The witnesses said it sounded like a 'stuck pig'. They said it wasn't human.

But it was.

Colt didn't need to read the briefing to know the police rolled in, lights flashing, tires squealing. She knew they probably treated this like any normal situation.

This was anything but.

This situation needed something more than cops, something more than covert ops, even. To know what was going on, you had to be special.

You had to be psychic.

So, any cop who rushed the door ended up lying on the ground in front of the factory, paralyzed. After the third wave of deputies went down, the sheriff realized what happened to anyone who got within twenty yards of the front door. They shivered. Their stomachs churned. They couldn't breathe. They felt things crawling on their skin; or a hot breath on the back of their neck; or fangs scraping the edges of their ears.

And the ones who kept going?

Standing in the corporate building on the other side of the parking lot, Colt scanned with her binoculars. Her circular view swung up through the crowd, across the yellow tape marking the edge of the psychic barrier, and to the few bodies still lying on the hot asphalt. She peered at a female officer who was face down, limbs twisted like a dead roach's spindly legs. Outside the police tape, firefighters had managed to get a lasso around the woman's foot. They'd been at it for hours, but there were still people left to fish out.

1

Synaptic overload. Basic psychic attack anyone with enough mental abilities can use. Undefended, it's like getting slammed on the back of the head.

Though, Colt had never seen it applied this way.

The briefing she'd received in transit said that, after the victims were pulled from the barrier, they regained consciousness. That was par for the course. Unfortunately, no one could get anything coherent from them. Some babbled, some cried, and a few just screamed and screamed until they were sedated.

Colt didn't like that. The barrier size alone was impressive, but even worse was how the people affected stayed affected after being pulled out.

She moved the binoculars. A drop of sweat slipped toward her lips. She blew it away. She'd been surveying the situation for the last twenty minutes, yet her arms felt heavy. She used to stand like that for hours and not feel a thing. Her whole body felt off. She told herself it was the plane ride. Sitting that long was why her legs and back were sore.

She rolled her well-sculpted shoulders forward, then back. Everything seemed sluggish. It felt like she'd spent five hours killing herself at the gym yesterday, but she hadn't. Goddamn if she didn't feel like she was getting—

She let go of the binoculars and ran a hand over her head. Her hair had gone from neatly tied to full-on crazy cat lady. Wasn't Texas supposed to be a dry heat? Goddamn humidity. Goddamn headquarters assigning her this detail. When this crap was over, she was going to fly back, walk into the Department of Scientific Investigation, find the highest ranking official she could, and give that suit-wearing bastard a synaptic overload of his own.

She sighed.

Goddamn getting older.

There was a thump in the chair next to her. "Orders, ma'am?"

She caught the tiniest trace of an accent, Mexican or South American. It didn't cover up that he wasn't asking out of politeness; the room was charged with anxiety. Field agents, strapped head to toe in gear, were milling about, finding things to keep themselves busy while they awaited orders. The Department of Scientific Investigation—also known as the DSI—was the government's cover agency for their psychic agent program.

Colt saw that, so far, the field agents were disappointed. They'd expected some tough-ass, ornery guy with a voice like poured gravel to come in, rip off the factory door with his psychic powers, and follow up with a huge, near-unbelievable showdown with whomever was the source of that barrier.

What they got was an athletic woman in her late-forties, wearing a button-down shirt, field pants, and lazily polished boots. She looked like she could use a nap, or a coffee, or first one and then the other. But the worst

2

part was she had done a lot of looking out windows and absolutely zero ripping doors off of hinges with her psychic powers.

Curious about the mental temperature of the room, Colt opened herself, lowering her psychic defenses to grasp errant thoughts drifting across the tops of people's minds. Mostly, people beginning to doubt the stories they'd been told about the great Special Agent Rebecca Colt.

But there was another emotion bouncing around which concerned her—eagerness. Quite a few of these young pups seemed to think this was a good opportunity to make a name for themselves.

"Ma'am," said the man in the chair.

She didn't like someone nipping at her heels. Go chase down your dinner somewhere else, Sparky.

She kept her eyes on the window. "Do you have any new intel for me?"

Sparky shifted in his seat. "No, ma'am."

"Then why would I have any orders for you?"

Emotions come off people in waves. Anger, frustration, joy and excitement, base and simple emotions are big waves. They wash over psychics and can overwhelm them. She'd expected that just now, but instead, she felt an uncomfortable creeping sensation in the muscles around her stomach.

Sparky was staring at the space between his boots. All she could see of him was a thick mop of inky hair. Complex emotions don't come in waves. They're more subtle and harder to read. But Colt knew how to tell the difference; guilt, fear, confliction.   He felt deflated.

Colt sighed.

"Barrier's still up," she said softly. "It's huge, bigger than anything I've seen."

Sparky looked up. His back straightened. "So whoever's making it?"

"Strong." Colt's eyes narrowed. "Enough that going in blind won't do me or anyone else any good."

"I have a team outside talking to the locals."

So, Sparky's got some authority? Maybe he wasn't so much an eager pup as much as a loyal one.

"Good." Colt raised the binoculars. "Keep them out of that barrier. They get anything useful, report it back to me." She untucked her shirt and a brief respite of cool air slipped across her stomach. "Then we'll make a plan for moving in. For now, it's sit and wait, soldier."

She expected a "yes ma'am," but Sparky was silent. When she glanced over, he was focused on her exposed stomach. She frowned.

"See something you like?"

"That's a nasty scar," he said, matter of fact, referring to the jagged, twisted, pale strip of flesh that started above her belly button and disappeared into her waistband.

Colt returned to the binoculars.

"Mission?" Sparky said.

"Yeah." She said softly. "You could say that."

Sparky's radio chirped and cut off his next question. He jumped to his feet. Colt noticed that, for his height, he moved with grace; more track and field than football.

"Go ahead," he said into the mic on his shoulder as he shuffled between the other field agents.

Colt tossed the binoculars onto a nearby table. Her hips shimmied as she pulled up the waist of her pants. She tugged her shirt down. Her breath came out through tight lips.

Calm down. Calm down, she thought.

She was used to guys staring at her; they're rude. But Sparky's comment had caught her off guard. The summer heat had already brought up dark memories. Mentioning the scar just made things closer in her mind.

The mission, she needed to focus on the mission.

Goddamn you, Dad.

"Agent Colt?" Sparky marched toward her. "We finished cross referencing all the vehicles in the parking lot against the employees in the factory and the offices."

"And?"

He nodded quickly. "There's an extra car."

The parking lot was God's cast iron skillet. There was no breeze, just waves and waves of heat rolling up Colt's body. It helped with the stiffness she'd been feeling, but it sapped her strength.

And it was slowly becoming obvious she didn't have the energy she used to.

Cutting behind the crowd, she tried to blink the Texas sun out of her eyes. Memories of her years in the desert with her father tickled at the edges of her mind.

Stop it. Now wasn't the time for a trip down post-traumatic-stress-disorder lane.

During their walk across the lot, Sparky talked, but Colt didn't hear a word. She just wanted to see the car. "Where is it?"

He pointed to the farthest corner of the parking lot.

"What's the name again?"

Sparky took a deep breath. "Samuel Bentley. 35 years old, married, two kids, high school graduate, been working at the plant for just under five years."

"Was he here to work?"

"No."

"Why not?"

"He'd been suspended."

Crap.

"Late for work. Lots of sick days."

Double crap.

"Trouble on the floor. Apparently he'd been drinking."

Crap, crappity-crap.

Sparky pointed with his chin. "That one."

Colt stopped dead.

Ford station wagon, fake wood paneling, tan paint the color of sand; its headlights—huge and round and sparkling like disco balls—stared at her. It was her dad's car. She was sure of it.

Unconsciously, her fingers drifted down, nails digging in around her scar.

Sparky yanked the passenger door open. He pulled back, raising one hand. Colt leaped back. The air hummed with telekinetic energy.

Sparky waved his hands in front of his face.

It was heat, trapped heat in the car. Just hot air.

Jesus, she needed to get a grip. What the hell was wrong with her?

Sparky looked away and tried to catch his breath. Colt snapped her eyes shut. Her molars clenched. She reined in the wild psychic energy that had poured from her, pulled it across her body, and walled herself off from the rest of the world. To anyone on the outside, it looked as though a sheet of hot air spun around her, then vanished. But inside, she dove into her own mind, just like the more experienced psychics had taught her when she'd started at the DSI. Her mind became a series of hallways, of passages and rooms. Systematically, she swept through the space, slamming certain doors and locking them tight. It wouldn't keep the contents of those rooms contained forever, but it would help for a while.

Good. Now open your eyes.

It wasn't her father's station wagon. That had been a '59. This was probably an early '70s model. The exterior was similar, but she peeked through the windshield and found the inside was different, too. Not modern by any means, but an upgrade from her father's. Opening the door, she found the bench seats weren't the cheap, scratchy cloth she remembered, but instead smooth, shining vinyl. It looked like an improvement, until she sat down.

5

Apparently, vinyl could reach temperatures equivalent to the surface of the sun. Colt hissed as she put her hand on the seat. The shock helped pull her back completely into the moment. For most, pain was something to be feared and avoided. But psychics knew better. Pain reminded you what's happening right then and there.

"It's a mess." Sparky bent down.

Colt replied with a grunt. Sparky dug through some papers in the well of the passenger seat. She already knew he couldn't find anything important, not like she could.

Breathing slowly, Colt raised her strong, rough hands to the steering wheel. Bentley's tense grip had worn grooves into it. Eyes closed, her fingers padded across them.

She may as well have stuck her hand in a light socket and pulled the chain.

Pain, fear, confusion, it leaped inside of her, along with Bentley's voice. Desperation.

What's happening? Panic. *What am I? Make it stop.* Thunder. *I can hear them.* Disorder. *I can't. Make it stop.* Anger. *I can work. The voices.* Inside. *It hurts. I hear them. I'm scared. Why?* Inside his head. *Why is this—What am I?* Terror. *I can't lose this job. What's wrong with me? Please. Oh god. I can't. I'm so scared.* Pounding. Pounding. *Make it go away. Help me.* Desperation. *Please, please, please.*

Someone help me!

She let go and everything Samuel Bentley had been for the last few weeks evaporated away.

Sparky grabbed the glove compartment latch. She already knew what was in there. But part of her hoped; if she were the praying type, now would have been the time.

Two bottles, one plastic and one glass, dropped to the car's floor with a hollow thunk.

All she could do was whisper, "Damn."

Sparky stared. "Whiskey?"

"Whisky and aspirin. Both empty. " She peered through the windshield to the factory buried in a psychic shell.

"Why aspirin?" he asked.

Colt swung her legs out of the car. "To help with the headaches."

"And the whiskey?"

Colt sighed and hoisted herself up. "Because the aspirin wasn't enough."

6

Something in the backseat caught her eye, an odd spot of pink and purple tucked down beneath the front seats. Her skin went cold.

Oh no. Oh god, no.

She dove into the backseat.

"Agent Colt?"

Colt pulled herself from the car and held up a floral patterned backpack, just the right size for a little girl.

CHAPTER TWO

"I'm going in." Colt unbuttoned her sleeve cuffs and rolled them up as she marched across the parking lot toward the barrier.

Just behind her, Sparky was checking his gear. "My unit can be ready in five."

"No."

"Agent Colt—"

"We don't have time!" She stopped and turned.

Sparky was staring, confused, his radio in his hand. Colt took a deep breath, then stepped toward him.

"This barrier, it's a defense mechanism. He's not able to control it, but he's not broken, not yet. He won't hurt her, not on purpose. But if your team busts in there, if you push him into a corner, he..." She looked Sparky in the eye. "He could do anything."

Sparky nodded and let go of his radio. Colt started again toward the factory. Sparky followed. Ahead of them, the rescue personnel moved aside, creating a pathway to the yellow tape sagging languid in the summer sun.

Right at the edge of the barrier, where people couldn't tread without their skin crawling, the DSI agents had set up a portable base camp. Just a few tables with a canvas pop-up cover over them. Colt grabbed a flashlight and clicked it on and off. She slipped it into a sleeve that her belt would loop through.

"I'll go in, find him, try to either reason with him or subdue him." She undid her belt and slipped the flashlight on. "If I can't, I'll take him down."

"I'll focus on getting civilians out."

"No need. Anyone inside is unconscious." She paused. "Or dead."

"Then I'm your backup."

Shaking her head, she grabbed a few other pouches and slipped them on. "That isn't a castle wall that needs to be scaled. It's a psychic manifestation of the chaos in Bentley's mind. It's his raw nerves, pushed out as far as they can go. Anyone who goes in there will end up like one of those stupid cops they're dragging out, or worse." She yanked her belt tight. "I don't have time for your machismo bullshit, alright, Sparky? Just stay here and—"

"Moreno."

Colt paused.

"Second Lieutenant Carlos Moreno, head of First Division Field Operations and team medical officer. Ranked first in my class for the DSI's psychic resistance training; trained field medic; five years mission experience; six years in the Marines; multiple deployments. And since I've taken charge, I haven't had one casualty in my squad. So stop thinking I'm just swinging my dick around."

There was no bravado in his words, no flash of damaged pride in his expression. He was all business right now.

Colt exhaled slowly. "See if those troopers have a shotgun with rubber slugs."

Moreno nodded. By the time he came back, Colt was ready. She waited for Moreno to finish giving the shotgun a thorough inspection. When he was done, she turned to the barrier and held out a hand.

A bed of stinging nettles pushed against her palm. Any normal person would have pulled back as though they'd touched something hot, but Colt knew better. She dropped her arm and focused. Around her, three or four inches from her body, a ripple of psychic energy zipped through the air, creating a visible shell that lasted for a second before vanishing.

She peeked back over her shoulder. The crowd of police who'd been watching stood gape jawed. Quite a few of them backed away. Moreno's eyes weren't big as dinner plates, but they'd do for a slice of cheesecake.

"Was that…"

"The wall," Colt said. Basic psychic protection. Anyone with controllable abilities could do it. And the stronger the psychic, the stronger the wall. With it in place, Colt extended her hand.

The nettles couldn't penetrate the psychic defense of her wall, though she felt them trying to work their way through. Taking a deep breath, she crept into the dead zone. Behind her, Moreno followed. Immediately, he sounded like he was having trouble breathing.

"Moreno?" she didn't turn back.

"I'm okay."

No he wasn't. His teeth were grinding. But Colt didn't stop or slow down. Moreno huffed, breathing Lamaze style, as they pressed on to the factory's front door.

Colt said, "Tell me about the girl."

"Elena Bentley, seven years old. We confirmed that the other daughter is with their mother."

As Colt had expected, talking, focusing on something else, was helping him.

"Mom said Elena is a real daddy's girl and that Bentley has a particular affinity for her. Up until recently, they were inseparable."

Outside, the sun beat down on the factory's egg white exterior. Behind the glass of the double doors, it was black as night. Moreno raised a key card to the lock, but Colt held up a fist. Psychic tendrils slithered forth from her wall. Stretching them beyond the door, she scanned for any type of consciousness.

9

Exhaling like a weight lifter after a set of curls, the tendrils snapped back. She gave the go ahead. Moreno swiped the card. There was a loud click as the doors unlocked.

"Power's still on," Moreno said, somewhat surprised.

"Yup," Colt replied, not surprised in the least.

"So why's it dark in there?"

Colt's only response was the sound of the door swinging open.

The hallway was wide and long. On the right, a wall of glass separated out the break room. The left wall was offices, dark as the rest of the building and just as quiet.

At the end was another set of double doors, these ones thicker and heavier, designed to hold back the sounds of the factory floor.

A few steps in, something crunched beneath Moreno's boot. He pulled back, aiming his flashlight down and casting a white circle across the floor. Glass; tiny, thin, curved pieces of glass sparkled in the beam. Moreno's light drifted down the hallway, following the shards as they made a column that stretched from one end to the other. He tilted his head back and shined the beam on the ceiling. The metal casings for florescent bulbs were empty.

"Check the wall," Colt said into the darkness.

Moreno examined the glass wall that separated out the break room and found it was lined with razor thin cracks. There was no point of impact, though.

"Did Bentley do this?" Moreno wasn't breathing heavily anymore, either.

Colt was impressed at how well he'd adjusted. She walked along the column of broken bulbs to the end of the hall. "Something pushed him, his ability pushed back."

"He cracked?"

"No." She walked to the heavy doors. "He popped like a balloon."

"Any chance he's all out of air?"

In the dark, Colt smiled a little. She sent her tendrils into the next room—the main factory floor. Bentley's psychic nettles attacked and her tendrils slithered back, fingers away from a hot pan. Colt exhaled. Her shoulders slumped, sweat ran down the chasm of her spine. She was already getting tired, but they were also getting close. The nettles were the only thing on the other side of the door, so with her nod, Moreno swiped the keycard and Colt pushed down the handle.

The door swung out fast and hard; something heavy was pushing from the other side. Colt scrambled back. An arm fell across her shoulder. Her eyes went wide.

She'd checked. She'd checked the room and hadn't felt anybody. What the hell was going on? Counter agent? Bentley hiding himself psychically?

A big man dropped his head against her chest, and Colt snatched as much fabric as she could on his chest. Twisting her hips, pumping with her legs, she used the man's tremendous weight to flip him over her shoulder and down to the ground. He hit with a flop. She pulled her hand back, balled it into a fist, and she prepared to strike when he tried to get back up.

But he didn't. He just laid there, face down to the floor.

Even though Colt knew he was dead, knew that he was just a body and she'd seen dozens of bodies, the shock and adrenaline surged through her veins.

First of all, most bodies didn't fall down on top of her. Second, how in the hell did that happen?

Crouching, she looked closer. The man's suit was wrinkled, and his skin had a chalky pallor. He'd been dead for hours. That made her feel better about being caught off guard, at least. But it didn't make her any less anxious about what was going on. Gently, she rolled him over.

"Jesus," whispered Moreno.

She couldn't blame him; he'd probably seen some action, some injuries in his time. But examining the man on the floor—Colt suspected it was the regional VP, Mr. Squealing Pig himself—she knew Moreno had never seen anything like him.

His face was warped, elongated by a jaw that was stretched to its utmost extent. His eyes were still glazed with madness and fear. Every vein and tendon in his neck stood out. He was frozen in a silent scream.

The tips of his fingers were a bloody mess. Colt examined one of his meaty paws and found the fingernails were missing.

She nudged the door open. In the dull glow from the factory floor's high windows, she saw lines like tar shadows on the inside of the door.

"He tried to claw his way out," she said softly, half to Moreno, half to herself.

"Why didn't he just open the door?" Moreno's voice was getting shaky again.

Colt risked a quick peek. His eyes were darting around, but he wasn't shivering, wasn't twitching. He was still keeping it together.

For now.

Her mind drifted to the residual anxiety and fear she'd felt in Bentley's car. The whiskey to settle his nerves. The barrier. The cops who had pushed through and passed out, waking up only to be sedated for their own good. And now the VP. There was a theme, and Moreno was getting caught up in it.

"Agent Colt?" Moreno didn't mean for a little droplet of spit to fly out, but it did. "Why didn't he open the door?"

"Because he couldn't," she said flatly, emotionlessly. She hoped Moreno would take a hint and calm down. "He was scared to death." Slowly, she stood and stepped over the body. Moreno, glancing one last time at the VP, followed.

The air drifting in from the factory smelled of machine oil and welded steel. There was a chemical odor, paint and sealant and industrial cleaning supplies. But over it all, Colt detected something else; a sweet and sickly scent, like ham gone bad.

Decomposition.

They stepped through the doorway. The factory floor spanned the width and height of the building. Machines and conveyer belts filled the space. The ceiling was a geometric spider web of exposed girders where huge lamps hung every fifteen feet or so. Just like the hallway, every bulb was blown. From the windows, so high up near the ceiling that their only real purpose was for ventilation, beams of light coursed in, casting sharp-cut shadows. At the back wall, a metal staircase ran up the wall. A walkway divided the building into two levels, and large offices made up the back.

But what really caught Colt's attention was the bodies.

Thirty, easily, were scattered throughout the huge space, draped over machines, dropped to the floor, curled up in corners. Pools of blood surrounded those with pieces of metal or plastic sticking from their throats, their mouths, their eyes. Others lay on the ground, arms and legs bent and twisted from the convulsions that killed them. But all of them, every single one, had screaming terror etched into their faces.

Colt heard Moreno's rapid breathing, the shotgun practically rattling in his hands as he approached from behind. Ebbing just enough energy from her wall, she built a psychic spike in case she had to knock him out. She knew he had to focus, use his training. She hoped he could push through.

His flashlight's beam panned across the room, moving up and down from one body to the next. She followed it, watching for a violent jerk in its motion. She wouldn't give him a second chance.

The white circle landed on a woman with a metal bar that pierced her throat and was coated with dried blood on both sides. Her hands still held one end, fingers woven into a tight death grip.

"H-h-h-how..." His voice was a breathy whisper, but at least it was a word and not a scream. "How... did Bentley... do this to... to them?"

Colt's spike was ready to fly at any second. "He didn't."

"They didn't do it to themselves!" He snapped.

Colt didn't reply. When Moreno figured out what she was—or wasn't—saying, his eyebrows crinkled.

"Wh-Why? Why would they do that?"

"For the same reason you're squeezing that gun so tight."

Moreno shut his mouth. His eyes, sharp and focused, jumped to her. "I'm not gonna kill myself."

Colt nodded. "Good, because I was just starting to like you."

He took a deep breath, blew it out through pursed lips, let go of the shotgun's trigger, and wiped the dripping sweat from his face. "Let's go," he said, again gripping the shotgun like a professional.

Colt started across the factory floor. Bentley wasn't here, and he wasn't in the front rooms, which meant he was in the back. The offices on the upper and lower level were dark. More hallways went back to another part of the building. She was going to need Moreno to help cover more ground.

"Keep talking," Moreno said as he shuffled along at the edge of her peripheral. "Tell me about what's going on."

"He's telaesthetic."

"There were over a hundred definitions of psychic abilities in the handbook."

There wasn't any movement in the offices to the left. "You remember empaths?"

"Yeah, they're a sensory type. Pick up and absorb the emotions of those around them."

"Telaesthetics are the opposite." Nothing in the offices to the right. Damn it. "They don't take in emotion, they put it out. Force it into others." The second floor was too dark to see anything. "These people weren't just afraid; Bentley's ability made their fears manifest in their minds to the point where they seemed real."

"Like waking nightmares or something, right?"

"Is that what you're experiencing?"

"No." He stepped over a pair of crumpled legs attached to a body which had been run the wrong way through the gears of a large machine. "It's more just... I don't know. Fear? Paranoia."

"How bad?"

"Enough that, a minute ago, I seriously considered shooting you."

She smirked. "The only thing that would do is piss me off."

Moreno chuckled, which gave Colt some comfort. Somberness crept back into his voice. "So what about Elena? She doesn't have psychic abilities, or training. Do you think she's—"

"There's hope," Colt said. "He loves her, so he may have subconsciously shielded her. Also, when people are related, they have a harder time using psychic abilities like this on each other." She paused. "Unless they really want to."

13

At the back wall, there were only two routes—down the hallway or up the stairs. Looking up to the offices, Colt noticed that the windows weren't just cracked; they were completely blown out.

Ground zero.

Exhaling like a yoga master, she wrapped her tendrils with her wall and sent them creeping up.

Holy crap. Muscles all throughout her body twitched and squirmed. A lesser person would probably have lost bladder control.

"Agent Colt?"

Stupid. Stupid, stupid, stupid. She'd completely underestimated Bentley's abilities. No, that was a lie. She'd overestimated her own. At least now she knew Bentley was up there, but that didn't mean Elena was too. She could have been anywhere in the building, holed up somewhere, hiding.

Colt signaled for Moreno to search the lower level. He nodded and disappeared into the hallway. Colt started up the stairs. Ascending was like moving through water. Every bit of concentration went into sustaining her wall and pushing back the terror that Bentley's subconscious was pumping out. This meant Colt was stuck playing defense; firing a spike or using her telekinetic powers would drain her wall.

She stopped. Glancing down, she curled the fingers of her right hand. Slowly, carefully, she drew energy from her wall. In her open fingers, telekinetic energy built. A waver in the air, a mist took shape. It was a handle, and a rounded body, and a barrel. There was no detail, but it was clearly the shape of a revolver.

Bentley's power attacked and almost made it through. The shape in Colt's hand vanished, and her wall solidified again. She frowned.

One shot. She would get one shot before the terror turned her into just another one of the bodies.

At the top of the stairs, she heard it; a voice, mumbling from one of the nearby offices. It was too soft to distinguish any words, but the cadence told Colt that the person was repeating the same things over and over again. Colt stepped toward the sound.

Bentley cried out, wild and random. The psychic pressure increased. It was like being pulled down to the deep end of a pool too quickly—Colt's sinuses and ears ached. Bentley's cry ended as quickly as it had come, and the pressure eased. His mumbling returned. As Colt drew closer, she could make out some words.

"I'm sorry. I'm... I'll fix it. I'll fix it. I didn't, I didn't mean it. Didn't mean it, didn't mean it. I don't... please. Please. I can, I can do it. I can still work. I need... I need this. Please. I'm sorry, sir. I'll put it back. I'll put it back. I'm sorry. Just give me a chance. It'll be okay. It'll be good. I promise. Please. Please, please."

14

At the edge of the office doorway, Colt stopped and peeked in.

Bentley's white t-shirt was half untucked and yellowed with sweat. His jeans were dirty. He may have soiled himself at some point. The smell was awful. The rising psychic energies inside of him and the anxiety they'd created had eaten away at whatever man he'd been as of just a few months ago. He was skin and bones, his eyes sunken, skin jaundiced, and hair thick with grease.

His eyes were bloodshot, the thick, red lines spreading up from his caruncle—the pink tear duct in the corner of the eye—like branches of a dead bush. He had tracks on his face where thick tears had run down through the dirt.

The pain, the exhaustion, they were the first signs that a psychic was either overusing their powers, or their powers were overusing them. Bloodshot eyes were the next. It was the body telling the user to stop, to back off. After that came tremors, sweating. Bentley was there, probably had been for a while.

She didn't see the signs of extreme psychic strain, yet. The sclera—the whites of the eyes—filling with broken capillaries, broken blood vessels appearing around the eyes from the strain, and finally, cerebrospinal fluid leaking through the ears and eyes as the strain on the person's brain literally rips it to shreds.

Colt had pushed herself far before, enough that it took weeks for the bruising to fade, but she'd never gone all the way. Once you hit that point, there was no coming back. For Samuel Bentley, there might be hope of recovery. But she had to stop him first.

The office was trashed, papers and glass and scraps of ceiling tiles all over the floor. A door connected this office and the next. The frosted glass was broken into a thousand spider webs.

Bentley paced in front of the desk. Behind it, slumped in a chair, was the body of a man in a shirt and tie. He didn't have the mask of terror that others in the factory did, but his eyes were rolled back into his head. Colt suspected this was the manager who had told Bentley about being suspended. It must have pushed Bentley to the breaking point. When it happened, this man had been lucky enough to die almost instantly.

As Bentley continued mumbling, he shuffled back and forth, picking up one item from the desk while accidentally knocking down another. He didn't even notice Colt.

But someone else did.

Sitting on the floor, tucked back into a corner, Elena had brown hair and huge blue eyes that were sunken and scared. When she caught sight of Colt, panic and fear and hope all moved across her face at once. Before Colt

15

could raise a hand, Elena gasped and sat up. Bentley stopped mumbling, looked at Elena's face, and turned on Colt.

"Who are you?" his voice was dry and cracked.

Colt tried to speak, but Bentley's ability honed in on her. The nettles wrapped around her and squeezed. Her eyes closed, and she turned her head.

"Do you work here?"

The room started swirling. She couldn't respond.

"I didn't... I don't know what happened..."

Colt put everything she had into her wall.

"I was just here to... something bad happened and I don't—"

"Sam," It was more of a grunt than a word, but he seemed to understand her.

"How do you know my name?"

"I'm..."

"I didn't do anything." He didn't yell it, but he came close. "I didn't do anything."

Her brain was suffocating. How the hell was he so strong? "Sam, you need to calm—"

"It was an accident." His words came out between sharp breaths. "I didn't... it just... I'm, I'm—"

"Sam."

"Go away." He said it like a child begging for a parent to stop yelling at them. "I can fix this, I can make it better. You just, just please go away."

In the corner, Elena whimpered. The sound punched through Colt's mind and sparked anger.

"I'm not leaving," she said, her teeth clenched.

"Go away," Bentley said again. Now he was pushing, purposefully, on her. And that just pissed Colt off.

"Not without Elena."

Elena who was crying. Elena who was scared. Elena was just a little girl.

Just like Colt had been when her father had taken her away.

Bentley's face twisted in despair. "Go away!"

Elena slapped her hands over her ears while sobs wracked her chest. Fat tears rolled from her eyes and fell where so many had fallen before.

And for Colt, that was too much.

Her hand snapped up. Like mist caught inside a perfectly clear bottle, the handle, the cylinder, the barrel running the length of her extended index finger. Her gun.

She felt the rush, the swell of her psychic force at the tip of her finger.

Her finger that was covered in dripping blood.

16

She froze. Confused, she stared at the crimson streaks running down from knuckle to knuckle. There was so much of it. What—where had it come from? Then, something moved across her belly, something warm and wet. A stain was growing, a bloody stain, right over her scar.

No.

Only, it wasn't a scar.

It's Bentley. It's his power.

It was an open wound.

It's not real. It's not.

A fresh wound.

Doesn't matter if it feels real, have to fight it. Have to—

"Kiiiiiiiddoooooooooo…"

Her father's voice, his deep, ragged voice rumbled against the door between the offices. Goosebumps exploded across Colt's body. She heard his heavy, thumping boots as he stomped toward the door.

"Kiiiiddoooo…"

She stood, shivering, as his silhouette appeared in the shattered glass. It was him at the end—emaciated, skeletal, his hair unkempt and sticking out. Him after years of running, of madness, of thousands of hours and just as many miles escaping something that wasn't even there; dragging her along, filling her with lies and fears and nightmares that would haunt her for every waking minute of the rest of her life.

His flat hands slapped the glass, and he roared, "Kiddo!"

Then he was on her, knocking her to the ground. He weighed so much, but maybe it's because she was so small, so young, only a teenager. She fought as he lashed out, grabbed and snatched and groped. Bourbon leeched through his sweat glands. His hot breath rained spittle across her face. He squeezed her throat, her arms, her breasts. She felt his bowie knife's blade tracing her stomach. He slid it down, down, down, moving the blade lower and lower, closer to the scar, to the wound, to where he'd already stabbed her once and was going to do it again and again until he got it right and made sure she was completely dead.

She screamed. Her arms thrust forward, sending a telekinetic wave. There was a metallic crack, the weight on top of her flew back, and the room shook.

Colt scurried across the floor. She glanced around the room, searching for the ghost of her father. The blood on her hands and abdomen was gone. It was just a scar, as it had been for decades. Her psychic wall rippled and rolled around her over and over again, fighting off the last of Bentley's infecting madness.

.

Reality slammed against her. Bentley had pushed the file cabinet on top of her as he'd fled. Now, it sat imbedded in the wall, a dent the size of a basketball hammered into it. But they were gone.

Snarling, Colt rolled over and pushed herself up. Legs still shaking, she left the office. Bentley's stinging nettles were waning, which meant he was moving away.

But he wasn't far.

CHAPTER THREE

Walking through the factory's hallways, Moreno's mind kept turning back to his grandparents' old farmhouse. He remembered the bed they'd made him sleep in after his parents had been deported. God, he'd hated it; so hard it made his back ache and so cold that no amount of blankets—and they only ever gave him one—could warm him. There'd been that window, big and old with warped glass that sent the moon's light wavering across the walls. An old oak tree nearby loved reaching out and scratching the window as the wind whirled. He remembered the animals in the barn, how by day they seemed so cute and fluffy and harmless, but at night, he'd imagined they were searching, snuffling the ground to find his tender young body and make a meal out of it. Every floorboard in the house moaned and popped in the dark. Darkness had surrounded him.

And on top of it all, he always really, really had to pee.

He kicked another office door in. Empty and dark.

As dark as that bedroom.

"Yeah, yeah," he muttered to nobody but his own mind. "I got it, fear, fear, fear. Message received." With a grunt, he kicked in the next door, knowing there would be nothing behind it.

His nostrils flared. Agent Colt had sent him away from the target, and he'd let her. Hell, he'd been relieved. The only thing that could have made him happier was if she'd told him to leave the building entirely. He'd done tours in Afghanistan, ugly ones. His unit had come under fire constantly. There were weeks where it happened nearly every day. He'd been grazed and singed by bullets, was at the edge of an IED blast that had killed out one of his best friends. It had been scary as hell, but it didn't keep him up at night. Afghanistan didn't pull him from sleep with a gasp and a cold sweat; probably because no matter how scared he'd been, no matter how much adrenaline had blazed through his veins, he'd put it aside. He'd stayed on mission. He'd put fellow soldiers and civilians before himself. For better or worse, he'd acted like a professional, and that gave him peace.

But at the bottom of those stairs, he would have abandoned a little girl to save his own ass. And so the farmhouse rose in his mind again, and he knew he wasn't going to sleep well for quite some time.

From way down the hallway, where he'd left Agent Colt, he heard the echo of a scream. His feet almost took off without him. He'd seen a sign for stairs. He could come up from behind and flank the situation. He wouldn't run away again.

He reached for the handle to the stairwell door, then froze. Paralyzed, stuck halfway between breaths, a tremor started in his hand and worked up his arm. Behind the door, he heard claws and talons and teeth dripping with ropes of saliva moving toward him. He backed up against the wall so hard it hurt. He watched, unblinking, as the door opened and a thing, a thousand things, the things that had made those sounds outside the farmhouse came out. Arms and legs, hooves and horns, slobbering jaws. They'd found him. They'd followed him. They'd waited for years for his blood, and now they wanted him because they were hungry hungry hungry hungry hungry hungry hungry...

Colt sprinted down a hallway, and shotgun blasts echoed. She tried to stop short, but too many things were going wrong with her body. She staggered to a halt and listened. It wasn't one or two pops. Moreno was unloading.

Oh shit.

Mixing telekinesis into her wall, she took off like a drag racer, propelling herself with both muscles and mind. She blew by the dark offices as she zeroed in on the sound. She entered the stairwell that reeked of black powder. One floor down, Moreno was firing shot after shot through an open door.

"Moreno!"

The gun continued to thunder, so she put her hands over her ears and hurried down the stairs. She stopped before the halfway point, the landing, because rubber slugs hammered against the wall and ricocheted off the top steps. Moreno was firing wildly, aiming at things only he could see.

When the shotgun stopped and all she heard was Moreno pumping of the stock and pulling a useless trigger, she stepped onto the landing. Metal and plastic clattered. The shotgun lay on the floor, a wisp of blue smoke rising from the barrel. She headed for the dark doorway.

"Moreno?"

A bullet ripped into the doorway, inches from her head. She threw herself against the inside wall. Down the hall, Moreno screamed like a terrified child and kept firing. Bullets shredded the doorframe. Colt closed her fists and started building a psychic spike in her mind. The second his clip ran out, she'd leap into the hall and—

The nettles attacked. Colt cursed as the spike dissipated so her wall could solidify. The gunfire stopped; Moreno was out. Colt leaned into the hallway, her flashlight's beam landing on Moreno's sweat-glazed face. He was forty, maybe fifty yards away. If she could make physical contact, she could spike him directly.

Babbling, crying, and whining, Moreno dropped the spent clip and fumbled with a new one. Colt bolted from the doorway. Moreno got the clip into his gun and yanked back on the housing. Colt pressed forward. He looked up screamed at her. Even though she spoke Spanish, she couldn't make out his words.

The pistol roared. The hallway blazed with flashes of white light. Colt ducked and swerved. The sound was like ice picks driving through her eardrums.

Halfway there.

Moreno squeezed the trigger. A bullet whizzed past Colt's head. She pushed hard on tired legs, swinging to the other side of the hallway. Eyes glazed with tears, Moreno stepped backward and fired as fast as he could. Colt went low. The barrel followed.

She dashed across the hall. A bullet sliced through one of her sleeves, missing the skin but leaving a hot, stinging line. She pivoted hard, moving to come in high and put the spike right into his face.

Five more steps.

A bullet pierced the outside of her thigh. Everything stopped. Her momentum lurched. Gravity doubled. Her hot skin went cold, and all the other pain in her body seemed pale in comparison.

One more...

The muzzle came up. She looked past it and pushed with her good leg, throwing herself forward with eyes closed and arms outstretched.

Moreno fired. The pin landed with a loud click on an empty chamber.

Colt's hand slammed against Moreno's jaw. Like water filling cracks in broken pavement, the spike rushed into his head. Her face fell against his chest. Her hand stayed on his face, against his skin, as they fell together.

She landed on the bed in the old farmhouse. The smell of mothballs and line-dried sheets filled her nose. Outside, the wind kicked up and the tree's skeletal fingers tapped the window. Colt was curled up, her skinny child's legs pulled against her chest. The darkness was spilled ink, blanketing everything.

She didn't belong there, so she leaped from the bed, her bare feet cold against ancient, warped floorboards. She ran to the door and pulled it open.

Sunlight slapped her in the face. The yellow bus that sat in the middle of the desert road shined like an ancient golden temple. She tried to breathe, to gulp down the dry air, and yanked at the light cotton clothes that wrapped her teenage body. In front of her, a line of Latinos waited to load onto the deportation bus. A couple embraced. The woman was sobbing. They waved at Colt, and she waved back. Her parents were going away. They were going away and she was going to stay here.

They climbed into the bus. She ran toward them, crying, but the earth exploded into a cloud of dirt and debris. The air became a solid, slamming wave. She was spinning. She was down. She was up. Someone was screaming. What the hell? What happened? Oh fuck, oh shit. An IED. It was an IED. Oh God, was she hit? Was she hit? She had to get up. She had to see if she could move. They were coming. They always came in after an IED, and she had to find cover, had to get the rest of her unit and move them to safety.

22

She crawled. There was shooting, so much shooting. Dust everywhere. She couldn't see. Up ahead, somebody, a figure, a body on the ground. She inched toward them. They were reaching out, reaching for her. She kept crawling, moved up and took the hand and got herself over them and gazed down into the woman's beautiful face.

She was glistening with sweat, but her lips were still pink. Colt thought her love looked beautiful like that, lying there, her black hair spread out against the white pillows. Her eyes, those big eyes so brown they were almost black, were staring up, right into Colt's.

She smelled so good. Colt still tasted her. She looked happy enough, but Colt worried. Had it been good? Had her love really enjoyed it? What was Colt supposed to say? Maybe she wasn't supposed to say anything. Maybe they were supposed to stay there and look at each other forever. Maybe that's what love really was.

Her love closed her eyes. Colt closed her own and leaned in, her lips parting and touching her love's.

Colt came up. The cardiac monitor was flat lined and emitted a continuous tone. Nothing. Dammit. Dammit !Lacing her fingers, one hand over the other, she slapped her palms down on the man's chest and began pumping. All around her, nurses were scrambling, grabbing at wires and searching for needles and shouting at each other. Colt ignored them.

Breathe you bastard, breathe!

She barked commands in a voice far too deep to be her own. No one really paid attention or did what they were supposed to do. Too many people were in the medical tent. The attack had been bad. How the fuck had they been caught off guard like that? Whatever. The guy here wasn't even from her unit. She wasn't even technically a doctor, not yet. Still, she had to do something. So, bending down, she pinched the man's nose and blew into his mouth. Coming back up, she checked the monitor.

No change.

All right.

Spinning, she grabbed a syringe. Turning back, she spread her fingers over the man's chest, counting his ribs. She found the spot and used her teeth to pull the plastic cover off the fat needle. She raised it into the air, point down, and slammed the adrenaline injection straight into his heart.

Colt gasped. Her eyes popped open. Back arching, she pulled away from Moreno's chest, throwing herself to the side. Disoriented at first, the hot, stabbing pain in her left leg brought her back to reality. Grimacing, she reached down. There was blood, a lot of blood. Her pant leg was soaked through. If she didn't stop up the wound...

Cold sweat ran down her skin. Her fingers trembled. Her vision faded in and out around the edges. Moreno's unconscious body was still. She hesitated, but only for a moment.

"Moreno."

Nothing. Wrapping her wall around her hand, she reached out and shook him gently.

"Lieutenant," she said, a little louder.

He didn't stir.

She dropped a fist on his chest. "Moreno!"

He jerked awake as Colt pushed herself into a half sitting position.

"Moreno, I—"

"No!" He kicked and, with a yelp of fear, reached down to his stomach, just below the belly button. "Dad, stop! Please—"

"Moreno." Colt tried to keep her voice down.

"I..." He blinked and looked around. "I wasn't me."

"Listen."

"I saw... he did, he did it to me and..." His hands were shaking.

She didn't have a choice. Touching his face, she slipped her wall around him and the connection they'd shared a moment ago began to re-establish.

"Carlos, I need you, okay?"

He stared at her, not sure of what to say, of what was happening.

"Your dad, he hurt you," he said.

Colt squeezed his arm and pulled up his memory of being in the tent, of saving the soldier. "I'm hurt, I need your help. Now."

Nodding, he snapped into action, grabbing Colt's flashlight and unzipping the small med pack at his back. Colt dropped to the floor, the cold linoleum practically sizzling against her feverish skin. Moreno knelt beside her.

"Sorry," he said as he tore the hole in her pants wider.

A tiny cry escaped her lips.

"You can move it?" he asked.

"Yeah."

"It went through, missed the bone. You probably have a torn—"

"Patch it."

From the med pack, Moreno grabbed a small plastic pouch. He ripped the top off with his teeth and dumped thick, cakey white powder into the wound. It felt like lemon juice. Colt clenched and hissed.

"Sorry," he said, flatly. She thought it was for the powder, but it was really for the fact that he had to rub it in.

Hard.

"Almost done." He had the gauze pad down and was wrapping her leg. "This stuff is self cinching and coated with a mild anesthetic."

"Great," she said sarcastically. "Get me up."

"Why?"

"So I can walk."

"I'll carry you out."

"No."

"Fine, you'll lean on me."

"Just get me up."

"You can't walk, not unless I numb it."

"Then numb it."

"You're going do more damage if—"

"Do it."

"You'll permanently—"

"That's an order."

Moreno's nostrils flared. Pulling a syringe from his med pack, he flicked the plastic cover off with his thumb and jabbed her with it. Instantly, a cool tingling filled Colt's leg. The pain didn't vanish, but it was the equivalent of stepping down from a migraine to a three-Tylenol headache.

"Help me up," she said softly, grabbing his broad shoulders. He hoisted until her good leg was beneath her. When she put weight on her bad leg, it was a weird feeling. She knew her leg was there, knew that it was taking weight, but it felt like it was filled with floating clouds.

"Okay," Moreno said, his face still close to hers. "Don't put too much weight on, you'll tear something."

Colt was silent. She took a small step. The bandage held. The pain was tolerable.

"Lean on me," he said, his hands floating around her waist.

In the distance, Bentley was still moving away, but slowly. Elena with him. Colt felt the girl inside of Bentley's presence, his cloud of fear.

"Let's get you out of here."

The cloud that had driven Moreno mad.

"Come on."

Colt sighed. "Yeah," she said. "Okay." Her fingers came up and touched his cheek, ever so gently. "Sorry."

The spike she sent was enough to knock him out but not enough to drop him cold. Moreno staggered back, eyes rolling up, and flopped onto the floor.

Bentley's cloud stopped moving. Maybe he was catching a breather. Whatever it was, Colt was grateful. She leaned against the wall and staggered forward. At the edge of the strongest part of his psychic cloud, she tightened her wall and pushed in.

Bentley bolted.

Colt growled. "Shit."

He was hauling a kid, and he was outrunning her. She allowed her wall to thin so she could put extra energy into her telekinesis, wrapping it around her leg like a brace. Bentley's nettles attacked. Colt gritted her teeth and fought them off as best she could.

Far down the hallway, a door banged. Colt found the open stairwell door and started climbing. She heard Bentley above, his huffing breath, his slapping shoes. Several floors up, hot sunlight poured into the stairwell. When Colt reached the top, she threw her shoulder into the roof access door. The Texas sun blinded her, and the waves of heat suffocated her. The world went fuzzy and she staggered. With her heart racing, she had to keep moving. If she stopped, she'd collapse. And if she collapsed, she wouldn't get up again.

Not until it was too late.

Ventilation shafts and air conditioning units dotted the rooftop. Dozens of police were just beyond the building's edge. If Bentley got too close, he could turn the entire crowd into a pack of terrified animals.

Extremely well-armed animals.

She hobbled toward the roof's far edge and felt Bentley's cloud weaken. Turning, she spotted him, pacing near the back of the roof. He was looking down. At what, Colt had no idea. There wasn't a fire escape or even a parking lot. This factory backed up to a smaller warehouse, maybe twenty feet apart.

Bentley ducked. When he came up, Elena was riding piggyback. He walked backward, facing the edge.

Colt's eyes went wide.

Oh no.

She dashed toward them. "Bentley! Don't!"

Eyes swollen from crying, Elena gazed back. Bentley half turned. Colt saw the panic in his eyes. He charged forward.

Colt dropped her wall and put everything she had into a telekinetic push. She moved like a rocket, but only for a few steps. The nettles pierced into her mind and stabbed at the muscles in her back, her arms, her legs. She grimaced. She was close, almost close enough to touch Bentley when he jumped. Colt dove forward, reaching for Elena.

Colt's stomach slammed against the gravel rooftop. Fingers clawing at the gravel, she cried Elena's name. But the girl's eyes were closed. Elena was screaming.

And so was Colt.

CHAPTER SIX

FIELDSVILLE, KANSAS
THAT SAME DAY

Mommy called, "Are you ready for pancakes?"

Vincent's reply was less a word and more a squeal of joy. He bounced in his seat and slapped his little hands against the breakfast table, which was mottled with old stains and glass rings from years of use. Sitting on a stool across the table, Mary Annette, Vincent's twin sister, beamed with excitement.

"Yes, Mommy." Her 'S' was slurred from the space where one front tooth had fallen out but her big kid tooth hadn't grown in yet.

With a little flair, Mommy tossed a pancake into the air, and it slapped on the boy's plate. Vincent made another noise that most people wouldn't think was words.

"Start with one," Mommy said.

He whined loudly.

"Vincent," Mommy's tone dropped two notes.

Mary took a deep breath. "Just wait." A child trying to be an adult.

"Mary," Mommy's tone went down another two notes. "Not your job."

Vincent smirked and stuck out his tongue. If Mary's eyes rolled any harder, she would fall out of her chair. Mommy turned, a plate in each hand, and walked across the room. Her stomach, round as a beach ball, reached the table before she could. She bent over to put the plates down, but winced and grunted.

"Little help here?" she said, her voice tight.

Vincent sat dumb. Mary leaped up and grabbed both plates.

"Thank you, sweetie."

Mary beamed.

Vincent only had one thing on his mind. "I want syrup."

Mommy's eyes narrowed. "How do you ask nicely?"

Vincent squeezed his lips shut before trying again, a little slower and quieter than before. "Can I have the syrup?"

"Can you have the syrup, what?"

"Please." Mary said quickly.

"Mary." That was as low as Mommy's voice could go.

Mary quietly went back to her pancake. Mommy went back to waiting quietly. When the silence became overwhelming, Vincent said, "Please," in a tiny voice.

Satisfied, Mommy shuffled back to the counter and returned. "Save some for your sister."

Taking the nearly empty bottle, Vincent's bottom lip stuck out. His mom rested a hand on his shoulder. Her skin felt as warm and soft as the pancake in front of him.

"We'll get more soon, sweetie," she said. "We'll go shopping today. Your daddy picked up an extra shift at the garage, so—" Her eyes, the same pale green as Vincent's, went wide. With a quick breath, she turned and moved to the refrigerator.

Vincent's fork hung in the air. His heart was going faster. "Mommy?"

Mostly empty jars clattered as the fridge door swung open.

His fingers rubbed against the fork. "Mommy?"

Behind the door, their mom muttered the words the kids weren't allowed to say.

His tummy felt like he was going down a big hill too quickly. "Mommy?"

Across the table, Mary was twisted, looking backward to the kitchen doorway. Vincent shifted in his seat. His chest felt too full. At the end of the hall, wood creaked and groaned as their dad's heavy feet plodded down the stairs. Mommy closed the refrigerator door with a thump that matched their dad's final step. The daylight that had filled the hallway, had streamed in crisp and golden through the glass storm door across from the stairs, winked out.

Vincent's chest rose in quick, shallow breaths that matched Mommy's.

Their dad filled the doorway. "My lunch ready?"

"Um," A bag of bread plopped down on the kitchen counter. Mommy stuck a jar of mayo under one arm and used the other hand to twist the lid off. "It'll be ready in just—"

"I gotta go."

"I know." The knife in her hand flipped back and forth on the bread. She used the other hand to pull back the tin foil covering a plate of roasted chicken from the night before. "Just a minute."

Dad grumbled and stomped across the kitchen. Dad's steps, his swinging arms, reminded Vincent of the pendulum in the old grandfather clock that sat in their hallway. Old and half broken, it didn't work unless you cranked it. And then, it swung slowly, slowly.

At first.

The cabinet door creaked as Dad pulled down a faded mug. "Is there coffee?"

"Um," was all Mommy replied.

The swinging inside of Dad quickened. Vincent didn't realize he was rocking back and forth in rhythm with it.

29

"No coffee," Dad grumbled. "Lunch ain't ready."

"I've been making breakfast."

The mug knocked hard on the counter. The knife slipped from Mommy's fingers. She had to use both hands to catch it. Vincent felt the thing inside his dad, back and forth, harder, harder, faster, faster.

"You done with that yet?"

"Almost." She stuffed chips into a baggie.

"I gotta go."

"Okay, okay. I can... you just get ready and I'll—"

"I am ready, dammit!"

Vincent's insides lurched. Dad's anger was waves of hot air from a campfire. Vincent knew what was coming, what would happen when those waves grew until they were out of control. Tears welled up in his eyes. His mom was afraid, so he was afraid. His dad was angry, so he was angry. The only one he couldn't feel was—

A hum filled the air. No, not the air. Vincent's ears. But it wasn't only there. It was everywhere. It was against his skin. It tingled.

Across the table, Mary was staring intently, her breathing slow and measured. "Daddy," she said, and with the words, the hum grew louder in Vincent's mind.

Suddenly, he felt afraid all on his own.

Dad bellowed, "All I needed was some damn coffee and my lunch."

"I'm sorry," Mom said. "I was feeding the kids and—"

"Cause they're the ones busting their asses at the garage—"

Mary's chin lowered. The hum became a buzzing. Vincent didn't like it.

"Daddy,"

"—working extra shifts."

"Daddy."

It was from Mary. It was from something she was doing with her head. Vincent felt it. He hated it. He whimpered.

"Gonna have two more goddamn mouths to feed and—"

"Daddy."

Mary's word sounded like a guitar string plucked too hard. Silence filled the room. Vincent turned away from his sister. Their dad looked strange, like when someone in a cartoon gets bonked on the head with a frying pan. His mouth was open, and he was just standing there.

Mary spoke slowly and clearly. "Go to work, Daddy."

"Mary Annette," Mom's voice shook. "You shouldn't talk to your—"

Without a word, Dad turned and walked out of the kitchen. The screen door banged behind him.

"Mommy?"

Outside, their daddy's pickup truck rumbled to life. Mary talked right over it.

"We can have pancakes now."

Mommy looked around like she didn't know what to do. She sniffed and wiped her nose. "Sure, honey."

Mary's little smile came back. Vincent didn't feel like bouncing anymore.

Again. Daddy was angry again. It was late. He should have been sleeping. Mary had been sleeping. Then, she'd felt it. Heat, rolling and pulsing. It wasn't like the warmth that came from Mommy. Mommy's warmth was nice. Sunlight. But it was night now. There was no sunlight. There was only Daddy making the house too hot.

She hadn't learned how to ignore the feelings, the strong feelings from other people. They didn't change her. They were on the outside. Like a sound or a color. They weren't on her insides.

But Vincent, she could hear him in the bunk above her, tossing, groaning. He wasn't like her. The feelings affected him. He couldn't control them. He needed to learn. If he didn't, Mary would have to teach him.

Daddy's feelings were back and forth, back and forth; angry, then sad, then sorry, then lonely, then angry again. If Mary wanted to, she could concentrate on him. She could practically taste the grownup drinks he'd been having. But she hated those drinks; the way they made him act, the things he said to Mommy. Mommy was too nice for that. Everyone should have been nice to Mommy, especially since she had babies growing inside her. Daddy wasn't happy with Mommy, and he wasn't being nice.

So Mary wasn't happy with Daddy.

She thought he should act better. Mary knew the right way to act, the way that made everything easier, that made Mommy happy. It would be better if he did the right things. But he was always making problems. Like this morning. That's why Mary sent him away; it fixed the problem. Mary wanted to fix the problems, but grownups always messed things up, they did all the wrong things. If Daddy just did what Mary wanted, all the time, there wouldn't be any more problems. Everything would be good. Everything would stay the same.

But things weren't staying the same, and Mary didn't like it.

Daddy's feelings, they got stronger. Mary knew what was going to happen. It had happened before. Down the hall, in her parents' room, Daddy's voice got big—real big. Mary couldn't tell what he was saying, because Vincent was moaning louder now. He twisted and grabbed the sheets.

Vincent's fists came down on the bed. Down the hall, it sounded like Daddy was giving a spanking, but Mary knew what was really happening. She heard Mommy stay silent.

For the first hit.

Vincent pounded the mattress again. Down the hall, Mommy cried out. Vincent hit it again. Mary heard a thump. She heard crying. She heard Daddy walking down the hall, his big footsteps on the stairs.

Mary got out of bed. In the hall, she heard Mommy still crying. When she reached the door, she peeked under. Mommy was lying on the floor, one hand holding her big belly. Her cheek was almost as red as her eyes.

Mary headed for the stairs.

Daddy was in the kitchen. He held another grownup drink and was saying bad words. Mommy had told him not to say those words in the house, but now he was saying them and thinking about Mommy at the same time.

He stopped when he saw Mary. The feeling inside him changed. He wasn't just angry anymore. He was something else. What was it?

"What're you doin' up?"

He was hard to understand, but Mary didn't listen to his words.

"You nee' somefin?" He was thinking about that morning. "Get outta here. Go tah bed." About how he'd done what she'd said. "Stop starin' an' go tah bed." How he tried to fight it, but couldn't. How he was helpless. "Get outta here!" How he was scared.

Daddy was scared. Mary liked that.

He threw the can on the floor. He took big steps toward her. His heat, his fire, got bigger. He was thinking about what he'd just done to Mommy. He was thinking he would do it to Mary next.

"Stop." She spoke into the connection, the invisible thread between them she'd made. Her words went straight down it and into him.

His muscles froze. All his heat turned into cold mist. He shook. He was afraid, but he pushed against her. He took a step. He raised his hand. Mary pushed, too. Like a Ferris wheel lurching to life, her irises turned.

"Stop," she said again, and he did, gasping, trying to speak through a stalled throat. He shook a moment, then stood still as stone.

To Mary, though, he was a piece of clay, something she could shape, she could change, she could do whatever she wanted with.

The fingers of his right hand curled into a fist. Mary knew he wanted to fight back, to make them stop. He panicked. The terror in his mind tried to force Mary out. She let her eyes spin and found the line that connected them, then followed it deeper into him, deeper, through everything. Daddy made a tiny, pathetic sound in the back of his throat. .

His fist jerked up, hitting just beneath his eye. He rocked, and the fist came up again, smacking his teeth and the point of his nose. His pain, the taste of blood in his mouth, came back to Mary through the line. She cringed. She had to keep that part further away. Soon, those feelings were just echoes.

Her eyes still spinning, Mary brought up Daddy's fist again. And again. And again. Things in his head cracked and come loose. Daddy was crying. Daddy was more than scared. He was terrified.

He was almost broken.

A punch set off bright pinwheels his eyes. He fell to the floor. The connection wavered. Mary squinted and commanded him to stand.

"N-no," he said. "I won't."

Mary frowned. She tried again. Daddy's legs moved just the way she wanted.   "No!" He dropped down again. "Ge' out. Ge' out of my head."

She walked to him. His face was right near hers. He was all sweaty. He looked scared. She felt it, the connection; she could go deeper. She could do more.   Slowly, she raised her hand.

"No," he whispered, "please."

She touched him. It was like pushing a door open. Daddy moved a little. He was shaky. Mary told him, with her head, to stop. He did. He stopped everything but breathing. Mary stepped back. Daddy's eyes looked different. They weren't moving. They weren't crying. They were flat, like a doll's eyes. And they would stay that way as long as she wanted.

Mary told him to get up, and he did. He didn't rock or slip. He got up slow and smooth. That made her happy. Daddy was finally being good.

But Mary was still angry at him.

So Daddy turned. He went out of the kitchen and through the mudroom. He didn't stomp his feet like a rude person. He closed the door quietly behind him, like a polite person should do. Outside, his pickup truck rumbled to life. Then, Mary told him to drive away for the last time.

When she couldn't hear the car anymore, but could still feel Daddy, knew he was doing what she wanted, she turned her thoughts upstairs, to her mother's bedroom.

To the two little minds Daddy left in Mommy's tummy.

If she could make Daddy better, she could make them all better. She could keep anything bad from happening to her and Mommy ever again.

CHAPTER EIGHT

THIRTEEN YEARS LATER

Invisible fingers crawled up the back of Amber's neck.

Oh god, not now. Please, not now.

It was stronger this time. It was like someone was actually standing behind her on the big empty sidewalk in the dark, working their hands into her hair.

Amber picked up her pace. The street was the kind of dark you only find in sleepy Midwestern towns. Streetlamps hung overhead, few and far between. Her apartment was six blocks away, but it was empty. She thought about turning back. The grocery store where she'd just finished her shift would still have people milling about. If she turned around, at least she wouldn't be alone.

But maybe whatever was sending out those fingers was back that way.

She kept moving, faster than before, and left the fingers behind.

Most stores were closed. Each time she passed by the big glass windows, she expected to see in the reflection someone behind her. But as she passed an antiques store, her bangs swinging side to side, she saw only her pale, scared face.

A streetlight's glowing circle enveloped her, but it brought no sense of warmth or safety. Still, she hesitated to walk back out into the dark.

Four more blocks to go. The fingers returned, wiggling behind her ears as though searching for something. She gasped and broke into a jog. The fingers stayed with her this time.

The first time, at the store, she'd outrun them. She'd been scanning some old biddy's white bread when something touched her arm. She'd thought it was the old woman trying to get her attention. When she looked down, there was no hand. She pulled back, confused. The feeling kept going. Up her arm. Past her elbow. Onto her shoulder. She'd stepped away from the register, thinking maybe it was a breeze, a bug, a spider web, something completely normal that could be easily explained and laughed away later.

But it hadn't been.

She'd scared the hell out of everyone as she screamed and ran to the employee lounge. When the door slammed behind her, the fingers stopped.

It had happened again when she was at the café on Main Street. It was her day off, and she'd gone for a coffee and muffin. A crowd of teens had just gotten off of school and stood behind her in line. Again, she thought someone was trying to get her attention. The invisible fingers didn't start at her arm that time. They went straight for her shoulder. When she realized it was happening again, she pulled back, left the café and started down the street. She'd thought she was losing her mind. Then the fingers faded, but not before she felt the breath—like someone at her ear, telling her a wordless secret. She'd choked and ran.

She'd gotten away again. Running seemed to work. But not this time. They weren't giving up. Every time she slowed down, even a little, they reached out for her. Two more blocks, then she would be home. She'd be safe there; she knew it. The fingers had never followed her home.

One of them squirmed beneath her earlobe. It worked its way up. She felt it press against the tiny hairs that lined the canal.

Oh god, it's going inside.

"No!" she screamed. Anger and fear rushed inside of her. Goosebumps broke out across her skin and, as they did, a ripple cut through the air in front of her like hot air rising from a grill. It spun around her so fast she breath, sure she would black out. But she didn't. Nothing happened, nothing at all.

The fingers were gone.

Exhaling, she didn't smile or laugh. She just kept moving until she reached her building. The cheap light above cast a sickly yellow tone on the glass storm door. Behind her jaundiced reflection, a shadow darted. Amber didn't turn around, just got her ass inside.

Slamming the door, she headed for the stairs and climbed to the second floor. At the end of the hallway, the shadow shifted again.

Something thumped behind her. She didn't look back. She couldn't look back. She prayed and hoped this was all in her head. She'd rather be crazy than have it be real.

At her door, the shadow appeared at the end of the hall, slithering into place, so thick the world beneath it vanished. There was a head and arms. It was a person, or something that looked like one. Because when she saw it, she felt those fingers pushing, wiggling against the air just a few inches from her.

And people can't do that.

She fell into her apartment. Before she slammed the door, another shape from the other side of the hall jetted forward. It hit the closed door and she stumbled back, panting so hard she didn't have the breath to scream. She couldn't take her eyes away from the door as she backed into the living room.

Something to her right moved. She tried to run. Pain bit into her arm, just above the elbow. A force pulled her, not the fingers, not a hand. It was thin and tight and wrapped around her arm completely.

She struggled to get away. Her free hand grabbed a doorway for leverage. If she could just get to her bedroom, she could block the door and

36

get out onto the fire escape. Then she could scream her head off. But she had to get away first. She had to pull.

Something jumped through the room, and it swirled around her free arm. The pain snapped, sharp and tight. It yanked her back, twisting her. The pain spun around her, wrapping her, tying her up. It squeezed her enough that the scream she'd saved couldn't even get enough air to come out.

Tears rolled from her eyes as she dropped to her knees. The shadow was there, inside the apartment, moving toward her. It was some grotesque thing, four legs, a wide body, two heads. One had messy hair, the other had...

Pigtails. Curly pigtails.

The four legs split into sets of two as the people stepped apart. They were thin, one shorter and one as tall as her.

Kids, teenagers. A boy and a girl.

What the hell was this? A prank? A joke?

But the fingers were no joke, and they had come from these kids.

"Why?" her throat was dry with fear. "Why are you doing this?"

The air pressure in the room increased. The fingers returned, and now they weren't just feeling around Amber's head. They were trying to push their blunt tips through her skin, through her skull. She closed her eyes and cried out, just like she had on the street. That ripple flashed around her again and the fingers were blown away.

The girl with the pigtails took a sharp breath. "Now."

Something hit Amber in the head. Not on the head, in the head. It never touched her bone or flesh but slammed directly into her brain. She felt pain and dizziness. The world spun. Ocean waves filled her ears, and bright lights filled her eyes. Her head dropped, but she could still hear them.

"Why didn't you do it?" the girl said.

"We didn't need to bring them," the boy replied.

"Clearly, we did."

"They're too young! They could get hurt."

"You would protect them."

Silence.

"Why didn't you do it?" the girl asked again.

"She... she's scared."

"She's dangerous."

"I don't think—"

"She blocked me." The girl's voice was flat, like she was reading aloud in English class a passage that she barely understood. "If she can do that, she can hurt people."

"Just because she stopped you?" said the boy, his voice going up and down, angry, then soft.

"She'll get stronger."

"I don't—"

"We did."

"Yeah, but—"

"They did."

Silence.

"What if she hurts someone?" the girl said.

Amber opened her mouth, but words wouldn't come. She closed her eyes and thought as loudly as she could, *I won't. I won't. I promise. I won't. I don't even know what's happening. Please, please, please.*

The girl said, soft and low, "What if she tries to hurt one of us?"

Please, please, please—

"Okay."

Amber's face scrunched. Tears formed in her eyes.

"All together," said the girl. "Now."

CHAPTER NINE

Vincent was counting the seconds. At the blackboard, Mr. Matthews droned on about the Roman Empire. Vincent made sure to look at Mr. Matthews' potbelly, instead of the man's eyes. They hid behind bushy eyebrows, like soldiers pausing in a trench. He feigned paying attention while smothering his ears with his palms. His skin and bones became seashells, and all he could hear was the rush of wordless noise.

At least, that's what his ears sensed. But behind his ears, voices whispered into him.

—*ew, did he look at me?*—
—*god, what a freak*—
—*should throw him outta school*—
—*total weirdo*—
—*scared just being near him*—
—*tried that on me, I'd-a kicked his ass*—
—*freak*—
—*practically killed that kid*—
—*gonna go postal on us or something*—
—*hate him and his stupid face*—
—*monster*—

Vincent tried to ignore them, but they were too close. He thought, if he could just hold out until the bell rang, he could run outside and get away from it all. Then tomorrow, maybe it would be different. Maybe they would stop thinking about him.

Yeah, sure. Like that had happened in the last four months.

But it was getting better, day by day. And if he could ride out the rest of the school year, make it to summer, maybe everyone would forget by the fall. Maybe he could just fade into the background and no one would bother him anymore. No one would think about him or what had happened.

What he'd done.

Somehow, he missed the end-of-day bell. Kids were shuffling around him, and Mr. Matthews was shouting out their homework. Snatching his backpack from the floor, Vincent went to wade through the crowd. Instead, the kids pulled back just enough to show how they felt about being near him. Vincent's jaw set. He lowered his head.

Fine. At last he could be the first one to leave. All he wanted to be as far from everyone else as they wanted to be from him.

"Vincent?" Mr. Matthews called his name as gently as he could. The other kids froze. Vincent kept his head down and barreled toward the door.

"Vincent," Mr. Matthews called again. "May I speak with you please?"

He stopped. Everyone was staring, their minds all focused on him and their thoughts fell like heavy rain.

—*what's he gonna say*—

—*oh my god*—

—*did he do it again?*—

—*did someone else get hurt?*—

—*was there another?*—

—*what*—

—*who?*—

—*a fight?*—

—*didn't hear*—

—*maybe*—

—*bet that kid died*—

—*monster*—

—*freak*—

"Excuse me." Mr. Matthews' voice slapped every kid in the room across the back of the head. "Are any of you named Vincent? No? Then keep those feet moving, or I'll double your homework and throw in a quiz next week."

The crowd dispersed. When the last one was out, Mr. Matthews sat in his creaky chair.

"Close the door, please." He didn't sound angry, but he didn't sound happy either. "You didn't take a single note today."

Vincent kept his head down. He knew Mr. Matthews was glaring at him, thinking about the muscles around his eyes and how tight they were. How his hands were fists. But he couldn't stop them from being so.

"Listen, I'm going to skip over the spiel about how what happened wasn't your fault, all right?"

Vincent nodded.

"Starting now, you need to pay attention in class, hand in your homework, and do the assignments. Got it?"

"Yes sir." The words barely passed Vincent's lips.

Mr. Matthews turned his attention to the papers on his desk. "Stop beating yourself up, son. It was a freak accident."

Vincent flinched.

"Remember your homework."

Vincent wanted to run from the room and through the hallway, but he forced himself to walk. Every person he passed, their thoughts were a strip of flint, and his brain was the match head. If he spent too much time in that hallway, he was sure his whole head would go up in flames.

But outside, sunlight warmed his skin. Around him, kids were heading in every direction, distracted, paying no attention to the freak boy. He jogged to the bike rack and, for a moment, his mind was clear.

A psychic finger tapped his mental shoulder. Turning, he saw Mary walking toward him. Mary made walking through a crowd look easy. It was almost like a dance, like every person around her was following some insanely precise choreography that got them out of her way with only inches to spare. Her long, skinny legs never broke their perfect stride. Her pleated, plaid skirt swung like a metronome. Her pig tails, dark brown and curlier than plastic ribbons on a storefront Christmas present, bounced as she marched through the mass of kids and over to her brother.

"Vincent?" she asked in the most cordial and proper of ways. Why was she like that? Why couldn't she just come over and kick him in the leg? Why couldn't she be a normal sister?

Ha, like she'd ever been normal.

"Vincent, I understand why you're upset."

Yeah, right.

"It was to protect us."

Like they needed protection.

Mary's tone shifted. "I don't like it when you ignore me. If you don't tell me what's wrong, I can't fix it."

Because Mary always knows what's best.

"I can't read your mind."

He smirked, knowing that drove her crazy.

"Please turn around."

He turned the front wheel away from her and threw his leg over the seat.

Mary's expression hardened, her eyebrows crinkling in the middle. "I said, turn around."

Yanking the straps of his backpack until they were snug against his body, he said, "Make me," then kicked off and pedaled furiously.

He raced past the sign for their school—Fieldsville High School, Home of the Bucks! The wind slipped around his face, through his hair, across the plaid shirt that hung on his skinny frame the way it would around a coat rack. Vincent's anger and guilt peeled away, carried off behind him like a twirl of autumn leaves. He zipped across lazy streets and leaped over low curbs onto strolling sidewalks. Cars hummed by, mostly pickup trucks and jeeps, and people walked here and there. Later in the day, there would be some traffic, people would be forced to drive five miles under the speed limit. But right now, things were free and clear for Vincent to race through.

Banking hard, his tires whirled as he cut down Main Street. If anywhere in town was going to be busy, it would be Main Street. The general

41

store, the shops, the café, the bakery, they all stood along this one road and, as much as Vincent wanted to be alone right now, Main Street was also the best cut-through to get to the other side of town. It led to the state roads, which bled into the farms that surrounded the town. Four months ago, Vincent would have headed that way. He would have swung underneath the highway overpass and listened to the freight trucks roll over him like mechanical thunder. He would have zipped over to the mall and run into the clothing store where his mom worked. She would have given him a hug and told him to get home to help Mary take care of their little brother and sister.

But the mall was where the kids from his school hung out, making noise and never buying anything. And near the highway too many people traveled, too many pairs of eyes could see him, and too many minds could be heard. So, he headed to the farmlands where there would be only quiet and sky. He was coasting now, finally finding true silence in his head.

A blip in his mind's radar went off.

Gently, he applied the brakes. Another blip. He hesitated, not sure what to do.

No, not what to do. What he wanted to do. The blip came again, a tiny psychic S. O. S. It was too far for him to get anything.

Unless...

He closed his eyes. It was weird, reaching with his mind. It wasn't stretching a limb; there was no weight, no gravity, yet there was sensation. The feelers slithered out and connected to the call. A frown slapped across his mouth. His eyes turned cold. He yanked the handlebars and drove back toward town. His legs pumped harder than before. He knew every corner, every sidewalk, and navigated with ease. The cars he zipped between didn't even have the chance to honk at him before he was gone. Dodging a changing traffic light, he almost crashed into a pedestrian. They shouted and waved angrily, but Vincent was a blur, already across the street and ducking down a thin alleyway.

The cry for help strengthened. Ahead of him was the Junior High School. From down the street, he could hear the crowd of kids. Some were screaming, some were laughing, some were stomping their feet and pumping their fists in the air. But most of them were chanting.

"Fight! Fight! Fight! Fight!"

The crowd was an arena of bodies. From beneath Vincent's cheeks, heat rose into his eyeballs. He wanted to calm down, needed to, but from inside the circle, the call burst out again, coinciding with a tremendous cheer from the kids. Vincent felt the pain through the signal, and inside him, the heat intensified into blaze.

Leaping from the bike, he ran into the crowd, smashing through them. Their excitement infected his mind, fueling the adrenaline in his veins.

Bursting into the center of the ring, he saw a local bully named Ashley standing over a dark haired boy, crumpled and dirty on the ground.

Vincent's little brother.

Charging forward, Vincent tackled Ashley from behind. They became a sloppy mess of flailing arms and swinging legs. They rolled around, Vincent so angry that he heard only the blood pounding in his ears.

That's when he felt it. Pressure, not heat or anger, but actual pressure building in his chest as though air was pushing through his muscles.

His fury pulled back, replaced by fear.

No. Please no. Not again.

He scrambled to get away. Ashley rolled over and leaped up, his fists ready before his eyes were open. Vincent stood, too scared to raise his fists.

He had to push it down, push down that feeling. If it got out...

He closed his eyes and waited for Ashley to start swinging, but the punches never came. When Vincent opened his eyes, he saw terror spread across Ashley's face. Not sure of what to do, he huffed, puffed, and took a quick step. Ashley pulled back, the way he would have from a barking dog.

That's when Vincent realized; the chanting, the cheering, the hooting and hollering and stamping of feet had stopped. The arena was silent. Thoughts trickled into his head. Then, they rushed into him like water freed from a dam. His stomach turned. His heart raced. He glanced around the circle, but everything was blurring. The kids were mixing together into one single thought, one feeling.

Fear.

Fear of him.

Vincent shook his head. He scanned his surroundings, trying to get his bearings. . Behind Ashley, two other boys named David and Travis were standing. They were Ashley's little cronies. Between the two junior bullies, arms being held behind her back, was a girl with eyes and hair the same color as Vincent's. One of her soft, freckled cheeks had a bright red slap mark on it.

All the noise, all the thoughts from the crowd evaporated from Vincent's mind. He focused on his little sister's red cheek. The world stopped spinning. The anger inside him came back, but as a simmering burn. He didn't charge the bullies. He just took three long steps, speaking one word with each.

"Let. Her. Go."

Travis 'chubby little cheeks shivered as his hands flew back. David stood there looking stupid for a few seconds before his brain finally got the message. The girl pulled her arms forward, then shoved Travis and David away from her. Not that they needed any encouragement to get farther away from Vincent.

Vincent turned to Ashley next. "Mess with them again." He raised his fist up near Ashley's face. The bully gaped at the pale bulging knuckles like they were grenades with the pins pulled. "And I'll do it to you."

Ashley nodded. After a few seconds of silence, Vincent's fury waned. The murmuring thoughts of the crowd crept back in.

"Get outta here!" He shouted. "Everyone! Go! Get!" A second later, all he saw was bouncing backpacks and the bottoms of sneakers as kids pushed and shoved each other to get away.

When everyone was gone, he helped his brother up. There were bruises and scrapes on his face from the fight.

"You okay?" Vincent asked.

His brother wiped a snotty nose on an arm and stared at the ground. His dark brown hair was a shaggy mess.

Vincent sighed. "I'm sorry. I got here as fast as I could."

His brother didn't say anything. He simply brushed off his clothes kept his head down. Vincent touched his sister's cheek.

"Does it hurt?"

She reached up and gently lowered his arm.

"Okay," Vincent said softly. "I'll walk you home."

CHAPTER TEN

The Kansas road was as flat as a sheet of paper in a breezeless room. Colt's government-issue car, some new model Hyundai, dull raincloud gray, hummed and glided over the smooth asphalt. As she swung into the DSI's field office, a symbol on the dashboard started flashing. She caught it just in time to not be startled when her entire car rang. A woman's prerecorded voice announced, "Call from seven, zero, three. Nine, six, nine..."

It was the DSI main offices in Arlington, probably about that performance review she hadn't done. Pulling into a parking space, she turned off the car and killed the voice.

The coffee pot held only the dregs; the day shift used to brew a fresh pot for her before they left, but they hadn't done that in a long time.

As she rinsed out the container, the last few people shuffled by. One or two of them offered a polite, cursory greeting. Colt's only response was a grumble. She pressed the brew button on the coffee machine.

Her cellphone rang again, same number as before. . She hit the big red "ignore" button and headed to her desk. Rolling back her chair, she peeked back and forth. There were still a few people milling about, gathering their coats and filing away the last of the day's work. No agents, no one with abilities.

No one she couldn't get to.

She broadcast a gentle push to the room. For a moment, everyone became so occupied with what they were doing that Colt was practically invisible. She could have taken off her top and not one person would have noticed. Instead, she used the freedom she'd created to sit down with a grunt and a flash of discomfort at the corners of her eyes.

She sighed.

Why the hell did she do that? It wasn't necessary. She was almost sixty. So what if she was a little achy sometimes? Well, all the time, really. So what if her knee had been giving her problems in the evenings? And the mornings. And the afternoons.

So what if she couldn't remember her last real assignment, the last foreign she'd chased down, the last wild car chase and alleyway shootout? The last time her heart pounded a cocktail of adrenaline and excitement into every vein, every inch, every nerve in her body?

She closed her eyes and leaned back.

So what if she wasn't any use anymore?

In her head, she felt a ringing telephone muffled by a pillow—except the pillow was her brain tissue. She listened to the psychic request and heaved a deep sigh. Now she knew who had been calling from the main offices.

Crap, this guy again.

It was ridiculous for him to request a psychic connection, but she knew that, if she didn't answer, he'd just keep at it. She opened the channel in her mind.

When her eyelids rose, a young, thin-faced man of Indian descent was sitting across the desk from her. He was wearing a salmon colored shirt and a heavy burgundy tie.

"Rakesh." She said his name with all the thrill and vigor of a person going in for a root canal.

"Hey, Agent Colt." He didn't give a little wave, but she was sure he wanted to. "I, uh, I tried to get you earlier, and, uh, I guess you were... um... I, I wasn't sure if you were on, on... an assignment or not so—"

That wasn't the right thing to put her in a good mood. "What do you need?"

Rakesh gave a big, "Oh, you know," kind of laugh. "Well, I was, was just finishing up on some, some stuff and I, uh, I wanted to get you... um, to get your opinion, your professional opinion, on some... some things, uh..."

Colt crossed her arms. This was the third time this month Rakesh had come calling to get her opinion on some things. He'd been at it for a couple of years now, ever since he'd called into the field office and Colt had the misfortune of answering the phone. The minute she'd said her name, he'd started stammering. Apparently, they still told stories about her in the DSI's basic training program, though no one had ever paid as much attention as Rakesh Pawar.

"And I figured," he said.

Colt wasn't sure if he'd been talking the whole time. Then again, it didn't really matter.

"Since you have, I mean, so much field experience and years and years under your belt—"

Colt's eyes tightened. "There a point here, Rakesh?"

He sat, gaping at her. "Yeah. Yes, yes sorry, I... it's the case Agent Geller is on. I can't... I've been trying to reach him and just... can't get a, a hold of him but—"

"Geller's on vacation," she said flatly.

Rakesh's mouth pulled into a little donut. "Oh." His eyes darted back and forth, landing anywhere but on Colt's. "Uh, I did not... Geller never told me, even though he's, he's supposed to... but that's fine. It's okay." He nodded a little too much to be convincing.

Running a hand over her face, Colt inhaled sharply, then paused. She was going to regret this. "What do you need?"

Rakesh was clearly shocked. When he recovered, he said, "Just, if you could get the word to Geller that there's been another incident, that'd be... I would, I'd appreciate it."

Incident? That was interesting. Event was DSI lingo for a one-time occurrence that simply hadn't been explained. Incident meant there was probable cause to assume something psychic was going on.

"What are the details?"

"Um." Rakesh's image reached out into thin air and moved its arms about. She heard papers moving around. His image flickered. He was having trouble focusing on her and the things in his hands.

"Female," Rakesh said. "Twenty-two, completely comatose. No prior medical history, no drug abuse."

Colt's interest waned. "I don't see how that's an 'incident'."

"Oh, well, it's the fourth case like it in the last three months."

Colt leaned forward. "All localized?"

"No, no, that's the, the interesting thing. All over the place. I mean, within, uh, all falling under your field office's jurisdiction, but—"

"First one, three months ago, where was that?"

"Uh."

The flip, flip, flip of paper. Didn't all young people use computers? Against Colt's will, Rakesh actually scored a point of respect.

"Tribune."

Colt looked across the room at the big map of Kansas hanging on the wall. "After that?"

"Larned." Flip, flip. "Then Bucklin."

She'd never heard of Bucklin. Standing up—suddenly those aches and pains didn't bother her so much—Colt walked to the map. Rakesh's image drifted along with her. He stuck his arms out, as though he were losing his balance. A smirk crept across Colt's face, but it faded while she mumbled the city names and dropped pushpins into the map.

"Huh," she muttered. No discernible pattern. "Most recent one, the woman, when did it happen?"

"She was admitted yesterday."

This was starting to look like a real case. Hit someone that has no psychic defense with a strong enough spike, and they can end up in a coma. But for the coma to last three months? The person doing it was extremely powerful, which meant they were probably well trained.

Colt grabbed a pin. "Where is she?"

"Prairie."

Colt paused. That was less than an hour away, which was good. What was bad was that every incident was hours apart. The pins didn't make a circle, or a star, or any other recognizable shape. They were random, with no central point or origin. That meant just finding a lead on whoever was doing this would be a ton of work. But, if she could find them, if she could bring them in…

"Agent Colt?"

How long had she been staring at the pins? She straightened her back. "Which hospital in Prairie?"

Rakesh looked through his papers. "General. Prairie. Prairie General."

Perfect. Colt rubbed her jaw. "Look, Geller's out, and it's sounding to me like this may be a bit… over his head. I've got a contact at Prairie General. Why don't I swing over there?"

"That would, that would be great!" Rakesh's enthusiasm broke through his attempt to control it. "I mean, I… I can't actually… it's Geller's assignment, and you're not really a field agent anymore so, uh, I—"

Colt pushed down the biting response that rose up inside her mind. "I'm just gathering intel, Rakesh."

Rakesh nodded. "Yeah, okay. Let's—yes, go ahead."

Colt nodded, smirked, and searched her coat pockets for her car keys. "Listen, while I'm headed out there, see what you can dig up on any possible leads in the area. Psychic potentials, traveling con-men, foreign agents, too."

"You think—"

"No, but I'd rather play it safe than sorry." What she really wanted was to keep Rakesh busy.

He nodded. "All right."

Colt headed for the door. The coffeepot was full. She walked right by it, Rakesh's image drifting along next to her.

"Anything else?"

Rakesh's eyebrows went up. "Well, since we're already here, I did see that HR has requested you complete a performance review. If you like, I could—"

Colt snapped her fingers. Rakesh disappeared.

CHAPTER ELEVEN

On the fifteenth floor of the DSI offices, Rakesh stumbled through a few more syllables before sputtering to a stop. The image of Colt was gone. And there were fingers in his hair.

Someone else's fingers.

"Uh." He tried to clear his throat in a manly way, but it came out sounding like a small mammal calling for more food pellets. "The, um... the connection was, uh—"

"Yes sir," Sandra said from behind him. "Agent Colt closed the psychic channel." Her voice was trim and professional, but there was a tiny bit of mischief dancing around on her tongue. She still hadn't taken her fingers out of Rakesh's thick, black hair.

"So." He scratched an ear. "Are we going to connect? I, I mean reconnect... with, with Agent Colt?"

"No, sir." She slid her fingers from his scalp and stepped away. He half stood, half leaped up and immediately began straightening his clothes and fixing his hair. He looked back and glimpsed her staring. He wasn't sure if he was feeling more excitement or shyness. In two needlessly large steps, he walked to the other side of his desk and laughed a breathy laugh.

Sandra just stood, a tiny smile resting on the edges of her mouth. Her hair, jet black and cut short, was buried beneath the birds' nest of wires and plastic that covered her head. The wires ran down to a control box, which was strapped to her back, just above her butt. The equipment was used to make her into a transmitter and even though it was terribly unflattering, Rakesh didn't even notice.

"So," Sandra said, unsnapping the headpiece's chinstrap. "You'll be working with Agent Colt?"

Rakesh turned, a boyish grin on his face. "Yeah."

Sandra smiled and shook her head. Rakesh's mind raced. Was it because she just took off the headgear? Did she think he was being immature? Wait, was she jealous? Did she even like him enough to be jealous? Damn it, why'd he have to go to an all boys school?

Playing it safe, he dropped the grin. "No," he said in a professional voice. "She's, uh, I just... just..." Why was he explaining? She'd heard everything he and Colt had talked about. But she was just standing there, short and curvy and cute, with her eyebrows up like she was expecting him to say more. He exhaled sharply. "She's an excellent resource, and I'm happy I get to use her."

Oh God. Use her?

How thick were his office windows, and could he throw himself through one?

49

Sandra bit her bottom lip. "I'm sure you are." She didn't need to be psychic to know what thoughts had passed though his head. The expression on his face said everything. "Is there anything else I can help you with, sir?"

"Uh..." He wished there was something else, another reason to keep her in the office for a little while, but nothing came to mind. Anyway, he needed to start researching those leads for Colt. Having Sandra about would be, well, more than just a little distracting. "No, no thank you. I think, yes, that's all."

As she walked out, Sandra's eyes drifted across the many photos Rakesh had hanging on his wall. She'd looked at them before. None were of his family or showing him relaxing with friends. Instead, most pictures were of him wearing tiny running shorts, usually a tank top with a piece of paper pinned to his chest bearing a racer's number. He was sweaty and ragged looking, and in many, he held a hand-written sign depicting the amount of time it had taken him to finish the race. He was always smiling, always proud. Some pictures went as far back as his military school days, where he was on the long-distance running team. Of course, none of the photos were of him and the team. Always just him.

A soft smile spread across her lips. "Have a good night, sir."

But Rakesh was already at his desk, focused and working.

CHAPTER TWELVE

The screen door's hinges whined as Vincent stepped outside. He'd set up his brother and sister with crackers and milk. They'd be fine alone for a while. He headed over to the old oak tree where his bike rested. The afternoon sun had heated the air, and Vincent enjoyed the gentle breeze slipping through his thin shirt. Throwing one leg over the bicycle's seat, he touched his toes to the pedal and prepared to push off.

From inside, a sound caught his attention. Through the kitchen window, he saw that they were getting glasses down from the cabinet. He waited a moment, listening for a crash, and stared at the old farmhouse where he and his family lived; at the old gray shingles covering the outside, cracked and peeling; at the rippled, old windows, sitting in frames sunken into the walls; at the roof that bowed in slightly and the walls that bent and sloped just enough to notice even at a quick glance.

The inside wasn't any better, but at least it was clean. His mother worked hard to make their house a home. There were cracks in the walls, slopes to the stairs, leaks in the pipes, and scuffs on the floors. From both the inside and out, the whole structure looked as though it were waiting for the last support to crumble.

But it had been like that since he was little. It seemed as though the house hadn't aged. People came out and worked on it; they fixed things and kept it standing, but they never seemed to actually improve it. It was like it was stuck, like it wasn't ever going to grow up.

He sighed, then his feet went to work. As he headed down the driveway, the sweet scent of the unkempt yard drifted across his nose and away on the breeze. Sweet grass and dandelions.

Hitting the street, Vincent took a hard left. He pedaled faster, and soon he was racing down the road. The same feeling from earlier, freedom from the problems of the world, washed his skin and bathed his mind. He was about to smile, but he remembered he should have been doing this an hour ago. He thought about Ashley and Travis and David. He thought about the look on his sister's face, her red cheek, the bruises and cuts on his brother's face. He thought about all the kids in the circle, how they had run away when he'd shouted. He replayed the terror in Ashley's eyes.

Inside him, anger pushed its way up toward the bottom of his heart, etching a hot scar across his insides. Below him, the pedals whirred and the chain buzzed as his feet pumped faster and faster.

They were all being stupid. This whole thing was stupid. No one knew what had really happened.

Not even him.

Why couldn't they just forget about it? Why'd they have to go after his brother and sister? They weren't involved. They didn't do it, and he didn't even mean to. It was just an accident. He never wanted to hurt anyone.

But he had. He'd hurt someone, bad. And it had been someone normal. Someone without powers.

The others, the ones Mary found, they were different. They were dangerous, Mary said so. But Vincent was starting to wonder. That last one, the woman they'd followed, she'd given him a look. It was the same look as Ashley, the same as all the kids in the circle. She'd been scared, so scared.

Of him.

Pressure, the same one he'd felt before, rose into his shoulders. It pushed harder, breaking the barrier into his arms. Vincent ground his teeth. No. He could hold it back, like he did earlier in the circle with Ashley. He didn't have to let it go. But it pushed, moving down into his elbows, toward his hands. He growled and fought it, but the pressure was winning, and suddenly he was afraid. That just made it go faster.

White knuckling the handlebars, he swung the bike off the road and onto a dirt path. The shadows of the trees blinded his sun-soaked eyes, and he jerked the bike to the side. Flying off the path, he crashed to the ground, his shoulder and hip sparking with pain. The bike, still between his legs, bit into his thigh.

Growling, he climbed to his feet. His hands balled into fists as he glared at the bike and shouted, "Piece of crap!" He kicked at it awkwardly, stomping on it and shouting. The pressure inside his arms waned and, after a few more kicks, it was gone. He wiped his face with his short sleeve and rubbed his shoulder, even though it didn't really hurt.

"Piece of crap," he muttered.

After a moment of silence, he reached down and pulled the bike up. Brushing away the dusty footprints, he tenderly set it on its stand, checking all the gears and brake lines. He felt the urge to tell it he was sorry, he didn't mean it, he wasn't angry at it, but that would have been stupid. Still, his lips made the words—tiny and soundless—as he cleaned some grass from the chain.

Undamaged, the bike rolled along next to him through the trees. The slow pace of one foot in front of the other was something he needed. When the path led to a small field, he left his bike against an old stump. Up ahead, one of the streams ran through the farmlands. The long, winding gully was four or five feet deep in the earth, the bottom a bank of pebbles. During storm season, it would fill to near the top. Now, the water ran half a foot deep.

Vincent paused. The field was part of an old farm, and there was a house on the property about half a mile away, but for all intents and purposes, the creek and surrounding areas were abandoned.

Still, he didn't want to take any chances.

With a little less reservation, he sent out his tendrils. Finding nothing other than a few gophers, he jumped into the gulley. The cold water lapped at the sides of his shoes as he straddled the stream. His feet were long and flat, as were his hands. He once told his mom those big feet made him feel like a clown. She'd said he was the handsomest clown she'd ever seen.

A smile spread across his face. In his mind, he heard her. She was humming the nameless tune that went up and down without care. Calm washed over him. Inching back and forth, he faced down the stream. His breath held. His face hardened.

A ripple shot out, like someone was dragging a stick across the surface of the water. Vincent shifted his feet. The ripple took off again but was faster and went farther. Rolling his shoulders, Vincent took a deep breath. He tried to think about his mom's calming song but knew that wasn't going to help. Instead, he thought about the bully, Ashley. In his chest, the pressure built. The pressure that had come before, during the fight three months ago. The pressure he was so scared of. The pressure that had leaped from him and hurt that poor boy.

He thought about how everyone was calling him a freak now. Their words, their fear and hatred for him bounced around his mind. The pressure moved from his chest to his shoulder, down into his arm. It was like something was pushing, straining to come out of him. He pictured his brother's face, scratched and dirty from Ashley knocking him to the ground. The pressure grew. He made himself remember his sister's cheek, red and hot and fresh from being slapped. It was in his forearm, almost into his hand.

He thought about Mary, her cold distance, and it pushed past his wrist.

He thought about the things she'd made him do, the people they'd hurt, that woman's face, how scared she was. It was in his fingers. It was pounding heat and energy, swelling the inside of his fingertips like the skin of a balloon ready to burst. His hand was a shaking fist. His body was trembling with anger and frustration, and he needed to just let it go and explode into the world.

And then, at that moment, he again pulled his mom's humming tune to mind.

With the focused clarity of an athlete, he opened his eyes and swung his arm up, throwing an uppercut against the air. The water of the stream burst upward, cut by an invisible racing razor, a psychic sword that sliced it down to the molecule.

53

The slash flew out awkwardly, at an angle, but that didn't matter. It had come under Vincent's control, under his command. And if he could call on it, maybe he could keep himself from calling on it.

He could never use it to hurt someone again.

Moving his feet, he swung up with his other hand. Another cut flew out, not as strong, but more precise than the last.

In the field, the setting sun glistened off the front tire of his bike. From down the dirt path, silent steps carried Mary forward. The breeze, eager to dance around her, teased her skirt as she came to the edge of the tree line. There, she stopped and watched.

Her face, a softer version of Vincent's, remained passive. Her eyes, so dark brown that it was hard to tell where her irises ended and her pupils began, stayed wide open as she listened to her brother slash the water over and over again.

CHAPTER THIRTEEN

Above Colt, Prairie General Hospital's florescent lights buzzed. The turning ceiling fans hummed in the quiet room. Machines blinked and blipped but made no noise. Heart rates were followed. Breathing machines inhaled and exhaled life into lungs, and the bodies lay perfectly still.

To Colt, Amber looked like a child. The young woman was placid and calm, but Colt knew that the last expression she'd worn was probably one of fear. Gently, she pushed aside a strand of hair, the rest of which had been neatly combed and pulled to the sides. There was no breathing tube in Amber's mouth, as her body was working perfectly.

The problem, Colt knew, was her mind.

It was gone.

Well, not gone, but not there either. Touching Amber's forehead, Colt stepped out of the room and into the young woman's head. It was terrifying; white void, no up, no down, no backward or forward. No air to breathe, yet no pull of a vacuum either. There were things there; it was an entire city, an entire world broken down into pieces so small they could be kicked down the street, then spread across the void. Sometimes so close they could touch, other times thousands of miles apart. And between each were ribbons, threads, strings stretched so thin they could barely be seen.

And they were screaming.

Howling.

Vibrating in fear and panic and pain. The place, the endless empty was filled with a noise that was the sound of death and life smashing together.

The pieces, the debris, they were Amber's mind. They were her thoughts, her memories. The threads were her emotions, her raw instincts, her passions and fears. They were her. She'd been broken. Torn apart. Shattered. Decimated.

Colt's hand pulled back.

This wasn't an accident. Whoever had done it, they'd pointed that psychic weapon at Amber's mind and pulled the trigger without hesitation. They'd left so little, there weren't any cohesive memories for Colt to figure out what had happened. There was nothing to read, nothing to see, nothing to sort through.

But there was something.

Amber had been a level one. A psychic. The kind of person that goes through life thinking that maybe they just have a knack for cards or always knows when a family member is sick. Colt felt it. And if she could feel it, there was a good chance the attacker had known too. In fact, it could have been the reason Amber was targeted. She and the other victims didn't have anything in common, but if they were all level ones...

This was a big case. Someone was hunting down level ones and taking them out. It could be a foreign or a sleeper agent, or maybe Colt was on the trail of a good old-fashioned sociopath. A shiver traveled up her spine. She was going to drag this bastard back to the DSI and throw him in front of the top brass. Maybe then they'd realize they still needed her at headquarters.

In a room filled with comatose minds, Colt had an easy time sensing the presence of someone coming through the door. She turned her head just enough to see his white doctor's coat flapping around pressed black pants; his black hair slicked back and his thick moustache well trimmed; his big barrel chest, which, she noted with an inward smile, he was puffing up just a bit as he walked toward her.

He held a clipboard with a manila folder, Amber's file. She'd called ahead to ask him for it. She'd called the hospital instead of his cellphone. The expression on his face said he was still unhappy about that, but Colt liked to keep business and pleasure separate.

When he stopped in front of her, arms crossed, he opened his mouth but paused, taking her in. Colt saw his face change. She wanted to reach out, to pluck the thoughts from the top of his head, but had promised a long time ago to never do that. Not to him.

"I know it's not coming here to see me," his voice came out from deep inside his chest. "So what has you so excited?"

"Who says I'm excited?"

His eyebrows went up, his chin went down. "Rebecca." His Columbian accent rolled her name out like a poem. "I have known you a long time." He said it so softly that she had to lean in. He smelled good, like earthy spices. His voice rumbled and came out smoky. "And I can tell when you are full of shit."

A laugh jumped out of her mouth before she could stop it. He laughed with her. When they were done, she waited until the corners of her mouth had relaxed. He still wore a trace of the smile, more in his eyes than on his lips.

Colt nodded. "Carlos, I'm sorry, but—"

"There's a case."

"Yes."

"And she," he nodded toward Amber, "is a part of it."

"Yes."

Carlos exhaled. "Now, you're not planning on filling my hospital with bodies, right? Because, honestly, I took this job to get away from that kind of stuff."

"And here I thought you wanted to stay close by."

She regretted it the second she said it. Carlos' cheeks flushed. Colt gave herself a little pinch—there was work to be done.

"I don't think Prairie has anything to worry about," she said. "Whoever is doing this, they seem to be moving around a lot."

Carlos looked back. His face was boxy and had aged well. Wrinkles plagued him as much as any man in his fifties, but he wore them like badges of honor. Colt had noticed the gray in his hair the last time they'd been together, but there was a bit more of it now. She liked it on him. What she didn't like was his grim expression at the moment.

"Someone did this to her, with..." He waved his fingers in front of his forehead.

Colt nodded.

"Can you help her? Or someone at the DSI?"

Colt didn't look away from his eyes, as much as she wanted to. "No."

Carlos straightened and, after a minute of thought, slipped the file from the clipboard and handed it to her.

"Anything unusual about her?" she asked as she read.

"You mean other than the fact that she's in a coma?"

Colt didn't reply.

"Blood work came back clean; no drugs, no alcohol. There are no aneurisms or clots in her brain. No hormonal imbalances or signs of chemical fluctuations. Other than the bruises, there seems to be nothing."

"Bruises?" Colt raised her eyes from the page file.

Carlos gave her an inquisitive look. She didn't mean to glean the thoughts from his mind, but it was so focused she couldn't miss it.

He was thinking she missed something; she never missed things. Was she okay? Was everything all right? Did something happen? Maybe she was getting too old for—

Colt pulled her own mind back and hoped Carlos hadn't felt or seen anything. Thankfully, his expression didn't change as he walked around the bed and pulled up Amber's sleeve.

Two purple lines, thin as fishing line, ran across her arm. The bruising around them was heavy, and the lines themselves were terribly dark.

"There are more," Carlos said. "Other arm, across her back, and on her chest."

"She was tied up."

"Looks that way. But it wasn't for very long. The bruises look bad, but they are surface. The muscles and bones beneath show no damage."

"How long until bruises like this heal?"

Carlos bopped his head side to side as he thought. "Depends on the person, but about a week."

The other victims at the other hospitals had been admitted more than a week ago, long enough for any bruises to fade. Hopefully, there would be something in their medical files. Colt reached out and touched the thin lines. Again, she felt an immediate connection and in the back of her head, she heard that horrible howling of Amber's void.

But there was no mind, no memories to tell whether these marks meant something, which Colt really needed to know, because she'd never seen anything like this before.

Her eyes opened before she took her hand away. For an instant, she saw a flicker of light, like dust caught in a sunbeam. Except it wasn't floating dots. It was a line, a wafting thread running from Amber's head, up, up, and disappearing into the ceiling. Colt followed it, confusion spread across her face.

"Rebecca?"

She turned to Carlos. He was gazing in the general direction, but he saw nothing. Colt looked back, but her hand had left Amber's skin. The connection was gone and the line with it.

What the hell was going on here? Had she imagined it? Could it have been something else?

She needed to know more.

"What about her history? Drug abuse, mental instability, genetic disorders, family problems, related illnesses or oddities."

"Unless it's in her file, I wouldn't know. Her primary physician should—"

"She's not from around here?"

"She was transferred yesterday."

This was new. "From where?"

"Ahh," he said as he thought. "I believe Fieldsville General."

Colt glanced at the folder. "That's not in here." She looked up at him.

He shook his head slowly. He was starting to see the same thing as Colt.

"Clerical error?"

"No. Having a transfer made involves a lot of paperwork."

"Huh."

As much of a pain in the ass as Rakesh could be, he was damn good at getting intel. This didn't match what he had found. That meant the file had been tampered with. Somebody was trying to get rid of evidence but hadn't done a very good job.

Colt's eyes tightened.

"Rebecca?" Carlos didn't seem to share in her enthusiasm. In fact, he appeared worried. She softened the muscles in her face and laid a hand on his arm.

58

"Relax," she said. "I'm fact finding." And inside, a part of her hurt for lying to him.

"And not on a mission?"

She let go of his arm and looked away, toward the door. "I have to..."

Carlos cleared his throat and stepped back, making room.

"Call me," he said, hastily adding, "if you need any help."

Colt faked a smile and headed for the door. She knew he was watching her go, felt his eyes on her back. He hadn't pressed her for more answers, hadn't demanded more from her. He trusted her, utterly and completely. And his concern was real; he'd seen her at her worst, and she knew it. With every step she took away from him, her jacket felt twice as heavy on her shoulders.

Her hand was on the door, but she paused. "Carlos?"

"Yes?"

"How far is it to Fieldsville from here?"

He hummed as he thought. Colt had been listening to that sound for years, and hearing it warmed her. "Knowing how you drive? Just over an hour."

"That's a long drive."

"Yes." He waited patiently for her to reveal where this was going. He always waited patiently, had since the warehouse in Austin. Since she'd been forced to take time off, been reassigned a dozen times, fought and struggled to keep herself in the game, and spent the entire time keeping him just far enough away that she could escape whenever she wanted to.

But she never had. And he'd always been there, waiting.

"It's late," she said. "I'm going to put a call in and have the office dig up the paperwork on the other victims. How about we grab a bite to eat and... take it back to your place?"

Carlos crossed his arms, smiled, and hummed a little longer.

The sun was a pat of melting butter on the horizon as Vincent rode his bike down the gravel driveway. The air temperature had dropped. Goosebumps rolled across his arms as he coasted to the end of the drive. His mom's old, red sedan was parked at an angle. He smiled when he saw it.

Still feeling guilty, he rested his bike against the old oak tree and went in through the screen door. Carrots and peas, potatoes and onion, all bathed in a thick sauce and cooked with beef; the smells permeated the hallways and rooms of the house. In the living room, Vincent's little brother and sister were playing a videogame. It was one where the players worked as a team. The twins' arms moved the controllers up and down in perfect unison as their characters advanced effortlessly across the screen.

In the kitchen, his mom was humming her nameless tune while she and Mary moved pots and pans about. Vincent stopped outside the doorway and peeked in. His mom was at the stove. Mary's shoulder flashed as she set something in the sink. Vincent pulled back, resting against the wall, closing his eyes, and listening to his mom's song.

A psychic tap, like the one outside the school, came to Vincent's mind. He rolled his eyes and accepted Mary's request.

I know you're there. Mary's voice tinny sounded in Vincent's head.

Duh.

Come in and say hello.

No.

We could use your help.

I said no.

Mom's had a hard day. Mary paused. *Come in here.*

No! The speed of the rising anger surprised him. *Don't tell me what to do.*

"Vincent, honey?" his mom said like a song, lilting up and down. "You out there?"

Dang it.

Vincent broke the connection with Mary. "Yeah." Closing his eyes, he pushed down the heat in his chest.

"Can you come in here, please?" the musical quality was gone; she was upset. He thought, terrified, that she'd found out about him and Mary, the people they'd hurt. But if that were the case, she wouldn't be busy making dinner. She'd probably be screaming and yelling. Or, more likely, crying.

Coming around the corner, Vincent kept his eyes to the floor. Nobody spoke for a while. There was only the sound of bubbling sauce and Mary's knife cutting vegetables.

Chop, chop, chop.

His mom was still at the stove. Her hair, dark as Mary's but wavy like his, drifted back and forth over her shoulders as she stirred.

"I heard about the school yard."

Double dang it. Vincent's gaze fell on Mary, narrowing sharply.

"And your sister wasn't the one who told me, so stop giving her that look."

His eyes dropped fast, and his cheeks flushed. Was it just her, or could all moms do that?

"You want to tell me your side of it?"

Mary slid celery—chopped into perfectly even, measured pieces—across the cutting board and said, "It wasn't his fault."

"Mary," their mom cut in. "I'm talking with Vincent."

Vincent almost sneered. He didn't want Mary's help. He didn't want anything from her right now. At the cutting board, her knife came down a little harder than before.

Chop. Chop. Chop.

Their mom turned around, wiping her hands on a dishrag. Vincent couldn't meet her eyes.

"Well?" she said.

He mumbled and stared at the floor.

"Excuse me?"

"I said," he inhaled deeply. "Ashley Brinks is a... a jerk." It wasn't exactly what he'd muttered, but he wasn't in the mood to wash his mouth out with soap.

She'd make him do it, too. He knew from experience.

From beyond the veil of his flopping bangs, two feet wearing white socks stepped up to match toes with him. The hands that held him as a baby came to rest on his shoulders. They pulled him down—he was taller than her now—and he felt breath like a warm summer's breeze as his mother rested her lips and nose against the crown of his head and kissed him sweetly.

"I'm proud of you," she said into his hair. "It must have been hard to not hit that boy."

All of Vincent's frustration and anger bubbled and dissolved into the air. She squeezed his shoulders.

"And if Ashley Brinks decides to mess with your brother or sister again," she leaned in. "I want you to kick his ass." She gave his arm a slap. "You have my express permission." With a swish of her hips, she returned to the stove.

This was a mom trick. There was no way she was serious.

"But..."

Grabbing a wooden spoon, she gave the broth a vigorous turn. "You did the right thing. If that thick-skulled Neanderthal is too stupid to learn his lesson, it's his own damn fault."

"Mom!" Vincent couldn't stop the smile that spread across his lips.

"He's lucky I don't come down there and do it myself." Beneath her breath, but above a whisper, she said, "Mess with my kids… I'll teach that little shit."

Vincent laughed but heard the thump of Mary putting down her knife.

"Mom, language."

"Oh, shut up." Their mom waved an arm at the kitchen doorway. "They're playing that game, can't hear a thing."

Mary sighed. "I think Mom is trying to remind you, Vincent." She tilted her head slightly. It was an affected gesture, practiced and polished. "That we have to look out for each other."

Their mom slapped her hands loudly against the thick, canvas apron around her waist. "All right, that's enough about that. I'm gonna go pick some tomatoes from the yard. Mary, finish the veggies. Vincent, you keep stirring this until it's all bubbly, then add a few cups of water. If you burn my sauce, I'mma burn your butt. Got it?"

Vincent nodded and took up the spoon. Behind him, Mary went back to chopping. Vincent worried that, as soon as their mom left, Mary would try to keep the conversation going, but both her mouth and her mind were silent. The only sound was her blade coming up and down.

Chop, chop, chop.

They stood there, as they had so many times over the years, within a few feet of each other. Yet there had always been a distance, a rift Vincent felt like he couldn't cross. He'd tried to reach Mary on anything other than a surface level. And recently, since she'd found those other people—the ones she said were dangerous—he'd felt that distance grow.

Still, sometimes, in quiet moments, he would say things, and she would smile at him the same way she did at their mom. But lately, he wasn't sure if those smiles were real.

Chop, chop, chop.

No, they were. They had to be. Mary was strange and distant, but they were twins. He was sure she loved him as much as he loved her. She just wasn't good at showing it. Or saying it. Or...

The silence caught him off guard. A feeling, like ants marching across his back and shoulders, made him turn. Mary was standing, frozen. The knife floated an inch from the carrot on the board. Her eyes were wide. Her mouth hung open the tiniest of bits. Vincent paused. He wasn't sure if she was even breathing.

"Mary?" he said. No response, but her eyes were slowly turning, round and round. He'd never seen her so focused on using her ability.

But what was she using it for?

His mouth closed. He opened the connection on his end. *Mary?*

Someone...

Vincent's stomach knotted. *Did... did you find another one?*

Mary's gaze drifted out, beyond their yard, beyond the town, into a place where Vincent couldn't follow.

Someone's looking.

What?

Someone's looking, she turned to him. *For us.*

Out in the yard, their mother's song echoed from a hundred miles away.

CHAPTER FIFTEEN

As Colt snuggled against Carlos' bare chest, her curly hair felt coarse against her skin. It used to be soft and smooth as satin. She closed her eyes and tried to push the thought away. She reminded herself that she'd just given Carlos the ride of his life.

"Wow," was all the breath he could muster.

"Yeah," she replied, smiling as they enjoyed the quiet.

His hand drifted up and down her leg. He stopped near the side of her knee, over the old scar.

"It doesn't look too bad," he said. "Considering I had to do it in the field."

It comforted her that he knew not to talk about the scar beneath her belly button, the one that ran down farther than it should. She kissed him through her pillow of hair. "You did a great job."

"Does it bother you?"

Why did he always have to play doctor? "Nope."

"Good."

She sighed. "Those were exciting times."

"Yes." He grinned. "But I'm glad they're over. I am too old for that kind of life."

Her fingers, combing through Carlos' salt and pepper chest hairs, stopped. For as charming as he could be, he was subtle as a bowling ball. And maybe because of the psychic connection from them touching, or maybe because she'd had time to think, or maybe because she hadn't had an orgasm like that in a few months, she started to think Carlos had a point. She'd jumped into this investigation, fired up and ready to go. It may have clouded her judgment. She'd only assumed the other victims were level ones like Amber. Hell, she'd assumed they were actually victims of the same crime. Their symptoms were the same, but that didn't mean it was the same thing. Coincidence did happen in this world, and it worked hard toward making fools of us all.

What if she was wrong?

From the lounge chair near the bed, an electronic ring pushed its way through folds of tossed clothing. Colt rose. Carlos' soft chest hairs tickled her nipples, and a shiver ran across her back and down her legs.

"You have to go?" she asked, nodding her head toward the ring.

"Not mine."

With a little effort, Colt got out of bed and walked to the chair. Her coat slithered through her hands as she searched for the interior pocket. No matter where she looked, it always seemed to be one fold away. Who the hell would be calling at this hour anyway? The DSI was basically shut down, and she'd left a notice at the field office that she was researching a case. And since she was currently in bed with Carlos, that didn't really leave anyone else who would want to call her.

Seeing a sliver of pale blue light through a tiny pocket flap, Colt yanked the phone out and checked the number.

Oh Jesus Christ and Judas on a tandem bike.

Rakesh.

"Do you have any idea what time it is?" she said into the phone.

"I, uh... no?"

"Wait." She snapped.

"But—"

"I said wait." She searched the chair for something to wear. Rakesh couldn't see her, but it still felt weird being naked and talking to him. Pulling Carlos' white undershirt over her head, she grumbled, "Is this important?"

"I, uh..."

If he said he wasn't sure, hanging up would be the nicest thing she would do to him.

"I have some, some new data for—"

"Why aren't you using a transmitter?"

"Well," he said, his voice a little hurt and a lot confused. "After hours, we're only supposed to use them for emergencies."

Colt opened her mouth, but the only thing that came out was guilty silence. Turning, she found Carlos' eyes. It wasn't hard, he'd been staring at her the whole time.

The night was over.

"I'm going to take a shower," he said. "A long one."

She nodded appreciatively at him. As he walked by, she thought he might touch her arm, maybe even tickle her butt cheek, but he didn't. The bathroom door closed, leaving Colt feeling more alone than if Carlos wasn't there at all. She waited until she heard the showerhead rush to life.

"What do you have?" she asked.

"Well," Rakesh replied. "Uh, there are no known foreign or sleeper agents anywhere near Prairie."

"What about Fieldsville?"

"Nope."

"Any known psychics?"

"I mean, they've got a population of about three thousand, so by the numbers there are... uh... gonna be about three or four level ones." Rakesh flipped through some pages. "There was a, umm, a ping on our radar about, about... oh, come on, where is it? Ah. Thirteen years ago."

"And?"

"And nothing. Long range detectors picked up a surge in psychic activity, but it was a one-time thing, so there was no investigation."

Okay, that ruled out some possibilities. "What about the other coma patients, find anything?"

On the other end, the papers stopped. "Get your computer out."

She fired up the laptop and logged into the DSI system. Rakesh directed her to an email he'd sent. The attachment consisted of several scanned documents. Most were filled out by hand.

"I managed to get the patient files, the police reports and," he paused. "The transfer requests."

Colt clicked from one document to the next. "Fieldsville General."

"Two of them lived within Fieldsville's city limits, two of them commuted in for work from neighboring townships. All four were transferred at the family's request and all by the doctors on staff at the hospital. No reasons cited for the transfers."

The seed of a frown was planted on her lips. Something was off here, but she wasn't seeing it yet. "Any notes from the Fieldsville doctors?"

"Standard medical jargon."

The frown grew. There had to be some mention of those weird bruises. But all the doctor's notes she could see were nice and neat, a lot of numbers and stats.

"What about the police reports?"

"Standard law enforcement jargon."

He giggled. Colt was not amused, but she had to admit that he was right. The reports were systematic, written up with only the details. No notes about the victim's homes or neighbors. Not a mention of the calls to the families. No personal notes from the investigating officers.

In fact, nothing personal at all.

Colt leaned back. "You couldn't find anything weird?"

"No," Rakesh replied. "Everything was in order."

"How in order?"

"Uh," he considered her question, but she already knew the answer.

Perfect order. Immaculate. Not a flaw among them, not even a spelling mistake. Everything was written in sharp, crisp handwriting that didn't waste a stroke. Multiple forms, filled out by nearly a dozen people, and everything was just right.

And that's what was weird.

Colt's frown turned upside down. "You're right. No way it's a foreign agent."

"Why not?"

Colt's eyes tightened. "An agent would know how to cover their tracks. The guy doing this has no idea the DSI even exists."

66

"Which... means... he has no idea you're coming."

"Yup." She made a note to never doubt herself again. And to stop listening to Carlos. Maybe she would sneak into that shower and show him she wasn't getting too old for some excitement.

But first, as much as it pained her, she had to say, "Good job on getting all this, Rakesh."

He tried to reply, but she didn't have the patience to sit through his stammering.

"I'll give you a call when I find something in Fieldsville."

His generous acceptance of her praise came to quick stop. "Don't, don't you mean, 'if' you find something?"

"Go home, Rakesh."

Silence, the kind where someone knows there's more to say, but it won't do any good.

"Night, Agent Colt."

CHAPTER SIXTEEN

"Night, Mom," Vincent said.

"Goodnight, honey. Love you." Her voice was softer than his pillow.

"Love you too."

She closed his bedroom door, and her first few steps resonated through the floor, up the chipped and smudged posts of Vincent's bed, and pulsed against his skin. They were a heartbeat to him, and their sound lulled his eyelids and eased his mind.

He rolled over, his bed's old springs chirping loudly. Scanning the room, he saw the shadows of all his piles; piles of dirty clothes, piles of clean ones, piles of unfinished projects, piles of magazines and books. His room was not filthy, not even dirty, but it was far from kept. He liked it that way. He liked to have his things, the few he had, out where he could get at them. It was only a couple of years ago that he'd gotten his own room. He wanted to make sure everyone knew it was his. That he was living there. That he was a person.

That he was more than just Mary's twin brother.

That he wasn't her.

Closing his eyes, Vincent breathed deeply. He'd done that thing earlier, the thing where he was able to shut out the voices of other people. It didn't last long, unless he focused on it, but it was working now. He'd wanted to do it at school, had been thinking about it for weeks, but he knew what happened when it went up. There was that weird ripple, that shiver of the air around him. If the other kids saw him wall himself off, they'd go back to thinking he was a monster.

Vincent's eyes opened and stared at nothing.

A monster.

Maybe...

There was a touch, like a fly landing on the back of his skull. He huffed loudly and squinted. Even with the wall, she could reach though if she was near. He saw her thin shadow creeping at his door. She pushed it open so gingerly it didn't make a sound. Clamping his eyes shut, he curled up under his blanket and spoke through the heavy cotton.

"What?"

Mary's voice echoed in Vincent's head. *We need to prepare.*

"For what?" he snapped.

Someone is coming.

"How do you know?"

I— She hesitated. *You have to trust me.*

The skin around Vincent's mouth drew tight. "Yeah. Right." He burrowed his head deeper into the pillow and tried to pretend she wasn't there.

Mary's head tilted to one side. *You should have used it on Ashley.*

Beneath the blanket, his fingers and toes curled.

He tried to hurt us.

His nostrils flared.

You had the chance to stop him. Just like you stopped—

"No!" He shot up, his face resolute. "I won't, okay? I..."

Her face was completely blank. He'd yelled at her, and she hadn't even flinched.

"Never." He went back to his pillow. "I'm never using it... any of it... again."

In the fractured moonlight streaming through Vincent's window, Mary's eyes drifted across the messy room. In every corner, in every available inch, was some stack of the things that her brother loved. Things that were ready to topple over, to crumble, if pushed just the right way. And when one of those little towers fell, it would take others with it, and soon everything would be broken apart.

Slowly, she pulled the door closed.

CHAPTER SEVENTEEN

Mary hadn't felt it again, not since last night. Brief, but powerful. Another mind, well focused. Trained? Yes. Organized. Someone probing in the mind of the woman in Prairie. They'd walked in the broken woman's mind effortlessly. How? Ah, physical contact. Mary kept forgetting. Touching. Skin warm and minds hot with emotions. Why did people touch so much? She didn't enjoy it.

The classroom she sat in was filled with boys. They wanted to touch her. The skin of her breasts, the warmth between her legs. Their minds were simple and blunt. Sometimes their imaginations were so strong she would find herself drawn into the stories in their heads. The touching, the fingers, the tongues, the closeness and contact did not bring excitement to her, but disgust. No one was allowed to come that close. She did not like it, so she pushed on their minds, sent them onto other things and other girls. She felt no desire to make contact with them or anyone else.

Except Mom. Mom was good. Mom was safe. Mom would not hurt her. She liked Mom and her hugs and the way Mom would run fingers through her hair. Pleasantness came with that, and love. Mom brought joy, and Mary wanted to keep it that way. She'd arranged things, worked hard to keep things the same. If Mom was happy, Mary was happy.

But the person, the psychic searching for them, was coming. Why? What did they want? How had they discovered the woman in Prairie? Things, they knew things. Mary hadn't been able to connect to this new mind, to burrow into their body the way she'd learned with others. This person knew how to protect their mind, how to block her. The woman in Prairie had blocked her. The others she and Vincent had broken were able to block her. They had resisted, and Mary couldn't have that. Someone who could resist could cause the life Mary had built to come apart, to change.

Mary hated change.

This new person, she couldn't stop them, not with her ability.

Vincent. Foolish. He didn't understand. She sensed him down the hall, sitting in his class. He was filled with heat lately, uncontrolled emotions. Just like their dad had been. He was angry yet fearful. Useless feelings, they led to nothing good. She couldn't comprehend him. He had protected their siblings from Ashley but had not used his abilities. But then later, he tried using it in the creek. Why? Mary needed him to use his power, to control it. Together, they could stop this person searching for them.

But he was not listening. Mary needed him to listen.

Problems. People were nothing but problems. Stupid, foolish animals. No one did the right thing, even when it was obvious. Mary could see it; it was all so easy. If only they all did what she said, no one would be unhappy. No one would get hurt, especially Mom.

If only she could—

Her eyes widened. Her breath held. At the front of her classroom, the chalk in the teacher's hand came to stop halfway through the loping curls of a word written in cursive. The kids sitting in the room all went silent. Their eyes glazed over. No one watched Mary stand. For them, time was frozen. They did not see her go to the window. They missed her eyes squinting, her nose wrinkling.

Her hands clenching into fists.

CHAPTER EIGHTEEN

It was the kind of road that faded away, stretched into the distance and became one with everything. With the grass, the sky, the tiny black line where the earth ended and the blue began. Colt had seen an aging metal sign with a route number a few miles back. But other than that, not much.

She loved drives like this. There wasn't another living soul within a mile of her. And, if there was, they were traveling in the opposite direction on the same straight road. They'd appear and be gone before she could even get a read on them. Being out in the open plains allowed her to fully drop her psychic walls, to relax a muscle that she'd been holding tense for so long, she'd forgotten there was any other way.

In the seat next to her, her phone sat, screen dark. She peeked at it and then at the odometer. In less than 20 minutes, she would be in Fieldsville. That calm, relaxed feeling ebbed.

She'd stopped about half an hour ago. Partly for gas, but mostly to stretch her legs. The little station and convenience store had been as dirty, depressing, and run down as every other one she'd stopped at in this part of the country. Hard times had come to Middle America a few decades ago and had never really left.

She'd put in a call to Rakesh to see what info he had on her destination. He'd been away from his desk then and hadn't called back yet.

Her eyes settled back onto the road. The horizon stayed flat, but she knew that soon she'd hit the outskirts of Fieldsville, a place that was potentially a hot spot for some kind of psychic activity. She'd learned the hard way what can happen when going into something blind. As the Hyundai eased down to sixty, Colt took a deep breath.

CHAPTER NINETEEN

The mounted TV in front of him was on, but Rakesh didn't see it. Beyond that, the large window reflected a ghostly image of his body as he bounced up and down, but he didn't notice it. Farther still, past the TV, past the glass, the city of Arlington was busy and bustling. The sun painted the walls of government and private offices with yellows and whites. Glass buildings glistened like Fourth of July sparklers caught in time.

Rakesh wasn't looking at any of it. He wasn't looking at anything, really. His eyes were open, but he saw long, winding paths, roads and sidewalks going up hills and down. His ears were filled with the mechanical whining of the rotating belt beneath his padding feet, the thump-thump of his sneakers coming down, the gentle whisper of his running shorts moving back and forth, back and forth. But he didn't hear it. Instead, he listened to his breathing. He listened to his heartbeat in the backs of his ears. He listened to the silence of the tenth mile of his run. He wasn't thinking, wasn't doing anything.

Just running.

"Sir?"

And now he was falling.

Coming in just shy of a miracle, Rakesh managed to lock one hand onto the treadmill's console. Beneath him, the belt kept spinning while his feet flailed about. His other arm shot out for balance, bobbing like a cheetah's tail.

"Sorry!" Sandra said. "I'm so sorry!"

Rakesh wanted to tell her that it was okay, but he was too busy desperately trying to smack of the stop button and kill the motor. When he did, the belt hummed itself to sleep. Rakesh gasped for breath. His sweat landed with plip-plop sounds on the treadmill.

Carefully, he stood. His running shirt, a polymer blend tank top, clung to his thin torso. The navy blue stripes down his chest flexed with each breath. The white was wet enough to be slightly transparent. Hands on his hips, he turned slowly.

Sandra was biting her bottom lip. With the stinging sweat in his eyes, Rakesh couldn't tell if she was embarrassed, stifling a laugh, or both. He made a weak attempt at a smile. He was really hoping she was there to work out, that maybe they would get a chance to chat. But instead he found himself facing a wild tangle of wires. And if she was wearing her transmitter gear, that could only mean one thing.

"Who..." He'd just gone from a seven and a half minute mile to standing still. His body didn't seem sure where it should be sending his blood. So after the world became very small, then very large, then normal, he blinked hard, ran his hands over his dripping face, and tried again. "Who is it?"

"I am so sorry, Rakesh. I didn't mean—"

He raised a hand, dropped his head, and tried to bring his breathing down slowly.

Deep breath in. Let it go slow. Deep breath in. Let it go slower. Control your breath, don't let it control you.

When he looked up again, Sandra said, "Agent Colt, sir."

And then his breathing stopped, if only for a second. His head bopped up and down. "Okay," he said softly. He couldn't sit because his heart was still beating too fast. So, he gestured to the treadmill next to his own. Sandra climbed up. Rakesh turned his back to her.

"Now," she began, but Rakesh spun and peered at her like a kid caught stealing a fingertip of icing from his own birthday cake.

"I..." he stammered. "I'm all sweaty."

Sandra smiled, genuine and warm. Flushed as he already was, Rakesh felt his cheeks redden further.

"Now," she said, gesturing for him to turn back around. Her fingers graced the edges of his black hair. "Just so you're aware." Her fingertips slid against his scalp. "She's driving."

"What?"

"So hold on."

"What?" he said, considerably louder.

He was used to the lurch, his mind being cast out across the psychic airwaves that few in the world could access. Sandra was a transmitter, a special kind of sensory type. If you were to put her in the center of a town, she could locate any individual she wanted to within a half-mile radius. Enhanced through DSI technology, Sandra could make instantaneous links over incredible distances. Like all high level psychics, she could use telepathy, the spike, and the wall. But her real talent came in taking Rakesh's mind for a ride on an incorporeal rollercoaster.

Usually, Rakesh would close his eyes and wait for it to be over. A big drop, some twists, maybe a corkscrew or a loop-the-loop if the agent he was connecting with was farther away. He didn't like it, but he'd gotten used to it.

Connecting to a moving target? With his eyes half open? It wasn't a rollercoaster. It was riding a bullet. It was being pulled halfway across America, around houses, through trees, over fields, this way, that way, and then slamming down into the seat of Colt's humming Hyundai. All in the time it took him to swallow back what little there was left in his stomach.

Colt glanced over as Rakesh's psychic projection appeared in the passenger seat. His hands and face were clear and detailed. His torso was like a comic book drawing that had been sketched and colored but needed a final inking. His legs were non-existent. The oddest part was how the light coming through the car windows didn't cast shadows across him. In fact, he had no shadows at all. He looked like he was sitting for a magazine cover photo shoot.

Which meant, when Rakesh reached out to stabilize himself and saw his hands go through the dashboard, Colt saw clearly the color in his face change.

"Don't you dare throw up in my car."

"I'm..." Rakesh let out a burp that came up from a little too low down. "I'm not in your car."

"Doesn't matter." Colt said, looking back at the road.

Rakesh took a big breath. "Don't forget I'm the one who writes off your mileage."

Colt had expected a "yes ma'am," an "of course," maybe even a "roger dodger." But she kind of liked snarky Rakesh better. Waiting for him to settle, she glanced over as his projection sat back in the seat and looked around. His eyes grew large.

"Wow."

"Welcome to Kansas," Colt said gently.

Colt took in the view as well, the flat, rolling sea of green cornstalks, their pulse set by the wind of the world. The sky was encompassing and unhindered. Miles and miles away, a single radio tower cut a thin line into the blue. Outside of that, it was a wash of light and clouds and farmland.

Rakesh leaned forward. "Wow," he said again, soft and breathy, the way a kid would. Thirteen hundred miles away, Sandra smiled and ran her fingers through his hair.

In the distance, specks dotted the horizon like ladybugs crawling through the grass. In a minute, Colt would drive into the outer edges of Fieldsville. She shifted in her seat again as though her leg was stiff. But it wasn't. She just felt... twitchy.

"All right," she said. "What have you found?"

"I..."

She knew that wasn't going anywhere good.

"I don't know."

She didn't snap or bark. Instead, she just watched as the ladybugs grew into well kept homes.

"Fieldsville," Rakesh said flatly. "According to the last census, general population at just over three thousand."

The homes were standard fare for Kansas, nothing fancy, not too big, and just a little bit quaint.

"Originally established as a farming town, it saw a boon in the seventies and eighties due to the manufacturing plants that moved in."

At a glance, Colt suspected every porch had at least one perfectly painted white rocking chair.

"It was mostly ceramics that—"

"How about you give me what I can't find on Google."

"Well," Rakesh said. "Local economy tanked a little more than twenty years ago."

And there were the white picket fences, the pickup trucks in the driveways. Maybe it was because Colt didn't have sunglasses on, but everything seemed to be... shiny. Clean. Waxed and polished and painted.

"The factories shut down around then and people—"

"Come on." Colt's voice wasn't laced with disappointment, it was drenched with it. But she hadn't meant it. She blinked and stretched her neck muscles, hoping to relieve whatever was causing her irritability. Outside, the huge fields between homes were disappearing. The manicured lawns were only just big enough to warrant a riding mower.

"Go deeper," Colt said. "I want the nuts and bolts."

"Yeah," Rakesh sighed. "But see, that's it."

Why was her back tensing up? "What's it?"

"That." Rakesh held up empty hands.

"What do you—"

"Twelve years," Rakesh said. "I looked at twelve years, Agent Colt. Internet and magazines and newspapers and blogs. I checked government funding, state funding, grant proposals, 501(c)(3) applications. I opened up every social media website. I saw everything. Everything that's gone into or come out of Fieldsville. Nothing. Not a single goddamn thing."

It was that odd feeling of having peed less than an hour ago but feeling like you may have to go again—only throughout her whole body.

"It, it, it... the place doesn't exist. I mean, it's there—"

"But completely inconspicuous."

"Yes!" Rakesh pointed at Colt excitedly.

Colt nodded. She left her palm on the steering wheel, but pointed her fingers at the windshield, and at the houses outside of that. Her tendrils stretched out.

Back in Arlington, Sandra's heart began to beat just a little faster.

Colt said, "Someone's made it invisible."

"Yes," Rakesh replied. "Well, no. I mean, kind of. They, you know, they still have, like, power and stuff."

"Uh-huh." Colt's tendrils didn't have to go far before she felt it.

"The electric company knows they're there."

Sparks in the air.

"Delivery trucks come and go. Life seems to, like, carry on, day to day. All while no major products are being shipped out, no huge money is coming in. Somehow they, they... I mean, hell, they even built a huge mall a few years back."

Colt watched shadows from trees and light posts slide across the hood of the Hyundai. "So things are going well in Fieldsville?"

"Yeah, but... you remember the doctor's notes?"

Colt responded with a distracted grunt.

"That's everything. Everything. I couldn't find one stray hair, okay? No lawsuits, no public health reports."

She could practically smell it, like ozone before a storm.

"I couldn't even find a parking ticket."

Colt checked one side of the road, then the other. "Sounds like a little slice of heaven."

"It sounds like it shouldn't exist."

The Hyundai's wheels stopped. Colt gestured out the window at the people peppering Fieldsville's Main Street. "Why don't you go ahead and tell them that?"

CHAPTER TWENTY

The muscles in Sandra's forearms twitched. She closed her mouth and swallowed.

Agent Colt? Her voice rang out in both Rakesh's and Colt's minds. She didn't even try to hide the fact that it was wavering.

"Yeah," Colt said aloud. "I know."

They were on the main drag of Fieldsville's downtown area. It was a two-lane road, bordered with tall, old-fashioned light posts, rising and arching down gently, ending in a golden bulb the size of a watermelon. The posts were painted the same shade of dark green as the leaves on the trees that dotted the sidewalks. Everything was stores, small with simple awnings and the names painted on the windows. Outside the corner coffee shop, two or three metal tables and chairs sat beneath umbrellas. A little farther down the road, a diner with fancy brickwork sat nestled next to a bookstore whose front door was surrounded by tables holding stacks of new and used books, all arranged, all displayed neatly.

People slipped in and out of shops. Colt heard door chimes—all real bells, nothing electronic or jarring. People were walking dogs. Out in the street, trucks and cars glistened in the morning light as they rolled by. Down at a cross street, a school bus lurched through the intersection. On the sidewalk, a few kids wearing backpacks hustled along. Others rode bikes calmly through traffic, no helmets.

But Colt focused on something else. Filling her ears was the humming of living things, the buzzing of ten thousand pairs of wings, a hive of insects just beneath the surface, all waiting to be agitated, to erupt. It was a tickling, like every inch of skin had fallen asleep.

A drop of sweat rolled down in front of her ear, slipping toward the nape of her neck.

"I'm putting up a wall," Colt said only a moment before the air around her shimmered, a wave of bent light rippling across her body. "Sandra? How are you now?"

I...

Her voice seemed distant. No, muffled. Like she was speaking through a closed window.

I don't know.

"What?" Rakesh asked anxiously. His projection had become slightly out of focus. "What's going on?"

"Sandra," Colt's eyes narrowed. "Be prepared to break contact if we have to."

Understood.

Rakesh's eyebrows crunched together. "Why? What—"

Colt turned and spoke quickly. "There's something here, all around us. It's..." She paused. "I've run into something similar before."

"When?"

"It was stronger, more concentrated than this. I'm not quite sure..." Colt's eyes wandered.

Rakesh leaned in. "Colt, when—"

"No back up," Colt said firmly. "I can keep this out with my wall. It's weaker, spread thin. But nobody else. Not this time."

Rakesh nodded. "Okay."

Leaning over the steering wheel, Colt gazed up at the rooftops and across the sky. "Sandra, what are the chances you can give me a little boost?"

I don't think that's a good idea, Agent Colt.

"I need to check something."

You're not a sensory type.

"I know."

There could be negative—

Colt huffed. "I know. Just do it."

Silence.

Sir?

Colt looked at Rakesh. He'd been staring at her. His image was still out of focus, but Colt saw the hardness spread across his face.

His eyes were glued to Colt's. "Go ahead, Sandra."

Yes, sir.

For Colt, it felt like warm sunbeams touching the skin around her eyes. She had to blink hard to readjust. Around the car, the world glowed in a layered pattern of auras. Everything, the trees, the cars, the buildings themselves, pulsated. It was less than Colt had expected. She'd thought a mist or a fog would hang over everything.

She thought it'd be like Austin, like Samuel Bentley's terror cloud.

Inside her head, behind her eyes and inside them, those sunbeams grew hotter. It felt like high noon on the beach in July.

The people walking the streets had auras, visual representations of their psychic energy. There were different colors, vibrations, shapes, and a dozen other things that Colt's brain couldn't interpret. In the back of her mind, Sandra's presence was trying to translate the sensory information into something Colt could process.

"Where is it?" she whispered.

Agent Colt? Sandra's voice, even coming straight from the woman's mind and spoken without breath, was thin and whispered. *The sky.*

Colt looked up. "What..." But then she saw it; a flicker, a single strand of spider's silk drifting through a pocket of light. A psychic thread, just like the one Colt had seen attached to Amber at the hospital. It was gone as

79

quickly as it had appeared, but before Colt could look away from that spot, another flashed at the corner of her vision. Then another, far off in the distance. Colt tried to follow them, to see where they were going. They existed in between the spaces of eye movements. The more she looked, the more she saw. Five. Ten. Twenty. Dozens. They were everywhere.

Not too far away, a single strand glimmered in the light, but didn't fade. Colt stared. It grew brighter, then thicker. Colt felt something, a pressure in her ears. The light whipped. The thread thickened into a strand of yarn and flashed neon green as it zipped over her car, vanishing behind it. The pressure on Colt's ears, not her actual ears, just inside of her mind, rocked her. Her eyes squeezed shut. She heard a crackling, like twigs breaking, and knew it was from the soft pink flesh of her eyes. Instinctively, she pulled her wall in and used it force Sandra out. The stinging, burning sensation diminished, but a tiny bit lingered, as though she had just finished chopping onions.

"Sorry," she said softly. "Sandra, I'm—"

It's fine. Sandra's voice was distant. Only a shred of their connection remained. *He's fine.*

When Colt opened her eyes and blinked back the tears blurring the world, she saw her hands, white knuckled, on the steering wheel. Rakesh's projected image was gone. At the edge of Colt's nose, a single runny drop of snot hung. Colt sniffled and rubbed her nostrils with the back of her hand.

Are you—

"Fine." Colt said. She breathed deeply, the way one would after sitting down from a long day of being on their feet. "Did you catch all that?"

Yes.

"And you can relay it to Rakesh?"

Yes.

Colt nodded. Outside the car, the world was normal again; no auras, no threads, no swirling colors of psychic energy. So much of what she'd seen hadn't made any sense, and that was just a touch of the invisible world. She wondered how life must be for Sandra.

A crowd of teenagers wearing plain shirts and simple jeans wandered by, their backpacks jostling. She heard their chatter through the closed windows.

"Sandra?" she swallowed.

The crowd of teens split apart at the front, moving like water around some obstacle in the middle of the sidewalk.

"Tell Rakesh that I'm sorry."

He says he would like to know what happened.

"Could you explain it?"

No, the teens weren't like water. They were like a school of fish, all moving together perfectly.

He also wants to know what the next step is.

The pod of bodies ended. As the last two slipped apart, Colt saw a girl standing there. She was dressed much the same as the other kids, simple plaid skirt, sneakers with white socks, white dress shirt with the sleeves rolled up. The girl's hair, dark as a stained mahogany dresser, was pulled up into two large pigtails so curly they were practically poof balls on the sides of her head.

"Information gathering." Colt said.

The girl peered in at Colt with eyes darker than the curly hair on her head.

"I want to know where this psychic energy is coming from."

He would like to know how you plan on finding that out.

The girl's eyes jumped up, above and beyond Colt's car. Colt heard a loud, single whoop of a police siren. In her driver's side mirror, she saw the silver grill of a police car approach her bumper. The headlights were big and round, the glass exposed. It was an older model, but she couldn't tell which one. Either way, the car glistened with a wax job that could make a Brazilian Model jealous. Quickly, Colt glanced back through the windshield. A block away, two puffy pigtails blended back in with the crowd.

She sighed. "I guess I'll just have to ask." Straightened her back, trying to stretch her leg—the ache had returned—Colt said, "Tell Rakesh he may get some calls. Whatever they ask about, just have him say 'yes'."

Yes, ma'am.

"Colt out." With a sharp exhale, Colt broke Sandra's connection.

CHAPTER TWENTY-ONE

"Agent Colt says—"

Rakesh replied with a raised index finger. He hugged the plastic trashcan against his chest, and it rumbled with his dry heaves. When the spasm stopped, the only thing that fell into the bin was spittle and sweat. Rakesh leaned back against the wall and closed his eyes.

Sandra stepped forward. "Should I get—"

"Whatever," he said, thin and weak and frustrated. The trashcan dropped to the floor with an unceremonious thump. "I just..." He buried his face in his hands. "Stupid," he said into his own palms. "So stupid."

Sandra smiled. She walked toward him and said softly, "Rakesh," but stopped when, from between his hands, Rakesh muttered:

"I hate psychics."

The room sat cold and quiet.

Sandra stepped back. "Is there anything else I can do, sir?"

Rakesh looked up. His glassy eyes darted around, coming into focus for the first time since the connection with Colt had been broken. "I... what?"

"If there's nothing else?" Sandra said, politely.

Rakesh's jaw flapped. "Um, I, I don't think—"

She gave a quick nod, turned, and started out of the gym. Rakesh watched in confusion. Her steps were tight and controlled. Her hand grazed the edge of a weight rack for support. When she was halfway to the door, the last few moments came into Rakesh's mind, rising from the fog.

"Sandra!"

She stopped and turned sharply, but when she saw him, his eyes both clear and aghast, his entire face screaming of embarrassment, she couldn't help but be a little bit soft.

"I..." His mouth moved around silent and unfinished words, as though testing each one out until he found the one that fit. "Next time," he said. "I'll listen."

She didn't respond.

"You know," he continued, choppily. "To, to you. About the, um, if, if there's another... I mean, I hope there's not. No, not, not with you. I mean, not not with you. I just—"

"Sir?"

He stopped. "Yes?"

She smiled. "Thank you."

He smiled, too. "I'm sorry." He took a deep breath. "I didn't... it, it's hard. There's so much."

"I know."

"Yeah." His eyes fell to the floor. "Clearly, I don't."

Sandra walked up to him. She wanted to reach out, to run the tips of her fingers through the hair on the back of his downturned head. "That's why I'm here," she said softly.

He looked up, into her eyes.

"I'm happy to help."

He smiled. "Thank you."

Sandra heard it, the beating of her own heart. In the air between them, she swore his heart was thumping loudly. Everything else around them fell away. Only the space between their gazing eyes existed. And it grew heavy, so heavy that Sandra felt it pulling her in. Pulling them both in. His eyes twitched back and forth. She tried to follow them. Was he leaning in? Was she? She saw the little beads of sweat on his forehead. In her ears, the blood pumped quickly. The air was charged with an electric bolt that would fire if they grew any closer. His eyes went big and wide. His mouth opened just slightly. The muscles in his body tightened, and she knew, at any second, he would—

A tiny burp slipped from Rakesh's lips. He threw himself to the side, found the trashcan, and threw up.

CHAPTER TWENTY-TWO

In her side mirror, Colt watched a pair of pleated khaki pants held up by a black and polished gun belt move toward her car. The officer reached out and touched the trunk, just beyond the plastic brake light covers. She knew police did that to leave their fingerprints in the event that something bad went down and they needed to prove they approached that particular vehicle, and from which side.

Colt took a chance and solidified her wall. The ripple through the air was minimal, and she doubted anyone coming up behind would notice it. Still, only a moment later, there was a not-so-gentle rapping at her window.

Colt peeled her left hand from the steering wheel. Thankfully, the shakes had left her already, which meant pushing her abilities wouldn't leave any permanent damage.

The window was still lowering when a deep voice, layered with a distinct down-home kind of accent, rolled into her car.

"Afternoon, ma'am."

Colt put on a little smile and a lot of lightness in her voice. "Afternoon, Officer."

The second the last bit of window vanished into the door with a thump, a long fingered hand came to rest there. He had to bend down, folding over like a willow branch, to look through her window. Colt guessed he was easily six-one, maybe six-two. His skin was the color of roasted coffee beans, and his hair had less gray around the temples than the wrinkles of his face led her to believe there should be.

"Is everything okay in here, ma'am?" He didn't speak slowly, but there wasn't any rush. He wanted her to hear every word.

Colt nodded. "Yes, Officer." Her eyes jumped the six-pointed badge hanging from his shirt, that same khaki as his pants. "Sorry, Sheriff."

The sheriff paused and stared. Colt did everything she could to breathe normally. Recognizing the badge may have been a bad move. His eyes, darker than his skin, jumped between hers.

"You feeling okay, today?"

Colt opened her mouth, and the laugh that came out was genuine. "Oh. The—" her finger waggled at her eyes, bloodshot from stressing her psychic abilities.

She sheriff gave half a nod, just up. He was ready to listen but not to believe.

"Allergies," Colt said and took a chance to sniff loudly, which she needed to anyway.

The sound was thin and wet and caused the sheriff to pull back the tiniest of bits.

"They're really up today," she said. "Not sure why."

The sheriff's eyes held on her for just a second, but then scanned around the car, spending a lot of time on the manila folders spread across the passenger seat. "You not from around here?"

Colt stopped her sniffling. She didn't mind holding her cards close to her chest, but that didn't mean the sheriff should assume she didn't know how to play the game. When she didn't answer, the sheriff's eyes stopped wandering and fell back to her. Colt offered a wry smile.

He already knew the answer, and she knew that he knew.

Taking his cue, the sheriff stiffened. "License and registration."

After she snatched the registration from the glove compartment, her hand drifted toward the inner pocket of her jacket where her DSI badge sat. But something tickled at her brain. It was how the sheriff was watching her, how his hand didn't hover over his weapon, but she could tell that it wanted to.

So instead, Colt handed over her Kansas driver's license.

"Just passing through today?" he eyed the license. "Or you here on business, Ms. Colt?"

Colt's wall blocked her from skimming his mind, but she didn't have to. In less time than it took a fly to dodge a swatting hand, the sheriff's eyes jumped to the folders and back. With a twist, Colt stuck her fingers into the top folder. Behind her, the sheriff leaned to the side, peeking.

Colt turned and handed him a picture of Amber. She expected the sheriff to snatch the picture from her, but he took it gently, making sure not to crease it. As he looked it over, nothing about his expression or demeanor changed.

"Her name is Amber," Colt said. "She went missing a little while back, ended up in a hospital in Prairie."

Nothing. The sheriff just listened. Colt still wasn't sure if it was a poker face.

"She's in a coma or something. According to her records, she was transferred from Fieldsville."

Just a nod and a low pitched "Mm-hm."

"I was hoping that maybe the doctors could give me some answers about what happened to her. Or maybe someone in town."

That got his attention. His eyes came up, alert and protective. "Is she family?"

Colt shook her head.

"Private eye?"

"Best in Kansas."

The sheriff nodded slowly, his face a blank. Normally, she would just reach out and give him a push, a little psychic nudge making him more inclined to be of assistance. But she was nervous. That weird feeling was swirling against her wall. So, instead, she had to do this the old-fashioned way, a good old stare down.

And Colt was not about to lose.

With a big, open-mouthed huff, the sheriff handed the photo back to Colt. "Can't say I know her." His tone was downright friendly.

"But do you remember her?"

He shook his head. "She ain't local, but that don't mean much. Hospital's a ways out of town. Anyone gets hurt on a highway in a 20-mile radius, they end up there."

"You think that's what happened?"

"Could be."

"Doesn't ring a bell?"

"Nah. Hospital's under my purview, but I don't hear about everything that goes on there. Troopers handle most of the highway stuff. I could give 'em a buzz, send the name along and see what they know."

"I'd appreciate that." Colt pointed at the sidewalk. "You think anyone in town might know what happened?"

Again, that protective expression crossed the sheriff's face. "Couldn't say for sure."

Colt nodded. "Small town."

The sheriff smiled as he watched the cars driving by. "Pretty quiet, though," he said, proud and affectionate.

"Word gets around?"

"I think someone would have said something."

Colt had lived in Kansas for a while now and, before that, she'd traveled all over the globe. Most small towns in America were quaint, charming, rustic, but just the tiniest bit frayed. They were your grandfather's tweed jacket, lovely and warm, but the colors blended, the lines were all soft, and there was always that one loose button.

From what she could see, Fieldsville's buttons were sewn on so tight, it would take a paring knife to get them off. Hell, she couldn't even find a piece of litter. And she was looking. Hard.

Her eyes narrowed. "Everything's so… neat."

"We have to keep things nice," the sheriff said, his voice drifting off a little. He seemed caught up in a thought, a daydream. His chest stopped rising and falling. He came back to the world with a smile and a quick breath. "Take Main Street down till it becomes the highway. It'll veer a few times, but stay on it. Go through the old factory district. After that, first thing you'll see is the mall on your right. Next crossroad, take a left. Hospital's a few miles out that way."

Colt nodded. "Thank you, Sheriff."

An "mm-hm," a nod, a pat of his hand on the roof of her car, and the sheriff was gone, walking back to his cruiser. Colt put the photo back and started the engine. She waited for the sheriff to pull out around her. He turned, nice and slow, at the next intersection. Colt noticed he wasn't looking back at her.

As she headed away from the shops of Main Street, she had to laugh. They even called their main street, "Main Street." Every storefront was filled, not a closed shop or empty space in town. There was an ice cream parlor, a bookstore, a toyshop without a single videogame in the window. It seemed like a perfect little town, the kind of place every parent wanted their kid to grow up in.

The small shops ended. There were a few bigger stores, hardware, grocery market, a little more modern, but none of them brand names. Ahead, the old factory buildings loomed. Fieldsville was finally starting to show some wear.

But that was it. After that, it was houses and highways and, after following the sheriff's directions, Fieldsville General Hospital. It was larger than she had expected. The main lobby of the three-story building was a big open space filled with chairs and potted plants. Colt stopped and tucked her hands into her pockets.

The farther she'd gotten from downtown Fieldsville, the weaker that buzzing sensation had become. The density of the air had fallen. Out by the hospital, it was like walking out of the humidity and into dry, machine-conditioned air. Colt had dropped her wall. . She couldn't hold it up indefinitely, and she was already feeling a little drained.

But here, closest to ground zero, Colt wasn't going to take any chances. No one was watching. Nurses and orderlies went about on their business. A few patients and visitors milled about.

A shimmer spun around Colt's body. It was the lowest-level wall she could produce. It wouldn't provide protection from psychic attacks, but it would mask her from detection. There weren't any signs of psychic activity, but whoever had put those people into comas had gotten them transferred out of the hospital. There was a chance the attacker worked there.

A few quick inquiries led her to the third floor. Stepping off the elevator, Colt walked into white hallways. Every fifteen feet or so, a watercolor painting of a flower or a field or a boat on the water broke up the monotony. The ward was shaped like an "H," with the nurses' station in the middle of the crossover. Behind the counter, a pudgy woman with short hair dyed a ridiculous shade of red sat with her head down, shuffling papers.

"Excuse me," Colt said. "I need to speak to the doctor in charge."

The nurse huffed loudly. "I'm sorry?" she said, even though she had heard full well.

This wasn't a stare down moment. Instead, Colt just whipped out her DSI badge. The nurse glanced at the badge, then back to Colt.

"Good enough?" Colt asked.

The nurse licked her lips and reached for the phone. Colt knew better than to grin. Putting her badge away, she pulled out a sheet of paper.

"This is a list of previous patients. Go ahead and pull their files."

The nurse simply reached up and took the paper—no argument or questioning. She typed and mumbled into the phone at the same time. With a short nod, Colt turned and leaned back against the counter.

And that's when she heard it.

It was an echo of a whisper in her mind. There were no words, nothing intelligible anyway. It was a sound, a feeling, an emotion carried on the invisible waves that only Colt could feel.

It was a child in the dark, the essence of fear.

While the nurse was busy, Colt stalked the hallway.

Come on…

A tingle spread across her brain. Like following the smell of warm bread to a bakery, she followed the sensation to a door that was slightly ajar. Inside, she heard the steady shushing of a respirator sending air into someone's lungs. Leaning in, she saw a figure lying in the room's only bed.

He was young, in that tender age she remembered so well that sat somewhere between childhood and adulthood. His tousled hair, the flower pots holding mostly stems, the balloons that had lost their lift and lay on the floor; he'd been at the hospital for a long time. Colt saw all that, but it was his sheets that really caught her attention.

They were perfect. He looked like a packaged good, a Twinkie in a wrapper. There wasn't a wrinkle around him.

The tingle resonated in Colt's mind again. She inhaled quickly, but blew out slowly. This could be anything. There were a thousand reasons for him to be in the hospital. Just because he was in a coma didn't mean he was another victim.

But if he was, Colt was going to take whoever did this back in pieces.

Nervously, she reached out. She remembered the experience of Amber's mind, and wasn't thrilled at facing something like that again. But if the same thing had happened to this boy, if he was a level one as well…

Someone down the hall called out, "Hello? Ma'am?"

Colt stepped out of the room and said, "Here."

From around the nurses' station, a young doctor stepped out. She was petite, wearing a standard white doctor's coat, and her thick black hair was in a loose bun held in place by a sharpened pencil and a ball point pen. Beneath her thick, black, plastic frame glasses, she appeared more than a little irritated. She didn't barrel down the hallway toward Colt, but she sure didn't take her sweet time either.

Colt nodded as the doctor approached but didn't receive one in return. Instead, the doctor glanced back at the room where Colt had just come from.

"I'm Doctor Foster," she said, her voice carrying a bit of a smoker's growl. "Is there something I can help you with?"

Colt pulled out her badge. "I'm Special Agent Colt with the DSI. I have a few questions."

"DSI?" Foster asked, one eyebrow going up. Way up.

"Department of Scientific Investigation."

Foster took the badge and stared at it. "Huh."

Colt waited. She loaded her come-back gun with every sarcastic response she had for the "I've never heard of that" every idiot gave her.

"All right." Foster nodded, handed back the badge, and smiled. "What can I do for you?"

Colt tilted her head. Foster wasn't being nice, she wanted to know what was going on and was smart enough to know playing nice was the best way to figure that out.

Colt liked her already.

"Do you have the list of patients I gave to the nurse?"

"I do." And she did. They were right there, on top of her notepad. She made absolutely no indication that she would be handing them over.

"Did you treat any of them?"

"I recognize two of them. The others were treated by different doctors."

"But they all had the same symptoms?"

Foster thumbed through the files as she spoke. "From what I can see, yes."

"Four people, all perfectly healthy, fall into deep comas for no apparent reason."

Foster dropped the pages.

"And nobody here thinks that maybe they should report that?"

"There didn't seem to be any connection," she said flatly. Apparently, she wasn't interested in playing nice anymore. Or mean. Or anything.

"Besides the fact that they all live or work in the same area?"

"There..." Foster's voice wavered. "There didn't seem to be any connection."

Colt paused. That wasn't a lie, but it wasn't the truth either. "So, why were they transferred?"

"The families requested it."

"Any particular reason?"

"No."

"No reason at all?"

"The families requested it."

Colt squinted. "The families, did they know about the other cases?"

"No."

"Why didn't you tell them?"

"There didn't seem to be any connection."

"And did you push back against the transfers?"

"No."

"Why not?"

"The families requested it." Without a blink, without a smile or a twitch. Completely passive.

Colt paused." How long have you been at the hospital?"

"Oh." Foster tick-tocked her head. "About four years now."

"You like it?"

A quick shrug. "Small town, relatively quiet, good people."

"You married?"

Foster's eyes tightened, and her head pulled back slightly. "I don't see what—"

"Just being thorough," Colt said.

With a big sigh, Foster held up her left hand to show it lacking any rings. "Nope." She used the hand to push back a loose bit of hair and adjust the pencil holding the bun.

Colt nodded slowly and waited a moment. "Was there anything else unusual about the coma patients?"

"No." Boom. Instant. Foster's entire body changed. Everything went slack. Her face, her eyes, they were dead. "There was nothing unusual about them."

Colt closed her mouth and took a long breath.

Not good. Foster wasn't even aware of how she was answering. Colt would bet that every doctor who had seen the victims was the same, probably the families too. Even the nurses could have been affected.

This wasn't normal. Colt could manipulate people, push on their minds and make them do things, but only when she was within range. This was a latent hypnotic suggestion, but extremely powerful. Basically, mind control. This was high level stuff. So whoever did this had a spike strong enough to blow a person's mind apart, could completely scramble Foster's brain and force a bunch of answers on her, and somehow left those weird, super thin, rope-like marks on Amber. Then, to top it off, they could find level ones like they had neon signs hanging over their heads.

When the child's whisper tickled Colt's mind, it roused her from her thoughts. She looked back into the room. He didn't fit the profile, but it was worth asking anyway.

"Why wasn't he transferred?"

Surprisingly, Foster didn't react robotically. Her face softened, and she leaned toward the open door. "What do you mean?"

"I mean," Colt said flatly. "Those other four coma patients were transferred. Why not him?"

"Because," Foster said defensively. "He's not in a coma."

Like hell he's not. She felt it, sensed how his mind was buried under a thousand layers of thick wool blankets, crying for someone to dig him out. She turned and started into the room. "He sure looks like he's in a coma."

"Well, he's not." She followed Colt in with quick, nervous steps. "Look, I'm going to have to ask you to leave."

"Why's he unconscious?" Colt pressed.

"He's...brain damage."

"Brain damage?" Colt peered at the boy behind the tubes and the respirator mask. "Where's the trauma?"

"Well, it's a strange case." She was nervous, Colt could tell.

"Tell me about it."

"I really think..." Doctor Foster pursed her lips, reached up, straightened the pen and pencil in her hair, and exhaled. "He was brought into the emergency room, completely unconscious. No sign of trauma, no injuries, nothing. We thought it was some sort of drug overdose or poison. But then, he started bleeding from his nose and ears."

Colt's eyebrows came together. "Aneurism?"

"Again, we thought so." Talking medicine seemed to be bringing Foster back to herself. "So we do a quick scan of his brain to find it, and..."

"What?"

"It wasn't an aneurism." Foster stepped to the boy's bed. She pulled out the pencil in her hair. "There was a cut." Her eyes snapped to Colt's. "In his brain." She traced a line in the air in front of the boy's forehead, just above the eyebrows. "Four inches long, perfectly straight, at a slight angle, from the frontal cortex all the way to the occipital lobe."

"You mean—"

"Filleted," Foster said. "It was...it looked almost surgical. There were no tracks or grains to indicate some sort of tool. It was like his brain just split." She put the pencil back.

This shit was getting weirder and weirder. Colt frowned. "How'd it get there?"

Foster shrugged. "No idea. Like I said, no trauma, no wounds, nothing." She looked up. It seemed that what they'd been talking about was dawning on her. The anxiety crept back into the muscles around her eyes. "Anyway," she stepped away from the bed and past Colt, heading toward the door. "We should go and let him rest. I'm sure—"

Colt didn't budge. "What happened before he came in?"

Foster turned. "I don't—"

"That cut came from somewhere. What was he doing right before he came in?"

"I..." Foster's fingers twitched. "It's not important."

Yeah. Right. Colt stepped forward. "What was it?"

"Just..." Foster's jaw fluttered. Her words seemed to be fighting their way out. "There was...an accident."

Colt watched sweat form on Foster's face. "A car accident?"

"No. It was..." Her legs trembled. The muscles in her face jerked and danced. "It was nothing."

"What was it?" Colt closed the distance between them. Even in the dim light, she saw Foster's eyes darting around. A battle was raging inside of the woman, Colt saw it. Fear and panic and her own mind pressing through the things forced upon her. "What happened?"

"A fight," Foster sputtered. Her chest heaved as she gasped for air. The pencil and pen on the back of her head bounced wildly.

"Like an argument?"

"No." Her shaking hands came up and rubbed at her neck, scratched at her delicate cheeks. "No. No. A fight with...a fist fight."

"And that's when it happened?"

Foster shook her head back and forth. Her body was twisting and writhing. A string of spittle shot from her lips, and she tried to push words out of clenched jaws. "Yes."

Colt was just outside arms reach of Foster. It was as far as she could go without breaking the wall she had up. If Foster couldn't take it, if she couldn't answer any more, Colt would take that last step. She'd drop the wall, grab Foster, and make a direct connection. She needed to know.

"Who was the boy fighting with?"

"I..." Foster gagged on her own throat muscles. "I can't. I can't." Her fingers scratched at her scalp, dug through her hair. The bun on the back of her head waggled and loosened. "I'm not allowed. I'm not... I can't..."

"Doctor Foster." Colt's voice dropped. She pushed her wall forward, used it to press on Foster. "Who did this?"

"It... was..." Her eyes shot up, eyes that were terrified and awake and, for an instant, they carried a simple phrase to Colt:

I'm sorry.

Foster snatched the pencil and the pen from her hair, brought them to the front of her face and jabbed them into her eyeballs. It happened so fast that Colt couldn't stop her. There was a thick squish like someone squeezing ripe peaches. Colt reached out. Foster reeled back and screamed in agony. Blood poured from behind her hands, erupting out of her eye sockets and running down her face. Across her cheeks. Into her mouth.

Colt touched Foster's arms. Electric guitar feedback screamed and wailed, pumped through giant amplifiers that were taped to Colt's ears and plugged directly into her skull. The shock made her stumble and almost drop to the floor. The world spun. She tried desperately to keep from throwing up. As she sat there, gasping and gagging, trying to shake off the psychic feedback, all she heard was Doctor Foster screaming.

And screaming.

And screaming.

CHAPTER TWENTY-THREE

Shouts and screams from a wave of kids washed over the front yard of Fieldsville High School. The final bell had rung a while ago, but Vincent had stayed back, waiting for the crowds to thin out. It was a beautiful day outside, and for everyone else, there were sports to play, friends to chat with, and homework to ignore.

Today had been better. The last thing he needed was to get jostled around, hear a bunch of thoughts, and start feeling flustered again. He'd been waiting near an hour, and finally the mass of legs and arms and backpacks were gone. Warm daylight streamed through the school's front doors to the dull brown tile floors. Vincent picked up his backpack and headed out.

There were still kids sitting on the stone steps, leaning against railings, laughing and shoving and flirting. A group of girls walked by. Before he could look away, one of the girls—a redhead with freckles across her pale nose—caught his green-eyed gaze. Vincent felt his face go red. Then white. Then green.

Here it comes. The girl would turn to her friends and whisper something. They would all peer back at him, disgust written on their faces and a hint of fear in their eyes. They'd pick up their pace. People would see. Everyone would stare. Everyone would think about him. Their minds would pound on him like hail, and he wouldn't be able to hold them out, and it would never, never end.

But the girl just turned away. She'd seen him, gazed right into his eyes, and gone on as though he were anybody else. A person.

A normal person.

The sickly parlor faded, and a grin, something that he hadn't worn to school for a long time, splashed across his face. He trotted down the stairs and grabbed his bike lock.

Mary reached out to him.

Again? Seriously?

Without looking back, he unsnapped the lock. "Go away."

There was no response, no voice from behind him; only a shadow that crept across his shoulder and dripped onto the ground in front of him. It started out at a normal size, but it grew thicker, heavier, wider. Something was wrong. The feeling, he'd been sure it was Mary, but now...

In a stance that showed he was ready for a fight, Ashley was behind him with his thugs, David and Travis. But something was odd. Ashley face wasn't the usual crinkled display of self-loathing. It was hard as stone, and his eyes were like marbles. David and Travis were completely stoic.

But Vincent couldn't feel any emotion from them. They should have been angry, or furious, or scared, or... or...

Something.

Vincent took a tiny step back and sent his tendrils out. He had to see.

Emptiness.

"What..." Vincent whispered.

Ashley's head raised, but his expression didn't change. "Run," he said flatly.

CHAPTER TWENTY-FOUR

The paper coffee cup was empty, but Colt tilted the plastic lid to her lips anyway. Her tongue probed the sharp edges of the drinking hole. She set the cup down on the metal table outside the little bakery. She closed her eyes and breathed deeply.

She heard shoes tap-tap-tapping behind her.

"Hello, Sheriff."

"So," he said it long and slow. "The DSI, huh?"

She sighed. This conversation never went well.

"Can't say I've ever heard of y'all."

Colt played with her coffee cup, then looked up at the sheriff. His poker face was back.

He said, "Wasn't even sure what it stands for," as his eyes locked on hers, probing for information. "Had to use the Google."

"We try and keep a low profile."

"That your standard operating procedure?"

"If we think it's necessary."

"What about misrepresenting yourself to local law enforcement?" His head tilted. "That a standard thing with you folks?"

Colt raised her chin a tick. "I believe we refer to that as retaining need-to-know information."

He nodded. "See, I refer to it as lying."

"Sorry if I hurt your feelings, Sheriff."

He laughed, breathy and soft, while he turned his head away. "Round here, that there's an arrestable offense." He stared into the distance. "So what's the story, Special Agent Colt?"

"Honestly?"

His eyebrows rose the tiniest of bits.

"I don't know. I thought it was one thing, but now I'm not sure."

"What do you know so far?"

"Not enough."

"What do you need?"

"A little bit of everything." She watched cars, the people go by. She looked beyond that, to things her physical eyes couldn't see. "I need to see the big picture."

"With what you got, can you answer me this? There something going on in my town?"

She nodded. "Yeah."

"Something bad?"

She paused. "Yeah."

"All right, then." He lifted his coffee cup to his mouth, pounded the last of the contents, and licked his lips. "You tell me what you need, and I'll get it for ya'."

Colt smiled. "Right now, I just need a little piece and quiet."

The sheriff nodded. "Yes, ma'am." He turned, without attitude or arrogance, and walked back into the bakery. She watched him go, appreciating how that went.

Agent Colt, said Sandra, who had basically been on psychic hold for the last few minutes.

"It's fine, Sandra. Put him through."

Colt felt Sandra's hesitation. Sandra had been working as a transmitter at the DSI for a long time. She'd connected with Colt on countless occasions under a variety of circumstances. But this was the first time Colt had ever asked for a minute to collect herself.

Rakesh's psychic projection appeared in the chair across the table from her.

"How you doing?" he asked.

"I'll live." Her eyes traced up and down his image. "You don't look too good."

"It's been...busy."

Colt smirked. "I guess I should say thank you."

"My pleasure. Under the circumstances—"

"Of course," Colt said sharply. She reached for the coffee again, but stopped when she remembered it was empty. That was okay though, because her hands had stopped shaking.

Finally.

She'd barely been able to stand after that insane psychic feedback. When the cops had shown up—dressed in those drab brown uniforms only small town law wears—the best she could do was hand them her badge and Rakesh's number, then try not to throw up on their boots.

The effects of the feedback were gone now, and Colt felt almost human again. But she'd had to keep her wall up since then. That damn psychic cloud was annoying her.

Rakesh leaned forward. "Have you spoken with the sheriff yet?"

Colt jerked her head toward the bakery's big glass windows behind her. Inside, the sheriff was talking on his walkie-talkie and grabbing several coffees. He and his men were going to be putting in a little overtime today.

"Just finished," she said.

"And?"

She sighed. "The people are real nice around here, you know that?"

Rakesh, unsure of what to say, opened and closed his mouth like a fish out of water. Colt reached into her jacket and pulled out a notepad.

"The boy in the hospital, his name is Henry. He was brought in about four and a half months ago."

Rakesh nodded. "That puts him before the other victims. What happened to him?"

"He got into a fight at school."

"And?"

"That's it."

Rakesh frowned.

"Vincent Domnall. Sixteen years old. According to eyewitnesses, Henry started the fight. He hit Vincent. Vincent hit back. Henry dropped. The end."

"That's it?"

Colt flipped the notepad shut. "That's it."

Rakesh shook his head. "I mean, the kid ended up in the hospital. How can—"

"No, Rakesh." Colt leaned forward. "That's. It. That's all I could get out of the sheriff. And his deputy. And the other guys on the force. Every single one of them told me the same story, word for word."

"B-but," Rakesh said. "It doesn't fit the profile. If he's sixteen, then—"

"I didn't say it was Vincent. I'm..." She pinched her lips together. "I'm honestly not sure. Some things point one way, some things point another. It just isn't lining up." She pocketed the notepad and stood up, much more slowly than she would have liked. As she turned away from the table and ambled down the sidewalk, Rakesh's image bobbed next to her like a balloon that had lost some of its lift.

"There are things that don't make sense," Colt continued. "Finding the level ones, those weird bruises, what happened to Henry's brain, this weird psychic density to the air, the amount of mind control that's been done to the people here—"

"What the doctor did to herself."

Colt inhaled deeply. "No kid could to do all that. Hell, no single person could do all that."

"So, what? A group?"

"I don't know, maybe. But whatever it is, Vincent is involved."

Rakesh nodded. When he hesitated, Colt knew where he was going. "No back up," she said sharply.

"Colt."

"Another day," she said, half demand, half request. "I can handle this." She wasn't sure if she could sell it anymore, but when Rakesh gave a dismissive wave, she knew he'd bought stock.

"I assume you got the address."

"Of course."

"Remember to take the sheriff."

"You know I've done this before, right?"

"Do you have a plan?"

"For what?"

"For... if you get there and, and you're wrong and Vincent is some super psychic."

Colt sighed loudly and turned around. The table was half a block away. Sitting on top was the empty cup she'd left behind. Raising her arm, she aimed her pointer finger at the cup. At the tip of her index finger, telekinetic energy built. In her curled fingers, the energy appeared, wavering and swirling inside the shape she knew so well. It was clear, the cylinder, the handle with its textured grip, the barrel and sight. She compressed the energy at the tip of her finger, halfway down the barrel, into a ball and molded it into a recognizable shape.

A bullet.

There was a pop, no louder than one of the little gunpowder snappers kids throw against the sidewalk on summer days, as the kinetic bullet fired. Her gun vanished. The coffee cup went flying, lid flipping through the air. A hole the size of a thumbtack was punched clean through.

Colt lowered her arm.

Rakesh's image rippled, disturbed by the psychic energy.

And that was a tiny one.

"Well," Rakesh said. "First you'll have to find him. It may not be as easy as you think. I mean, he could be anywhere. And if he knows that someone is prying into things, there's a good chance you'll never fi—"

"Move it!"

Colt whipped around. The boy, arched over the handlebars of his bike, pumping like a madman, was nothing but a blur of sandy blonde hair. She stepped back as he flew by and missed her psychic wall by an inch. Watching him speed off, she completely missed the three other boys following close behind him.

They careened around her, their tires buzzing. Colt dodged them but as the last kid tore past, Colt's arm grazed his shoulder. Her eyes shut, her body tensed.

Psychic feedback. Lighter this time, because of how little contact there was, but it was there; same as with Doctor Foster.

Opening her eyes and forcing her frozen lungs to exhale, Colt watched the four boys head down the street, away from town.

"Rakesh," she said as she rummaged for her car keys. "Rakesh, are you—"

He's fine. Sandra's voice, shaky and startled, sounded in Colt's head. *It was only for a second, so I don't think—*

"Good," Colt said as she ran to her car, eyes glued to the boys as they raced off. "When he shakes it off, tell him Vincent isn't going to be that hard to find."

CHAPTER TWENTY-FIVE

"Are you—"

"Yes!" Rakesh held up a hand in Sandra's general direction. He couldn't really find her properly, because a hive of pissed off hornets swarmed inside his head. Hunched over, he stumbled around the room as though he'd clocked his forehead on something hard and was trying to walk it off.

Actually, that would have been far more pleasant.

The feedback had come through Sandra for only an instant, but because Rakesh had absolutely zero psychic defenses, there were some lasting effects. Sandra, on the other hand, seemed fine, almost as though it hadn't happened at all, which was odd since she'd spasmed and shouted when it hit. Of course, Rakesh didn't really have the faculties to consider this. He was too busy trying to focus his eyes.

Sandra slowly moved toward Rakesh. "Can I help—"

"No," he responded, gesturing again with his raised hand. "No, thank you. I... I'm okay. I am." He wasn't, but he didn't want her touching him right now. Part of him, a silly, childish part, was afraid that it would happen again. Standing straight and filling his chest, Rakesh calmed himself down.

Sandra stood with her hands folded in front of her. Though her back was rigid, her head was lowered, and the tangle of colored wires hid her face. Rakesh regretted snapping the way he did.

"Sandra," he said, apologetically. But she didn't respond. Rakesh shook his head. He probably didn't say it loud enough. "Sandra?"

Still nothing. She was still. Weirdly still.

Rakesh's voice went from soft and sorry to curious but cautious. "Sandra?"

Her face popped up quickly. A glassines washed away from her eyes. "Yes?" she said as though waking from a dream.

Rakesh paused.

It must have been the feedback. She was having some delayed effect or something. Whatever the hell that was, she seemed fine now.

But did she?

"Are you," he started. She was giving him a strange look, as though she were seeing him for the first time. "Did the, um, the feedback..."

"Yes?"

"Are you okay?"

A light switch went off inside her. A warm smile spread on her lips. "Yes." She blinked. "Thank you for asking."

Rakesh felt a little better, but in the back of his head, there was a little noise. "Good." It wasn't the hornets buzzing or the feedback. "I'm glad." It was a little subconscious alarm telling him something was wrong.

And it wouldn't turn off.

CHAPTER TWENTY-SIX

Vincent gasped out the word, "Crap." He'd hoped that either Ashley or one of his thugs would get knocked down by that lady on the sidewalk. He'd seen her from down the street, walking around talking to herself. He'd slowed down so the others could close the gap. At the last minute, he'd shouted and swerved. The dream was that she'd swing her arms out, Ashley and his punks wouldn't have time to change course, and bang, problem solved.

But, of course, it didn't work. They were closer than before, and it didn't look like they were going to stop. Vincent had seen on TV that sometimes sled dogs would run themselves to death under command of their master. He wondered if these guys would do that.

Banking hard, Vincent swung around a corner, off of Main Street.

All right, let's see you try this.

Another hard turn, and he leaped off the curb. His body bobbed and weaved as he slithered between the bumpers of moving cars. By the time the drivers were honking, Vincent had already jumped onto the next sidewalk and swung a ninety-degree turn into an alley.

His feet pumped as brick walls became a rusty red blur. He came within inches of trashcans and dumpsters. His eyes teared up in the wind, and he forced them to stay open. He rushed toward the end of the alley, and the street at the end was crowded. There was no way he could cut through the traffic. He coasted. Shifting, he drifted so close to the wall on his left that he felt the bricks radiating the heat they had absorbed from the noonday sun.

The alley ended. The sidewalk began. Vincent hammered to the right and dove into the street. Behind him, a car slammed on its brakes and honked. When he saw an opening, he lurched out and cut across the lane. He hovered on the single yellow line that separated the direction of traffic. Cars swerved as much as they could to give him room, and Vincent did the same. The wind broke against each vehicle with an angry "shush".

Ahead, an intersection with a light changed from his direction to the cross traffic. Vincent pumped the pedals to match the light. In that moment when all the lights were red, he exploded into the empty space and made a hard left. Back at the intersection, which was already almost a block away, someone leaned out of a window and barked his name.

Slowing down and finding a shallow groove in the street, Vincent narrowed his eyes. His tendrils went out.

He found them as easily as they seemed to be finding him. Even with all the cutting and swerving, they'd stayed right on him.

Their minds were not empty, but hollowed out. The inside of their heads were a long cellar staircase, and down at the bottom, they were calling out, scared and shallow. He pulled back the tendrils. Chills spread across his skin. He remembered that feeling, remembered it from a long time ago, but he couldn't place it. Whatever it was, wherever it had come from, whoever had done it to them, he knew it was bad.

He also knew they were getting closer.

Bending down, he burst up and jumped to the sidewalk. Across the street, Ashley, David, and Travis flew out from a cross street and rode parallel. Vincent didn't look at them, didn't even acknowledge their presence. He just pumped. They were directly across from him. He saw them in his peripheral. Holding his breath, he fired a psychic spike that missed by a mile. Even if it had hit, he was too distracted to give it any kind of punch.

Frowning, he buckled down and pushed his already burning legs.

Just as Ashley jumped the curb to cross the street, Vincent cut through an empty parking lot littered with cracks and crabgrass. His tires rattled as he leaped over curbs, growled as he zipped across a patch of grass, and squealed as he slipped into the tight, curved driveway of one of Fieldsville's failed factories.

Hanging off the side of his bike like a stunt rider, Vincent hunkered down to pass beneath a chain that was spread from one of the loading dock's walls to the other. He steered toward the ramp at the end of the loading area, went up, and dove through a doorless double doorway.

He dodged the few remaining machines, rusted and falling apart. The room was huge. It smelled like an old basement, and everything was covered in a layer of dust. It was so thick on the floor that his tires left clear streaks. He'd hoped to hide behind one of the machines, but a blind man could have followed those tracks.

Vincent squeezed the brakes and spun sideways, throwing a cloud of dust into the air. His foot hit the floor, and he stood, panting, sweat pouring down his face and body beneath his shirt. The air was thick and stagnant. It pressed in on him as he waited.

Out in the loading dock, the buzzing of tires approached.

Vincent snapped his kickstand down and stood, staring at the door. Slowly, Ashley and his thugs appeared at the ramp. They walked up in the same formation they had ridden in. Their steps, their swinging arms, everything was synchronized. When they came into the empty factory, they didn't look around, didn't examine the room. Instead, they headed straight toward Vincent.

One last time, he sent out the tendrils. Their hollowness, their nothingness, was all he found.

"Why?" he asked.

None of them responded. Their hands opened and closed, searching for the perfect fist.

"I don't want to do this," he said as his hands did the same. In his shoulders, the pressure was starting to build. "Please don't do this."

Ashley lowered his chin. "Then stop us."

Slowing his breath, Vincent's mouth closed and tightened to a thin line. He stared with hard eyes and, spreading his feet, took the same position he'd had the day before.

At the creek.

CHAPTER TWENTY-SEVEN

The only sound Colt heard was the perky "bing!" of the Hyundai telling her the door was open with the key in the ignition. She ignored it and stood, one foot out of the car, searching.

She'd felt the psychic spikes. There were three, rapid fire. Unfortunately, figuring out which way they'd come from was like figuring out which way a gunshot had come from in an open space. She'd hoped there would be more, but it didn't seem like that was going to happen.

The quaint stores of Main Street had given way to large concrete buildings. To Colt's left was a two-story hardware store and a storage facility. To her right an empty parking lot, the asphalt cracked and grass growing through. It was the lot to a rundown factory. She saw broken windows and even a bit of badly done graffiti.

Damn.

Whoever had fired those spikes was either hiding behind a wall or was out of reach. Not to mention that the psychic density was reducing her normal range. It was like searching in fog.

The Hyundai kept reminding her, ever so politely, that the key was still in the ignition. Growling, Colt yanked it and slammed the door.

Following those brats had been harder than she'd expected. They'd torn through the busiest streets they could find. One minute, she had them, and the next, they were cutting a corner and diving into alleys. They'd even split up in an attempt to lose her. The one boy, the one who'd shouted at her, he seemed to be the leader. The others followed but eventually split away. He'd probably sent them off as a diversion. It didn't seem likely that a kid could come up with something like that, but there was a very good chance that this was not a regular kid.

At one point, she'd lost them entirely. Then, a tiny ping on her psychic radar. It wasn't a spike. Somebody was using tendrils without masking them. Rookie mistake. Then one spike, a weak one. That had led her to where she'd felt the bigger spikes.

Moving slowly, she checked for disturbances in the tufts of grass at the edge of the sidewalk. There were cracks and chips, some initials carved long ago into the cement while it was still wet, but nothing of major interest. As she headed back, she saw a thin black streak at the entrance to the parking lot.

The tire mark was fresh. Looking up, she saw the broken windows of the empty factory looming overhead.

Great. She'd had such good experiences in factories before.

Her psychic wall hardened.

She found the bikes easily. Three of them lay on the ground of the loading dock, thrown down carelessly. It set off an alarm in Colt's mind. The bikes had kickstands. In a town like this, kids don't just drop their bikes. Bikes are the closest thing to freedom and kids usually take good care of them.

Either these kids were in a major hurry, or...

She made her way up the ramp, turning sideways as she neared the door. Her right hand curled. Her index finger pointed. A tiny glimmer, like the world just slightly out of focus, in the rough shape of a gun appeared in her hand. Slowly, she walked into the dim factory floor, her finger leading the way.

It was eerily quiet. The sound of every footstep bounced off the concrete walls. Thankfully, it didn't look anything like the factory in Austin. Three sets of sneakered footprints and one thin line of bike tires marked the floor. The feet overlaid the tire marks. The sandy-haired boy had gotten here first, she was sure of it. Any of them could still be here. Moving with angled steps around one of the large pieces of abandoned equipment, Colt caught sight of something near the back of the factory floor.

One of the boys lay on the floor, his head lilted to one side and his arms spread wide. There was small pool of red blood on the floor beneath him.

Colt stepped out, her eyes checking every corner, glancing at every shadow. When nothing moved, nothing happened, she raced in.

The other two boys were close by. They were all on the ground. No red puddles oozed out beneath them, but she saw the dark liquid on their shirts and skin. As quickly as she could, she kneeled down by the closest. He was breathing and the pool of blood wasn't growing, at least not fast enough to see.

She pulled back from her wall just enough to give the boy's body a telekinetic push, rolling him so she could get a good look. A cut, a perfectly straight cut, went through his shirt and into his skin. It was clean, like it had been made by a razor blade, and not deep enough to be life threatening. But he was going to need stitches. A lot of them.

The other two boys both had similar cuts; all shallow, nothing deadly, right through their clothes and the skin beneath. There was no bleeding from the nose, nothing coming out their ears. It wasn't the same as the boy, Henry, in the hospital with the gash in his brain.

But it was close enough.

The psychic cloud was stronger near the boys. Colt frowned. Even with her wall up and tightened, she couldn't keep it out. So she knew that what she was about to do was stupid, but she wasn't sure if she'd get another opportunity. Focusing everything she had, she reached out and touched the

107

boy's head. Immediately, she had to let go. The psychic feedback had filled her head too fast to get anything.

Looking around, she saw the footprints from the scuffle. There were also streaks, pencil thin lines slashed into the dust. Someone had tried psychic spikes to knock the boys out. But it hadn't worked, which was weird because spikes that could create a kinetic response was impressive. So, were these three psychic too? Did they have walls up?

No. She hadn't gotten any thoughts or memories, but she could tell just from touching the one boy that he wasn't even a level one. So why the hell didn't the spikes take these kids out?

Rubbing her face, she followed the lines back to a central point. Some footprints and a set of tires led out to the side, heading through the only other door exiting the factory.

Colt took a deep breath, pulled out her cellphone and notebook, and dialed a number.

"Hey, Sheriff," she said, her voice echoing back to her ears again and again.

CHAPTER TWENTY-EIGHT

Vincent was getting better. Mary saw improvement. His ability was more focused, more precise. But he hesitated. She couldn't have him doing that. Emotions were holding him back. Why was he afraid? That power was so great. Using it only made sense. Stupid Vincent. If he couldn't be relied upon, he had to go. If he couldn't be good, he could only be bad.

Problems, problems, problems. All or nothing, that was the only answer. Vincent still had potential. But the woman, the one who'd come, she was something different. Such skills. The barrier, more flexible than Mary had thought. Good to know. Mary needed to be stronger. This woman, this person, Mary could learn much from her. There were things Mary had never thought of. If she wanted to be better, she would have to observe more.

The woman was getting closer. Searching, searching, searching. A meeting was inevitable. A confrontation was out of the question. Another plan, a different approach. The woman had pushed in on the bully. Mary had pushed back. Just like with the doctor. It had worked. A tiny bit, the tip of her pinky finger, that's all Mary needed to get through. She wasn't used to wiggling in slowly. But it could be done. Patient. She had to be patient. And then there was the other mind she'd found. So far away, but she felt the connection. She needed to work on that one. So many, so many minds to play with. Soon. Soon all her problems would be solved, and then Mary could make it so nothing ever had to change.

CHAPTER TWENTY-NINE

Vincent stood in the shade of the overpass near the mall, a tiny breeze tickling his skin. The thin, wordless roar of traffic overhead grew enough at times to match the sound of the blood pounding in his ears.

Across the grassy area, across the parking lot, his mom was working her afternoon shift. Inside his chest, his heart beat hard enough that he felt it against his sternum. Every few seconds the muscles in his feet, in his legs, in his arms and back and shoulders would twitch as though he were about to take a step; as though he were going to go to her.

Teeth grinding, he used the inside of his elbow to rub his eyes; eyes that definitely weren't crying, because only kids cry for their mommies. And though Vincent wasn't exactly sure of what he was becoming, he knew that he wasn't a kid.

Not anymore.

CHAPTER THIRTY

Finding the door to Rakesh's office slightly open, Sandra pushed it gently and leaned her head in. She heard a manic tap-tap-tapping as Rakesh's fingers flew across his laptop's keyboard. Stacks of papers surrounded him, which wasn't unusual, but he seemed more disorganized than normal. He'd shoved all of his regular paperwork to the edge of his desk and was currently combing through several teetering heaps of freshly printed documents.

Sandra cleared her throat so quietly that Rakesh couldn't hear it over the shuffle of paper. "You needed to see me, sir?"

Rakesh started to say something, but he barely got the first word out. Sandra had removed the transmitter headgear that normally made her look like a Rastafarian swamp witch. With a clear view of her pixie haircut and deep brown eyes, Rakesh just stared like a caffeine addict at the first pot of brewing coffee.

Sandra smiled a cheeky smile. "Sir?"

Rakesh blinked. "Yes. Yes! Sorry. Yes. What?"

"You said you needed me?"

His heart skipped a beat. "I...I did?" When? Did it slip out after the weird feedback thingy? Was he completely out of it? He didn't remember saying it.

"Yes," she replied. "For your report."

Rakesh's eyebrows went up, and the fear that had clamped around his chest vanished. "Yes! The report. Yes. I need you, um, your...just, just come in. Please." He dove behind his computer screen and breathed as many sighs of relief as he could without being obvious. In the doorway, Sandra curled her smile into her mouth and pinched down gently on it with her teeth. She stepped in, closed the door, and straightened her dress with a fast tug.

"How can I help you?" she asked.

"Well..." Rakesh, back in the saddle of something he was actually comfortable talking about, began moving papers again. "I am trying to put together as much as I can on Fieldsville."

Sandra nodded and gave a little, "Mm-hmm." She loved how studious he was.

"Looking for any anomalies in the area, any disturbances."

He was so focused, so driven.

"Checking the local papers, the sheriff's records."

"Uh-huh." And when he worked, he got the cutest little ridge right above his eyebrows. She thought it made him distinguished.

"Basically, anything from the past sixteen years we can get our hands on."

The pinched smile rolled out from Sandra's teeth. "Sixteen years?" she asked calmly.

"Yes," Rakesh said with a grin. "That's when—" Something was strange. Why was Sandra standing so straight, like a statue or an armed guard or something?

"That's when, what?" she asked matter-of-factly.

It was odd, Sandra's bounce, her edgy punkiness was gone. And her eyes, they were so...

"Vincent," Rakesh replied, pushing back the silence that had leaped into the room. "He's sixteen."

Sandra nodded, but didn't respond. Rolling his chair so his legs were beneath the edge of the desk, Rakesh searched for a fleshy part of his thigh and, when his fingers found it, pinched hard. His face didn't change a bit.

"So," he said with a small smile, even though the pain in his leg was intense. "I was just gathering up everything I could find on him, and I was wondering if there was anything you might have to add."

Sandra turned her head slightly, but it was mechanical, as though it had been rehearsed in the mirror a thousand times in an attempt to make it look normal. "Why would I have something to add?"

Rakesh shrugged. "I know you got a big jolt of that, what did you call it, psychic feedback? When it happened, did you manage to, I dunno, get anything?"

"Get anything?" she repeated.

"Yeah, thoughts or feelings or...maybe a connection?"

Sandra's head lowered slightly, and she stared at Rakesh hard. Under the table, his finger shifted and drove his nail into the skin. If he pressed any harder, he'd start bleeding. But still, his face didn't change.

Eventually, Sandra raised her head. "No. I didn't receive any thoughts or feelings. Just psychic noise."

Rakesh nodded. "Positive?"

"Yes. I didn't receive any thoughts or feelings. Just psychic noise."

"Alright. That's all I needed."

Sandra turned and started for the door.

"Oh, Sandra?" Rakesh called.

She turned to him. Her eyes were glossy, as though she were dreaming but awake.

"I, um, that dress. It looks nice on you."

With a blink, the sheen in her eyes was gone. Red rushed into her cheeks. "Thank you," she said though a tiny grin. "Sir." She turned and her hips, which had been level, shifted and bounced with a wonderful swagger as she left the room.

When the door clicked shut, Rakesh's fingers released. He hissed loudly and rubbed the spot where he was sure there would soon be a massive bruise. It was a technique he'd learned when he'd joined the DSI. Even non-psychics had to receive special training to help them avoid psychic attacks and interrogations. They'd been taught what to do if a psychic was trying to hear your thoughts on a low level, meaning they weren't actively burrowing into your head; something you would definitely notice, mostly because the sensation was akin to someone taking a corkscrew to the side of your skull. A low level reading could be blocked if you had a ton of synaptic activity going on. The easiest ways to achieve that? Pain. And if that pain is something that you're causing yourself, so much of your brain power is being taken up on trying to make the pain go away, the only thing a psychic can get is a mess of random subconscious messages that don't make any sense.

That was exactly what Sandra had gotten just now, because Rakesh was sure she'd done a cursory scan.

But... why?

Leather. A touch of exhaust. Warmth from the steel surrounding her and the rumbling engine in front of her. Polish that didn't come from a spray bottle, but instead shoe polish and a hint of oil applied with love and affection, and hours with a cotton rag, spent going back and forth, back and forth.

"Wow," Colt said as the sheriff's cruiser hummed. It was like being inside of an upright bass, bowed slowly and delicately. Colt felt every inch of the car working together. This thing wasn't like her Hyundai or any car she had driven for a long time. It didn't zip over the road. It didn't glide. The cruiser's wheels dug into the asphalt like runner's toes, grabbing for purchase.

"This is an original." She knew it when she ran her fingers reverently along the inside door panel. She didn't pick up any memories, but a lot of latent emotions crept through her mind. Most of them good, some of them great. This car had gotten a lot of time and care.

"'69 Polara," the sheriff said. He beamed with pride.

"Restored?"

"Just kept up."

The sheriff turned the wheel, and the tires crunched while they rounded a corner. They were drifting through the suburbs just outside downtown Fieldsville.

"It was my daddy's car. He was sheriff for forty-five years. Day I got the star, he gave me the car."

Colt responded with a "Hmm" as her smile faded. The sheriff didn't glance over; he didn't need to. Any further discussion on the subject of fathers wasn't going to be good for anyone. Instead, he let the silence settle, giving Colt whatever space she needed.

The houses here were quaint, but not as classic as the ones out in the fields where they were headed. Just like those farmhouses, though, Colt saw polished cars in driveways, trimmed lawns. Not a stray abandoned couch sitting in the sun. Not a single home in desperate need of a paint job.

"You all work hard," she said.

"We have to keep things nice."

"Must have been difficult, when the factories shut down."

"Things got bad for a while."

She thought about the bustling Main Street. "Seems like you all bounced back."

"Yeah," the sheriff said with a sigh. Even though he sunk lower into his bucket seat, Colt could tell that the muscles in his core were primed and ready for action. It was as though, underneath his calm swagger, a little needling voice was keeping him on edge.

"We've done pretty well. Keep to ourselves, try and buy everything local. The town really came together a while back."

"When was that?"

He thought a moment. "Ten, twelve years ago."

Colt was surprised. "That recently?"

"Guess so." He half laughed. "Sounds silly, but it seems like that's the way it's always been."

"Anything in particular happen around then?"

He opened his mouth and, just like Dr. Foster had done before she'd gouged her eyes out, it seemed like the words that wanted to come out just couldn't find their way. Colt watched him struggle for a moment. She was tempted to send out a tendril, to extend her wall and give the sheriff a little push. But she was damn tired. They'd left the downtown area, and the psychic needles in the air were receding, but still she had to play it safe for now. She decided to move onto something else.

"Didn't you all have the mall built around then?"

Instantly, the conflict within the sheriff dissolved. "Nah. That was years later."

"Doesn't seem very down home to me."

"Yeah, but it was good for the town. Made a lot of jobs. Brought in some money."

"People from other towns come in?"

"When they need to."

"To work?"

"Yeah." He paused. "Well, no. Not really. Seems like most everyone that works at the mall lives in Fieldsville."

"Not too many outsiders, huh?"

"Now, it ain't like that. People come through here all the time."

"How many of them stick around?"

The only response came from the cruiser's engine going from a hum to a growl, then dying back down. This time, it was Colt who gave the sheriff room to fill the quiet.

"So, Agent, what is it exactly we're looking for?"

Colt thought. "Tell me about them."

"Who?"

"The Domnalls."

"Well," and the humming engine eased back. Beneath the tires, gravel crunched. "Why don't you just go ahead and get acquainted with them?"

They were down the driveway quickly. Colt tried getting a good look at the house, but the angle of the sun splashed a golden glare across the windshield. When the sheriff's cruiser lulled to a stop, she pulled the handle and stepped out.

Goddamn, she was beat. It was just past six o' clock, and she felt ready for a good night's sleep. That denseness in the air had returned, and it was giving her a headache. It didn't help that the psychic feedback lingered like ringing ears after a rock concert.

She joined the sheriff, taking special care to keep him just outside of her wall. The sheriff took the sunglasses from his long face and put them in his shirtfront pocket. He wasn't just tall and thin, he was like the iron framework of a skyscraper.

As he led her around the Domnall house, Colt scanned the front porch.

Now things were getting odd.

The second step was clearly broken and had been for a while. An old porch swing hung on rusted chains. No piles of junk or broken windows, but lots of chipped paint, old wicker furniture in need of repair, a railing missing bars, and a crap ton of weeding that hadn't been done. There was a brittle quality to the home. It was dilapidated. It was unkept.

It was broken.

"You've been here before."

"Few times," the sheriff replied. "Had to bring Mr. Domnall home on a couple of late nights, after the dozen beers in him decided it would be fun to drive his truck into a gulley." He sighed. "That was before his accident, though."

"What happened?"

"One night those beers got tired of the gully and decided hittin' a tree at sixty-five would be more fun."

"I take it he wasn't wearing his seat belt?"

The sheriff shook his head.

"Anything since then?" Colt asked as they reached the side door. "Domestic disturbance, child services, anything like that?"

The sheriff adjusted his belt and shook his head. "Nope." He banged on the screen door's frame "Thirteen years ago I came here to tell Mrs. Domnall she was officially a widow. Haven't had to come back since."

Colt shifted her eyes toward him. "What about Vincent and that fight?"

The sheriff stared at the door and went, "Hmm," before knocking again. A teenage girl with curly pigtails and brown eyes answered.

Not just any teenage girl, though. It was the one Colt had seen in the street, the one that had stared at her. The girl peered at Colt, then at the sheriff, then back to Colt.

"Hello there, Mary," the sheriff said softly. "Your momma home?"

Mary stared at Colt another moment before she shook her head and said, "No. She's working a double today." She said it factually, like a grown up would. "Just us kids."

Colt looked inside and saw two other children in the den. They were younger, and neither were the boy who had flown past her on the bike, but the little girl had the same color hair and the same eyes. This was definitely the right house.

"Is Vincent here?" Colt asked.

Mary's big round eyes, her deep, deep brown eyes, widened at the mention of her twin brother's name. "Who're you?" she asked coolly.

"I'm..." Colt paused, gave Mary a good once over, and decided to treat her like an adult. Pulling out her badge, she said, "I'm Special Investigative Agent Colt with the DSI."

Mary ignored the badge and kept her eyes on Colt, who was having trouble looking away. Those eyes were bottomless.

"Is that like the FBI?"

"Sort of." The denseness in the air muffled her ears, and the ringing was like white noise lulling her to sleep.

"What do you investigate?" Mary asked.

Before Colt could answer, which she was going to happily do, the sheriff raised a hand.

"All right, Mary. How 'bout we ask the questions here."

Mary broke her locked gaze. Colt closed her eyelids and pinched the bit of nose between them. She felt as though she'd almost dozed off there.

Damn, today was a long one.

"Agent Colt asked you a question, Mary."

"Yes sir, sorry sir." Mary glanced back. Colt saw brown eyes. Simple, plain brown eyes. Not bottomless pools.

"Vincent's not here, ma'am."

"You know where he is?" the sheriff asked.

"No, sir."

Colt squinted. "Earlier today, Vincent was seen riding through town with Ashley Brinks. You have any idea what they were up to?"

Going thin lipped, Mary said, "No, ma'am."

"You have any idea how Ashley and the other boys ended up in the hospital after that?"

"No. No, ma'am." She was completely clamming up, but she wasn't giving prerecorded responses like Doctor Foster and the sheriff's men had. Mary was hiding something, but Colt wasn't sure what. Her instincts told her to send out the tendrils, maybe even probe Mary's mind, but a little voice in her head said it was too risky. She'd gotten two tastes of that psychic feedback already and wasn't interested in a third. People all over the town seemed to have been hit with some kind of psychic whammy, and Colt was sure Vincent was somehow involved. There was a good chance—a very good chance, that little voice told her—that Mary was just another victim.

Or, maybe she was just covering up for Vincent because they were siblings.

Letting out a long breath, Colt tried to relax her body. She leaned in a bit and softened her voice. "Mary, can I ask you a question?"

Mary didn't drop her mask, but didn't say no.

"Things haven't been completely normal around here, have they?"

A tiny crack appeared in Mary's mask.

"And Vincent, he's not acting like himself lately."

The crack grew wider, spread across Mary's face.

"I bet you've seen him do...things." She had to be careful what she said in front of the sheriff. Mary hadn't shown any signs of being under control, but the sheriff had. She leaned a bit closer and almost whispered to Mary. "Things normal people can't do."

Mary took a step back. The cracks in her mask were opening wide, and what Colt saw beneath was not fear, but wariness. She'd pushed too hard. Mary seemed so adult, but she was still just a kid. Colt wanted to put a comforting hand on Mary's shoulder. But was that the right thing to do? She hadn't spent much time with kids and wasn't comfortable with them. Being a mother hadn't been an option for her. Not because of the job, the hours, or how she'd joined the agency when she'd been just a little older than Mary. It was because of the day the world around her changed. It was because of the moment she'd had to grow up, when her powers had come all at once in a hot, angry, terrifying burst. When she'd gotten the scar on her belly.

Looking at Mary and her siblings, Colt became acutely aware of how she really wanted to make sure that none of them ever had a day like that. But pressing the issue wasn't going to help. Mary was keeping secrets, and she was keeping them for a reason. The best Colt could do was show her that she understood.

"If I'm right about Vincent," Colt said, "there are people who can help." Standing up straight, she put on her professional voice. "When Vincent comes home tonight, don't tell him the sheriff and I were here."

Mary nodded.

"Just give the sheriff a call and let him know."

Mary nodded again. She didn't smile or frown, she just stared intensely. Colt looked into her eyes and again found herself fascinated with how deep they were.

"I don't know where he is," Mary said, her voice steady as a metronome. "You believe me, don't you?"

She knew Mary had been lying before, had seen it in the girl's face and heard it in her voice, but now, she wasn't so sure. She felt conflicted, but eventually her gut won out. Colt gave the sheriff a "let's go" nod and walked off without a word, letting the crunching gravel beneath her feet be Mary's answer.

"What will you do?" Mary's voice called from the doorway.

Colt turned.

"If you're right about Vincent." Her fingers tightened around the screen door's frame. "Will you take him away?"

Colt chewed on her words before she answered. "Only if I think he's going to hurt someone."

Mary nodded once, slowly, and then disappeared into the house, the door closing behind her.

"Can you have your men keep an eye out for Vincent?"

The sheriff huffed. "Shouldn't we just stake out the house?"

She couldn't tell him that Vincent may be able to detect anyone watching his house before he even got there, so she just said, "It won't work."

"You want an A.P.B.?"

"No. Just let me know if someone spots him. Don't approach him, don't try and bring him in. If he runs, don't try and stop him."

The sheriff's eyebrows came down so far that his eyes almost disappeared. "Now hang on. I brought you here 'cause you said Vincent may be connected to what's goin' on with them people in the hospitals."

"So?"

"So you didn't say that he may be the one doin' it. If that boy's dangerous, I need to know."

Colt opened her mouth. This was always part of the job that she hated. The sheriff deserved the truth. He deserved to know what was happening in his little town. But if she told him, he'd think she was nuts and throw her in a jail cell. Or, at least, he'd try until she spiked him unconscious.

"I'm not sure," she said. "Not yet. I need to find him first. But, if he is dangerous, then it needs to be me who deals with him. You and your men aren't—"

"He's just a damn kid." The sheriff growled.

Colt drew half a smile on her face. "Kids are capable of a lot more than we give them credit for." She saw that he wasn't satisfied with that, but it was the best she could do. "Now," she said, yanking open the door to the cruiser. "Where am I gonna find a hotel that doesn't have stuffed animal heads on the walls?"

CHAPTER THIRTY-TWO

By the time Vincent rounded his driveway, the sun bled out across the horizon. . The kitchen and den glowed peacefully while the rest of the home sat dark and vacant. No shadows milled about behind the curtains. Vincent thought about how it looked like nothing more than a huge dollhouse, a toy, an imitation of a real home.

Halfway down the driveway, he stood on the pedals and coasted. Across from the side door, a huge oak tree stood sentry. Mary was there, waiting behind the tree. He felt her presence. He thought of turning around, pedaling away as fast as he could, but it would do no good. He'd have to come home eventually, and she'd still be waiting for him.

But he had to try something, anything, to avoid speaking with her. So instead of taking his bike to its usual resting place by the tree, he pulled up beside the porch and dismounted there. He hoped that, maybe if he went in through the front, someone would notice. They never went through the front door, hadn't for years. Their mom would have to notice. She'd realize something was wrong. She'd ask him what it was, and he would open up to her. He'd tell her everything about Ashley and his gang, about the fight with poor Henry, even about the people in the hospital and how they got there. He'd wanted to tell her for a long time, but it wouldn't work unless she asked; not unless she suspected. If he just came to her with it, she'd never believe him. But maybe if he gave her a sign...

"You're in trouble." Mary stood at the edge of the driveway. Vincent didn't look at her, but he felt her eyes on him, hard and cold as steel.

"You gonna rat on me again?"

"The sheriff came by."

Vincent's heart leaped into his chest. He turned quickly and found Mary with her arms crossed. One of her legs was bent and rested behind the other. Her expression surprised Vincent; she looked genuinely worried, concerned even. It was strange, Vincent wasn't sure if he'd ever seen her this way before.

"There was someone with him," she said. "A woman from the government. She was asking a lot of questions."

"About what?" Ashley? Henry? The people in the hospital?

"You."

Vincent stared deep into his twin sister's eyes. She was telling the truth, that much he knew.

Mary took a deep breath. "She knows."

"How much?"

"Enough." She began walking around Vincent in a slow circle. "She knows you're different. She said she knows people who can help those... like you."

"Like me," Vincent said sardonically.

"She said she's going to take you away."

"Like, to jail?"

"I don't know. But I don't think you'll have a choice. If she finds you..."

Vincent, his chest filling with quick, shallow breaths, stared at the ground. His eyes darted back and forth as he thought. From inside the house, in the back where the kitchen sat, there was a muffled bang of pots and pans. He held his breath and listened, straining his ears to hear just a murmur of his mother's humming.

But he couldn't. The only thing he heard was the blood pounding in his ears and the sound of Mary's feet crunching gravel as she crept closer.

"Vincent?" The word should have been gentle, kind, soft and comforting. Instead, it was a noose tightening around his neck.

Giving the song of his mother one more chance to find him, but finding himself without it, Vincent turned and faced his sister. *What do we do?*

Mary's lips curled at the edges. *We do what she said.*

Vincent craned his head, his eyes narrowed with confusion.

We call the sheriff.

Colt had known there was no point in searching for Vincent, but that's exactly what she'd spent the rest of the evening doing. She figured he had to be skilled enough to put up a wall, even a basic one, and become undetectable to her psychic radar. It didn't help that sensory abilities weren't her strong suit. So, she'd done her job the old-fashioned way.

She'd driven.

And driven.

And driven.

Every highway, every country road, every little dirt path she could find that was wide enough for her car. She'd driven by his place several times, even headed to the mall when she saw a bunch of kids outside of it. But Vincent wouldn't be hanging out with other kids. If he was as powerful as she thought, he wouldn't be interested in socializing.

He'd be interested in dominating.

The Hyundai bounced slightly as Colt slowed. Thick neon reds filled the evening sky out front of the motel where she had checked in a couple of hours ago. The sheriff had recommended it; just outside town limits, which was important if Colt wanted to drop her wall and get some sleep.

Her room faced the road. Even though there were available parking spaces near her door, she cruised through the lot and made her way around back. It was standard protocol to never park near her room. If she did, it would be easy for anyone trailing her to watch her get out and go to her door. Parking as far away as possible, preferably with some sort of visual obstacle in the way, meant they would have to follow her and, in doing so, make themselves obvious.

Getting out of the car, she hissed. She didn't feel any of that weird psychic humidity, and the last of the feedback was gone. However, after driving around all day, her left knee was really starting to ache. She gave the limb a minute to stretch, and the pain slowly ebbed from sharp to dull.

She'd parked at one end of the lot, on the back of the L-shaped building. She wondered if the office had some aspirin to buy, but it was in the opposite direction as her room, and she really didn't have it in her to go the extra distance. She was beat; her muscles hurt, her joints hurt, her everything hurt. In fact, screw protocol, she was taking a shortcut to her room.

A hallway divided the building at its bend. Outside of walking the building's perimeter, it was the only way from the back parking lot to the front. Walking through it, past vending and ice machines, her brain bounced around everything she'd taken in earlier.

122

If Vincent was actually controlling all those people himself, making them do and say things they would never do, there was only one explanation: he was a puppeteer.

Colt didn't want to believe it, mostly because it was a genuinely scary idea. Puppeteers were rare, and she'd never faced one. She flashed back to the factory in Texas, to how Samuel Bentley had infected all those people with his fear. A puppeteer was worse. A puppeteer didn't just push their uncontrolled emotions onto people; they took total control of them. And with what happened to Doctor Foster, it was looking like that was the case.

But something was wrong. Things didn't add up, one thing wasn't pointing to another. Yes, Vincent could be a puppeteer. He was young, so he'd have trouble controlling people with basic psychic abilities, like level ones. He'd get frustrated and lash out at them, try to remove them. But then, how did he even find the level ones? It's not like they went to his school. And the boys, Henry, and the three in the abandoned factory. How did he cut them? And why? Couldn't he just control them?

And the bruises; she remembered the bruises on Amber at Prairie General. Henry didn't have those. The boys at the warehouse didn't have those.

This didn't make sense. He couldn't have sensory abilities, and be a puppeteer, and make those cuts, and cause that kind of bruising. It just wasn't possible.

It was getting darker out. The chrome railing for the stairs at the end of the building, the ones that led to the second floor, glowed red as coils on an electric stove. The walkway for the second level overhead had no lights beneath it, so Colt needed to look down to make sure her keycard was facing the right way. She held the keycard up over the swiper but stopped when she saw movement in her peripheral. A figure with long arms and legs in a khaki uniform approached her.

Colt smiled a professional smile. "Evening, Sheriff." She hadn't gotten a call, so what was he doing here? If he was coming by hoping to charm her into a good time, he was barking up the wrong tree. "What can I—"

Intent to kill; it came off the sheriff and hit her like a packed snowball, hard and stinging. His hand came up to his holster so fast Colt barely saw it. She slashed the keycard down, hammered the handle, and pushed. The sheriff unloaded his revolver and Colt felt the air around her split. The bullets barely missed as she fell into her room. The wooden doorframe cracked, exploding shards. She hit the floor, tucked, and rolled. Up on her knees, she shoved her hand forward and kinetically slammed the door just as the sheriff appeared in it. With a twist of her wrist, the deadbolt locked. An instant later, the door shuddered as the sheriff put his shoulder into it.

Colt kept her hand out, holding the door telekinetically. Outside, the sheriff stepped back and kicked. The cheap wood snapped and splintered, but Colt's kinetics held it shut while she stood and extended the forefinger on her other hand. The door thumped rhythmically, and as Colt's gun went from invisible to foggy to a solid block of gun-shaped white kinetic energy, she waited for just the right moment.

Colt released. When the sheriff kicked, the door burst inward easier than he'd anticipated, and he was thrown off balance.

Colt didn't give him the chance to stand up straight.

She fired the bullet—molded wide and flat—and the sound was marching drum bass drum hit too hard, dull, heavy, and percussive. She hit him in the chest, and it launched him backward, his legs catching the front bumper of a parked car and the rest of him pounding a sheriff-shaped dent into the hood.

Colt didn't see where his gun went, but it didn't matter; he'd exhausted the cylinder. Also, he wasn't getting up anytime soon. . She lowered her hand, and the psychic revolver dissolved as she walked through the door. Outside, people were leaning out of their rooms and gaping at the scene.

Colt took a deep breath. "Nothing to see here. You should all go back to your rooms."

Everyone relaxed and closed their doors peacefully. Colt ground her teeth and bent over. She gasped for breath. She felt it; that was too much. Her eyes would be bloodshot for hours, and as soon as her adrenaline came down, she'd have the shakes. Pushing on that many people was like barbell squatting twice your own body weight, and it was only going to get her a few minutes before it wore off.

Stepping up to the sheriff's limp body, she reached out to touch him and see if she would get that same feedback she'd gotten from Doctor Foster and the boys at the factory.

Headlights flashed across the parking lot. Tires squealed as two police cars swung in from the highway at full speed. One car turned and headed around the back of the building, the other came straight toward her.

Before the squad car could come to a stop, Colt raised her hand, her gun appeared, and she fired. The squad car's windshield went white as a snowball and half caved in. The car swerved right, then left, and crashed into a parked car. Colt raised her hand to where the driver would get out.

The passenger window blew outward as the shotgun inside went off. Colt ducked, but the shot went wide anyway. The forestock ratcheted back, and Colt sprinted for the stairs. Behind her, another shotgun blast took out a room window. Glancing over her shoulder, she saw the cop running toward her and aiming at the same time. She turned forward and ducked as another shot ripped a chunk of concrete out of the wall two feet away.

Her feet pounded up the stairs. She reached the top, gripped the rail, and pulled herself onto the walkway. The shotgun cop reached the base of the stairs and fired, pellets sparking off a metal post near her head. He followed her up, firing again. She stayed close to the wall, and he couldn't get a decent shot. Eyes forward, she sprinted down the walkway toward the turn. She took as big an inhale as she could and headed straight for the railing that surrounded the second level. Slapping her hands on it, she vaulted over.

The wind whipped around her as she slowed her fall with telekinetic hands. When she hit the ground, she rolled forward to absorb the remaining shock. She stood, twisted, pointed, and her gun appeared. The instant the shotgun cop reached the railing, she fired. An invisible sandbag hit his face with enough force to knock him up and send his body crashing to the walkway.

Movement caught Colt's eye. Two brown uniforms raced down the stairs. They must have followed shotgun cop. Colt aimed at one—well built, black, young—but he drew quickly. His gun's muzzle flashed, and a bullet whizzed just over Colt's head. She threw herself toward the parked cars and the sidewalk beneath the walkway, shooting telekinetic bullets while she ran. She punched two holes in the wall and the cops returned fire. Gunshots rang out as she vaulted a car, landing on the walkway and breaking into a full run. She felt the cops following. Fortunately, it was dark enough beneath the walkway they couldn't get a clear shot.

The skin of her hand burned as she gripped the wall and swung her body into the vending machine hallway. Dust and stone sprayed into her face as one of the cops missed her fingers by inches. Her heart pounded so hard it couldn't skip a beat in surprise. Adrenaline pumped fire through her legs and pushed sweat out of every inch of her skin. She was in full combat mode, her senses at their absolute peak. A warning siren went off in her mind. Her feet weaved to the side, and she leaped behind vending machine. Its glass shattered as a bullet tore into it, right where her head had been a moment before.

She spun out, dropped to one knee, and threw both hands up; index fingers wrapped in semi-transparent revolver barrels. The pops from her bullets were small but rapid, a wild attack on a punk rock snare drum. The cops ducked behind an ice machine that shook as Colt's invisible bullets made it look as though someone had taken a ball-peen hammer to it. She turned, her breath slightly caught, and broke for the end of the hallway. Behind her, a shotgun was cocked and fired, but not before she could slip around the corner and disappear.

Spinning, Colt pressed her back against the wall right next to the hallway. Her ears rang from the shotgun blast, but she sensed the two cops running toward her. She balled up a psychic spike in her palm.

The young, black cop burst from the hallway. Colt smashed her hand into his face. The spike was a direct hit, a stun gun to the brain. Eyes rolling up into his skull, limbs flailing, he was unconscious before he hit the ground.

The other cop —short, stocky, Hispanic, shaved head—raised his shotgun. Colt aimed her open hand at the gun and clenched her fist. The cop's finger yanked back, but the trigger wouldn't move. He tried it twice more, but Colt's telekinesis held it in place. She stepped forward, another psychic spike building in her free hand, and swung. The cop, his face an emotionless mask, ignored his failing weaponry and ducked to avoid Colt's hand. He switched his grip on the shotgun and brought the shoulder stock around, aiming for Colt's head. She leaned back, then ducked as he jammed the butt of the stock at her. She spun around his side and behind him. The cop turned. Colt was there, her guard down, completely open. He lifted the shotgun's stock and swung hard. At the last second, there was a strange blur, as though Colt had gone out of focus, and she disappeared.

Not moved. Disappeared.

The cop stopped and looked around. She was gone. Then, she was next to him with her hands at her sides, like she'd been there the whole time. He stepped back and brought up the shotgun's barrel, but Colt went all fuzzy and vanished again.

Keeping the gun up, the cop checked in every direction.

Nothing.

He turned to his left, then swung the shotgun to his right. Colt appeared out of nowhere. One hand clamped around the gun while the other slammed a spike into the cop's face. His body stiffened for a moment, then dropped to the ground, leaving the shotgun in Colt's hand.

Her shoulders rose and fell as she huffed heavy breathes. She pumped the shotgun until all the shells had clattered to the hallway floor, then dropped it. Blowing hard from tightly pulled lips, she looked and listened to the suddenly still and quiet night.

No sign of reinforcements.

Quickly, she bent and touched shotgun cop's head.

Feedback. It still stung her brain, but not like before. She was learning to tone down the effects of it. But it was still there.

Damn.

Standing, her left knee stung. She grimaced as the joint popped but sighed as the stinging faded afterward. Her legs ached to hell. Walking as quickly as she could, she got into her car and headed for the highway.

126

The other kids were noisy, always noisy. Their words, words, words were nothing but chatter bouncing off the school hallway and into Mary's ears. Their minds were too jumbled, too messy, streaked with emotions and desires and pointless thoughts. They were all the same, all unaware of the cruelty that life could hold, all naïve about how fragile things were. Mary knew, understood how fast things could change and how, if you didn't work to make the changes you wanted, things would go wrong.

And in Mary's world, things were going wrong.

The Agent, Colt, was still alive. She'd sent the sheriff and his men, but it wasn't enough. Colt was strong. Mary had watched through the men's eyes. She'd seen how Colt used her abilities. So strong, so skilled, dangerous, dangerous. How had she vanished like that? Mary seethed. Something she'd never seen. Something she didn't know. It infuriated her.

All around, the minds of the students buzzed. Wild tales about the shootout banged against her ears. It was gunfire. No, bombs. It was police. Terrorists. A psychotic pipe-bomb-wielding lunatic. Spies. A bank robber. And—from that one strange boy whose mind was so disheveled Mary made a point to normally avoid it—aliens.

She crinkled her nose and shoved away their useless thoughts. She had to focus. Colt was still pursuing. She'd found Mary but hadn't seen the truth yet. Colt was focused on Vincent. Good. Good. Vincent was scared of Colt. Perfect. She could use that, use them. It would take a little more. She felt it, the tiny crack in Colt's wall. Mary had picked at it, chipped away while they spoke at the house. And every time Colt searched inside people, every time she found the feedback, Mary got in a little bit more. But she needed more time. Then she could fix it. She could use Colt to push Vincent. And if Vincent refused to be pushed, she could use Colt to kill him. Mom and her siblings were safe. No one would take them away. No one would take her away. She just needed the chance to work her way in.

A quick squawk from the announcement system silenced the hallway.

"Mary Domnall," said an old woman with a thick Midwestern accent. "Please report to room one-oh-five. Mary Annette Domnall, please report to room one-zero-five."

Mary tilted her head, then smiled.

Perfect.

CHAPTER THIRTY-FIVE

"He never came back to class?" Colt asked.

"Nope." Mr. Matthews leaned back in his chair, his arms folded across his chest. As Colt walked around the room, he watched her intently.

"Didn't ask permission?"

"Didn't say a word."

"Did anyone talk to him before he left? Say anything to him?"

Mr. Matthews shrugged. "The only thing that anyone is talking about is what happened at the hotel last night. You wouldn't happen to know anything about it, would you, Agent?"

Colt paused. She looked Mr. Matthews up and down. "How many tours did you do?"

"Two."

"What division?"

"Twenty-third division, light infantry."

"You work with any covert operatives while you were there?"

"Escorted enough to know one when I see one."

"I'm just here to gather information."

"That's what they said. But they always kept their hands in their pockets and checked the corners, too."

Colt smiled. The students must be terrified of this guy. "What happened right before Vincent ran out?"

"Don't know. I was facing the board."

"Are you sure?" Colt's wall was up, but she sent a tendril out and gave Mr. Matthew's mind a little refresher. He opened his mouth, but before he could answer, there was a flash in his mind. He was back, reliving the minute before Vincent jumped up and ran out. He was at the board. He felt the chalk in his hand. He heard the murmuring behind him, every syllable, every little smack of their lips as clear as if the kids were stage performers putting on a show.

"Mr. Matthews?" Colt asked politely.

"There," he said softly, "there was... someone had an aunt staying at the hotel. They watched from a window, saw strange things. Something about a car being... its window getting smashed by nothing. And a person who..."

"What?"

Mr. Matthews shook his head. "They said the person flew or floated or something like that." He chuckled softly. "How ridiculous is that?"

Colt faked a smile. "And that's when Vincent left?"

"Yup. Ran out before I could stop him."

Colt cocked her head. "Ran?"

"Like someone had just opened fire on him."

Again, something that didn't fit into place. If Vincent had sent the sheriff and his men, he would have already known she was psychic. Hearing about it shouldn't have shocked him. So why'd he run? She raised her chin to speak, but a knock at the door cut her off.

Mr. Matthews stood with a grunt. "Come in."

Mary opened the door slowly. She held her books to her chest.

"Thank you for coming, Mary. This is Special Agent Colt."

"We've met." Colt stepped uncomfortably close to Mary. Hiding behind those books wasn't going to help. "Your brother has a talent for not being wherever I look for him." She bent forward. "You know where he is now?"

Mary shook her head. "No. Sorry."

Colt straightened her back. "I'd like to talk to Mary alone for a minute."

Mr. Matthews frowned. "I don't think that's a good idea."

Colt glared. "Your principal—"

"I really don't care what she said, I'm not about to let you interrogate a minor without an adult present."

"It's not an interrogation."

"Then what is it?" Mr. Matthews huffed.

This was ridiculous. She could just push on him, and in a flash, he'd be walking down the hall to get a Jumbo Honey Bun out of the vending machine in the teacher's lounge. Unfortunately, he'd eventually come to his senses and come storming back. The last thing she needed was the town up in arms about some government agent sneaking around, luring children into dark rooms.

"I just want to ask her some questions," Colt said as politely as she could, which was about as politely as a growling Doberman.

"Not without an adult," Mr. Matthews hammered.

Colt was just about to reach out and psychically knock Mr. Matthews around when Mary spoke up.

"It's all right," she said with a strong voice.

Both Colt and Mr. Matthews looked at her.

"You can go, Mr. Matthews."

He shook his head. "Mary, I—"

"It's okay," she said. "I trust Agent Colt. You can go."

He seemed eager to protest further, but the wind slowly left his chest and his shoulders dropped. He nodded and stepped aside. Mary walked past him into the room, and with one last harsh glare at Colt, Mr. Matthews headed out and down the hallway. When he turned a corner, Colt closed the classroom door.

Mary sat in the front row, her thin body tucked in the space behind the desk. Colt felt like smiling. It was basic physical language. Mary was doing anything she could to create a barrier between them. This kid was hiding something.

Leaning back against the door, halfway across the room, Colt stuck her hands into her pockets. She let the silence afterward hang like a dead pendulum. Behind her, through the door, she heard hoots and hollers, sneakers yelping against linoleum, lockers closing and classroom doors being bolted shut for the night. It was a life Colt had barely known. By the time she was high school age, she was hunting down secret agents in foreign lands. She'd been doing this for a long time and knew exactly how long to let Mary sit and stew before saying anything.

"What happened at the hotel last night is the talk of the town."

Mary kept her eyes on the desk. "Yes, ma'am."

"You've heard the rumors?"

"Yes, ma'am."

"You think any of them are true?"

"I don't know..." A tiny smile appeared on Mary's lips. "Probably not the one about aliens."

Colt chuckled and pushed herself away from the door. "You know the sheriff and his men were after someone, right?"

"That's what I heard, ma'am."

Colt plopped herself down on the outside of Mr. Matthew's desk and stared straight at Mary's lowered head. "Did you know that someone was me?"

Mary's expression of disbelief was beautifully calculated, the kind of face that only a teenage girl, a master of manipulative emotions, could make. "But why would—"

"Don't," Colt said, her voice a karate chop on the girl's throat.

Mary's jaw wavered. Her lips wrinkled as they pressed together. Her eyes shimmered as tears built, growing fat and heavy, dropping down and landing in the shifting folds of her wringing hands.

She choked and said, "I'm sorry."

"They tried to shoot me."

Mary's chest fluttered, and her throat made little noises. "I'm sorry."

"They tried to kill me, Mary."

"I said I'm sorry!" Her hands slapped loudly against the cheap, lacquered desktop. Colt just stared. The fire in Mary's eyes faded. After a moment, she said, "I...I had to tell him."

"Had to?"

Mary looked up. "He's my brother."

130

Colt nodded. Either Vincent hadn't controlled Mary then, or he was still in control of her now. Colt had a hard time believing Mary was being manipulated at that moment. The emotions she was showing, the way she was acting, most puppeteers stripped away their target's emotions. The only emotions the puppets have are the emotions of the puppeteer. Colt turned away while Mary sniffled and sobbed. Just like she did during their first meeting, Colt's heart ached in a way it hadn't for decades. Mary seemed so small, so fragile. Colt wanted to pat Mary's shoulder. No, she wanted to hug her. She wanted to comfort her. She wanted to whisper sweet words and soothe her. With a shift of her hips, Colt again became aware of the scar on her belly.

She wanted a chance at what she'd never had.

"I didn't think..." Mary said as she wiped away tears. "I mean, I guess I did but...but..." she stared right into Colt's eyes. "Please," she said softly, "you have to believe me. I didn't want anyone to get hurt. You have to believe me."

Colt sighed deeply. Of course she believed Mary. How could she not? "Mary," she said softly, "your brother is dangerous. You know that, right?"

Mary nodded.

"And you know the things he can do?"

Mary hesitated, but nodded. Her tears had stopped falling, and she was getting herself together. Colt decided it was time for the ten-thousand-dollar question.

"Can you tell me?"

Mary looked up. "Okay, but you're going to think I'm crazy."

Colt felt the edge of her mouth pull up into something resembling a grin. She wouldn't think Mary was crazy, and not just because Colt had been dealing with the unbelievable longer than the girl had been alive. Mary could have told her that Vincent was an alien from Alpha Centauri, and Colt wouldn't think her crazy. Mary was a good kid.

"He," Mary began, a breath filling the space between words. "He can hear stuff that...he knows what people are thinking."

"Anything else?"

"I've seen him...I don't know how to describe it. It's like, this thing that shoots out and—"

"A spike," Colt said. "It's called a spike." This wasn't important. She needed more. "What else?"

Mary, who had seemed eager to talk about those simple things, as though she were speaking sultry secrets to a confidant in the dark, looked away.

"He..." She wrapped her arms around herself and a shiver ran across her chest. "He makes people...do things."

131

Colt nodded. "Like what?"

"Things...things they would never do on their own." Her lips pulled tight. "The people around him, it's like he controls them or something. Like they're—"

"His puppets," Colt finished.

Mary glanced back, her eyes wide. "Yeah," she said softly.

Colt's eyes narrowed, and she turned away, anger growing inside of her. "So that's why you told him about me."

"No," Mary said casually, as though Colt had misspelled her name and she was simply correcting it. "It doesn't work on me."

"What do you mean?"

Mary sniffed and shrugged her shoulders. "It doesn't work. He's tried it, bunches of times, but nothing ever happens." Her lips pulled tighter, her face grew cold. Her eyes floated out of the room and into memory. "Over and over again. All he wanted was to control, to do what he thought was best. But no matter how much he strained...it never worked." She blinked and looked up, her face going soft again. "Not on me, I mean."

Colt leaned back. She'd never heard of something like this before. Puppeteers can control anyone around them. Only people with powerful psychic abilities of their own can fend them off, and even that's difficult. A basic wall won't do it. If Colt were to spend time around a puppeteer, they'd slowly seep their control into her, worm thoughts into her brain. She'd have to actively push back the person's ability; she'd have to know they were doing it to stop them.

So how the hell was Mary immune? Because they were twins? Or was possible the girl had some latent psychic ability? She may even be able to block Vincent's control entirely. If Colt could get at that, could just scan Mary's mind—

Mary's eyes went wide and she jerked back in her chair. "No!" She almost screamed it, the kind of scream a girl would use when a stranger reached out from the shadows to drag them in. It was fearful yet commanding and Colt's psychic tendrils pulled away instantly.

Mary raised her arms in a defensive position. Colt thought she saw an angry fire burning in the girl's eyes, but it was gone so fast she couldn't be sure. The shout had surprised her, yet she was more startled at how she'd reacted. Normally, she'd have just paused, then kept pushing. Why did she retreat so quickly?

"Don't do it," Mary said. "You can't."

Colt's jaw tightened. "Why?"

"Because," Mary paused, "he'll know."

"Vincent?"

Mary nodded. "We're connected. When he's close, I can feel it. And he can feel me. It's always been that way."

Colt nodded. That would explain why Mary was immune to Vincent's ability. They were on the same psychic wavelength, so to speak. It would be like two ocean waves, equal in size and strength, meeting each other going different directions. There'd be a crash, and both waves would dissipate. Of course, this didn't help Colt. It wasn't something she could duplicate within her own mind. But it did give her an advantage. Since Mary was immune, she could put her trust in the girl.

"Listen," Colt said. "Vincent has already hurt people, and he's going to hurt more."

"If I could have stopped him, I would have," Mary's words rolled down her chin and across her chest. They crept along the desk and floated into Colt's ears like tiny burrowing insects. "Believe me."

"Of course. But I need to ask you to help me."

"You know I want to help you, Agent Colt."

"I do, but this may become dangerous. And when everything is over, I'm going to have to take your brother away. I can't promise that you'll ever see him again."

"I'll help you, I promise."

Colt nodded and said, "Thank you, Mary."

"I'm on your side, Agent Colt."

"Right," she replied, the words simply forming in her mouth and coming out without thought.

"You can trust me."

"I do," Colt said, her voice flat. "I trust you completely, Mary."

Against her chest, Mary's chin wrinkled as a smile spread across her lips. "Perfect," she whispered.

CHAPTER THIRTY-SIX

In the sunbeams that poured into the empty factory, dancing specks of dust drifted through Rakesh's psychic projection. They were in the factory where Colt found Ashley and his thugs. The police had taped off the whole building. It was quiet and empty, and it would stay that way as long as Colt needed it to.

"Are you sure this is the best plan? Why don't I send in some backup?" Rakesh asked, his voice not echoing off the factory's walls as it should. Colt paced and listened to the sound of her own footsteps.

"Wouldn't do any good. I'm the strongest in the area. Anyone else he could potentially control."

"I could have a team out there in four or five hours. Even if he tried hiding, our sensory types could—"

"He'd bolt. He's strong enough to know they'd be coming. He's got a bunch of people in this town under his power. Any random person could drive up, he hops in, they drive off. Then it's a national manhunt for a teenage kid."

"If he's that strong, he'll know you're trying to ambush him," Rakesh replied.   She nodded. "It's fine if he knows I'm here. One on one, I can take him."

Rakesh sighed audibly. This wasn't what he wanted to be talking about. He wanted to talk about how weird Sandra had been acting, how she'd tried to read his mind, how every time he mentioned the case Colt was on, she suddenly became serious. But considering she was currently transmitting between his mind and Colt's, that wasn't really an option.

"All right," he said. "How's the sister?"

Mary was standing in the loading dock area, hands folded in front of her skirt.

"She's fine. I told her I had to make a call, then we'd try and bring Vincent here."

"And she's okay with this?"

Colt spoke without thinking. "She just wants what's best for her family."

"But she understands what this means?"

"She just wants what's best for her family."

His lips squeezed together as Colt's indignant tone stung his ears. "I know that, Agent Colt," he hit every consonant in her name extra hard. "I want to make sure that she's aware of the ramifications of her actions. If she were to change her mind and—"

"She won't," Colt said firmly.

"I'm just saying—"

"She," Colt hammered, "won't. I trust her."

Rakesh's eyes opened wide. "You barely know her."

Anger flared in Colt from nowhere. "It doesn't matter! At least she's trying to help."

"And I'm not?"

"I don't think helping your career counts."

Rakesh stammered. "Excuse me?"

They were so busy arguing, snapping personal attacks back and forth, the world around them fell away. Colt didn't notice how Mary's shadow slithered up to the edge of the doorway. Mary didn't peek, but stepped right into plain sight. Her face was a finely practiced mask of nothingness. She stared at Colt, her chin lowering slowly. After a moment, her eyes drifted through the air to the sunbeam breaking through the broken window, to the same spot where Colt saw Rakesh's projection.

On the other end of the argument, Rakesh stood in his Arlington office and yelled at the air in front of him. He never noticed how, behind him, Sandra's body grew stiff as she inhaled deeply, how her face twisted in an expression of pain, then fear, then faded to a look of placid release. Sandra's eyes closed and, when they opened, they were no longer her eyes.

They belonged to someone else now.

"You do whatever you want," Rakesh barked. He was done with this; done with this argument, done with this case, done with Colt, done with Sandra, done with everything. "Handle this as you see fit because, clearly, you don't have any respect for me or the fact that I am simply trying to protect you."

Colt growled through clenched teeth. "I don't need help from some wet behind the ears—"

"This conversation is over," Rakesh said. "I expect a full report tomorrow morning. Don't contact me before then."

"Just keep your nose out of my damn business until then," Colt replied.

"Fine."

"Fine."

Rakesh's head turned back. "Sandra, end the connection. Now." He made sure to keep turned so that Colt wouldn't even get to look him in the eye before his image faded away. Behind his closed eyes, the factory, the sunbeam and Colt all dissolved like grains of sand through a sieve.

Had the whole world gone bat-shit crazy? First Sandra tried to read his mind, and now Colt, the coldest, hardest, most professional agent he had ever seen, was completely emotionally ensnared in a case? He knew she didn't particularly like him, but that was totally out of line, even for her. Everything about this was bizarre.

He rubbed his face but stopped cold when he realized Sandra was still there, standing behind him. He didn't need to look to know that she was staring at him, her eyes drilling tiny holes into the back of his head.

He felt it.

"Uh," he grunted. There was a strange energy in his office suddenly. He sensed it coming off of her. It wasn't a psychic thing. It was...

He was creeped out.

"We're done," he said, trying to sound like her boss instead of her prey, which was how he felt at that moment. "And I have, um, a lot of paperwork to do. So..." He peeked over his shoulder. He saw her flat face, her lips drawn in, her eyes piercing and intent on him. Those little wrinkles around her eyes, the ones he thought were so cute, came back with her grin. But they weren't hers. They weren't right.

"Of course, sir," Sandra said. "I just wanted to make sure you were okay."

Rakesh faked a smile and waved a hand in the air. "I'm fine, Sandra. I just...I have a lot to do."

"Of course, sir," she repeated. She left the office, not bouncing her hips, not looking back with a slightly devilish stain in her eyes. Nothing.

Sandra had left the building.

So who had moved in?

CHAPTER THIRTY-SEVEN

"I heard you shouting."

Colt started. Rakesh's image had faded only seconds ago, and her heart was still pounding. Mary's sneakered feet padded silently across the dusty floor.

"I hope you're okay," Mary said.

Colt's mind was still reeling from the argument. What the hell had just happened? She never got fired up like that, especially with people at the DSI. She might be gruff and tough, but she was a soldier, for god's sake. She was trained better than that.

Taking a breath, she muttered, "It's fine. My supervisor and I...he thought you shouldn't be involved." And now that she thought about it, Rakesh was right. Mary wasn't an agent. She was a kid. And Colt barely knew her. What was she thinking bringing—

Mary squinted. "I need to be here."

Colt nodded. Then shook her head. "I, I don't think—"

"If I'm not here, Vincent won't come."

Colt's breathing slowed. "That's right."

"So you need me."

"Yes." Of course she did. But it was still a bad idea that—

"And you trust me, don't you Agent Colt?"

Face softening, Colt nodded. "Of course I do." She did. She really did. Rakesh was an idiot. How could she not trust Mary? She had to.

She absolutely had to.

A smile, one that was tiny but hid big things behind it, spread across Mary's face. "Good. Are you ready? Should I call Vincent?"

Colt's hands slipped into the pockets of her coat. There, they wiggled and flexed, then fell loose and prepared.

"Go ahead."

CHAPTER THIRTY-EIGHT

Vincent didn't know where else to go. After he'd run out of class, he'd jumped on his bike and sped away as fast as he could. He couldn't stand it anymore. Something had happened, something bad. Mary had done something, and now the whole town was talking about it, and Mary was acting like everything had gone wrong, and he just didn't know what to do anymore. Mary had said she was going to send the sheriff, that he would take care of her.

But the government woman had powers too. And Mary hadn't just sent the sheriff and his men to talk. She'd sent them to kill.

Mary was a killer.

He'd done things, terrible things, but nothing as bad as that. He never wanted to hurt anyone, but that didn't matter. The government woman was coming for him. She thought he'd done it all, and really, he felt like he had. This was all his fault. Mary had done things too, but he'd never said no. He'd never told her to stop. He'd just sat back and did what she said, and everything that was happening was happening because of him.

What if he couldn't stop the woman from taking him? What if she locked him up in a cell for the rest of his life? He'd never see the town again. His home. His family.

His mom.

The bike's spinning wheels had carried him away. His eyes looked without seeing, simply working to keep him from crashing into anything. He'd pedaled so hard he was sure he'd stripped the gears. The pounding in his chest drove his legs like unrestrained pistons. He'd needed to go faster and faster because, no matter how far he went, the fear and guilt chased right behind him, threatening to squirm through his skin and into his head.

Into his heart.

He'd gone to the mall first. He thought about going in to see his mom. He needed to see her, even if just for a minute. She wouldn't be angry about him being out of school. She'd know something was wrong. She always knew.

The parking lot had been half empty, the asphalt warmed by afternoon sun. Yet Vincent had felt so cold inside. He'd stopped just outside the entrance. In the sunlight, the white stone the massive building was made of seemed to shimmer and glow. It was so clean. So pure. So sure and solid. He'd stared at it a long time, his mouth a frown and his eyes loping down.

He didn't deserve it.

Monsters don't deserve love, even from their moms.

The entire way from the mall to home, he'd walked. Along the two lane highway, down the local roads, through a small field where his bike had cut a path for his favorite short cut. He'd heard the cars go by but hadn't glanced up once to see them. There'd been so far to go, so much time to think, and yet he couldn't remember a single thing that had crossed his mind in that time.

So he was at home, his bike resting against the old oak tree outside. His little brother and sister sat at the living room table while he sat on his bed, head hung as precariously as the towers of things that filled his room. The toys and comic books and magazines and unfinished models and half collections of baseball cards or playing cards or whatever else had gripped his fancy for a short time of his childhood, they all sat and waited to be touched, to be finished, to be a part of his life again. He stared at them with eyes that shimmered like the surface of a lake. The pointless things he had loved so much. He knew now he could never go back to them. They were the things of boys. Of people.

Not of killers and monsters and, and, and weak, spineless, useless piles of garbage.

He stared, and his chest heaved. He stared, and his nose wrinkled. He stared, and his hands clenched at the sheets on his bed, the knuckles turning white. His teeth ground against one another, and the pressure behind his ribcage swelled. His fingers squeezed so tight that sparks shot through his skin, his muscles, his bone. The pressure crept through his shoulders, into his arms, down to his hands. It pushed at the edges of his skin, desperate to escape. When the first tear ran down his quivering cheek, he opened his mouth, swung his arms out, and roared like the beast that he was.

There was a sound like a thousand pairs of hands all clapping at once. Two towers shattered and exploded, cut clean through the middle by a telekinetic blade so sharp it could slice molecules. Pieces flew in every direction as he slashed his hands again, bellowing a wordless curse. Two more towers burst. His arms swung over and over, towers splitting and severing and crashing to the floor around him.

He stopped when there was only chaos left, all his dreams and loves spread across the floor in pieces. Things settled in the room. Quiet moved in. His siblings didn't come, didn't check on him. He was completely alone.

Until he heard Mary's voice inside his mind.

Until she told him there was hope.

His head raised. His eyes, red and swollen, blinked with sharp clarity. Taking a deep breath, he stepped off his bed. Beneath his sneakered feet, an action figure of a hero he'd emulated as a child crunched loudly.

At the bottom of the stairs, the twins were waiting for him, their bodies standing straight and tall. They watched Vincent as he descended, her with emerald green eyes, him with eyes as brown as walnut shells.

Outside, a pickup truck pulled in. The twins headed out first. Vincent stood in the doorway, looking back at the home in which he'd grown up, the place he loved. His gaze slipped to the edge of the kitchen door.

Darkness, silence, nothing else.

The twins were already climbing into the truck. Mr. Matthews, eyes as flat and lifeless as dinner plates, was closing the doors from the outside. Vincent climbed into the passenger seat as Mr. Matthews got behind the wheel. Without a word spoken, without a single acknowledgement of any type, they all buckled in simultaneously.

CHAPTER THIRTY-NINE

It had been too long. The sky was a match head bursting to life in slow motion. The air was still warm from the afternoon sun, but night's gentle breath was beginning to blow.

Colt stood in the street, the loading dock to her right. The wall to her left had several dumpsters overstuffed with packing materials and old junk from the factory. They would make excellent cover if Colt needed it.

That is, if Vincent ever showed up.

Movement to her right, atop the loading dock, caught her attention. She didn't turn her head, didn't even move her eyes away from the end of the alleyway. "You should stay inside."

"Will it be dangerous?" Mary asked from the factory's open doorway.

"If he fights back."

"He will."

"He will," Colt repeated.

Mary glanced down the empty alleyway. "He's strong."

"I'm sure."

"Stronger than you think." Mary's voice was a thin as her eyes. "You have to strike first, or he'll get you. He'll have you, and then he'll make you do things."

"That won't happen."

"It will, if you don't stop him right away. He doesn't care about anyone. Not even our family. He's a monster."

"A monster," Colt repeated. In her mind, the image of Vincent burned hot. He had hurt so many people, Amber and the others, Henry, Ashley, Doctor Foster. He had caused so much pain.

"You have to stop him," Mary said flatly.

"I have to stop him," Colt replied.

"Do whatever it takes."

"Whatever it takes," Colt repeated.

"Stop him," Mary whispered.

"Yes."

Mary's eyes gleamed. "Even if you have to..." Her head snapped up, wide eyes flying to the end of the alleyway. At the same time, a wave of hot air rushed over Colt's skin. Only, it wasn't hot air.

No way.

No way a kid could be that strong. He's not even in view, and she felt him. Either he wasn't trying to mask his presence, or he was so ridiculously powerful that his psychic energy couldn't be contained. Colt hoped for the former but prepared for the latter.

All of her psychic feelers reeled in and wrapped around her body. The air around her shimmered as she put up the thickest wall she could. Out of the corner of her eye, she saw that Mary was still on the loading dock.

"Promise me," said Mary hurriedly. "Tell me you'll ki—"

"Get inside!" Colt barked.

Mary closed her mouth and slowly moved into the factory. Colt took a moment to reach into her own mind. Invisible fingers found handles to mental doors and gates and slammed them shut. Threw the bolts. Drew the chains. If Vincent could put out this much power, she had to put her mind on total lockdown. A skilled puppeteer can find any opening, any weakness in a person's mind and force their way in. And once they're in, there's almost no getting them out. They're like an infection. By the time you realize they're there, you're too sick to fight it.

The loading dock was silent a moment, the sky at the end of the alleyway a pulsing red and orange backdrop to the edges of the building. Then, in that warm, living light, a shadow appeared.

Vincent.

He was a little shorter than she expected. Taller than Mary by three or four inches, but that was all. When he'd peddled past her on his bike, he'd seemed a flurry of gyrating, chiseled limbs and a taut torso like a coiled spring. Seeing him now—standing with his sneakered feet sticking out from under rolled and cuffed jeans so high they showed off dirty white socks; skinny arms and sinewy neck not even able to fill half of the short sleeves and collar of his plaid button down shirt—he didn't seem like a menace, a monster, a controller of people and a sociopathic killer.

He looked like a kid. A kid who carried bags of anger and pain beneath his emerald eyes; a kid who already had frown lines on his face; a kid who was tired and frustrated and who, frankly, looked like he was terrified to be standing there.

Around Colt's index finger, the telekinetic gun wavered.

"You're her?" Vincent's voice wasn't powerful and booming or smooth and devilish. It was tense. It broke with a pubescent shift. "The lady, or, woman with the government?"

Colt nodded. "I'm Agent Colt, with the DSI." Something wasn't right here. Why was he scared? His emotions were palpable. They were fused in deeply with the power that pulsed around him. Colt didn't need to be psychic to know that Vincent was teeming over with more feelings than he knew how to handle. She saw it in his face, in his body language, in the pit stains beneath his arms. His breath moved in and out through his nose so quickly that he had to take a purposeful breath before shouting.

"Is it true...what Mary told me?" he paused. "Are you here to take me away?"

Her mouth opened to reply, but suddenly she was beginning to doubt. He wasn't acting like a puppeteer. His power was completely untempered, raw, and exposed. He wasn't focused. He wasn't methodical. He wasn't an emotionless sociopath. There'd been no attempt to probe her, to search for a weak spot, to take control and make her his slave.

Something was wrong.

Her shooting hand loosened.

Vincent was still staring, his eyes wide with need. "Well?"

It didn't matter. Colt still had a mission, and all of the evidence pointed to Vincent. She knew he was involved, and with the things that Mary had said...

It was like a flash-fire on the inside of her skull. Just the thought of Mary, the mere passing of her name through Colt's mind and all of the words, the warnings, Mary's insistence that Colt end things, that she did whatever it took; those things overtook Colt and pressed all of the doubts out of her mind.

Vincent was the puppeteer. Vincent was a monster.

Vincent had to be stopped.

The psychic revolver reformed, clearer and more detailed than it had been in a long time.

"Yes," Colt said flatly. "You have to be stopped. You've hurt too many people." She tightened the muscles in her core, prepared to move and dodge when he lashed out, when he attacked.

But he didn't. His bottom lip pulled up, almost like he was ready to cry. A crease, a deep crease made from more worry than a child should feel, appeared between his eyebrows. His mouth closed, and his head tumbled forward. Floppy hair fell down, almost covering the Adam's apple that bobbed while he swallowed whatever it was he was feeling.

There were words which left Vincent's mouth covered in thick layers of guilt and remorse. They tumbled across the ground, and though Colt couldn't make them out right away, she figured it out.

"I'm sorry."

A shudder moved through him, running down to his feet and back up to his chest. It filled him with air and pushed his face up. The sadness was washed away. His muscles were set. His eyes did not flare and roar with anger, but simmered like coals.

"I'm not going with you," he said.

Colt opened her mouth to reply, but Vincent cut her off.

"Let's go."

Colt's eyes went thin and then thinner again when she realized that he wasn't talking to her.

143

Two shadows stretched out across the ground behind Vincent, sliding up the brick walls. The figures moved in from around the corner and came to take their places behind Vincent. They were shorter, thinner, and had eyes that were flat and dead.

Vincent and Mary's younger brother and sister.

Of course.

That's how Vincent was able to completely smash the minds of the level ones he put into the hospital, three psychic spikes hitting in unison could devastate a person. It also explained how they were able to locate those poor people. Vincent was amplifying his power using his siblings. The three together would be like a radio tower sending out radar waves, which they could triangulate until they'd zeroed in.

The twins walked in perfect synchrony, arms and bodies swaying like timed pendulums. Colt's wall was up, but she took a chance and opened a tiny window to reach through. She almost smirked, the way people do when they hear an answer they already know is coming.

Feedback, loud and piercing, stabbing at the ends of the nerves in her mind. The kids were definitely under Vincent's control, which meant she wasn't fighting three people. She was fighting one person who had three bodies at their disposal.

The siblings stopped, spread feet and hanging arms, standing in a line, Vincent in the middle. The younger twins were emotionless drones, their faces betraying nothing. Vincent though, his chest heaving and his nose wrinkled, seemed to be boiling over with both anger and trepidation. He was waiting. No, hesitating. No...

Scared.

And once more, the thought jumped into Colt's mind and softened the muscles around her eyes just the most miniscule amount possible.

Something was wrong.

With a sharp exhale, Vincent threw a psychic spike. The twins followed suite, their own spikes coming milliseconds later. The dirt and dust blanketing the alleyway kicked up as the spikes flew toward Colt. Before they reached her, the doubt she felt, the concern over Vincent's odd behavior, was shoved aside.

Time to work.

Colt hardened her wall. The spikes hit it dead on, their kinetic force dissipating across the wall and creating a curved crease in the alleyway dust. Colt didn't need to glance down to know that Vincent's spike had pushed hardest against the wall, had even managed to bend it slightly. That level of power was incredible, but nothing that Colt hadn't seen before.

On the other hand, Vincent had clearly never seen a wall like Colt's before. While the twins' faces were still masks, Vincent's eyes were practically popping from his head. For a second, she was sure the boy was going to say something like "Whoa!" or "Cool!"

Instead, he snapped his trap shut and lowered his head. The energy he'd put out earlier, the wild and untamed fire within him, boiled up. Colt felt it in the air and was about to make a move when Vincent fired again.

Their timing was better. All three spikes came at once. Again, dust kicked up like tiny whips snapping across the ground. Again, all three slammed into Colt's wall and splashed across it. But this time, Vincent's hit hard enough to make the wall shimmer in the air. For Colt, it was like standing with her body against a door while someone hit the other side with a sledge hammer. Her eyes widened and, when she felt Vincent building up that energy again, decided she wasn't going to give him a third chance.

The siblings' shots flew out all together, Vincent's moving to the front and the twins' coming up to deliver an aftershock effect. They tore across the ground, blasting the last of the dirt aside as they sped toward Colt's wall, ready to pierce it and explode like a psychic missile. They reached the wall and passed through without a hint of resistance, heading straight at Colt's still, waiting form.

Which vanished in a blur. .

It was like an over-enthusiastic arm gesture in a photograph. There, then gone. The spikes flew across the ground, past the nothingness that had been Agent Colt, and continued down the alleyway.

The twins turned out, looking to the sides, their eyes sharp and focused. For the first time, expressions lit their faces. They were shocked, but concentrating on the task at hand. Between them, Vincent stood dumbly. He even blinked hard, as though his eyes had betrayed him.

Colt wasn't surprised. This technique was pretty high level. It was the same thing she'd done to the cop at the hotel, and it worked on both psychics and non-psychics alike. Simply put, Colt had moved before Vincent and his siblings had even fired those last spikes. Before she took a step though, she sent out a psychic image—similar to the projection of Rakesh—and imprinted it on the outer surface of the kids' minds. It happened as fast as the flash from a camera, and if the people weren't expecting it, they'd get taken in. After that, she'd moved. Because the kids were focused on her psychic image, or afterimage, they never saw her skirt around and end up right behind them.

She grabbed the twins' shirts from behind, yanked as hard as she could, added some telekinetic force for good measure, and launched them back toward the alleyway entrance. Their arms flailed around her as they fell, but they weren't able to grab hold. As they crashed to the ground and skidded across the asphalt, Colt kept her eyes on Vincent's turning head. The expression of surprise on his face was genuine, but it didn't matter. Cold had

145

promised Mary she would stop him, and that's exactly what she was going to do.

Bringing her arm back, Colt lunged forward. In her palm, a spike strong enough to take down a foreign agent was balled up. Vincent's eyes were wide, his arms coming up as though he were cringing away from a flying dodgeball. Colt planted her foot, twisted her waist, and thrust her arm; her aim perfectly lined up to pass between Vincent's forearms and slam both her palm and the spike into his face.

Gotcha.

There was a zippering sound, like plastic gift wrap ribbon tied around itself and yanked tight. Pain shot across Colt's outstretched arm. It was dragged to a stop, inches from Vincent. There was a line, a deep groove, all around Colt's forearm. The sleeve of her shirt was pressed down, wrinkled against her skin. And there, in the crease, Colt saw a shimmer, a flicker of light like when the sun catches a single strand of a spider's web.

It was a rope. A gossamer wire. A psychic thread composed of compressed kinetic energy and made into physical form.

For the first time in a very long time, Colt was stunned.

This was something completely new.

Her eyes traced the nearly invisible line back to the hands of Vincent's younger brother. The boy was on his side, his arms out and his fingers pulled tight. Colt began to turn, but an equal pressure caught her other arm. Looking down, she saw the same groove around her other arm. Only when she followed this one, it led to Vincent's sister.

When they were falling. That's what all the flailing was about. They weren't trying to grab her. They were spinning these threads.

She was so sure she'd fooled them with her afterimage, but it turned out she was the one who got caught.

And she had no idea what to do.

The twins simultaneously launched from the ground, telekinesis pulling them up the same way it had lifted Colt in the hotel parking lot. They spun as they rose and, in doing so, wrapped the threads around themselves. Colt's arms were pulled back and she was dragged away from Vincent. Instinct kicked in, and she lowered her stance, dug her feet in to keep from losing balance. Behind her, the twins landed together, graceful and smooth.

"Now!" Vincent's voice exploded in front of her. Colt came completely out of her state of shock. She thought Vincent was going to spike her but then realized she was horribly wrong.

The twins jerked their arms. The threads buzzed as two psychic spikes flew through them. There was no defense. The threads were as good as physical contact. Even with her wall up, Colt couldn't stop the spikes from hitting her dead on.

Her entire body spasmed. Sparks and pinwheels erupted across her vision and the world spun inside her head. The twins' spikes weren't that strong, but they struck deep. In the time it took her to fall to her knees, Colt slipped in and out of consciousness. The only thing that kept her up was the tension of the threads around her arms and the decades of training in her mind and body.

The city outside of Rakesh's window had been dark for almost an hour. Gazing at the boxy skyline, he thought about how the sun would be setting on Colt in a matter of minutes. By now, she should have made contact with Vincent.

He hoped that kid kicked her ass.

He'd heard the stories about Colt, about how difficult she could be to work with. They weren't even close to true. He'd never met such an unprofessional, self centered, egomaniacal...

Drumming the desk absent mindedly, his fingers sent ripples across the countless pages and file folders he'd been pouring over since their argument. He'd gone over it again and again, examined every file, every scrap about Vincent a dozen times. But always with eyes that didn't really see. The truth was, he was just trying to distract himself, trying not to think about what was really bothering him.

What the hell got into her?

Across the room, a photograph from over a decade ago stared at him. In it, he was wearing his military school uniform. He was standing with a rifle tucked snuggly against his shoulder and his diploma in his hand. He wasn't smiling.

A feeling of unease washed over him.

No. What the hell got into him?

Everything about this case was wrong. The way Colt was acting, the evidence not adding up, the fact that every piece of information Rakesh had pointed to Vincent being anything but a puppeteer.

Yes, Vincent seemed to be a poster child for a budding psychic problem. The fight at school, his dropping grades, his complete lack of social interaction with other kids. Everything showed a kid who felt isolated and angry toward the world.

But not one who wanted to control it.

That's what made puppeteers so dangerous; they always started small, controlling those around them. But soon, they were after entire neighborhoods. Then towns. Then cities. And eventually, they wanted the whole world doing what they desired.

Rakesh flopped back in his chair. His gaze rolled over to the phone and stayed there. His fingers twitched, but instead of pressing buttons, he brought them up and rubbed his face.

The stubble bit into his fingertips like cactus needles. When was the last time he'd shaved? Showered? Eaten a real meal?

Screw it. He's just a kid. She can handle a kid. He would come in tomorrow, and everything would be fine.

Pushing himself up, Rakesh shook his legs out. He'd been at his desk for the last two days straight. He needed a good run to shake away that strange feeling. But it would have to wait. For now, he was going home.

He picked up a stack of papers on his desk and tapped one of their sides, straightening them all out and putting them back neatly. The different stacks coalesced and pretty soon he was able to see spots of his desktop again. As he shifted all of Vincent's school reports to one side, he noticed a folder that appeared untouched.

It was Mary's file. A smirk crept across Rakesh's face. Here was a kid after his own heart. While Vincent was steadily building a rap sheet that any juvenile delinquent would be proud of—or certain laissez-faire special agents—Mary's entire folder couldn't have had more than eight pages. He flipped it open, suddenly realizing he hadn't even looked at it yet.

Mary was exemplary. She had straight A's. She didn't have a single blemish on her school record. No detentions, nothing. From what he could see, Mary was...

He paused.

Mary was perfect.

Not a complaint. Not a single citation. Not an assignment turned in late or anything except a perfect score. One hundred percent on every standardized test. Perfect attendance record. It was like Mary could do no wrong.

Or even if she did, nobody was allowed to say anything about it.

Oh shit.

He dropped the file, grabbed the phone and hit the speed dial for Colt's cell. It didn't even ring, just clicked and went straight to voicemail.

Dammit.

It was late. The building was probably close to empty, but a transmitter would be on for the evening shift. Dialing down to their department, he whispered a quick prayer that it wasn't Sandra on duty tonight. He couldn't stop thinking about that creepy vibe he'd gotten from her earlier. The phone rang. Rakesh promised himself that in the morning, if Colt was still alive and Mary was in custody, he'd figure out what was going on with Sandra. But right now, he had to...

"Huh."

It just kept ringing. He ended the call, got a new line, and tried again.

Same thing. No answer. Nothing.

Hanging up the phone, his fingers hovering over the receiver a moment while he looked around. His windows had become black mirrors, reflecting the bare walls of his office. Outside his door, the open area filled with cubicles and copiers was dark and quiet. The only sounds were the ventilation system and his own breathing.

149

With a shake of his head, he stepped away from the desk. There had to be someone downstairs. Maybe their phone wasn't working. Maybe they'd gone to the bathroom. Didn't matter. He'd take the elevator down and go to see for himself. If there wasn't a transmitter, maybe one of the scientists or technicians could activate Colt's phone remotely. He had to at least try.

His office was built into the second level of a large open room. The cubicles sat in the middle. Two staircases ran up the walls, mirroring each other. At the top of the stairs, a pathway rounded three of the four walls. It had private offices like his, but there were also hallways that led to other second-level walkways in the neighboring cubicle areas. The fourth wall was made entirely of glass and overlooked the city. Like the windows in his office, the stacked panes made a giant two-story mirror as black as settled tar.

With his hand sliding down the faux wood railing, Rakesh sped down the stairs and through the cubicle farm. He wasn't running, but any faster and he'd have to call it a jog. His eyes were so focused on the end of the hallway, near the elevator, that he didn't see the janitor mopping the floors until it was too late.

His dress shoes squeaking loudly, Rakesh reached out for anything he could to keep from dropping. His fingers found the janitor's sleeve, and for a second, it looked like both of them were going to end up on the floor.

"Sorry!" Rakesh shouted, his hands clutching at the janitor's shoulder and his feet stuttering on the floor. "Sorry, sorry, sorry. I—"

"Watch it!" The janitor, a good four inches taller than Rakesh, narrowed his icy blue eyes and pulled away.

Rakesh held his hands up, palms exposed. He had more important things to do than get into an argument. Also, the janitor had the distinct appearance of someone who preferred to argue with his fists.

Booking it to the elevator, he swiped his security badge and took a long, long ride down. After several more swipes, a fingerprint scan, a retina reading, and near a half dozen computer controlled doors, he was into the lower levels of the DSI.

It was like any other government facility; there were a lot of ceiling lights, very few signs, absolutely no windows, and countless rooms and offices with locks that required clearances ranging from sensitive to presidential to open. At the massively heavy door, which led to the labs, a guard was sitting on a chair, snoring lightly. Rakesh frowned and swiped his card. The huge door slid into the wall with a hiss. The guard didn't even stir.

Just another day at the super secret, underground, hidden spy base.

The lower levels of the DSI were where the scientists did their research. It was also where the tech monkeys—or electronic engineers, as they preferred to be called—built all the crazy machines and devices that studied, measured, assisted, and amplified the abilities of the agents.

150

Rounding the corner of a T juncture, Rakesh stopped. The door at the end of the hall, the one that led to the transmitter's office, was open. Inside, the room was still. He waited a moment, hoping someone would wander out, heading to the vending machines or the bathroom.

Nothing.

Damn.

Slowly, so slow that it seemed silly, he began toward the door. It dawned on him that a hell of a lot of horror movies started this way. So when his fingers reached out, touched the door and gently swung it open, he was relieved to find it not only glided silently on well-oiled hinges, but there wasn't anything or anyone inside ready to jump out at him.

What was there, though, didn't make him feel too much better. Pieces of equipment were everywhere. The headgear and power supplies that the transmitters used appeared as though they'd been taken apart. Wires were sticking out, and pieces seemed to be missing.

Suddenly, he wanted very much to pull out his cellphone and call Colt. Unfortunately, he'd have to go all the way to the upper levels to get reception. His heart beat a little harder. Taking a deep, long breath, he tried to keep the muscles in his neck from tensing.

This could be anything. Maybe there's a problem with the equipment, so they're at the lab getting it fixed.

It was definitely a jog that took him to the short flight of stairs which led to the Research and Development Division. The lab's curved wall was made with frosted glass, through which shadows of tables and machines could be seen. This was the lab where they made enhancement technology. If someone was getting transmitter gear fixed, they'd be here.

Over the sound of his own footsteps, Rakesh noticed the silence. Some sort of drilling or screwing or mechanical beeping usually came from the lab. But right now, the air was thick and dead.

Double damn.

As he rounded the bend, he noticed something lying on the ground, sticking out of the lab's doorway.

It was legs. Human legs. Legs wearing brown loafers, black socks, dress pants, all blanketed by the bottom of a white lab coat.

Rakesh froze.

He wanted to wait, to give the legs a chance to move. A thousand excuses for someone lying on the floor ran though his mind, and all of them gave him permission to ignore what he'd come across and leave without a second thought.

Too bad he didn't believe a single one.

Through the soft buzz of computer monitors, towers and cooling fans, he heard something from inside the lab. Something organic. Something alive. A person's voice.

"Gak," it said, again and again, as though the person were choking. But there was no thrashing, no sounds of movement. Just, "Gak."

Oh damn.

Rakesh opened his mouth and exhaled quietly. His dress shoes ticked and tapped, and he trotted over to the doorway. The rest of the body on the floor came into view. It was one of the scientists, a big, barrel-chested, mostly bald black guy. His arms were out to the side, and he lay on his stomach. His eyes were half open and glazed over. At his head, a liquid pool shimmered on the floor.

Drool. It was drool, not blood. The scientist was alive, just unconscious.

As the room came into view, Rakesh saw desks and tables and benches filled with equipment and notebooks. The back wall opposite the door was covered with computer setups; monitors, touch screens, blinking lights, things that beep and go ping and all sorts of panels for other stuff to be plugged into. Not a lot of this caught Rakesh's eye though. He was busy staring at the woman.

She was older, wearing a lab coat, had a bush of crinkly red hair, and stood stiff as a board. A worktable in the middle of the room was completely covered with stray wires and gear. It blocked his view of her feet, but he could assume she was up on tiptoes.

Her head was tilted back, and her eyes bulged so far out they almost touched the lenses of her cat's eye glasses. She twitched and shivered and from her tense throat, more of those "gak" noises escaped.

Rakesh leaned in and saw that something stuck out of the back of the scientist's red hair, something straight with...with smooth, silken skin.

He didn't recognize her at first, maybe because she had her back to him, maybe because she was standing so straight and firm, maybe because she didn't have a nest of wires covering her short, jet black, pixie hair cut. Or maybe it was because he had a hard time believing the Sandra he knew would grab a co-worker by the back of the head and spiking them into unconsciousness.

Unfortunately, that's exactly what she was doing.

The red-haired scientist dropped. Her skull hit the floor with a dull thunk. Rakesh winced.

Lowering her arm, Sandra moved away from the woman and disappeared from Rakesh's view. Slowly, he leaned to see what she was doing.

The mess of stray wires on the table led back to the headset Sandra normally wore. There were at least four times the normal amount of colored, insulated wires it usually had, several sets bound together into massive cords. The small, wearable battery packs had been replaced by what looked like cooling towers that were plugged into various flexible metal tubes, which ran all around the room. Some went into outlets. Others traced up the walls into vents. These ones had thick, looming, rolling steam pouring out, seeping into the vents and across the ceiling.

Behind it all, against the back wall, Sandra was systematically plugging the different bunches of wires into computer banks and panels. As she did, lights flared up in the machinery, blinking and oscillating. Rakesh heard the humming from the electronics grow louder and noticed the steam being vented thickened.

Looking around, Rakesh's eyebrows pushed together. *What the hell is she doing?*

"Making modifications."

Rakesh almost had a heart attack and very nearly wet his pants. Simultaneously.

It was Sandra's voice, but it wasn't. It was her vocal chords, her mouth and lips and tongue, but it wasn't her voice. The speech pattern, the inflections, they were completely wrong.

No, not wrong. Someone else's.

She didn't turn, just kept working. "This equipment is amazing, but I'm sure you're used to it by now." She plugged in a heavy coil and several electronic needle gauges on a nearby computer screen jumped to life. "I didn't know how to use it, so I had to search the minds of these two." She waved an arm in the general direction of the scientists. "They were very helpful."

Rakesh opened his mouth. Here was the part where the hero was supposed to make a witty retort, say something cool and calm that got under the villain's skin.

He had nothing. His mind raced, trying to figure out what to do. Physically, he could take out Sandra, but there was no way he could get past her psychic abilities. He wouldn't get halfway across the room before she spiked him into oblivion.

Wait a minute. They were maybe thirty, thirty-five feet apart. She could have popped him already.

Unless...

A corner of Rakesh's mouth twitched. Taking a deep breath, he stepped into the doorway. "What..." He swallowed and tried again. "What are you doing?"

Sandra turned. Rakesh wanted to run but waited. Sandra stared, as if weighing the options.

No, not the options. The distance.

Her eyes, cold and glassy, met his.

He was right. She didn't have complete control of Sandra's abilities, and that meant she couldn't throw a spike. Not yet, anyway.

"I already have Agent Colt," she said simply, factually. "She failed her mission, and you failed to stop it from happening."

A wave of heat spread across Rakesh's face. By his sides, his hands curled into loose fists. "I doubt that," he said, trying to sound confident. "Colt, she's tough."

"She'll be finished in a matter of minutes. After that, there's no one left to stop me."

Rakesh smirked. "Oh yeah? I dunno," he stepped into the room, "there's a lot of agents working here. Whole upper level is just full of—"

"The upper levels are empty."

Rakesh's smirk slunk away.

"I can't use all of Sandra's abilities, but I know what she knows. Agents are either out on assignment or have gone home. It's only the night shift, of which you were not supposed to be a part." She turned back to the panels and wires. "That doesn't matter, though. By morning, this building and everyone in it will be mine."

Rakesh stopped. "What about me?"

"You have no abilities. There's nothing you can do to stop me."

"I can warn people."

Sandra stopped plugging. "You won't even leave this room."

Rakesh stood straight. "You're wrong."

Sandra half turned, her head cocked in a mock of curiosity.

"There is something," Rakesh said, "something I do really, really well." He took a deep breath and lowered his chin. "I can run."

"No," Sandra said emphatically. "You can't." Her hand came out fast, curling in the air as though she were grabbing a pole. Tightness pressed in against Rakesh's leg instantly.

What? Telekinesis? Telepathy? An illusion? How did she...

Looking down, he saw a hand, a thick, sausage-fingered, dark-skinned hand, grabbing his leg just above the ankle. The unconscious scientist shifted on the ground, using his free hand to push himself up slightly. Slowly, robotically, his head turned. The drool still smeared across his face, he gazed up at Rakesh with the same cold, dead eyes that sat in Sandra's head.

Rakesh gasped.

Oh damn.

CHAPTER FORTY-ONE

Everything was dark. The asphalt's burning heat bled through Colt's pants, and she focused on it. The pain gave her bearings. She sought out the searing tightness of the twins' psychic threads around her arms. When she found it, she knew where the kids were. She squeezed her eyelids shut. When she opened them, the darkness had illuminated.

And Vincent was right in front of her.

He inhaled. Colt put everything she had into her wall. His spike slammed into it, and Colt rocked backward from the force, but that's what she wanted. The threads went slack. With a quick twist of her wrists, she got her fingers around them. The second she did, she felt it.

The connection went both ways.

Good.

Colt filled her wall with telekinetic energy and kicked it forward. It knocked Vincent back and took the wind out of him. As he fell, Colt squeezed the threads and fired. Her spikes created a tsunami of psychic energy that raced back and slammed into the twins. The two jerked back, yelped, and went limp.

The threads around Colt's arms disintegrated. She caught her balance and grabbed at her tingling limbs. In front of her, Vincent was almost on his feet, taking huge gulps of air. Sweat ran down his cheeks and dripped from his chin. Colt sensed the psychic energy swirling within him, a fire with a gust of wind rushing up through it. Instead of anger in his eyes, she saw fear and desperation.

Fists clenched, Vincent jerked up and threw a spike. Colt's wall deflected it effortlessly. She prepped herself, expected him to send another, but he just stood there, his face slowly falling. He knew he was beaten. .

Colt launched a spike. Vincent barely had time to raise his wall. Colt stepped forward and let fly with another, then another. Each time, Vincent's wall weakened. Each time, more of her spike's energy made it through. She pushed him back. He stumbled, his eyes squinting. Colt built up her psychic energy, then sent it sailing through Vincent's wall.

His knees buckled. His eyes roll up into his head and he fell, his dangly arms and legs folding beneath him.

One more spike, and he would be unconscious.

The sun had drained from the sky. At the end of the alleyway, streetlights that hummed to life. The world had been hot and livid when Vincent had shown up, but now cold, colorless light etched its way across the walls and ground. Shadows sunk into an abyss-like darkness. The air around them grew cool and edged, sleek and sharp.

Her footsteps echoing off the alleyway walls, Colt approached Vincent as he squirmed on the ground. He got his knees beneath him, and a string of spittle stretched to the ground.

"Please," he said.

Colt's eyes narrowed.

"I'm sorry," he said through a clenched throat.

Something gripped at Colt's stomach.

"I'm didn't..." His voice fluttered. "I didn't want to hurt anyone but...but...I couldn't stop..."

Colt's eyes widened. The sparkling drops gathering beneath his downturned face weren't sweat, but tears.

"It just happened. I'm sorry. I'm sorry! I promise," he gasped.

Colt's mouth gaped.

"I promise I won't do it again."

Her hands loosened.

"I don't wanna go. I don't wanna leave."

Her heart hammered.

"I want my mom."

Her skin chilled.

"I want my mom."

Colt practically scrambled away.

"What are you doing?" Mary's voice grabbed at the back of Colt's neck.

Straining, Colt turned. Mary was in the alleyway, her plaid skirt having turned into a crosshatch of grays and blacks streaked with thin red lines glowing like fresh blood in the moon. Her huge brown eyes blinked but showed no emotion.

"You little bitch," Colt said.

Mary's impassive face twitched. The invisible hand on the back of Colt's neck burst into a thousand little fingers that raced up and down Colt's body. She gasped. It was the miasma, that humming presence that Colt had felt since she'd arrived in Fieldsville. Mary had picked away at her from the beginning, and now she'd found every chink in Colt's psychic armor.

"I believe," Mary said, raising her chin slightly, "you made me a promise, Agent Colt."

Mary's tendrils rushed into her body and filled her with a great storm. Her mind rolled and toiled but would not settle.

"You said you would help me."

Colt's head filled with a roaring sound, a thousand of her inner voices all speaking different things at the same time.

"You said you would do whatever it took." Mary's voice was hard and straight, a pole pushing Colt deeper into the turmoil of her brain where she

156

was telling herself to fight against the gathering winds, to stand fast, drive through. But her own voice was one of countless others, and those words were swallowed up.

Colt squeezed her eyes shut until they stung and forced them open.

"Now do it." Mary's voice was as cold as iron. She was standing, her hand in the air, fingers outstretched. Her huge brown eyes were glowing and spinning like pinwheels lit with green flame in the night.

"Kill him."

The voices echoed and repeated Mary's command over and over, and they all were becoming Colt's. No other idea could make it through. She could consider no other notion.

Kill him, the voices battered against her.

She wasn't aware she was moving.

Kill him Kill him Kill him Kill him.

Vincent struggled to stand. His face was red and swollen. His eyes still burned with the tears he had shed.

Kill him Kill him Kill him Kill him Kill him Kill him Kill him Kill him Kill him.

His shaking hands wiped snot away from his nose.

Kill him Kill him Kill him Kill him Kill him Kill him Kill him Kill him Kill him Kill him Kill him Kill him Kill him Kill him.

He was completely lost. Confusion spread across his face.

She stopped turning.

He was tired.

She raised her arm.

He was scared.

In her hand, her revolver appeared. At the end of her finger the kinetic bullet hardened into a point.

He was being betrayed—

Her muscles tightened.

—by the person—

The bullet wavered.

—whom he loved.

The voices roared, *Kill him Kill him Kill him Kill him Kill him Kill him Kill him!*

No.

The storm stopped.

Not again.

Colt dug down, found a tiny drop of herself that was still free, and used it fire off a spike that flew screaming through her own mind, shredding Mary's control. It felt as though her nerve endings were spread a dozen paces away from each other, then pulled back in by the gravity of her core.

157

And the instant afterward, she was a statue of flesh and bone. The world became a photograph in her eyes, a picture of Vincent staring at her outstretched arm and telekinetic gun, his face frozen in the expression one bears as they realize there's no running from the danger that approaches.

An expression that she'd worn before.

Colt blinked. The photograph vanished. Vincent trembled. Tiny gasps of his breath rung in her ears. A single drop of sweat ran down her face. Across her body, Mary's countless greedy fingers jabbed and pushed and squirreled around, desperately seeking an opening where they could climb back in.

This was beyond control. It was beyond invasive. It was torture. It was abuse.

She'd been violated in ways she had never thought possible.

And she was furious.

She turned with eyes like flaming arrow tips and swung her loaded psychic gun.

Mary yanked upward, as if lifting a weight.

The muscles in Colt's arm contorted, raising her gun. The bullet fired with a thunderous clap, flying feet over Mary's head and smashing into the brick wall of the factory, blowing a hole the size of a beach ball into it.

Mary didn't even flinch.

Colt struggled to lower her arm. "Fuck." Her tricep was so tight that if it kept going, something was going to break.

Fine, if she wants to play a game of push...

Colt focused her telekinetic power and spun her hand in the air. Yards away, an invisible force grabbed Mary by her outstretched wrist and twisted.

Hard.

Mary cried out as her joint was wrenched to the absolute limit. She lost the psychic hold on Colt's arm.

Muscles slackening, Colt twisted her outstretched hand. The telekinetic hold on Mary's wrist responded, twirling back the other way. Mary saw it coming. She rolled with the rotation and landed in a crouch. She snatched at the muscles in Colt's leg. Colt stepped back and brought her arm down. Mary's wrist dropped, pulling her toward the asphalt.

Both of them stood, muscles shaking, jaws clenched, locked in a grappling contest; Colt holding Mary on the outside, Mary holding Colt from within.

But unlike Mary, Colt had been here before.

Colt spun, releasing the telekinetic hold on Mary's limbs. Mary's balance wavered, and in that moment, Colt extended a leg, throwing a kinetic spin kick into Mary's gut. The psychic grasp on Colt's muscles evaporated as

158

Mary flopped back on the ground. Colt raised a misty gun, but Mary snatched the limb and pulled it across Colt's body. Colt tried with her other hand, and Mary countered the same way. Mary flicked her wrists, and Colt's arms flew out, stretching wide.

Colt raised her leg again, but Mary had already seen this trick. She released Colt's arms and forced Colt's leg to jerk up. Colt used a telekinetic force to turn it into a back flip that landed her on her knees. She punched both fists forward, sending telekinetic strikes down the alleyway. Mary released her hold on Colt and scrambled as the telekinetic strikes sailed past.

Limbs free, Colt stood with a grunt. At the end of the alleyway, Mary rose as well, her usually neat-and-trim hair falling wildly across her face.

Mary's face was no longer a mask of passive indifference, but instead, it seethed with disdain and contempt.

Colt couldn't help but grin.

All right, she thought it loud, with the hope that Mary would hear. *Let's see what you can really do.*

As if in response, Mary breathed deeply and lowered her hands to the side. Colt prepared for an attack, but Mary's hands danced in the air.

Shadows shifted on the ground. Two lumps pulled up into the colorless light of the night.

The younger twins.

They stood not through muscle, but by their telekinesis. Their arms dangled and their heads bobbed, their joints made of rubber bands. Then, with a hard flick of Mary's fingers, their bodies stood straight and their heads came up. Even in the dark, Colt could see their eyes.

There was nothing. No thought. No soul.

They were empty. Hollow.

They were puppets.

Colt fired first. The spike was fast and hit Mary's wall with a thud. The girl stepped back. Colt prepped another, knowing that just a few more would break through, but stopped when Mary sent the twins out.

Their speed was incredible; lifted and driven forward by telekinesis, the two covered the distance of the alleyway in seconds. They raced toward Mary and crossed each other as they dashed past her. Colt saw it then, how their fingers almost touched, and knew they were passing a thread between them. As they spread further apart, heading to each side in an attempt to clothesline her, she crouched and sprung upward.

With a telekinetic push, she easily cleared eight feet. In front of her, Mary stepped back. Colt's hand was up and a bullet ready to go. Mary managed to tense the muscles in Colt's arm enough to change the shot's angle, but Colt had counted on that. The bullet was like buckshot, breaking into a dozen smaller parts as it flew. One hit Mary's shoulder and sent the girl

159

stumbling. It wasn't enough to put her down, but it probably hurt like hell. Immediately, the muscles in Colt's arm became hers again.

Behind her, the twins flung their thread up into the air in an attempt to catch Colt as she landed. But she'd seen that coming, too. As she hit the ground, she snagged the psychokinetic line and fired off a spike down each side. The twins broke the line immediately, disintegrating it in mid air, then touched fingers and came at Colt again.

Before they could take two steps, Colt fired. The shot hit the boy in the leg. It was strong enough to bruise the bone and send him toppling to the ground. He went down without a sound, without a whimper or cry.

Colt's temper flared.

The thread between the twins pulled tight as the boy fell and the girl stumbled. Colt moved in as fast as she could, a spike balled up in her palm. The girl let go of the thread and began spinning another. She dodged Colt's thrust by inches, her sandy blonde hair floating as Colt's fingers grazed it. Her lithe body lilted, while her fingers spun thread after thread into the air.

With a growl, Colt snatched the threads as they wrapped around her. She yanked hard. The girl fell toward Colt. Another swing of the arm, back the other way, and the girl was completely off balance. One more pull and the girl was dragged in. Colt grabbed her by the front of her shirt, spun halfway around, and threw. The girl flew across the alleyway and crashed into a dumpster. There was a sharp metallic bang, and she dropped to the ground, unconscious.

And that only left...

Mary's spike hit Colt from behind, striking her wall like a boxer's punch. Turning, Colt stared at the girl.

The puppeteer.

The real monster.

Mary's normally balletic posture was gone. She was half slouched, one hand on her wounded shoulder. A dark shimmer of fresh blood seeped between Mary's fingers. It was a flesh wound, but it had been enough to break the girl's stoic resolve. The mask was gone, and Colt saw what lay beneath.

Shaking, blazing eyes, curled lip, clawed hands, Mary's rage at being denied had consumed her. Snarling, the girl launched another spike. It splattered like a snowball against Colt's wall.

"Vincent's was stronger."

Mary's fists clenched. She howled and reached out, her fingers aimed at Colt's body.

But nothing happened.

Mary snatched at Colt over and over again.

"That's not going to work anymore."

Mary pulled together her psychic fingers into the point of a great lance, which she aimed straight at Colt's chest. She thrust forward with a command for Colt's heart to wrench itself and push every ounce of blood up into Agent Colt's brain until it burst.

But Colt wasn't there. There was only a blur, then nothing.

Mary's eyes widened. Her face went slack. She held her breath.

"Here."

Mary turned, only to see the back of Colt's hand crash across her face. Mary reeled. Before the girl could right herself, Colt brought her arm back across, slapping Mary's face. Mary screamed and fell. All of her gusto, all of her arrogance, was gone. She was just a teenage girl, and Colt was kicking the shit out of her.

Colt snatched Mary's shoulders and drove her knee into the girl's gut. Mary's screams stopped. Colt drew her leg back and drove her knee in again. She looked down. Mary's mouth was twisted in a silent groan. Her hands shook, and her eyes clamped shut as tears rolled out of them.

Huffing, spit flying from between her lips, Colt shoved Mary's curled body away. The girl fell in a pile, her legs kicking as she desperately tried to fill her lungs. Colt stood over her, gazing down with professional apathy.

Squirming on the ground, Mary managed to take a breath and let it out with a pitiful wail.

Colt reached out with a foot and pushed Mary onto her back. "Shut up."

Mary lashed out, scratching and clawing at Colt's leg like an animal. Colt dropped a telekinetic blanket made of lead, pinning Mary's arms and head to the ground. Colt stared at Mary's face, filthy with tears and dirt, swollen and red from the slaps. But her eyes were cold and sharp as polished blades. Colt had never seen anyone hate something so much as Mary hated her right then.

Raising a hand, index finger straight, Colt pointed right between Mary's eyes. "I'm going to keep my promise," she said softly.

Mary went quiet and watched Colt's hand.

"I'm going to stop the monster." The air in Colt's hand swirled, then tightened into a perfect, semi-transparent revolver.

Mary's eyes snapped shut.

"No!"

Colt turned. Vincent's fist was coming right for her. Instinctively, she pulled back. Vincent stumbled as his punch flew wide, but he reeled and came back again.

"Get away!" he shouted as he swung wildly.

Colt knocked his arms away. Behind Vincent, Mary was getting up. Colt ducked a wild swing and slipped past Vincent, heading for Mary.

161

Hands snatched at the back of her shirt.

"No!"

For his size, Vincent was strong. He managed to bring Colt to a stop by dropping to one knee and yanking.

Growling, Colt threw a round kick into Vincent's side. He shouted in pain and let go of her. As he dropped, Colt started to reach out to him. She knew he didn't understand. Mary had tricked him.

Dammit... Mary.

Whirling, Colt saw the girl stumbling toward the end of the alleyway. Mary's fingers were twitching, pulling at something or someone that Colt couldn't see. Whatever it was, it wasn't going to be good. Exhaling quickly, Colt raised her arm and lined up the shot.

The air behind her ignited with raw psychic energy. She turned and found Vincent's eyes. He stared at her hand, following the line to the back of Mary's head. He gaped at his brother and sister, collapsed to the ground. Inside of him, Colt felt the floodgates open. The energy pulled in, rushed into Vincent's body, driven by his pounding heart into his shoulders and down into his hands.

Colt stepped back. Vincent leaped forward, a primal scream rising from his throat. His fist was clenched and pulled back. The psychic energy rushed up, like flame and heat and force, trying to escape from his flesh and bone. Her eyes went wide. Her head leaned back to dodge the punch. Vincent's fist soared past her cheek, missing by only inches.

But that was close enough.

There was a pop like a leather belt folded in half and snapped against itself, and pain erupted in Colt's cheek. Stumbling back, her eye above the cut clamped shut from the pain and she felt the warm splash of blood running down her face.

He attacked again, aiming for her chin, but missed by a wide margin. There was another snap of air, and Colt felt that same instantaneous slice on her chest, inches below her collarbone. Her shirt split open, a six-inch slice cut into it. Her bra strap was severed, and the gash on her skin, long but shallow, stung. Her white shirt was already sticking to her skin as blood, dark as tar in the black and white world around them, seeped out.

Outside. The cuts happen outside his range.

When Vincent came in again, his arm arching wide and high, Colt stepped forward instead of back. She stopped his swing by hitting high on his arm near the elbow. Her other hand landed flat against his chest.

It was less of a bullet, more of a telekinetic medicine ball. The percussive force blasted air in every direction. As Vincent flew back and skidded and rolled across the ground, a cloud of dust rose in the white fluorescence of the alleyway, a million specks of light all swimming with each other.

Colt watched through the dust as Vincent slid to a stop. Her entire body ached. The cut on her face bled like a fountain, and applying pressure was like stabbing herself with a white hot knife. She felt the muscles in her legs flapping. Her left knee throbbed as she walked, staggered really, toward Vincent. She was approaching her limit.

Just one clean spike, and he'd go down for good.

Pushing himself up on shaky legs, Vincent gazed up at Colt for a moment. He seemed about to say something when a thunderous mechanical roar filled the entrance to the alleyway behind him.

Colt threw her arms up as headlights blinded her. Peeking through her fingers, she looked to where the thudding of the engine was bouncing off the brick walls. There, in the glow of the headlights, a silhouette stood.

Mary.

A car door opened. Shadows moved about in the edges of the light. Colt checked the alleyway. Both twins were gone. By the time Colt turned back, Mary was walking out of the light. Colt started to bring her pistol out, but Mary vanished into the darkness.

"Wait," Vincent said as he tried getting to his feet.

There was a metallic thunk as the car door slammed.

"Wait," Vincent said again into the light.

The engine revved.

Vincent staggered forward. "I'm coming, I just—"

The engine thumped as it shifted gears.

Colt's arms lowered. Before her, Vincent stood, beaten and broken, his body a shadow against the headlight beams.

Oh God.

The tires screeched like a thousand enraged birds. .

Adrenaline fired into Colt's body. She broke into a full sprint just as the tires caught the ground and the truck lurched forward. Vincent stood dumb, his only attempt at escape a simple step backward as his sister directed the truck to bear down on him. Colt's heart hammered. Her arms pumped. Her feet slammed against the ground, and as she came upon Vincent's back, her arms wrapped around his thin frame. Her mind dug deep down into the absolute last of its reserves to find enough energy to get her and Vincent into the air, just above the headlights and the hood of the metallic death that barreled toward them.

A blanket, her own psychic wall mixed with telekinetic energy, engulfed them as they rolled in the air and slammed into the truck's windshield. Colt screamed in pain, Vincent in fear. Their bodies went up,

163

leaving the shattered and snowy white windshield beneath them as they passed over the top of the cab and crashed onto the street.

Brakes locked. The truck's tires smoked as it dragged to a stop. On her back with Vincent pressed against her chest, Colt pried one eye open. Through her tears, she found what looked like the back of the truck, pointed her gun, and began firing. She heard the pinging of metal being dented and the crack of the rear cab window. After more than a dozen hits, the truck shifted gears and tore out of the alleyway.

The sound of the engine faded away, and Colt lowered her gun. For the next minute, the only sounds she heard were her own labored breathing and Vincent's sobs, muffled against her chest.

CHAPTER FORTY-TWO

Ever since Rakesh met Sandra, he'd daydreamed about her reaching out for him. Of course, in these fantasies, her embrace had been slightly more passionate than it was now.

Now, it was more of a lunge.

She was going for his head, just like the poor redheaded scientist. She was going to, figuratively, suck out his brains. If Rakesh was lucky, he'd end up like the big bald-headed guy on the floor, whose hand was vise gripped onto his ankle.

So, armed with the knowledge that he would be done for if Sandra touched him, Rakesh reacted in the most natural way possible.

He squealed.

Having never been in an actual fight, the best he could do was to flail his arms about, trying to both attack and defend at the same time. As a result, he stumbled back. The tension against his ankle shifted to the rim of his tan wingtip shoe and his foot came loose. His leg swung up, the shoe popped off, flew straight across the room, and smashed directly into Sandra's face.

If, at that moment, Sandra weren't under the control of a sociopathic teenage girl who was intent on using her to dominate the world, it probably would have been pretty funny.

Sandra did not find it amusing.

She halted her lunge and grabbed her face. The scientist on the floor imitated the movements perfectly. Scrambling, Rakesh caught a glimpse of blood trickling from Sandra's nose. He also caught a glimpse of the anger in her eyes and decided it was best to get up and haul ass. In seconds, he was up and sprinting down the hall, one foot slapping a hard sole and the other slipping because of the smooth, cotton sock.

Through Sandra's eyes, Mary watched Rakesh disappear down the hallway. The pain and shock from being hit in the face had muddied the connection a moment. Mary wanted to send Sandra after Rakesh, but Sandra was the one thing holding Mary's mind in the building. So instead, the young girl pushed herself deeper into Sandra's mind, gaining access to new causeways of Sandra's psychic ability.

Under Mary's command, Sandra raised her hand. As she did, the redheaded scientist rose from the floor, invisible strings of psychic control pulling at her muscles and moving them to Mary's will. Sandra raised the other hand, and the big, black man also stood.

Mary couldn't see through the scientists' eyes. Her power wasn't fully realized.

Yet.

Through psychic commands delivered like orders over a radio, she sent the scientists after Rakesh. Sandra went back to the machines, plugging and unplugging wires.

Her drones hard at work, Mary reached out with Sandra's ability and began stretching psychic fingers deeper into the building.

CHAPTER FORTY-THREE

For the first two hundred yards of the hallway, Rakesh's body didn't seem to be working any better than his mind.

Oh crap. Oh damn. Oh hell. What do I do? What do I do? Do I call someone? Colt? Do I call her? But Sandra said—no, don't do that. Forget what she said. But if Mary's here—not Colt. Colt's busy. Who else? Ummmmm... wow, I need to socialize more. Dude! Situational awareness! Okay, no calling. Not yet. What about, do I get out? What about—shit, do I evacuate the building? Yes! Good idea. How, how do I do that? No clue. Okay. Bad idea. Next idea. Um, police. Call police. Have them come... to a government facility... that technically isn't supposed to exist. Stupid idea. Stupid, stupid, stupid.

Rounding a corner, Rakesh's sock-covered foot went out from beneath him, but he caught himself on the wall.

There'd never been anything like this before. Who the hell would be crazy enough to take on an entire building filled with people who could read your mind, wipe your memory, and make you think you're a twelve-year-old Austrian yodeling prodigy? The employee handbook didn't cover infiltration by a puppeteer who's using the transmitter you'd like to take to dinner as their personal slave-making machine!

His legs pumped. With a loud squeak, his un-shoed foot skidded out from beneath him again.

Dammit! Get it together. Focus. Form. Center. Come on. Stop being an idiot.

Quickly, his core muscles tightened. His arms stopped swinging madly. His hands became loose fists and stayed out, never crossing the centerline of his sternum. His legs went from knee raises to kick backs, using nearly all of their energy to push him forward.

He transformed from a flailing fool to a tuned machine. His heart rate came down, and with the torrent of blood and adrenaline waning, his thoughts became clearer.

Step one, let security know. They're reduced at night, but they still carry guns. Or stun guns. Or something. Whatever, doesn't matter. They're armed. Step two, there's a phone at the guard's station just outside the security door. One call to the central, and they bring in a whole legion of agents to shut down Sandra.

No, not Sandra.

Mary.

Sweat beaded across Rakesh's forehead when he reached the security door. "Hey!" he shouted at the guard on the other side, who was probably still asleep. "Security breach!" As he touched the card to the sensor, the gears shifted in the wall. "Get on the phone!" In just a second, he'd be across the door, have it shut, and be calling in the cavalry. "Hey!" With a whoosh of pressurized air, the door split in the middle. "There's a—"

The guard was at the door, arms raised and pointed at Rakesh's chest. Rakesh looked up, past the man's wrinkled sleeves, to his eyes.

His cold, flat eyes.

Oh, damn.

Tiny barbs hit Rakesh square in the chest. Fifty thousand volts of electricity pumped into his muscles. It was like a full body charley horse. He saw white and black and red and yellow and spots and stripes and nothing and everything all at once.

He wasn't even sure how he'd fallen. He only knew he was down. Static filled his ears. Hands fell upon him, and he felt himself being rolled over.

Sharp pain stabbed his chest as the guard yanked out the Taser's tiny metal barbs. He couldn't move, couldn't respond to the pain, but his eyes did pop open.

The guard was standing over him. He grabbed the keycard and tossed it down the hallway. Out of instinct, Rakesh's gaze followed the card. Where it landed, the shadows of two figures came around the corner at the far end of the hallway. .

He had to run. He had to get away, but his legs squirmed like unearthed worms. The static was clearing from his ears. He had to do something before the two scientists got there, before they could drag him back to Sandra so she could suck his brains out, too.

The guard bent down, dug his hands into Rakesh's collar, and hauled him up. Rakesh's arms were more useless than his legs. They flapped about, slapping at the guard's hips.

"The Taser isn't there, Rakesh." The guard's throat was filled with gravel, but carried the intonations of Mary. "It wouldn't do you any good anyway. It was one-time use."

If his tongue hadn't been the equivalent of a fish flopping on dried land, Rakesh would have said something mean and biting. Instead, he focused all his capacities at getting control of his limbs. Squeezing his eyes shut as tight as he could, he opened them and checked the hallway. Redhead and big bald were on their way, maybe a hundred feet to go. Rakesh's heart pounded in his chest. With every beat, he reclaimed another inch of his own body. Sloppily, his fingers slid around to the back of the guard's belt.

"The pistol is in a special holster, and I doubt you know how to remove it. You're defenseless. Just give up."

One hand clamped down on the guard's shoulder. The other pulled away from the belt and found its way to the guard's neck.

"I don't..." Rakesh slurred, "need a gun...to stop you."

The guard's hands tightened around Rakesh's collar. "No?"

"All I need...is this." His hand rose and swayed just at the edge of the guard's peripheral vision. Rakesh waited until the man turned and saw him waving the guard's security badge and keycard in it.

With a grunt, Rakesh drove his knee between the man's legs. . The guard half shouted and half coughed, then dropped Rakesh onto wobbly legs.

He pushed off the guard and scampered for the security door. Behind him, redhead and big bald started running. With a full body heave, Rakesh slammed the guard's keycard onto the sensor. The guard reached out, his fingers like claws, just as the security door closed.

Panting, Rakesh lifted the sensor. Beneath it was a numeric keypad. He punched in his own security code, closed the sensor, and touched the card to it again. There was a loud thump as the doors went into full lockdown. The keycards the scientists had wouldn't be able to open the door from the inside now.

Grinning, he reached out for the callbox that was next to the sensor.

"Ha," he whispered. "I guess you're not as smart as you—"

His fingers stopped in mid air.

The landline phone was smashed to pieces.

"Okay," he said. "You are that smart."

His muscles felt like they were made of mud, but he had to get moving. Mary's puppets weren't hammering on the door like mindless zombies. In fact, they hadn't even tried to get it open. That meant they were already heading toward him another way. Mary had access to the bottom floor's layout in the guard's head. They would be taking the most direct route to him.

No, they would be setting up to cut him off.

Minutes. Five at the most, two at the least; that's what he had to get to an elevator, get to a higher level, find an office, make a call, wait for reinforcements, and hide. Anyone he ran into could be another of Mary's puppets.

His brow crinkled.

How the hell did she get the guard? If she could just take people over, why hadn't she taken him?

His eyes opened wide. Sleeping, the guard had been sleeping. That meant his conscious mind wasn't active and Mary just slipped right in. That meant no taking any naps, not that he was planning on it anytime soon.

After all, he had work to do.

"Okay." The word came out like a puff of smoke. His back tightened. "Come on." Tilting his chin back, he closed his eyes and breathed deeply.

"Run," he told his legs, which had carried him through marathons, through hundreds of hours of training where he'd run up and down more stairs than any human being had any right or need to climb.

"Run!"

His arms cut the air by his sides as he sprinted down the hall. The stairs were about three or four hundred feet away, but there were a bunch of twists and turns to get there. Reaching out, Rakesh dragged his hand against the wall and tried to slingshot himself into the next hall as fast as he could.

He was a hundred feet out. As turned the second-to-last corner, he skidded to a stop. The hallway ended in a T juncture. A shadow was splashed across the wall. Someone was standing there, near the elevators and stairs, waiting for him.

Damn.

Snapping his head back and forth, Rakesh searched for the closest door. Slapping the guard's keycard across it, there was a loud beep, and a single red light appeared. The shadow started moving. Turning fast, he tried another door.

Beep.

Damn!

The shadow thickened and Rakesh heard footsteps along with some other sound, a high-pitched squeaking. Maybe it was another stun gun charging up or some crazy weapon one of the scientists had built. Whatever it was, it sounded terrible and Rakesh really, really didn't want to be it anywhere near it.

As the shadow crept to the edge of the juncture, Rakesh dashed to another door and slapped the keycard. There was a pause. Sweat dripped down from his head and splattered across the floor. Feet appeared at the end of the hallway. Rakesh held his breath.

The light flashed green.

He threw himself against the door, spun inside, and slammed it.

It was pitch black for a moment before the motion sensors turned on the lights. He was in a small office. There was a bare desk and an empty filing cabinet but no phone or computer. That explained why the keycard gave him access. There wasn't anything confidential in here, so there was lighter security.

He wanted to growl, to shout and curse, but outside, the squeaking and footsteps grew louder. Rakesh closed his eyes and opened his mouth wide. He sucked in air and exhaled as much as he could. He had to slow his heart rate, to stop the blood from pounding in his ears so he could listen.

Through the door, he heard a grumble. The squeaking stopped, and a gruff voice barked, "The hell is this?"

Rakesh's eyebrows pinched together. He knew that voice.

170

Out in the hallway, the janitor he'd run into earlier grumbled something else. In the room, Rakesh let out a quick sigh and opened the door a fraction of an inch. The janitor was a few feet away, bending down, examining the droplets of Rakesh's sweat.

Yanking the rolling mop bucket closer, the wheels cried out desperately for oil. Rakesh almost laughed, and he pulled back from the door so he could go out and warn the man to get out of the building.

"Hey!" The janitor barked loudly.

But not at him.

Rakesh shut the door and pressed his ear against it.

"One of you spill something down here? I just did these floors an hour ago. I don't need to be doin' them again."

There were footsteps, more than one pair. Rakesh prayed that it was someone else, some other person working late.

"We're very sorry," said three voices in perfect unison. "Let us help you with that."

"Oh no, no," said the janitor, sardonically. "I'm not gonna get written up for causing trouble."

"We insist," said Mary's puppets.

Rakesh held his breath.

"Listen," snapped the janitor. "Next time, don't—hey! What're you—"

Rakesh closed his eyes.

"Get off me!"

The hall filled with the sounds of stamping feet, of skittering shoes and rustling clothes.

"Stop it!"

Mary's puppets were completely silent. The janitor went from speaking to grunting to wordless cries, from fury to fear. And then, from cries to screams. He screamed as though acid had just been injected into his veins.

Inside the room, Rakesh pulled away from the door and clenched his fists. He wished he could will the sound away, but the janitor just screamed nonstop as though his lungs could never empty of air. Rakesh covered his ears with his hands until the janitor's voice gave out. When silence fell, he peeked into the hall.

Mary's puppets were standing around the janitor, their hands grasping at his head. His eyes were rolled up, and his mouth was open in a noiseless scream. His body twitched and shivered, but soon he went limp. The puppets lowered him, and he stood. Mouth closing, the janitor looked up with eyes that were as flat and cold as Sandra's.

171

The puppets, all four of them, stood a moment. Then, orders received, they moved at the same time. Redhead and the guard headed left down the hallway. The janitor marched back toward the elevators. Big bald reached into his pocket and took out his keycard. A jolt of fear leaped into Rakesh's heart, but big bald stomped toward the next office over. With a touch, the door unlocked and big bald disappeared into the room.

Rakesh closed his eyes.

If he could get big bald's keycard, he could maybe get into an office with a phone. But that would require a direct confrontation. Though he didn't have to be afraid of the brain wiping thing—it looked like it took all three of them to pull that off—there was no way Rakesh could overpower that guy. Mary was smart, putting the biggest and strongest in charge of the door-to-door. Even if he were a fighter, Rakesh had the odds stacked against him. He had to come up with something else.

Outside, he heard a door close. Big bald lumbered across the hallway and went into the office there. He was being systematic, and that meant Rakesh's room was next. He didn't have a choice, there would be only a few seconds before big bald came back out. He had to move.

There was the beep. Rakesh watched as big bald vanished into the room, the door swinging shut behind him. The moment the latch hit, Rakesh yanked his door open and dashed out.

Right into the mop and bucket.

It was the antithesis of grace. Rakesh stumbled, scampered, then smashed into the floor. By the time he realized what he'd done, it was too late. Big bald came out of the office and headed directly toward him. Rakesh pushed himself up to run. At the end of the hall, the janitor came around the corner.

Damn.

Thick hands grabbed Rakesh by the back of the shirt and swung hard, slamming him face first into the wall. Big bald pulled him back to do it again. Rakesh swung back and tried to put his elbow square into big bald's nose. Instead, the attack just barely grazed the man's cheek. Rakesh tried twisting, turning around so he could get a better angle. Big bald flattened Rakesh's back against the wall.

Lifting his leg, Rakesh jammed his foot into big bald's ample gut. It wasn't a kick, and it wasn't a push, but it was something in between. There was just enough force to pull himself free of big bald's hands.

As he turned, he saw the janitor dashing toward him. Rakesh tried to turn, but his shins found the bucket that had rolled into the middle of the hallway. The bucket tipped, and Rakesh tipped with it, sticking a landing in the world's worst downward-dog yoga pose.

Murky, soapy water splashed across his wrists, soaking his sleeves and the floor. The janitor hit the puddle at full speed and actually managed to get airborne before he came down into the suds.

Rakesh tightened his abs and tried to pull himself up, but big bald chose that moment to throw a heavy kick into his side. Hitting the floor, Rakesh slipped and skidded on the edge of the puddle. Something hard dug into his shoulder, and he heard the clatter of wood nearby. Big bald dropped down, straddling him at the waist. Rakesh pulled his legs up, trying to push the heavy man off of him, but couldn't get the leverage. Big bald's sausage fingers searched for his throat. With one hand, Rakesh struggled to keep the grasping digits away from his neck. With the other, he reached out into the puddle.

Big bald found Rakesh's neck, but Rakesh found the mop. A shower of dirty water rained down as he jammed the mop head into big bald's face. They struggled there a moment, but the flat part of the mop's head worked its way under big bald's nose and pushed the man away.

Rakesh stood, holding the mop in both hands like a knight wielding a sword. Big bald lurched in, and shouting, Rakesh swung as hard as he could.

Right into big bald's shoulder.

There was a loud snap, which, for a moment, Rakesh believed was big bald's arm. Unfortunately, when he looked down, he saw that it had been the mop breaking neatly in half.

"Oops," he said softly.

Big bald lunged. Rakesh stepped back and turned, hoping to avoid being driven into the wall again. Big bald staggered around, his feet hitting the edge of the soapy puddle, and went back. Arms flailing, the massive man came down on top of the janitor, who had just gotten his footing. There was a tremendous smack as the back of big bald's head hit the floor, and a crunch from the janitor's body beneath. Rakesh, finally getting his balance back, glanced down to find both men motionless.

Panting, he peered one way down the hallway, then the other.

There were no signs of redhead or the guard.

Bending down, he grabbed the broken mop handle without the head. Then, skirting around the puddle, ran toward the elevators. Behind him, he heard a soft groaning coming from underneath big bald.

CHAPTER FORTY-FOUR

Slivers of smoke rose as the redheaded scientist soldered another set of wires to the monstrous headset on the table. Sandra pulled massive cables across the floor and led them to a chair at the center of the room. In unison, they stopped their work and looked up.

The others, scientist and old man, what happened? Mary couldn't feel them. Even with Sandra's power. Incredible power. Mary was glad to have it. They were unconscious. Knocked out. When they woke, she would have them again.

Rakesh. Annoying man. He had gotten away. Where was he going? Not back here. He'd run away to call in help. That meant going up. The elevators. That's where she would find him. He was more trouble than she'd anticipated.

Deep inside Sandra's sandbagged mind, a spritely smirk appeared.

Mary felt. Sandra pushing back. Mocking her. Proud of Rakesh. So she sent her power down to that bit of Sandra. She tore at it, slashed it until Sandra's mind was still and silent.

Able to focus again, Mary sent a new order. On a sublevel beneath the lab, a door opened into a dark and steamy hallway. The guard walked from a stairwell and headed for a series of large digital readouts and fuse boxes. He opened the panels and watched as six displays showed the current level of the elevators. One caught his eye—the one that was headed toward their floor.

Back in the lab, Sandra's body returned to her work while the redhead exited to intercept the annoyance.

CHAPTER FORTY-FIVE

"Come on," Rakesh said. "Comeon, comeon, comeon, comeon."

The elevator dinged at each floor on its way to him. Soon he'd be on his way to the upper levels where there were offices he could get into with the guard's keycard. All he had to do was get up there.

With a thump, the elevator arrived, and the doors slid open. Rakesh was about to leap in but stopped.

The other elevators were dinging. He checked their floor displays. They were headed toward him, too.

How stupid could he be?

One more step and Mary would have had him. She'd sent every elevator down there. And in his eagerness, he'd almost fallen for it.

He smacked the button for the top floor and stepped out. As the elevator doors closed, he jogged down the hall. He yanked open a heavy door and noticed a sign bolted to the wall.

IN CASE OF EMERGENCY, USE STAIRS.

He managed a grin.

His heart pounded in rhythm with his feet. After being knocked around, his head throbbed, and the muscles around his spine were tense and sore. His back and sleeves were soaked with soapy mop water, and he was acutely aware of his scent—a strange combination of lemony fresh and swampy stink. He was getting the shivers from being wet, but also from the adrenaline running through his system. He couldn't stop his hands from shaking. He throttled the mop handle just to give his fingers something to do as he climbed the stairs.

Making sure to temper his breathing, he checked the numbers spray painted next to a door. Only six floors to go before he was out of the sublevels. Soon, he'd be calling for help. Soon, he'd have the entire forces of the DSI charging in. Soon, he wouldn't be alone in this.

A stitch formed in his left side. Right now, it was an annoying little sting, but Rakesh knew that, if he didn't slow down, it would become a bowie knife twisting between his ribs.

He reached another floor. Five more and he would be out of the sublevels. Chewing on the inside of his lip, he stared at the door. As much as he wanted to get out of the sublevels, he had to think about the long game here. Even if he called in for backup, it would take some time for them to get there. He couldn't risk burning out now. The stitch needled him again. Slowing his feet, he reached out and checked the stairwell door. It swung open, no keycard needed.

The hallway was dark and lined with office doors, which didn't have keycard sensors. Panting, he jogged to the closest office. The lights kicked on, and there, on the desk, was a phone.

Rakesh smiled. "Yes," he said, picking up the receiver. "Thank you, G—"

Nothing. No dial tone. It was dead. Completely dead.

His smile fell, and he dropped the receiver to the floor.

They'd cut the lines or at least shut down the system. There were no phones and probably no computers either.

He flopped onto the desk, his forehead resting against folded forearms. Without a way to reach anyone, he didn't know what to do. . Running and climbing had gotten him nothing. Mary had seen through him, had predicted his next step.

There had to be another way. There was always another way. Think. Think. Something in his pocket, pinched between him and the desk, pressed into his leg. His eyes popped open. Leaping up from the desk, he reached into his pocket and yanked out his cellphone.

Maybe, maybe he… what floor was this? Maybe he was high enough.

The screen came to life, and Rakesh looked with hope to the upper corner.

No signal. It was at least another six, maybe seven floors before he was out of the sub levels.

Everything ached. Everything hurt. Still, he pressed on, returning to the staircase. Just a few flights of stairs. If he made it just another few flights, he could call in the cavalry.

He could do this.

He had to do this.

His feet beat a slow, steady rhythm on the stairs. He kept an eye on the phone. The second the slightest hint of a signal bar appeared…

Keep going. Keep going.

Lower level seven.

Lower level six.

No signal. Rakesh's muscles were beginning to feel numb.

Lower level four.

Lower level three.

His feet, his heavily calloused feet, stung from hitting the hard concrete stairs. The phone bobbed up and down, but the screen didn't change. He watched and listened for a ping, a knock, a beep that would indicate he had a signal.

Lower level two.

Lower level one.

Come on, you son of a—

176

Three or four levels down, a door burst open. The sound struck Rakesh's ears like a whip. He stopped and waited.

Someone was there, standing in the doorway. They were listening. Standing as still as he could, Rakesh breathed slowly. There was a pause, and the sound of the door creaking shut danced up the stairwell. Rakesh closed his eyes and grinned.

RING!

He tossed the phone in the air as though it had come to life and tried to bite him. Frantic fingers reached out for it, fumbling and sending it farther, and farther, and farther away from him before it clattered down the steps, falling into the space between the stairs, down two whole levels, and crashed.

Rakesh didn't move until he heard the footsteps from the stairwell down below. Then, he burst. Running as fast as he could for the phone before the puppet could reach it. But his legs couldn't carry him the way he needed them to, and whoever was coming up the stairs was fast. Rakesh was only one level away from the phone, but a shadow jumped around the stairs below.

Crying out, he threw himself at the closest door, shoulder first. Running into the hallway, he whipped around corners, unsure where he was going. He was screwed. Cellphone was gone. Mary had control of the building. He didn't have any other choice now. It was only a couple of levels to go before he reached the upper floors. If he could get up there, maybe he could get out of the building. This was it, his last chance. He had to escape.

This floor was set up like the floor he worked on, hallways of offices leading to big, open cubicle spaces. If he could get to one of those, he'd head straight for the exit and get the hell out of the building.

Lowering his head, he dug deep and sprinted. The next hallway would lead him to the upper staircase, like the one where his office was, and after that he would be able to get out.

Cutting around the corner, he didn't see the janitor before they collided. They both went down, a mass of swinging arms and legs, and Rakesh felt the sear of carpet burn on the side of his face. The janitor laced arms around his neck and torso and pulled. Rakesh fought desperately, wildly. He beat at the janitor's sides, kicked back with all his strength, even got his teeth into the man's arm and bit down on the wet, soapy sleeve.

They stumbled farther down the hall. Rakesh gasped and grunted and growled; he clawed at the janitor's arms. Planting his feet, the janitor pushed hard and drove the top of Rakesh's head into a wall. Snarling, Rakesh put his feet against the wall and pushed off, down the hall, and onto the raised walkway above the cubicles. They hit the railing and, together, went over.

There was a tremendous thump as they came down onto a desk in the cubicle area; pencils and markers and sticky notes and paperclips went flying as the janitor landed on his back, Rakesh on top of him.

Rakesh bounced and tumbled to the floor. The world spun inside his head. Looking up, he saw the feet of the desk and, for a moment, wasn't really sure what had happened. Blinking, he came to. The janitor's arms and legs hung over the edges. The man's fingers twitched, but he wasn't trying to get up.

Rolling clumsily, Rakesh stood. It took three or four tries to get his legs beneath him. Even after that, the best they could do was carry him shakily as he headed for the exit.

Almost there. Almost...

He stopped and hobbled back to the janitor, then dug into the man's many pockets.

With a small smile, he pulled out his cellphone. Tapping a button, the screen—now cracked—lit up.

No signal; because why would it be any other way?

"Damn," he said softly as his flopping feet began carrying him in a lazy jog toward the exit.

CHAPTER FORTY-SIX

Colt had wool blackout curtains for eyelids. The quiet of the Prairie General Hospital hallway, punctuated by tiny taps of padded feet and regular clicks of computer keyboards, wasn't helping to keep her awake.

She was wrecked. The last time she'd felt this bad had been... hell, she couldn't really remember. Granted, she'd never been hit by a car before, but still, she wasn't just sore or tired. She didn't need a bandage for her boo-boos and a little rest to feel better. Her bruises were going to last for weeks. Her muscles were going to ache for days, and when they finally stopped, they wouldn't be stronger because of it. No matter how much she hated the idea of it, no matter how much the thought scared her, there was no way around it.

She'd made a mistake, a huge one. Her ego had gotten in the way.
Again.
And that hurt even more than the injuries.
Though, not by much.
"Middle initial?"
The curtain eyelids pulled back, and Colt raised her head. "Sorry?" she looked up and found herself staring into the leaves of a potted plant that took up most of the counter, which she was leaning against for support.

Behind the plant, a nurse who was only a decade or so younger than Colt raised an impatient eyebrow. "The patient's middle initial?"

What ever happened to bedside manner? Colt's entire torso was wrapped in bandages. She had bruised ribs. Creams on her arms dealt with the friction burns from the twins' psychic threads, and she had more bandages over those. She'd had to get stitches on her cheek where Vincent had psychically cut her, and she had a series of butterfly bandages across the shallow gash on her chest. Her entire shirt was stained with blood, and until a few minutes ago, she'd been hooked up to an I.V. bag to help with the dehydration. Not to mention she was on the strongest pain medication they could give her without making her sleepy or loopy. She couldn't take anything stronger because, unfortunately, she still had work to do.

"I don't know," Colt replied, rubbing her face.

On the other side of the plant, with its big fat palm leaves, the nurse gave an indignant huff. "Well, I'm gonna need that to get him into the system."

Those blackout curtains turned into shutters, the kind that snap shut with a bang and can take off a finger if one isn't careful. Shoving the plant down the counter, Colt glared at the nurse. There was no need for psychic abilities. The message was clear.

Do. Not. Fuck with me right now.

It was so late that, technically, it would soon be early. After Mary and the twins had sped off in their pickup truck, Colt had dragged Vincent to her car. He'd been awake but completely out of it, in shock most likely. She'd buckled him in, leaned his weeping head into the corner between the headrest and the doorframe, and watched him curl into a shivering ball. Then, she put the pedal to the metal and got the hell out of Fieldsville.

The little Hyundai had torn across highway asphalt. Along the way, in the silent hum of tires on road, Vincent's whimpers and sniffles had given way to sobs and heaves. Then, the occasional deep inhale. Then, pure silence. He hadn't slept. Colt had watched his reflection in the window, his empty eyes staring into the passing and shifting blackness around them. He hadn't said a word.

She was lost, sitting next to him. She'd dealt with victims before, but never someone so raw, so exposed. Vincent's emotions were mixed with that incredible psychic energy he had. They poured out of him and pressed against Colt. One moment his heart pounded with fury and rage, and the next, it fell so far into itself that it seemed to collapse and vanish like a dying sun.

She'd wanted to comfort him, to talk to him, to simply let him know that she was there for him, that he wasn't alone, like she had been all those years ago. But between the physical pain she felt and the emotional pain Vincent was throwing at her, it took everything she had to keep the car on the road.

At some point, a shimmer of air had passed around Vincent as he'd pulled up his psychic wall. He'd curled up under it like it was a blanket. Until then, Colt had been able to see the side of his face. After that, all she could see was his back.

She didn't cry but hadn't felt so close to doing so in years.

Without words, Colt's expression carried the experiences of that night to the annoying nurse sitting at her little computer. The woman pulled back slightly, her raised eyebrow dropping in shame.

"I... I'll just leave it blank for now."

Colt nodded, then slid the plant back between them.

From down the hall, toward Vincent's room, she heard the sound of dress shoes tap-tapping on linoleum. Wiping away the look of death she'd given the nurse, she turned and saw Carlos coming toward her. She was hoping that his barrel chest would be held high, puffed out and stomach pulled in, attempting to make himself look good for her. She wasn't feeling amorous, but it would have meant that things with Vincent had gone well.

Clearly though, they had not.

Carlos was carrying his clipboard. He had on a doctor's face, and Colt knew a bunch of questions that she couldn't answer were coming her way.

180

She pushed back from the counter to meet him. Pain, sharp and stabbing, attacked her left knee. Carlos rushed over.

"Are you—"

"Fine." Colt held up a hand to stop his hands from taking her shoulders. She grasped at the glowing embers that burned in the tiny spaces between her bones. "I'm fine."

Carlos pulled his arms back, but did not move away. A frown pulled the ends of his moustache down. "We should get that X-rayed."

Rubbing furiously, Colt shook her head. "It's stiff."

"I don't—"

"It's stiff," Colt snapped. She breathed heavily in the silence between them. "It was a long drive and... and a long day." Slowly, she put weight onto the joint. The embers were gone, and she was able to stand up straight. She saw the way Carlos looked at her. The doctor's face was gone; this concern was personal. Colt felt touched. A tiny smile hit her lips.

"I'm fine," she said softly.

Carlos nodded. He turned to hand a file to the nurse. Colt looked away, the moment of her smile passing into time.

"How is he?" she asked.

Taking a deep breath, Carlos crossed his arms. "What happened to him?"

Colt's face went slack.

"Is it the same thing that happened to you?"

It was an unprofessional question, and that made it so much harder to answer, so she didn't.

Carlos's jaw jutted forward. "Then maybe, because I'm not sure what's going on here, I shouldn't be discussing his condition with you."

"Doctor Moreno, don't make me get out my government I.D." She tried to say it playfully, but it still came out as a threat. She couldn't help it; that was her nature.

He glared at her. She couldn't blame him. He was right. He'd always been right. All those years ago, he'd been right. Her actions had cost him, them, so much. And yet, he'd always stuck with her. So here, standing in the hospital hallway, battered and bruised and aching, she'd done nothing but let him down again.

But it didn't matter. There was something more important right now. She put her hand on Carlos's crossed arms.

"Please,"

Sighing, Carlos's stubborn face softened.

God, she loved him so much.

"His injuries aren't severe. Some bruising, some abrasions and scrapes. He's exhausted and dehydrated, but nothing that won't resolve itself with time."

Colt nodded. A slight weight lifted from her shoulders.

"But that's not the problem."

Colt looked up.

"He's in shock. Whatever happened… he won't talk about it. In fact, he really isn't speaking. A couple of yeses and no's, but that's it."

Nodding in the direction of Vincent's room, Colt asked, "Is he awake?"

"Yes."

"Good. I need to speak with him."

"I would like for him to get some rest first."

"I'm sorry, but it can't wait." Turning, Colt made sure to put her weight onto her good knee first. She skirted around Carlos' large frame but stopped when she felt his hand on her arm.

"Rebecca," he said. "Vincent is… does his family know what's happened?"

Colt stared straight ahead, down the white, sterile hallway. "They are what happened."

She walked away, and Carlos's fingers slipped limply from her arm. He watched as she headed slowly down the hall, a subtle limp affecting her stride. He sighed and lumbered down a different hall.

Standing at a crossroads of hallways, a simple left turn would have taken Colt to Vincent's room. Strangely, she just couldn't seem to make it. Instead, she stood impotent, leaning against a mounted box that housed a large fire extinguisher. The metal felt cool through her shirt, and she tenderly rested her aching ribs against the side of it.

She had no idea what she would say, what she could say. How was she going she tell a child that she needed to leave him there, alone, in the hospital while she went out and hunted his sister down? How was she going to tell him this was going to end badly, that she was going to have to stop Mary and all her puppets once and for all?

How was she going to tell a young boy that he was about lose the people closest to him, that she was going to have to kill them all?

In comparison, the aches and pains in her body seemed so trivial.

With a grunt, she pushed herself up. Her left knee made a grinding sound as she walked, and walking wasn't taking the pain away as it had always done before. Maybe Carlos was right about that X-ray.

Vincent's room was dim. The monitors next to his bed beeped and booped, creating a tiny theme song that played to the beat of his heart. The back of the bed was raised, but Vincent's head was flopped to one side.

Between the song of the monitors, Colt heard his tiny sleeping breaths. He snored a bit too, and the sound brought out a smile on Colt's face.

At least, the side that didn't have stitches.

She'd always been told that children were angelic when they slept, but it wasn't something she'd ever really seen until now. He appeared so delicate, so fragile and helpless. It was funny to her, considering just a couple of hours ago, he'd been smacking her mind with spikes stronger than any kid his age had the right to fire. But now...

She stood by his bed and, peeking out the doorway, pulled up a wall. She wrapped it around her hand, pulling it as close as she could. Reaching out, she hesitated in the air a moment. It felt unnatural, strange, but the urge inside of her was just too strong. Stretching her fingers, she gently touched Vincent's sandy hair, brushing it away from his forehead. Her skin grazed his, and a rush of the dark dream that plagued his mind slipped into her. Colt frowned and pushed her wall out, washing it over Vincent.

"It's okay," she whispered with a voice that she'd never used before. "It's okay."

The darkness slipped from Vincent's mind, and there, as he drifted away into mental white noise, was a thought mumbled on Vincent's lips.

"Mom."

Colt was honored. She shushed gently and petted his head. When his thoughts settled, she stood up straight, stepped back, and sat in the soft chair next to the bed. She watched him until she, too, was deep asleep.

The cellphone in her pocket buzzed before it started ringing. It wasn't nearly enough time for Colt to wake up and answer it, but it was enough to get her moving. The electronic imitation of an old-fashioned ring bounced around the room. She scrambled to find which pocket the damn thing was in. Yanking it out, Colt pressed the answer button.

"He-Hello?" It took a considerable amount of effort to find the word in the foggy haze that filled her skull.

"Colt?" said a voice, a panting, strained voice.

Pulling herself from her chair, Colt started across the room. "Uh, I..."

"Colt, are you there?" the voice said. "Can you hear me?"

Behind her, Vincent stirred but did not wake. Colt took the phone away, shook her head, and tried to rub the sleep away from the muscles in her mouth and tongue.

"Come on, Colt! Can you... damn it, maybe I'm not high enough. Colt!" The voice pushed the speaker so hard the sound crackled.

Frowning, Colt came out of her haze and pulled the phone up. "Rakesh, this is not a good—"

"Yes!" Rakesh shouted with glee. "Ha ha! You can hear me? You've got me?"

"Rakesh," Colt snarled. "I don't know what this is about, but—"

"I can't believe it," Rakesh was sighing, gasping.

Colt could practically hear his smile.

"Oh thank God," he said.

The look of confusion on Colt's face was one she only used for special occasions. "What the hell? Are you drunk?"

On the other end, Rakesh gulped in air and panted. Then, between inhales, he said with a voice that carried no joy, "Mary."

The word snapped down on Colt's heart like a bear trap. "What?"

"Mary," Rakesh repeated. "She's here."

"What do you mean she's there? I just saw her a couple of hours ago."

"No, no, not her. Her... her mind."

Colt shook her head. "I don't—"

"Sandra's a puppet."

Colt froze. Fear wanted to grip at her, but her training had been better than that. "Tell me everything."

CHAPTER FORTY-SEVEN

The lighter sparked and gave life to the tip of the cigarette. Carlos pulled in deeply; the first puff was always the best. His eyes closed, and as the smoke poured from his nose and lips, the tightness in his chest floated away with it.

The sky was still dark, but the stars had begun to blink out, one by one from east to west. The sun wouldn't rise for another hour or so, but already a gentle warm breeze heralding daybreak danced across the hospital's back entrance.

To his left, down the ramp that led to the parking lot, someone inhaled.

A woman stood with her back to Carlos. She was so still that he hadn't noticed her when he came out. He'd been caught up in his own head, but he still should have seen her, especially since she was wearing nothing but a hospital gown.

Carlos coughed purposefully as he faced her, but still she did not move. A breeze rippled the blue gown across the backs of her long, thin legs and danced playfully with her flat, brown hair. Her stillness, her absolute lack of even the smallest muscle twitch, was unnerving.

"Excuse me," he said softly.

The woman didn't react.

"Are you alright?" As he walked closer, he started to feel as though he recognized her. But he knew his patients, and none of them looked like her. "I'm Doctor Moreno. Are you a patient here?" Obviously she was a patient, but was she from another floor? Another ward? "Are you okay? Do you need some help?"

He reached out to touch her, but stopped. The wind had blown her hair to the side, and a he caught a glimpse of her cheek, of her nose and the corner of her eye. Suddenly, he knew where he'd seen her before.

The coma ward.

With choppy movements because her muscles hadn't been used since she'd arrived there, Amber turned toward Carlos. A drop of blood trickled from the inside of her ear. In the darkness, it was black as molasses. But Carlos didn't even see the blood. He didn't notice how her fingers, long and thin, curled quickly around the lighter, which hung limp in his hand. When she brought it up and flicked the wheel, the orange light danced across her face, and Carlos saw even more clearly the blue eyes that he couldn't stop staring at.

Dull, flat, emotionless eyes.

Doll's eyes.

"Perfect," she said, and the world around them burst into yellows and oranges.

CHAPTER FORTY-EIGHT

Moving her jaw back and forth, Colt rubbed the tips of her top and bottom canine teeth together. On the other end of the phone, Rakesh was silent.

"Where are you now?" she asked.

"I just got into the garage. I'm going to my car and—"

"Go back."

"What?"

Colt's eyes tightened. "Get back inside."

"Are you out of your goddamn mind? I just got out of there."

"And now you're going back in."

"Why?"

"Because," Colt said flatly. "You have to stop her."

"Like hell I do!" Rakesh said, high and thin. "I'm calling in every available agent and having them come down on this place like a swarm of psychic locusts."

"Rakesh, think about it; Mary has already taken over Sandra, who's a high level psychic. She's spread her ability to people who don't even have psychic powers. If she can do that, she can take over anyone she encounters."

"Yeah, but—"

"What happens if her little drones get their hands on someone really strong? What if she gets a telekinetic? Or a pyrokinetic? What if she gets control over a teleporter and zaps Sandra straight into the Oval Office?"

Rakesh fell silent.

Colt took a deep breath. She knew she was asking a lot. She knew he'd already been through so much tonight, but considering he had zero training, she had to admit that he'd actually performed pretty well. However, he needed a plan, and she had one.

"Use your administrative codes to lock down the building. They've already cut communications, so you don't need to worry about that. Then, you're going to need to get a weapon."

"Where will I—"

"Use the guard's keycard. Go to the main security desk. Get anything they have."

"Okay, but what am I supposed to do with it?"

Colt pressed her lips together. "You'll need to do something that causes a diversion, pulls Sandra's drones away from the lab where she's working."

"Okay."

"Then, you need to isolate Sandra."

"Got it."

"Then you need to kill her."

Rakesh paused. He didn't even breathe. "No."

"Rakesh,"

"No. There has to be another way."

"Rakesh,"

"I can knock her out or, or hit her with a stun gun or, or—"

"Rakesh."

"Colt, I'm not going to..." He froze, either because he couldn't fathom the act, or because part of him already knew it had to be done; he'd just been hoping someone else would do it.

Colt spoke clearly and crisply, trying to make this a conference call instead of a death sentence. "Knocking her out won't be enough. Even if Sandra is unconscious, Mary can still use her like an amplifier. There needs to a complete signal separation."

Breathing heavily, Rakesh frowned and squeezed the phone with angry fingers. "I'll lockdown the building," he said. "I'll get the drones away. But I am not going to kill her. I'm going to find another way."

"Rakesh," Colt said it softly and sadly. "I'm sorry, but Mary is just too strong. Anyone that's been exposed to her, that's she's attached herself to, they..." She stopped, a thought noodling at the back of her brain.

Attached to. The threads she'd seen all over Fieldsville.

The one she'd seen at the hospital.

"Oh no," Colt whispered.

"Colt?" Rakesh's voice seemed to come from a thousand miles away.

Across the room, Vincent inhaled sharply and sat up.

Colt lowered the phone, and Rakesh's voice was lost in the sound of wild beeps from Vincent's heart monitor. Vincent glanced around, his eyes wide. Finding Colt, he froze.

"She's here."

Halls away, someone screamed. Colt tossed her phone on the chair and ran to the doorway. People were running by, nurses and patients and doctors, all of them heading away from the same place.

The nurses' station.

Colt's eyes went thin. "Stay here." She pointed at Vincent, who was throwing off the sheets. "Hide in the closet, and don't move until I come to get you."

"But—"

"Hide!" Colt barked as she ran into the hallway, slamming the door to Vincent's room behind her.

Fighting the rush of people, Colt suddenly knew what a salmon at spawning season must feel like. Every time she banged against someone, her

188

body sparked with pain and her mind sparked with their thoughts. She never got anything clear from them, just that they were afraid.

Colt threw up her wall. It didn't matter if people saw it. They were in a panic and wouldn't think twice about it. Pushing forward, she made it to the hallway intersection and turned the corner.

Thirty feet away, next to the nurses' station, Carlos was standing on shaky legs. The entire right half of his body from the waist up was shirtless. The exposed skin wasn't the wonderful tan that Colt knew, but was burned, blistered and blackened in places. Scorch marks ran up his neck and onto some of his face. The hair on the side of his head was almost completely gone, and his ear was shriveled like a piece of chicken left on the grill too long. His right arm was cooling lava, black and caked on top, but cracked with lines of hot red beneath. His right hand was curled into a fist, held at the wrist by his unburned left. He trembled and twitched and was clearly in a severe state of shock. He should have been lying on the floor in agony. Instead, he was standing as though a taut rope were tied to the top of his head.

And Colt knew why.

Fingers, long and thin, were squeezing his left shoulder. Behind him, a figure stood, feeding him the psychic command to stand up. Colt saw part of Amber's head, but was more focused on the ball of fire that Amber held in her other hand. It was an orange sun the size of a baseball, wavering and dancing and licking back and forth. . It floated, inches from her palm, the air shimmering around it from the heat.

Pyrokinetic.

Colt's gun swirled to life, and her finger pointed.

"Down!" Amber shouted from behind Carlos.

Colt stopped.

"Hands down, Agent Colt, or I cook him alive."

It wasn't a bluff. Pyrokinetics used their own psychic energy as fuel for the flames. As long as they had oxygen and a spark, they could generate nearly infinite amounts of flames.

Slowly, Colt lowered her hand. When it reached her side, Amber stepped out from behind her hostage.

Bloodshot eyes and blood seeping from her ears.

Colt spoke loud and clear. "You're pushing her too hard, Mary. Her mind wasn't ready to use that power."

"It doesn't matter," Mary's puppet replied. "I only need her long enough to eliminate you and Vincent."

Colt nodded. "I heard about what happened at the DSI. Seems like my friend Rakesh got away."

"He'll be dead soon."

"I don't know." Colt shook her head. "I wonder if you're spreading yourself too thin. Maybe you can't control as many people as you thought."

Amber sneered. "Soon I'll be strong enough to make anyone a puppet. Even Rakesh. Even you."

Colt spread her feet. "That's not going to happen."

"No?"

"No." The fingers of her left hand flicked, telekinetically hurling the huge potted plant that sat on the nurses' counter. It smashed against Amber and sent her sprawling sideways into the wall, black soil and thick chunks of red clay pottery falling everywhere.

Jamming her arm out, Amber sent a burst of flame. But before it even traveled two feet, Colt fired off a powerful spike that tore across the ground. The spike shattered Amber's wall and hit hard enough to roll her eyes up into her head. Colt shot an open palm out, knocking Amber back through the hallway. The fireball vanished in a puff of smoke. Amber's limp body and Carlos's knees hit the floor at the same time.

Colt ran to him. "It's okay," she said as she caught him before he fell. His burns were even worse up close, and his left hand was still locked around his wrist. "It's all right. You're going to be okay."

Carlos shook and gasped. "I can't," he stuttered, his teeth chattering. "I have—"

"Don't worry," Colt said. She searched for anything she could use as a cold compress. "Without the fire, she can't hurt us."

"She's got me. I can't..." Carlos said through his quivering jaw. "I'm... I'm sorry."

Colt stopped what she was doing. "What?"

Carlos looked up, his eyes tearing, but not from the pain. "I'm so sorry."

The fingers on his right hand, charred and blackened, opened with the crinkle of carbonized flesh. Colt tilted to the side and saw there, sitting delicately in his palm, a half crushed cigarette.

Still burning.

Her eyes went wide. Behind them, down the hall, Amber rose as though drawn by strings. Her hand shot out, fingers spread.

It was instantaneous. The tiny cinders at the end of the cigarette bloomed into a furious explosion of yellow and white flames. The air thumped as all the available oxygen was sucked in. The flame engulfed Carlos, scorching him to the bone. On instinct, Colt pushed back. The flames caught her limbs, and she felt the sting of burned skin, but the pain wasn't nearly as bad as the sound.

The sound of Carlos screaming.

Rolling away, Colt stopped on her stomach. She pushed up with fatigued arms and tried to sprint toward Carlos. Sweat broke out across her body, but she didn't care. The heat from the flames would have made anyone else pull back, but she didn't care. Carlos was screaming and throwing himself around, and she had to save him. But the flames that were eating him alive spun up into a wild, twisting column that snaked through the air and reached out to smother her.

Colt grabbed her wrist and pointed her finger. The gun spun into the air, but it was hazy. She was exhausted. She fired a kinetic bullet, wide and flat, into the heart of the flaming column. It pushed through, pulling the air behind and causing the column to cave in on itself. Then, reaching out with both hands, she gripped at the air and pulled hard, ripping down the suspended ceiling above Amber, sending metal frames and white tiling crashing around her. The flames from the column spread across the desk and the ceiling. Emergency alarms sounded, and the fire sprinklers went off in the hallway. Water rained down, snuffing out the fiery column. Colt ran to the charred mass on the floor that had been Carlos.

A layer of steam was rising from his body. He no longer screamed or moved. He no longer felt pain, or joy, or love.

Colt dropped to her knees.

He was gone.

The pooling water quivered, shook and rolled as if, beneath the floor, a giant speaker was blasting out long, low-frequency notes. .

Colt's fists clenched, and her body trembled. Tears streamed down her face. She breathed in tiny gasps. The vibration spread from the floors around her into the walls. Everything rattled. The paintings on the walls clattered, a few of them crashing down. Colt made tiny little grunts, high-pitched prayers and pleadings to anyone, any god that could bring Carlos back to her. The walls nearby cracked. The floor beneath her snapped, then bowed, then dropped an inch against her uncontrolled telekinetic force. The light fixtures in the ceiling exploded in a chain reaction. The reverberations of her pain traveled throughout the entire building and, as she began to completely lose control, the pipes in the ceiling above her wrenched and twisted. The water falling from the sprinklers was suspended in the air.

She couldn't feel anything but pain, deeper and hotter and worse than anything she'd ever felt. Even when little Elena Bentley had died. Even when her father had died. Even when her mother had died. Nothing, nothing was worse than this, and she didn't know if she could do it, if she could hold back as she had her entire life. She needed to scream. She needed to finally let go and bring the whole goddamn building down on top of her and the bitch who'd done this and snuff out this pain because it was too, too much.

191

And then, just as she was letting it all go, letting everything she had inside of her spread, her tendrils extended in every direction, searching for nothing particular but finding something important.

Vincent. He was down the hall, watching her, watching to see what she would do with the rage and pain that was swirling and storming within her.

Her fists relaxed. The rattling of the walls and floors ebbed. The unbridled telekinetic power coming from Colt was reined in and, as she placed herself atop it, her trembling body calmed.

Down the hall, Amber was unburying herself from the ceiling tiles. Taking a deep breath, Colt stared down at Carlos.

"Goodbye," she whispered.

She flew up like a mousetrap snapping. A spike balled in her palm, she bent low and charged in with a growl. She pulled her arm back as she drew closer, and closer, and closer until she was just feet away from Amber.

Fire shot through her left leg. For an instant, Colt thought maybe Amber had hit her with her pyrokinetic abilities. Then, she realized the pain wasn't coming from the outside. Her growl turned to a gasp, and her knee crunched loudly. The muscles around it flexed, but it was as though they had nothing to grasp, nothing to pull on. Before she could do anything, her entire leg went out from beneath her.

A thousand hot needles stabbed from every angle around the joint. She couldn't open her eyes. She couldn't unclench her fists. But she heard the hissing of the air around her. She felt the oxygen being drawn away and gathered for another fiery burst.

She couldn't get away. As the air around her rippled with pure heat, she held her breath, curled up, and wrapped herself in the same telekinetic blanket that had protected her from the windshield of the pickup truck.

The reformed flame column hit her hard. She tumbled all the way down the hall. Any part of her skin that was exposed seared with an instant sunburn. The water from the sprinklers kept her clothes from igniting, and she slid down the hallway with a wet screech.

When the tumbling ended, when the column moved outside of Amber's range of control and dissipated into the air, Colt opened her eyes. She was at the hallway intersection. Trying to push up, her palms slipped and she fell to the floor again. The world around her drifted into spots of blackness. Her eyes rolled in their sockets. Her hair, some of it soaked from the water and some of it dried from the heat of the flames, stuck to her face. The stitches on her cheek had burst, and blood was running out from under the bandage, mixing with the water that poured down from the ceiling. Her left leg had gone almost numb, and her right leg was shaking so much that she couldn't even put weight on it. She gasped at the steamy air. Her stomach

192

churned, and nausea overwhelmed her. The skin beneath her clothes, soaked through by the sprinklers, prickled into goosebumps.

She was done. Her focus was lost in the miasma of pain and adrenaline. She used what little telekinesis she could gather to slowly drag herself up onto her elbows.

When she got there, her head raised enough to see the edge of a red, metal box that hung on the wall in the intersection. Putting all of her weight on one trembling elbow, she reached out with her other arm and used her mind to open the door of the fire extinguisher case.

"Really?" Amber asked. "A fire extinguisher?"

Colt rolled her head. Through thick-clumped strands of wet hair, she saw Mary's puppet walking, bare feet silently padding through the water, flames slithering around her like endless red pythons that drifted on the air. Amber was close enough that she could have turned Colt to ashes, so why hadn't she?

Amber stopped. "Where's Vincent?"

Colt smirked. "It must be hard. You could never control him, but at least you could always keep tabs on him."

"Where is he?"

"Does it drive you crazy?" she coughed. Her entire torso tightened. But the sound covered the fact that her telekinetic fingers were twisting the fire extinguisher, rotating it against the metal brackets that held it. "Knowing you're not all powerful?"

The puppet's fire spun faster, glowed brighter. "Tell me where he is, or I will burn down this entire building."

Agonizingly, Colt pulled herself up and flopped into a sitting position. Her chest shivered. Her fingers twitched, and the fire extinguisher leaned from the wall. "It's not even that he you're not all powerful." She looked up, through the puppet's flat blue eyes and into the dark brown ones, which hid there. "Your spike? I've met ten year olds that can do better." She laughed. "He's stronger than you. And you're scared."

Amber inhaled through her nose slowly. She took a step, a single step, toward Colt. Her hand raised and, around it, the fire swirled hot and hungry. "When I'm done," she said simply, "no one will ever threaten my family again."

The flames gathered, compressed and condensed into a single ball of white-hot fire. Colt's eyes went wide.

From the hall off to the side, the water that had begun to pool erupted up in a thin line that leaped four feet in the air. The spike cut through the air and hit Mary's puppet dead on. It was a haymaker, a ten-pound medicine ball thrown by a major league pitcher. The psychic force slammed Amber's brain, overloading it and breaking all concentration. She

193

rocked back, hard, and fell against the wall. The miniature sun in her hand evaporated, leaving only a lingering whisper of flame at her fingertips.

"Stop it!" Vincent shouted from the hall.

Amber's body jerked. Mary's commands spread down to the woman's individual muscles, forcing them to flex. She rose with a series of spasms, a stop motion animation made by a madman.

Vincent's fists jerked as he fired off another spike. Amber had just enough time to get up a wall. The spike connected with a loud crack. Vincent started walking, firing a spike with every step. Amber raised her hands, straining to keep her wall together. Only a dozen feet away now, Vincent closed his eyes, dug down deep and, with a shout, let fly.

Like a pane of glass, the wall shattered. Amber dropped back.

"No," Mary whispered through Amber's mouth. The puppet's eyes closed tightly. Her jaw clenched so hard her entire head shook. The blood poured from her ears. From her squeezed eyelids, a thick crimson liquid trickled down.

Colt froze.

Blood mixed with cerebrospinal fluid.

Mary was killing her.

Amber's eyes opened. The capillaries in the whites of her eyes had burst and turned a sickly crimson.

Colt's lungs filled. "Vincent!"

The puppet leaped away from the wall, spreading her arms. All around her, the flames burst to life, larger and wilder than they had been. Colt rolled back, pressing herself against the floor. Vincent dropped, his anger replaced by fear.

In the center of the swirling fire, the puppet's face was cold.

Colt reached a shaking hand toward the fire extinguisher. It lurched forward and flew from the box. "Vincent!" Colt shouted above the roaring and hissing flames.

He turned.

"Cut it!" she shouted.

He shook his head and scuttled backward.

Colt used every bit of strength she had left, telekinetic and physical, to throw the tank over Amber's head. It arced slowly, flipping end over end. Vincent watched it, hesitation holding his heart.

But his fist closed. His breath held. And, with a grunt, he swung.

There was a sharp metallic ping followed by a concussive bang. The world around them was enveloped in white smoke. One half of the extinguisher slammed into the floor, the other punched clean through the wall, just next to Colt. The yellow light of the flames persisted a second but were swallowed up and vanished within a cloud of fire-retardant gas. Vincent dropped and covered his mouth. From inside the gas, Amber gasped and coughed.

Colt opened her eyes and scanned the thick white cloud. She squinted, and found Amber's shadowed form. Jamming her arm out, Colt took aim.

"I'm sorry," she whispered, so softly only she heard it.

With a flash, her gun appeared, and she fired. In the white cloud, a spray of red erupted from Amber's head, misting into the air as her body collapsed.

The cloud drifted to the floor. There were pops and crackles as the gas from the extinguisher caused ice crystals to form. Both Colt and Vincent sat still while it settled, catching their breath and slowing their racing hearts.

Groaning, Colt dragged her good leg beneath her. Sliding her back against the wall, she pushed up to a standing position. Vincent watched as she used her arms to put her left leg slightly off to the side, as her face winced in pain and her hands shook. He saw how she closed her eyes and bit the inside of her lips, how she took deep breaths and gained control of herself. How, even through the most awful of pains, she managed to keep going.

How she fought.

How she never gave up.

She dragged against the wall, hopping on her good leg, using anything she could grab for balance. As she hobbled past Amber's body, she paused to glance down. Then, her eyes rose. Vincent followed her gaze to the body burned into a blackened pile. .

Looking away, Colt shuffled along the wall.

"Where are you going?" Vincent said.

She didn't stop.

Vincent stood up. "Where are you going?"

Another one-legged step.

Vincent paused. "I'm coming with you."

"No, you're not."

"She's my sister."

"Vincent, I'm going there to—"

"I know."

Colt stopped. "No you don't." She faced him. He was so thin and his face seemed much more shallow than just a few hours ago. "Not just her."

"They're not—"

"They're puppets," Colt said. She had no time, nor strength, left for empathy.

Vincent took a deep breath. "I'm coming."

"No!" Colt barked. "She's insane."

195

"Yeah, I know. But that doesn't..." He swallowed. "You said it. She's weaker than me, but I let her tell me what to do. I hurt all those people because I thought I was protecting others." His face, his eyes, steeled as much as they could. "And now, because of me, the last person that means anything to me is all alone."

CHAPTER FORTY-NINE

The parking lot was barren except for a few scattered sedans and pickup trucks. The air was still chill from the night, but in just a couple of hours, that would change. Soon, the day shift would arrive, opening the mall's doors and getting their shops prepared for another day of intermittent weekday customers. But for now, the front door remained locked while the side doors—painted to blend in with the walls—opened to release the night shift.

Tasked with restocking shelves and unloading new merchandise, they left without vigor. There were a few words exchanged, a "good-bye" or a "see you later," that were only half met with responses. After that, it was dragging feet, yawning maws, and the sound of digging for car keys.

From inside the dented pickup truck with its cracked windshield, Mary watched her mother walk toward a beaten red sedan. She felt the minds of the people in the lot. She was not controlling them, but there was a tether, a psychic thread that led to each of them. Whenever she wanted, she could pull that thread and they would be hers. Everyone was hers.

Except Mom.

In the middle of the white sea of Mary's eyes, surrounded by streaks of bloodshot veins, her irises spun. Out in the parking lot, everyone stopped and turned toward the red sedan.

CHAPTER FIFTY

Rakesh had heard screaming, Colt yelling at somebody, then nothing but sounds of chaos. He'd killed the line, knowing that whatever was going on, it was related to Mary. Either she'd shown up at the hospital, or she'd sent puppets there.

How many people could this kid control?

Quietly closing the door to his office, Rakesh checked the massive windows behind his desk. The sun had started to rise. The city was waking bit by bit. Lights flickered on in rectangular windows, and shadows moved about on the streets. Headlights were no longer lonely ghosts drifting through the night. Rakesh didn't have much time. The early birds, the government folk who showed up before six so they could leave before three, would be arriving soon.

He listened at the door and, hearing nothing, rushed to his desk. Yanking out his gym bag, he unzipped it and pulled out the things he needed. First came the sneakers, then his water bottle and a protein bar. It wasn't until he saw the food that he realized how hungry he was. He was shaking so badly that he couldn't tear the wrapper, so he used his teeth. One hand jammed the chalky bar into his mouth while the other worked at getting his sneakers on.

It was painful. His feet had taken as much of a beating as the rest of him. Running barefoot had flattened his arches enough that the sneakers felt uncomfortable. But he could go faster now, if he had to. Hopefully, though, there wouldn't be too much more running.

The protein bar was hitting his stomach like a brick, and he knew the little burst it gave him wouldn't last long. It was strange. He'd run marathons with only water and sports drinks. Yet here he was, muscles spent, adrenaline depleted, energy drained.

Shaking his head and smiling, he understood how years of living like this, how a lifetime of running and fighting and fear could harden someone. He was starting to get how Colt could do the things she did.

The smile faded.

The things that she had to do.

The things that he had to do.

The weight of it was so oppressive, he wasn't sure he could stand. But he did, even if it was bit by bit.

He would find another way. Something would happen, something would change, he would see something that he hadn't seen before and, in the end, he would find another way.

He had to.

Closing his eyes, he took a long deep pull on his water bottle. With a kick, the gym bag went back under his desk, and he slipped out of the office.

With the phones and computers shut down, he had to find another way to lock down the building. But Mary's puppets were still working, which meant that at least some of them had computer access. The guard's keycard would allow him to use just about any system that was still on, and he had a good idea where to find one.

The vinyl painted stairs squeaked beneath his sneakers. Going down was easier than climbing, and when he reached the door to the main lobby, his legs felt good and warmed up. It was amazing what a little rehydration could do.

Stepping into the hallway, Rakesh looked at the numeric floor displays of the four elevators. Each one was moving. He had to assume the people inside were Mary's puppets, probably searching for him floor by floor. For all he knew, there were dozens of puppets in the building, and for every minute that passed, there could be more.

The lobby's exterior wall was made of thick glass nearly two stories tall. In the middle of the room was a modern lighting fixture of some kind, not fancy enough to be called a chandelier, but not just a series of florescent bulbs either. Rakesh had always thought it looked somewhat like a bird's nest, the long stems of the lights twisting around one another and in a bizarre oval shape while the bulbs stuck out, creating an orb of light. After he'd been with the DSI for several years, he'd realized it was a loose imitation of the human brain.

The security desk was an oval shaped counter with one entrance at the back. Behind it, one on each side, were the large archways which led into the building.

Gliding his back against the wall and moving toward the edge of the archway, Rakesh stopped when movement caught his eye. A guard was working inside the security desk. The man was tall and lanky, his skin the color of chocolate milk. As he moved from one side of the desk to the other, Rakesh noticed the glowing screens of the computers. They were up and running, showing information on the elevators and the security system.

But if he could see everything that was happening, that meant...

The guard turned to check another monitor. Rakesh leaned out, just far enough to see the man's flat, dead eyes.

Another puppet to add to the collection.

Seriously, how many people could that kid control?

Sliding back toward the stairs, Rakesh stopped and peered at the elevators. The hallway had the lobby at one end, and a T juncture with another hall at the other. Moving to the elevator farthest from the lobby, Rakesh looked up.

It was close, just two floors away. The others were all higher up. Rakesh glanced down toward the lobby, took a deep breath, and hit the up button. A mechanical rumbling echoed down the shaft and through the door in front of him. Snapping his head, he looked toward the lobby. No guard. Good.

There was a tiny puff of air from the crack between the doors. With a whoosh and loud bell chime, they opened wide. Reaching in, Rakesh hit the button for the top floor then dashed toward the end of the hallway, praying he made it around the corner before the guard saw him.

Scampering around the wall's edge, he stuttered to a stop; tiny hopping steps kept his sneakers from squeaking. There he waited, breath held. He heard the tap-tap of the guard's shoes on the tiled floor. The hallway was filled with electronic static and a loud beep.

"Someone has accessed elevator three from the lobby." The guard's voice was a clear East Coast accent, probably New Jersey. The other three Rakesh had heard earlier—big bald, redhead and the other guard—they'd spoken with a Midwest accent and a healthy dollop of Mary's smugness. So why did this guard sound different? And why was he talking into a walkie-talkie?

Sandra's voice came through the speaker. "It is most likely Rakesh. Where is he going?"

Another voice, the guard who had zapped him at the security door, came though. "Elevator three is headed to the roof." His voice had lost the Midwest accent.

She'd finally hit her limit, spread herself too thin. They were just following orders now, another ant digging a tunnel. Which meant Mary wasn't seeing through their eyes, wasn't aware of their every action. The connection had grown so weak that they were probably endlessly loyal, but she couldn't communicate to all of them psychically. Rakesh half-smiled.

"He is attempting to alert the authorities," Sandra said, still speaking with Mary's accent. Of course she wouldn't let go of Sandra, she was the linchpin to Mary's plan. "Go to the roof, others will meet you there. Corner him and bring him to me."

"Understood."

There was a click of a doorknob and the squeak of hinges. Rakesh waited until he heard the thump of the stairwell door closing before he headed to the security desk.

The computers were still up, and with a quick swipe of the stolen keycard, Rakesh brought up the entire building's security grid. He cursed quietly. He'd hoped he could cut the power to the lower levels, mainly the labs, but everything down there was hooked up to some kind of independent generator. He also couldn't disconnect or even find the computer programs

Sandra and the scientists were messing with, so that was out, too. He thought about triggering a fire alarm, turning on the sprinklers and maybe shorting out whatever they were building in the lab, but that would send a message out to the fire department, to the police, and to the top brass of the DSI. People would come running, and Mary could pick and choose who she wanted to brain drain.

Damn.

A few quick keystrokes brought up the lockdown screen, but his fingers hesitated. No one could get in, but no one could get out. He was locking himself into the building, into the fight, into the fact that he had to stop them.

No matter what.

He couldn't look as he typed his password.

Speakers throughout the building erupted with fuzzy warning sirens. Gears and cogs spun into action, levers released, deadbolts fired. Every exterior door the building pulled shut and clicked loudly, sealing itself. The grand windows that covered the front of the lobby darkened as steel shutters fell like the eyelids of a tired child. Six thumps rumbled from the hallway behind the security desk as the elevators automatically stopped, impotent and inert in their shafts.

And then there was silence, but only for a moment.

Grunting, Rakesh spun from the desk and tore through drawers, cabinets, searching for anything and everything that could help him. With the elevators shut down and the puppets having rushed the roof, he figured he had a minute, maybe a bit more, to get the hell out of there and figure out the next step. The code he'd entered was his handler code. He had access to tons of classified materials, so his security level was higher than anyone else in the building right now. Without him and his password, they couldn't do anything about the lockdown.

That meant they were going to be searching for him extra hard.

He snatched up the stolen keycard, and his eyes caught sight of a walkie-talkie sitting in its charger. He grabbed it and noticed the large, black door beneath the chargers, about the height of a mini-fridge, that wouldn't open but had a keycard slot on the front. Quickly, Rakesh unlocked it.

The worry on his face dissolved under a small grin. "Oh, damn."

CHAPTER FIFTY-ONE

The stalks were high and summer green, rocking back and forth in the wake of the speeding car. To Vincent, his forehead pressed against the window, the tires rolling on the flat asphalt sung a song of white noise. He felt every yard, every foot, every inch that the tires crept forward, though they never seemed to go fast enough.

The walls of corn rippled like a sheet snapped across a bed. His bed. His blankets, unkempt and unmade. His house, broken and split, always teetering, always hanging by a thread. Threads. His brother and sister. His mom.

Mary.

Closing eyelids shut out the morning sky. He waited for the rush, the pulse of anger that would start in his belly and work its way into his chest, push pressure into his shoulders, then spread into his arms like tentacles that could not be wrested down. But it didn't come. Instead, his breath drifted out, impotent and unused. He felt like a spent bullet's shell.

"You okay?" Colt's voice filled the Hyundai's cabin too quickly.

"Yeah," Vincent replied. "How much longer?"

"Thirty, thirty-five minutes till we hit Main Street."

Vincent stared through the windshield but watched Colt in his peripheral. Her hands were steady on the wheel. She wasn't white knuckled, wasn't tense, just focused. A white gauze pad the size of a playing card was taped to her cheek and her right hand was wrapped, the bandages up her fingers to the first knuckle. It looked like a boxer's wrap, but Vincent knew it was there to help treat the burns she'd gotten.

Her other cheek had a bandage too, long and thin, from where Vincent had cut her back at the loading dock. Beneath her coat, beneath the new white shirt and blue jeans she'd gotten out of the trunk, there were more bandages. And wraps. And stitches. She was bruised and burned and must have been hurting, but she didn't show it. Her face was clean, her expression set, her hair pulled back tightly into a ponytail. Even with the bandages, she looked frighteningly professional; Vincent saw the sharpness in her eyes.

Glancing down, he became acutely aware of how shabby he was. They'd washed his face and arms at the hospital, but he still looked like he had just crawled out of a garbage can. Brushing his pants a couple of times, he tried to get rid of the dust, but it just rubbed in deeper. His teeth pressed together, the muscles in his jaw flexing and holding. Bending over, he tried rolling the ends of his jeans up. One of the cuffs had ripped, so no matter how firmly he folded it, it flopped back down and hung loosely around his ankle. His breath came hard through his nostrils. He closed his eyes and squeezed his hands into fists.

202

Nothing. No rush in his ears, no hot pressure working through his chest. It was weird and scary. Just yesterday, and the days and weeks and months before, he would have completely lost his temper over the smallest thing. But now, the cuff that wouldn't fold didn't seem to matter. Maybe he was starting to learn, had been forced to learn, what was really worth getting angry about.

He thought about Mary, and he knew the empty casing he was still had some powder in it.

Colt glanced at him. His eyes were puffy, and his hair was a mess, but his color was better. She'd convinced him to eat; blackmailed him, really, by telling him he couldn't come unless he ate and drank. After all the confusion, Colt had managed to take a couple of nurses by the arm and push on them. They'd treated her and Vincent, cleaned them up, bandaged her wounds, and brought them all the food and sports drinks they could find. They'd also given Colt an injection of a strong painkiller to take the edge off. She knew it would make her loopy, so she'd also had the nurses bring the strongest, blackest coffee they could brew.

Her knee felt like it was packed in wet sand. A cortisone shot was controlling the swelling, and the leg was in a brace. The thing was more complex than it had any right to be, with metal crossbars that added support on the sides. But hey, it wasn't a cast, and she could walk around.

Well, limp around.

With a long sigh, Colt stared at the road. They were at a complete disadvantage. Mary may have gotten knocked around back in the alley, but she'd had time to recover. Colt was running on fumes and coffee. And Vincent, even with a hell of a spike, had zero training.

Granted, that wasn't always the most important thing. You learned a lot more about someone seeing how they acted in the field, and Vincent had pulled through when she needed him. If they could put together a solid plan, there was a good chance they could take down Mary.

"Vincent," she said. "Is there anyone else who can resist Mary?"

"Just me and our mom."

Colt nodded. That simplified things. This wasn't a go-in-guns-blazing kind of deal. There were higher stakes here. Vincent had bigger priorities, and she was going to help him, even though the agent side of her brain— logistical, methodical, well-trained—told her it was the worst idea possible. Vincent wasn't the big picture. Him saving his mom didn't help the overall scenario. She should have been focused on the threat. Even if Vincent's mom died, even if Vincent died, those would just be two more minor deaths, sacrifices for the greater good.

But she didn't give a shit. It was stupid, impulsive, emotional and completely illogical. It was personal. No one had been there for her, to save her, protect her, keep her family from being torn to shreds. But here she had a chance. Vincent had a chance.

It wasn't professional, but it was right.

It also told Colt exactly where Mary was going to be.

Right by her mom.

"We'll head straight to your house. You get your mom and get out."

"What'll you do?"

"I'll take care of the rest."

Vincent's teeth clicked together as his jaw snapped shut. He crossed his arms and pushed himself back against the seat.

Colt softened her voice. "I think it's better if—"

"Yeah right," he snapped.

"Vincent."

"You don't get it," he growled, "she's my sister."

"I know."

"No," Vincent turned and leaned across the car, "she's my sister! She's supposed to care about me! We're... we're supposed to..." His hands waved in the air, grasping at the racing thoughts within his mind. His emotions pulsed and grew. "We're a family, and we should all love each other, but she—"

"Vincent."

"You don't know!" he roared. "You don't know anything!" He cried, a shout and growl and yelp all at once. Her betrayal overtook him. His fists beat at the car around him, pounding the door and the seat. If his psychic batteries were charged enough, he would have torn the interior to shreds. His thoughts, the ones he had no words for, beat against Colt's mind. She felt the conflict inside him, how he despised and loved Mary all at once. How his entire self was being split down the middle. She saw images, flights of his mind where he punched Mary, smashed her face into the ground, beat her into a pulp and got her out of his life forever. But then he also wanted to hug her, to see her laugh and smile, to sit at a dinner table and play games with her and be happy for the first time since he could remember. All he wanted was for them to be a normal family, but Mary had stolen that. She'd taken their lives and twisted them, bent everything to her own will and stripped away any chance of them just being happy.

And then, just as quickly, another thought came into Vincent's mind. One he'd had before, one he'd said at the hospital, but had also been avoiding facing it full on for as long as it had lingered within him.

He'd let her.

Every step of the way, he'd followed along. He'd moaned and groaned about it, but had he ever said no? Had he ever told her to stop? Had he ever done a damn thing to hold his family together? She'd called all the shots. She'd made all the decisions. All he made was excuses. He could have done something, could have fought back for once. Just once, that's all it would have taken. One argument, one outburst, one moment of him standing up to her, and this whole thing, this whole mad, mad world that they'd created, wouldn't have been there.

But he hadn't. Because he was afraid. Because he was hesitant.

Because even though he had more power than he knew what to do with, he was still a coward.

Silence filled the car as his fit ended. Vincent dropped his forehead against the window's cool glass. The tide of emotions pulled back, and his thoughts receded from Colt's mind. She tried to think of something to say, but it was so close, so familiar. Beneath her shirt, under the bandages and balms and bruises, the scar on her belly itched and burned.

What else was there to say?

"When I was a kid—"

Vincent gasped. His body went tense, and all of the swirling inside him shifted. Colt felt his fear and quickly looked at everything she could. A pop, a camera's flashbulb of sunlight pinged off something in the corn. Colt slammed on the gas just as a car ripped through the stalks, missing their back bumper by an inch. If Vincent hadn't reacted to its presence, the Hyundai would have been t-boned.

The sheriff's car, Colt recognized it right away, swung out onto the road, fishtailing for a moment with light blue smoke pouring off its spinning wheels.

"Ahh!" Vincent shouted and pointed at a squad car erupting from the shivering wall of corn just ahead of them. It was not trying to force a collision, but an interception. Colt jammed the wheel to the right. There was a bang as the squad car jumped up from the grassy strip onto the hard asphalt. Its front wheels slammed down, the entire car rocking on its shocks. Its engine roared as it pushed forward, trying to come up next to the Hyundai. Colt swerved just enough to get two wheels into the grass but keep them straight.

"Ohh!" Vincent shouted, pointing as the green veil opened and a third car ripped through, traveling almost parallel to the road and sliding up toward the passenger side. Colt tried to jump out of the grass, but there wasn't enough time. The squad car slapped against the Hyundai's side with a bang of splitting fiberglass and the squeal of metal on metal.

"Mary!" Vincent screamed as he pulled away from the impacted door. "It's Mary!"

"No shit!" Colt snapped.

The squad car bounced off their side and came in for another swipe. Colt let it hit them, relaxing her arms just enough that the squad car pushed them up over the lip of the grassy drop-off and up onto the road with a shower of gravel and dust. The squad car's tires hit the edge, and as they pulled away to build up a bigger swing onto the black asphalt, Colt extended her arm. In the squad car to the right, telekinetic hands grabbed the wheel and spun it so hard that the driver, Mary's puppet, was hit in the face by his own shoulder. The car tore a hole in the corn and vanished.

Another crunch of crumple zones doing their job sounded as the squad car on the left drifted back, then hammered the trunk of the Hyundai. Colt's head snapped back into the headrest, a dull throbbing splashing across the inside of her neck and the base of her skull. It was like the pain of a five hour-long headache all hitting at once. Forcing her eyes to stay open, she gripped the wheel and swerved into the other lane. Tires squealed behind them, and the squad car followed, revving up for another hit.

The Hyundai didn't have the horsepower to outrun the squad car, and she was pretty sure that the sheriff's car—keeping pace behind the squad car—was even faster. Any second now, the sheriff would see an opening, gun it, and come rolling up to flank them. Even without Mary in complete control of the officers, having only her consciousness manipulating them into perfect synchronicity, these were country boys she was going up against. They'd grown up racing tractors, riding dirt bikes, and driving on every kind of road there was. Colt wasn't going to outrun them or outmaneuver them.

That really only left once choice.

As the squad car roared behind them, Colt swerved back across the road, pushed the accelerator as hard as she could, and punched the button for the sunroof. She shouted Vincent's name over the sound of wind pouring into the car. "Grab the wheel!"

His hands gripping the dashboard, and with his hair flapping wildly in the twirling breeze inside the car, Vincent gaped at her with confusion spread across his face.

"Take the wheel, keep it straight, put the gas down as far as it'll go. Got it?"

Vincent shook his head. "I don't think I can—"

"On the count of three!" She shifted in her seat.

From behind, the squad car crunched against the Hyundai's trunk.

"Three!"

"What!?"

Colt let go of the wheel. Reaching up, she grabbed the lip of the sunroof and pulled herself up. Vincent dove across the car and snatched the wheel. They were going so fast that his tiny touch changed their angle instantly.

Thinking Vincent had swerved to avoid the squad car, which was once again bearing down on their already crushed rear bumper, Colt shouted,

"Good job!" through the sunroof. Below her, Vincent shimmied up and sat between her legs, holding the wheel as tightly as he could.

"Oh my god." He said it fast, like it was one word. "Ohmygod, ohmygod, ohmygod."

Wind pressure is an amazing thing, and when you're going down a straight road at over ninety miles per hour, it feels like someone is hitting you with a fire hose. The lip of the sunroof pressed against Colt's waist, digging into her pelvic bones. Her loose hair flapped wildly against her face. The bandages that had been taped so diligently to her cheeks threatened to tear away. Still, she kept her eyes open. The squad car was on their butt, and the officer in the passenger seat had his gun out the window. He wasn't aiming at her, but at the back wheels of the Hyundai. Colt reached out and clenched her fist. Telekinetic fingers grabbed the officer's wrist, cranking it until it was facing backward. The gun went off and the bullet grazed the roof of the sheriff's car with a quick spark.

Leaning into the sunroof hurt like hell, but it freed Colt's other hand. She extended it and grasped at the squad car's wheel, but she couldn't turn it. The driver gripped it tight, bringing his knee up into it and holding it firm. Colt snarled. Mary was so deeply connected to her puppets that there was an instant transfer of information, and she'd already seen this trick before. Colt concentrated, tried to draw up more telekinetic energy. Normally, she'd be able to wrench the wheel away, even just enough to drive them into a ditch would be fine. But she was splitting her attention between the wheel and the officer's arm, not to mention the fact that she was still exhausted from the fight at the hospital.

The whipping wind was cool in her armpits. Sweat trickled down from the back of her neck. She didn't know how much longer she could keep this up. The driver was stone faced, his eyes flat and unblinking; he could hold that wheel all day if he needed to. The officer in the passenger seat got his free arm out the window and was using it to pull his gun hand back down. Colt ground her teeth, but the guy was stronger than he looked, and soon the pistol's barrel was coming into view. She continued to struggle with him, but only until he'd gotten her lined up, an inch away from his sights.

Both her hands released. The shooter's arm dropped quickly, another bullet missing completely. The squad car shivered on the road as the driver took control. The shooter brought the gun up, but Colt pointed her index fingers, and in each hand, a misty revolver appeared.

Invisible bullets rained down on the squad car like ball bearings shot from a paintball gun. The windshield spider-webbed with thick white lines that reduced visibility to near zero. In the Hyundai, Vincent squawked at the sound.

The squad car swerved back and forth, but Colt stayed on it. Her hands, flexing with each shot, shifted to the passenger side and focused there. The windshield on that side twisted and bent inward. It turned white as snow. Then, tiny dark spots appeared as the bullets ripped through. She saw flailing arms for a minute, then the movement stopped. As the squad car swung back, coming not just behind the Hyundai but passing it slightly, the driver leaned out his window with his pistol ready. Colt fired first, the telekinetic bullet cutting across his forehead. Colt saw a spray of red as his head whipped back and his arms waved. The knee he'd been using to hold the wheel jerked, and the car snapped wildly back across the lanes. Colt reached out, tried to grab the wheel and right the squad car, but it was too late. The car drove itself into the ground. There was a smashing, a shattering of glass and a crunching of steel and bones as the squad car flipped up, then came tumbling down onto its roof.

Sparks flew up from the Hyundai's roof, inches from Colt's waist. Her hands went up reflexively, but she instantly lost her balance. Inside the car, Vincent screamed and ducked his head as the sheriff kept firing. The Hyundai wobbled on the road. Colt growled and barked, "Straight!" down at him.

"Ohmygod, ohmygod, ohmygod!" He screeched, his hands flipping the wheel back and forth. Colt heard the wheels beginning to squeak, felt the inertia pulling the car farther and farther with each shift of direction. They were fishtailing and Vincent couldn't compensate.

Another bullet hit the roof near Colt, this one close enough that the Hyundai's gray paint flew against her skin like tiny dull knives. The sheriff was bounding up on them, leaning out his window, right arm crossed over the left and holding his pistol. Colt grabbed the roof with one hand, bent her knees as much as she could, and twisted her body around. She reached for the Hyundai's wheel with her hand but grabbed it telekinetically.

"Stop!" she shouted into the car. "Vincent, let me—"

The bullet hit so close to her hand that she felt the heat from it. Startled, she pulled back, letting go of the roof and the wheel at the same time. The car jostled heavily to the left, and for a moment, Colt thought she was about to be thrown from it. Vincent was panicking, screaming something unintelligible inside the car. Another bullet came so close it cut a line in her sleeve. The car lurched. Colt completely lost her footing. Vincent was crying, shouting that he didn't know what to do. Colt tried to speak, but the back-and-forth motion was making her nauseous.

She couldn't focus, couldn't get her brain straight. Everything was happening too quickly. Her legs were smacking up against Vincent. Every time they did, she felt his panic rush into her. She had to keep some kind of wall up, to keep them separate. But she couldn't control anything, not even

208

herself. She clawed at the roof, fear overtaking her. She was scared, more scared than she had been since she was a kid. Her mind flew to places it shouldn't, and just as she tried to pull herself together, the Hyundai swung to the side. She came down against the roof hard, her head smacking the steel. Everything went fuzzy.

At the wheel, Vincent watched as the road swayed back and forth, powerless to stop it, terrified and angry and sorry and desperate. One of Colt's legs swung into him. He reached to push it out of the way, and his hand locked around exposed skin. Instantly, the leg, the wheel, the windshield and everything else vanished.

CHAPTER FIFTY-TWO

On the lower levels, the buzzing alarm echoed throughout the hallways, each cry bleeding into the next. With her hands buried in a mess of colored wires that hung on a metal oval ring, Sandra looked up. Big bald and redhead moved in unison with her. Sandra glanced at the walkie-talkie on the table nearby.

There was a faster method.

Closing her eyes, Sandra focused. Through her, Mary flexed the mental threads that connected her to the other people in the building. Sandra's face quivered, and a vein in her forehead swelled.

The eyes and hands and mind of the guard in the basement became Mary's to use. She used him to check the security system and found most of it to be inaccessible. Everything locked down faster than she could have the guard counter it. Quickly, she glared up where the shut down command had come from. When she saw the lobby terminal, anger boiled inside of her stomach.

And the guard's stomach.

And Sandra's.

And big bald's, and redhead's, and the janitor's, and the half dozen other puppets she had created in the building.

She had assumed Rakesh had run away because he was a coward. But it had been a trick. He had a plan that went against her will. Nothing could have irritated her more. Still, Rakesh hadn't ruined her plans. The building on lockdown didn't matter.

Or did it?

This wasn't something random. No, Rakesh was smarter than that. Mary had underestimated him. She had to accept it. He was smarter than her. Finding him was a priority, partly to stop whatever he was planning, partly because she savored the idea of adding that intellect of his to her own.

In the lab, the muscles around Sandra's eyes pinched together. To Sandra, it felt as though fingers were working their way up from her stomach, through her throat, clawing at the back of her tongue, grasping her uvula, and pulling hard. They pushed against the backs of her eyeballs, needled behind her eardrums, twisted past her sinuses. Mary's power worked its way through her, and soon, every security guard in the building stood still, their heads shaking and their throats gasping as Mary stripped their brains for information.

The lower and sub levels were powered independently. The generator was on the west side of the basement floor. The computers were controlled by a central CPU storage room on the east side of the floor above the generator. Using the stolen keycard and his administrative password, Rakesh could open any exterior door he chose and seal it again. He could not access the elevators, and would have to use the stairs. This meant that either he was going after the power, the computers, or he was going to bring in outside assistance through one focal location.

There wasn't time for this. Mary had other things to focus on.

She needed more.

Sandra gasped. The fingers that had probed her insides grew into hands. Then into wrists. Then into arms. It was like something was clawing its way through every orifice she had.

In Mary's mind, the images from every set of puppets' eyes faded into focus. They were shaky, as each puppet was quaking, but soon she saw hallways, offices, conference rooms, break rooms.

And Rakesh.

It was only a moment, a second where her puppet stopped shaking and looked Rakesh in the eye before he lunged forward. The puppet, and Mary too, heard the crack of electricity arcing between the tiny metal heads on the stun gun. Then, there was nothing but sharp pain, cutting like a thousand knives. Throughout the building, the puppets all spasmed and twisted and screamed together. In the lab, Sandra clawed at her neck and face, a wild animal trying to tear away a caught and injured limb. It was too much for her, Mary's ability pushing through and the intense connection to the puppets. . As her mind began to crack, to reach a point where it would shut down rather than endure, Mary slipped her psychic fingers away from the puppets and back into Sandra.

The puppets staggered, their eyes seeing only white, and their minds filled with nothing but nothing. Sandra gasped and choked. Her throat was seared from trying to scream the screams of all Mary's puppets. Her fingers, still hooked like talons, hung away from her scratched and bleeding face. The blood vessels in her eyes had burst. Around her sockets, purple and red veins like lines of infection webbed her skin. For a brief blink of time, her connection with Mary wavered, and Sandra's brain reached into itself and extended a tiny and shaking finger to the reboot button that would kick Mary's consciousness out. Traces of life and thought and feeling and color crept up from behind Sandra's irises.

But Mary returned and stamped Sandra's will, dragged her down to the depths of her own mind, and buried her beneath insurmountable psychic pressure. The hint of life in Sandra's eyes faded. The gasping in her throat stopped. Her head dropped, then cranked sideways.

"No one..." Mary's ragged words barely made it out of Sandra's trembling mouth. "Find him." Spittle dropped from her lips. "No one... not allowed... how dare he." She reached for the walkie-talkie on the table, but Sandra's body was still in shock. She collapsed, madly grasping at the table's

211

smooth steel surface. She snarled and snapped, biting her lip. Mary tasted Sandra's blood.

Mary stopped. Sandra stopped. The puppets, who had been standing or leaning limp and lifeless, came back to life. Redhead and big bald blinked and helped Sandra up.

Mary quelled her rage. It was hard; not only had Rakesh caused her to feel the pain of the stun gun, but he'd caused her to almost lose control. Whether the building was locked down or not didn't matter. Whether Mary had a dozen puppets at the DSI or a thousand wasn't important. Her control over Sandra, on the other hand, was vital. Her access to the equipment in the lab was paramount. Whatever else happened was insignificant. But Rakesh had almost taken Sandra away from her, and that meant he absolutely had to go.

Sandra grasped the walkie-talkie. "Rakesh is near the third floor, on the north side of the building. Find him. Kill him." She dropped the walkie-talkie on the table.

Beep. Buzz. Crack.

"Why Mary," Rakesh's voice blurted through the speaker. "You sound... shocked." He laughed before letting go of the call button.

Sandra pressed the button and hissed, "Rakesh,"

"Oh yeah," he said. "By the way, third floor? Long gone." His words came out two or three at a time between labored breaths. "You didn't expect me to stick around, did you?" His voice, even through the speaker, had a chamber's echo to it.

He was in a stairwell.

"It doesn't matter where you run, my puppets will find you and kill you." The arrogance in her voice had returned, but there was something else behind it.

Anger. She was angry.

"I dunno," he said. "Using the walkie-talkies? I'm starting to wonder, you really strong enough to pull this off?"

Sandra stood, her legs more sure now. Beside her, redhead and big bald went back to the computers and masses of cables and tubes and pipes that filled the room like an overgrown mechanical digestive system. Sandra stuck her free hand into the tangle on the table where all the tubes and wires coalesced and said, "I have more than enough power to deal with you."

Over the speaker, a heavy door opened with a bang. "Maybe," Rakesh's voice oscillated. He was running in a stairwell while talking. "But what about Agent Colt?"

"She will be dead soon, too."

"I kinda remember you saying something about that before." There was another bang, then a pause. His voice strained as though he were peeking around a corner. "According to Colt, things didn't go quite like you planned."

Across the room, big bald and redhead were working together over a series of touchscreens. The hum in the computer banks grew steadily louder.

"I underestimated her. I don't make mistakes—"

"Underestimated?" Rakesh seemed to be on the move again. "She smacked you around like a little bitch."

Across the room, redhead jammed a thick pipe into a connector much harder than necessary. In the basement, the guard slammed open a doorway and headed toward the generator room. Throughout the building, Mary's puppets thumped and banged with snarling faces as Sandra's placid and glassy eyes rippled with a current of fury.

She took a long breath through her nose and said, "I don't make mistakes twice."

Rakesh's voice leveled out, as though he had reached the landing between two floors.

"Seriously? Come on, kid. You can't even handle me."

Sandra picked up a pair of needle nose pliers and went back to the nest of rainbow wires. "You are nothing more than an annoyance."

"An annoyance that you can't catch," he said behind the bang of a door, "can't stop," his voice bounced, "and can't predict."

Arrogance dripped from Sandra's lips as she said, "Your plan is obvious."

"Ha!" She discerned his smile through the walkie-talkie. "You don't have the first clue what I'm up to. And even if you do figure it out and try to catch me, I'll just get away like I have every time."

"Luck."

"Nope."

"And it will run out."

"You see," bounce, bounce, bounce, "when you say things like that, it lets me know something."

Sandra stopped, her eyes moving just slightly toward the walkie-talkie in her hand. "What's that?"

"You're scared."

Sandra's hand tightened. "You're wrong."

"Oh yeah, you're scared."

She heard his even steps as he ran down a hallway.

"Of Agent Colt, of me, of your plans completely falling apart," he said.

The pliers gripped a wire so tightly that Sandra's hand shivered. "You really do think too much of yourself, Rakesh."

"You're just a scared little girl, Mary."

"I am not a little girl." The wire came away with a metallic snap.

"Did you really think you were ready to play with the adults?" Smooth voice, another landing. "Sure, you took over some Podunk town in Kansas. Big deal. This is the DSI. This is the big leagues." Thump, thump of steps. "You can use all the fancy words you've taken from grownup minds, put them together to sound like you know more than everyone else. But when all this is said and done, Colt is gonna swat your butt and send you to your room without supper."

Sandra's lip quivered. "She is nothing compared to me."

"She's been showing you up left and right! And I've been stuffing it in your face all night." Creak of a stairwell door. "Without psychic powers, I might add."

Slowly, Sandra lowered the pliers to the table. Her eyes half shut, and she leaned in to the walkie-talkie. "If you're referring to the lockdown, it hasn't hampered me in the least."

Another door. Another hallway.

"It hasn't hampered me in the least," he said in a mocking tone. "Sorry to tell you this, kid, but I've got you right where I want you."

"Is that so?" her eyes closed, and the psychic threads between her mind and the puppets shivered.

"Oh yeah. Another floor or two, and that little arts and crafts project in the lab is coming to a close."

Sandra focused. Mary's message, her orders, zipped out to all of the puppets in the building. All at once, a dozen people stopped what they were doing and moved toward a singular location. Even redhead and big bald stopped what they were doing. Their jobs were almost done, and Sandra could finish that work. Mary wanted Rakesh taken care of. She wanted him dead. She wanted to take control of him and force him to cut his own gut open, then pull out his entrails and watch them splatter to the floor as he bled out.

The walkie-talkie crackled. "What's the matter, Mary? Are you scared?"

He was so sure of himself, and it infuriated her. She did not push the button, but said, "You don't even know the meaning of the word."

"You gonna run and hide?"

"Mostly because no one has ever taught it to you."

"Maybe you should go and get your mommy."

Sandra stopped. That ripple came back to her eyes. All the puppets picked up their pace. Raising the walkie-talkie, she spoke slowly. "Maybe you shouldn't have let me count how many levels you went down."

There was quiet on the other end.

"See you soon, Rakesh."

214

The metal table thumped as the walkie-talkie came down. Stepping over coils and beds of wires and cables and tubes, Sandra made her way across the lab. Without redhead and big bald working, it had grown quiet. The computer banks in the walls still hummed. Pipes, threaded through punched holes and running wildly about the lab, carried super cooled air to the spots where the cables and wires amassed, plugged into every possible part of various machines. Moving about the computers, Sandra pressed buttons, flipped switches and checked the many monitors that hung from the array. Everything was ready.

With a simple tap to a screen, the entire room began to vibrate. Several floors down, hundreds of computer bank fired up. A half dozen emergency generators kicked on. In the lab, the lights dimmed and flickered as electricity was drawn away and focused into the bizarre network Sandra and the scientists had created. As the pipes grew colder from the air inside, the room grew warmer, and steam drifted up lazily, hanging languid and lethargic against the walls.

The screens flashed with numbers and figures, but Sandra did not gaze at them. There was one screen, the largest in the room, which flickered and flipped between different images. It seemed to be a grid, a tangle, something that zoomed in and out quickly. Touching modules on the screen, Sandra adjusted the fluttering image until it became coherent.

It was a map, displayed over black with city streets as red veins and city limits as blue arteries. The map settled, focused down with the DSI building at the center. As the graphs, the pie charts, the numeric percentages displayed on the other screens increased, the map on Sandra's screen zoomed out slowly. In seconds, the entire city block was in view. Within minutes, the map would show the entire downtown area, then the city, then the county, then a good portion of the state. If the scientists' calculations were correct, Mary had less than ten minutes until the majority of the Mid Atlantic would be displayed.

Turning, Sandra walked around the table. With delicate dancing fingers, she touched the modified headgear. Only a few more minutes, then her plan would be complete. She would be unstoppable. Nothing mattered after that. Not Vincent, not Agent Colt, not...

The walkie-talkie sat silent. It had been too long, one of the guards should have checked in. Mary had released total control over the puppets, simply given them their commands and set them to work. But there had been no word. Rakesh should have been captured by now. With Sandra's hand, Mary picked up the walkie-talkie and raised it to her lips.

"Put it down." Rakesh's voice was so soft she barely heard it over the hum of computers and the hiss of pipes.

CHAPTER FIFTY-THREE

Vincent opened his eyes. He was in a house in Connecticut, sitting on the floor in a little white dress, playing with his dolly. In the bright kitchen with the white and black linoleum floor, his mommy was making something big for dinner. She was working extra hard, which meant...

The front door opened, and Daddy came through. He was in his uniform and carrying his duffel. He'd been gone a long time. Vincent ran across the shag carpet, calling to him. Daddy reached out, and the world dropped out from beneath Vincent's feet. Daddy called back, "Kiddo, Kiddo," and swung Vincent, laughing, through the air.

Then the spin ended, and a world of green sleeves enveloped Vincent. He rested his face against Daddy's stiff cotton lapels. Looking up, he saw a smile spread across Daddy's face, but not across his eyes. There, the muscles did not pull up. Vincent saw the thick bloodshot in Daddy's eyes, and the bruising around them. Frowning, Vincent burrowed his face into Daddy's shirt.

When he lifted his head away, it was from a pillow and he blinked away the haze of sleep. It was dark, middle of the night dark, but the sounds. Shouting. His parents. Loud. Louder than ever before. And different. Angry. Daddy was angry. And mommy, she was ... a crash. A small one. Mommy screamed. Vincent sat up. A big crash, huge, Earth shaking. Mommy's voice so high and loud that Vincent felt his tummy go all tight. He wasn't sleepy anymore. More noise. Thump, thump, thumping. Someone was coming. Why wasn't Mommy yelling anymore? The door, someone was at the door. The handle shook. Vincent pulled back, curled up, shivered. The door swung open, and a light as intense as the sun blinded him.

As his eyes adjusted to the mid-day desert sun, the hot air outside the car blasted him. What the heck? Daddy was there, holding the door. "Come on, Kiddo," he said. Vincent uncurled his long, skinny, hairless legs. He stepped out of the station wagon. Another motel. He smelled. How long had it been since he'd had a shower? As he stood and stretched, he noticed Daddy staring across the parking lot. Across the street, at the little diner, at the people sitting inside, drinking their coffee and eating egg salad sandwiches. Unlike Vincent, it wasn't hunger in Daddy's eyes. "Get inside," Daddy said. Vincent started to argue. Daddy put his hand on his back. "Move," Daddy said. "Now." Daddy shoved, and Vincent lurched forward.

His feet skittered on the sandy path. Behind him, Daddy smiled. "Left, right, Kiddo." Vincent huffed and wiped the sweat from his forehead. The sun had finally started to rise, and it was getting hot. They'd been running for an hour, and another hour's worth of steps still waited for them. Even so, Vincent smiled. Daddy was so much happier out here, away from people, so Vincent was too. "Pick it up, Kiddo," said Daddy as he moved past. Vincent pumped his legs and arms, but couldn't keep up. Daddy swept by, leaving puffs of dust and sand with each step. Vincent's smile faded. His face twisted. His leg quivered, and he staggered to a stop. He put his hands on his knees, sweat from his face raining to the desert ground, rocked back, and sat down.

The chair creaked in the tiny cabin. Humming softly, dimmed so as not to distract, exposed bulbs hung from the ceiling. Outside, a coyote yowled at the dusk.

The chair squeaked.

"Stop squirming," said Daddy.

"I'm sorry."

"You have to concentrate," said Daddy.

"I am."

"You have to focus."

"I am."

"Imagine a wall," said Daddy.

"I am."

"Get ready."

"Daddy?"

"Are you ready?"

"I'm... I'm not."

"Focus, Kiddo."

"I can't."

"It's coming."

"I can't, Daddy. I—"

"Think of a wall, Kiddo."

"I can't do this."

"It's coming."

"Please, Daddy."

"Get ready."

"I don't like this."

"Stop talking and focus."

"I don't like it. Please."

"It's coming."

"Please don't. I don't want to do this anymore."

"Focus, goddammit!"

"Daddy, I can't!"

"I'm doing it."

"I'm sorry! Please don't do it!"

"Here it comes."

"I can't! I can't! Please, Daddy. I—"

Daddy's face tensed. A dash, a swish of the dirt on the floor between them, and an invisible palm slapped the surface of Vincent's brain. Everything spun, and he dropped.

His fingers dug into the sandy ground, and it worked its way into the wraps that covered his hands. Blood dripped onto the earth beneath his downturned face. Sweat trickled on back of his neck beneath his long hair. Just out of reach, Daddy's bare feet bounced up and down. "Get up," Daddy called. Vincent's jaw clenched. "Come on," Daddy said. "You're going to learn to fight, one way or another." Vincent pulled his bare feet beneath him, dragging lines in the sand. He stood on shaking legs. He came up to Daddy's chiseled, lean shoulders now. Daddy was smirking, but not in the kind of way that made Vincent want to laugh.

"Guess you can't do this either, huh, Kiddo?"

Vincent dug his toes in, crossed his arms in front of his face, and dove forward. He hit his father square in the chest.

Water splashed around him. He pushed through, running against the rain and wind. Arms cross over the paper bag in his arms, he tried to shield it from the downpour. Under flickering fluorescent streetlamps, he moved his worn sneakers across the parking lot. Fishing the motel key from his jacket pocket with chilled fingers was like solving a puzzle. The bag slipped, but he caught it in time. It would have been so much easier if he could have just knocked.

The TV produced the only light in the room. The news had been on for two weeks, and nothing had changed. He sniffled. Instead of reaching for a tissue, he put his hand inside the bag. Out came a sub sandwich wrapped in butcher paper. Vincent walked across the room to where the shifting, jumping colors of the world's happenings washed over the gaunt figure. For a moment, Vincent wasn't sure where his dad's limbs ended and the chair's began. His fingers dug at the sandwich's paper, found the tape, and pulled it away. The smell of sliced meats, shredded lettuce, oil and vinegar filled the room. The figure didn't stir.

Vincent put the sandwich his dad's lap. "Dad?" he said softly, trying to coax the glassy eyes from the screen. "You should eat. It's been days. Please?" His father's hands remained motionless. Vincent adjusted the sandwich, made sure it wouldn't fall, just in case. Standing, he peeled off his wet jacket and hung it by the door. Without wanting them to, his hands covered his face. Even though his dad was there, he cried like only the lonely do.

A voice startled him. It wasn't the heavy voice of a man, but it was too deep to be a child. He glanced up. The bright ceiling lights of the burger place bounced off the white walls and polished, laminated tables, stinging his already tired eyes. The boy standing by the table was about his age, wearing a

218

uniform. Vincent had seen him behind the counter when they'd come in for a pit stop. Vincent tried not to wipe his wet eyes, but failed. "What did you say?" he asked the boy. "Are you okay?" the boy said. Vincent nodded but didn't put any effort into the lie. The boy smiled at him, a soft smile. "Do you need anything?" the boy asked. The boy's eyes were warm and inviting, and Vincent found himself staring into them for longer than he should have.

Just as he was starting to enjoy the closeness of the boy's body to his own, something moved in the corner of his vision. It happened fast. His dad appeared from out of nowhere, getting between him and the boy, voice strained and low. Vincent started to stand, to explain, to tell his dad nothing was happening, that it was just a boy. A hand shoved him down. The boy started to come forward. Vincent couldn't stop him, and he couldn't stop his dad from turning his eyes, already etched with thick red veins, on the boy. The boy stopped, eyes rolling up. To Vincent, it appeared as though the boy were drowning in the middle of the room. Dad stepped toward him. Vincent leaped up, shouting for him to stop. The boy's body shook. Vincent grabbed his dad, pulled at the back of his shirt, but couldn't stop him. The boy's head jerked. A fluid the color of blood, but thicker than it had any right to be, ran from the boy's ears. He screamed. His dad grabbed Vincent's arm and pulled him back. People in the restaurant stood and gawked. His dad swung an arm. Faces went slack. Eyes closed. Heads drooped and landed against tables. Behind the counter, a phone receiver slipped from a woman's hands. Vincent struggled as his dad pulled him toward the door. Craning his neck, Vincent glanced back in time to see the boy stop shaking, let out a final breath, and drop.

A cop hit the ground, and dust clouded around his blue uniform. His gun skittered from his hand like a flat stone across a calm lake. Vincent slapped the cracked windshield. His head was throbbing and something warm and wet and salty had crept into his eye. His body shifted, trying to right itself in the seat. The station wagon was sideways, resting on the passenger side. Vincent wrapped his fingers around the steering wheel and pulled himself up. The driver's side door was already open, framing nothing but the bright blue sky. Vincent peered through the windshield. The two cop cars, the ones that had found them just a few miles from the burger place, were both crashed as well. One was upside down. Vincent watched, mesmerized by the tires that still spun against nothing. From one of the shattered windows, another cop was pulling himself out. Wiping the blood from his eye, Vincent looked back.

Vincent's dad blurred and disappeared.

Grabbing the doorframe, Vincent kicked his tangled legs. With a thump, the glove box opened. An empty bottle of bourbon fell and joined the broken window. Vincent looked down. The handle of the sheathed bowie knife hung lazily. Outside, someone was yelling, shouting fearful warnings. Vincent bent quickly. The knife held in his teeth, foot jammed into the steering wheel, he lifted himself onto the battlefield.

The cop was pinned. His father stalked the man. Vincent dropped the sheath as he ran in. It was a mistake. His father turned. Vincent moved the way he'd been taught. His dad was fast, faster than Vincent had ever seen him move. The hits were blurs. The knife was in Vincent's hand, then it was gone. When it returned, it came point first. The blade felt cool against the warmth of Vincent's insides, but that vanished in the pain that followed. The blade stung as it pulled back, leaving nothing but an empty space in his abdomen. He didn't have time to look, didn't have time to realize he was being thrown down before the ground stole the breath from his lungs. His eyes opened and watched as the blue sky went black. As skeletal as it had become, his dad's frame blocked the world and overshadowed all. A flesh noose locked around Vincent's throat. His dad's skin was hot as an iron skillet, or was it that Vincent was suddenly cold? There wasn't enough blood to make his ears pound. His dad's words dripped along with strings of spittle. "You traitor," he said, "talking to them, telling them about me. I told you. I told you! They're after me. They're after us. I thought, I thought I could, I could trust you..." His dad's madness had completely consumed him. "You're just like your mother. And now," his father raised the knife, "you're going to die like her, too."

Vincent thrashed and kicked. He clawed at the ground, searching for something, anything he could use. When his fingers found something solid, he swung it as hard as he could. The revolver, the one dropped by the dead cop, cracked across his dad's face. The fingers around Vincent's throat loosened. Vincent's feet pulled up close, dug into his dad's stomach, and he pushed. Fire raced through his insides at the knife wound. He'd ripped something inside of himself, but it didn't matter. His father stumbled back. Vincent brought the revolver up and held it just like his dad had taught him. He took aim and his fingers clenched, but he waited a moment too long. The gun kicked, but his dad was two feet to the right. Vincent tightened his shoulders and shifted. The gun kicked, but his father was to the left and farther back. Vincent followed and fired. And fired and fired and fired. His father appeared before him, eyes lowered. Vincent leveled the sights and pulled the trigger, dropping the hammer against nothing but a spent shell.

His dad took a step.

That cold feeling sunk deeper into Vincent's body. His hands trembled. He pulled again.

Another step.

Ice grew in Vincent's muscles, worked down in jagged points toward his bones. The gun clicked, and clicked, and clicked.

His dad turned the blade around, getting the grip just right.

Vincent couldn't get enough air, couldn't stop his whole body from shaking.

The blade shimmered. His dad's eyes were black as well bottoms. He was steps away. He wasn't going to stop.

Vincent cried out. Even knowing the bullets were spent, he jerked the trigger anyway. The cylinder rolled over uselessly, again and again.

His dad's head tilted to one side.

"Please, please, please, please."

His feet stopped.

Vincent froze.

"Goodbye, Kiddo."

His dad dove. Vincent squeezed the gun, closed his eyes, and pulled the trigger with a scream.

"Please."

There was no kick back, but the air around him thundered. When the silence drifted down soft as settling dust, his eyes opened. The silhouette of his dad blocked the glowing embers of the sun's slow descent into the hills. In the middle of the shadow, a beam of light slipped through the hole where his dad's heart should have been. As his father dropped, the man's face restful for the first time in over a decade, Vincent leaped to catch him.

He grabbed the Hyundai's steering wheel. In front of him, the road rolled back and forth, serpentine. The skin of Colt's leg was warm against his fingers. Vincent blinked. He let go and peered into the rearview mirror. The sheriff's car was tracking behind them. He listened. Colt wasn't shooting. He felt. The muscles in Colts legs resting against him were loose, her feet tapping for purchase instead of gripping. He took a deep breath.

His hands locked on the wheel. The car didn't jerk, but slid smoothly until they were riding the yellow line, bits of tire smoke drifting back behind them. Colt's leg pressed against his shoulder. With a grunt, he fired a thought straight into her brain.

Wake up!

Above him, Colt stirred. Screaming lead death ricocheted off the roof of the car. The sheriff was shooting again. Vincent steered the Hyundai to the right side of the road, keeping them closer to the gun's blind spot. It would only last a few seconds, then Colt would be in prime firing position. She still wasn't up, wasn't fully conscious. Vincent decided on a more direct approach.

Colt barked as Vincent's teeth dug into the back of her leg. The image from the rearview mirror of the sheriff's car closing in smacked her visual cortex. Everything in her head lined up, and her mind was instantly at full attention. She didn't even look, just flipped her arms out, pointed her fingers, and the misty revolvers appeared. Psychic bullets pinged off the hood of the sheriff's car, smashing his driver's side headlight and knocking against his windshield. Even with the barrage, the sheriff managed to get another shot off. It skimmed the roof near her head. She smelled the distinct odor of burned hair.

Jesus, this guy was tough. He could drive, he could shoot, and even without Mary controlling him, Colt had a feeling that he'd still be calm and collected. When this was all over, she was taking him back to the goddamn DSI and turning him into a field agent.

That is, if she didn't end up killing him in the next few minutes.

Below her, Vincent was coaxing the wheel back and forth, always working to keep her out of the sheriff's firing area. And when she ended up there, he used the pedals to increase and decrease the distance, change the angle, do anything to give Colt the advantage. Basically, he was driving like she would have.

Colt kept low, twisted her aching body, and popped off shots at the sheriff's windshield. Her telekinetic bullets had a ton of kick, but their range was limited. Their power decreased considerably faster than a physical bullet, and the sheriff picked up on that. He dropped back to a distance. His windshield cracked, fractured and chipped, but if Colt wanted to white it out, she would have to let the telekinetic energy amass at her fingertip and fire off a big shot. If she had two minutes, she could punch a hole in his engine block. Unfortunately, she didn't have two seconds.

Her bullets were weakening. The revolvers in her hands wavered in and out of sight. She felt the red lines creeping into her sclera, headed toward her irises. Next, her hands would start to shake. Her knee ached, even through the cortisone shot and the pain meds, and she wasn't sure how much longer she could stay up in this position.

She paused her barrage, only for a second, and the sheriff made his move. The front of his car lifted as he gunned the powerful engine inside. Colt saw the shift of his body behind the cracked windshield. He was going to lean out, get a clean shot.

Wrapping her left hand around her right wrist, Colt poured all of her psychic energy into one hand. The revolver there took on a bit of color. It looked almost real, just semi-transparent. She fired the shot, slamming the sheriff's car loud and heavy. It was bigger, but she couldn't do it rapid fire. And the sheriff caught on fast.

Instead of backing off, like Colt had hoped, the sheriff pushed in. Colt focused hard and pounded out another shot, but he read her movements and jerked to the left. It hit the frame of the car, not the glass, and left a deep dent. He swung to the right, exposing the driver's side. If Colt had a shot ready, she could have popped him right there. Instead, he fired first, missing her by inches. Colt flopped on the roof, covering her head with her arms. The sheriff only got off the one shot, but he was swinging back to the left of the road already. It was a good strategy, and eventually it would work. With every second, his car drew closer. Colt didn't think he'd get her on the next pass, but it was a good bet he'd pick her off on the one after that.

Lips pressed together in a tiny pink line across his face, Vincent held the steering wheel with arms as straight at yardsticks. His mind was clearer than it had been in months. And, when a few hundred feet away, the wall of corn shredded and the squad car Colt had sent spinning off earlier leaped out, Vincent didn't even flinch.

Smeared brown and green from dirt, leaves and stalks, the car plowed over the manicured lawns. Fence after fence shattered against its front bumper. Lawn chairs jumped and spun through the air as the car angled itself on a collision course with the Hyundai.

"Hey!" Vincent shouted as loud as he could, but got no response. "Hey!" He looked up, trying to catch Colt's eye, but she was too focused on not getting shot.

To the right, a wooden swing set burst into dozens of pieces as the squad car drove through it. The spinning red and blue lights atop the car were wrenched off with a metallic screech. Even though the grill and front bumper were twisted and folded over onto themselves like a failed piece of origami, the squad car's front rose up, and the engine hammered hard.

Vincent's fingers danced on the wheel. He went to swerve to the left, but the sheriff was roaring up past their blind spot. Colt used a buckshot bullet, riddling the sheriff's car with dents. But the sheriff's crept his bumper up to the edge of Vincent's driver's side door.

A loud clap cut through the engine noise. The Hyundai's rear window disintegrated. Vincent jerked down. The Hyundai swerved to the right. Vincent pulled the car to the left, forcing the sheriff to pull away. Looking up, Vincent saw a cloud of white cotton stuffing sticking out from the shredded headrest. The bullet had missed him by inches.

The squad car ripped through another fence, and Vincent heard it now, its damaged engine struggling like a spent horse driven by its rider to death. The squad car bounced through a small duck pond and headed for the last fence between them. To the left, the sheriff advanced, bringing his passenger window almost in line with Vincent's. Colt was shouting something. Her shots ravaged the sheriff's car, but he refused to relent. The last fence to the right shattered. The sheriff pulled up. The squad car leaped the ditch between lawn and road. The sheriff's gun rose, steady and true.

Screaming, Vincent slapped one hand against Colt's leg and zapped a thought into her brain.

Hang on!

Both sneakered feet hit the brake pedal as hard as they could. Colt flailed at the roof of the car as she toppled backward, her butt pushing down on Vincent's shoulders. The Hyundai's tires screamed against the asphalt. On the right, the squad car clipped their front bumper, tearing the headlight away as it bounded across the road. The squad car slammed into the sheriff's and sang metal carnage. Tires from both police cars shot into the air. Glass sprayed like water from a lawn sprinkler. Splatters of liquids, red and black and clear, gushed like blood from severed arteries. The cars tumbled over each other, falling away from the road and into the ditch. Then, from the ditch to the fences. Then, from the fences to the yards where, slowly, they settled.

Squinching his eyes shut, Vincent clenched his teeth. The steering wheel bit into his cheek, Colt's weight pinching his head in place. He growled and pushed against the wheel, but he couldn't lift her.

"GeOphh!" he said through lips made of pressed Play-Doh.

Colt . gasped as she pulled herself up. The edge of the sunroof had left an indent just beneath her shoulder blades that went from her shirt to the bandages, to her skin, through her muscles, and down to her bones. She was lucky that she hadn't broken her spine. If it hadn't been for Vincent's warning, her lower back would have hit the sunroof opening and folded her like a rag doll. So she managed a tiny smile as she rested her forehead against the roof of the car.

"Good work, Kiddo," she muttered, her eyes only half open.

"What?" Vincent called from below.

Colt opened her eyes. The words she'd said fluttered in the air around her, taking a moment before slipping into her ears. Her heart stopped a moment. Pushing herself up, she grunted.

"I said—"

CHAPTER FIFTY-FOUR

"Move it." Rakesh's voice filled the lab. "Put it down, Mary."

Fingers tightening, Sandra lowered the walkie-talkie and faced Rakesh.

He looked terrible. His dress shirt was dirty, wrinkled, soaked through with sweat and murky water. His hair was slick but a complete mess. All she could see of his face behind the 9mm pistol were his dark brown eyes. At first they were pinched tight, focused and intense. But, upon seeing Sandra clearly, they went wide.

"What... what did you do?" His voice did not break, but she heard the hairline fracture beneath its surface.

Sandra gestured to the mottled skin around her eyes, as well as the dried blood that had seeped from her ears. "I've forced her abilities to increase. These are the side effects."

She waited for Rakesh to respond, but his face did the talking. His eyes drew tight again, but now she saw that it was anger drawing the strings.

He knew this wasn't really Sandra. It was her body, it was her throat saying those words, but it wasn't her. She was still in there, somewhere, buried deep inside. But right now, she wasn't going to come out. He'd hoped, truly hoped, that when she saw him, when they came face to face, that his image would give her the strength to fight back, to wrest control away from Mary and put an end to this. It was a silly thing to think, but he couldn't lie— it had crossed his mind.

Though, there was still one more chance.

Tilting her head to the side, Mary asked through Sandra's lips, "How did you get away?"

"I didn't have to, I never went downstairs."

"What?"

He couldn't help it, a little smile snuck onto his lips. "I've been on this floor, opening and closing doors and pretending to jog."

Sandra's face showed no reaction, but her eyes twitched. "Then you've only put off your death by a couple of minutes." She took a quick breath, her eyelids dipping slightly.

"Don't!" He stepped forward, aiming the gun at her face. The movement caught her attention, which was exactly what he wanted. "Don't close your eyes or, or blink or, or, or go cross-eyed, because I will shoot."

Sandra stood still, unnaturally still, and stared at the gun. Rakesh's hand wasn't shaking. His voice wasn't quivering. That was not the threat of a man brought to the edge.

When Rakesh was sure Mary wasn't sending out a call to her puppets, he took a long breath. "Good," he said, his voice pulling down with intent calm. "Now, I want you to let Sandra go."

There was a slight pause before Sandra said, with a flat monotone, "That's not going to happen. I'm quite fond of this particular body. Her ability suits my needs very well."

Rakesh nodded. He waved the barrel of the gun toward the large computer screen behind her, the one displaying the ever-growing map. North Carolina was just coming into view, along with the Pennsylvania/New York border. "You're going to use her, going to boost your signal and take over the entire world, huh?"

Sandra did not seem impressed. "No, she's not strong enough for that. Even with the modifications I've had your scientists make to the equipment here," she gestured toward the cannibalized headgear. "Her maximum range will have a radius of approximately four to five hundred miles."

Rakesh shrugged sarcastically. "Oh, is that all?"

"There's no stopping this, Rakesh." Sandra tilted her head. "If you give up now, I would let you live."

Rakesh's fingers opened and closed on the grip. "Get out of her. Now."

Sandra's lips pulled into a wry grin. "Why, so you can get in her?"

Rakesh's mouth opened, but nothing came out.

Sandra tilted her head. "This body of hers is quite nice." Her hands went to her hips, but didn't stay there; they glided, up and down along her curves. "And so... mature." Her fingers graced the bottom of her round breasts. "Being in here as long as I have, I've gotten to experience some new things."

"Stop it," Rakesh said, anger wiring his jaws together.

"I've felt what happens to her physiology when I make her look at you." Her hands kept moving, sliding across a stomach that twisted and rocked like a slow motion belly dancer. "The sensations are quite... intense." A hand slipped down, just below her waist. The other cupped at her breast, worked its way in between the opening of her shirt. "You know, I could let you have her, Rakesh," she said, her voice a smoky whisper. "I could make her do whatever you want. Just tell me how you'd like to fuck her and I—"

"Enough!" Fury stained the word. Now his hand was shaking. "Let her go, or I will—"

"No, you won't." Sandra's hands dropped as though her arms had instantly fallen asleep. The sultry quality to her voice vanished. "If you had the stomach, you would have shot when my back was turned." She took a step forward. Rakesh stepped back. "You're a coward. Scared. Unable to act

226

even though you know the consequences." She looked past the gun, past Rakesh's fire and into eyes that seemed to almost be pleading, begging for this to end. "You're weak," she said, hammering at his resolve.

A whimper, tiny and thin, left his lips. Though he did lower the gun, it was only after lowering his head.

"Very well," she said, accepting his defeat. Turning away, she walked to the metal table in the middle of the room. "But no worries, Rakesh. In a minute, you'll forget your fears." She slipped her hands through the wires, onto the metal grasps of the headgear and lifted it. "You'll forget your pains. You'll forget that you ever even fought against me, or that your cowardice was the reason that I won." Raising the mad crown of wires and cables, Sandra smiled.

White fire lit up her brain as Rakesh jammed his stun gun into the base of her neck. As her body jerked, the headgear dropped and bounced on the table. Rakesh pushed hard, leaning into her back with one arm. He held the button, pumping an electrical current into her body until she was flat against the table.

He stuffed the stun gun back into his pocket and dragged her away from the table. She wasn't unconscious, but she made no effort to fight back. Rakesh wasn't sure if he'd severed the link between Mary and Sandra, but he couldn't count on it. He laid her on the floor. Reaching into his other pocket, he yanked out a thick, industrial zip tie. Rakesh made a loop around the exposed pipe running floor to ceiling near the door, stuck Sandra's hands through, and cinched the tie shut.

He'd never planned on shooting Sandra, but Mary hadn't known that. Originally, he'd planned to wait for her to turn her back, then bum rush her and hit her with the stun gun. But when she'd gone for the walkie-talkie, he had to stop her before she could hit that button. A bit of psychological games later, he figured she would make the mistake of turning her back on him. Now that he knew what she was after, he could stop her without having to hurt anyone.

Even before the headgear had become a rat's nest of colored wires, Rakesh couldn't have told anyone how it worked. Now? It was a thousand times more confusing. But he didn't have to make it work.

He had to make it not work.

And that was considerably easier.

Behind him, Sandra stirred, a groan slipping between her lips. Rakesh put the pistol down on the table. He didn't have much time. Holding down the headgear with one hand, he grabbed a handful of wires with the other and pulled as hard as he could. There was a snap, a couple of sparks, and the wires came loose.

"No," Sandra muttered behind him.

Rakesh ignored her and grabbed one of the thick bundles. He strained and ripped it free. On the computer screens, graphs dropped and numbers fell.

"No!" Sandra shouted.

Rakesh grabbed another handful, but before he could pull, Sandra's shout turned to a scream. Then to a howl. Then to a deathly screech. Rakesh spun. She was there, on the floor, her head shaking and her teeth bared and grinding so hard that the gums turned white. The veins that ran thick beneath the skin of her forehead slipped down like the roots of a mango grove into her cheeks and jaw. Blood, thick and crimson, ran from her eyes and sprayed out from huffing lips. Rakesh grabbed the gun. Sandra's eyes opened. He knew what was coming.

Scrambling sideways, he dodged the psychic spike. It sliced through the miasma of steam that veiled the floor. Rakesh stumbled wildly, running up to the wall. Another spike missed him by inches. Rakesh pushed off the wall and ran back to the table. Sandra continued to screech and fire spikes, one after another. Mary had forced Sandra's brain, strained it against all reason so she could use the spikes, but had little control over them. They curved and sliced through the air like amateur golf balls.

Rakesh flipped the table onto its side and ducked behind it. The spikes pinging off of it were so strong he felt the vibrations in the steel. Huffing loudly, he scanned the room. The headgear had fallen on the other side of the table, and there was no way of getting to it. He was completely pinned down. Sandra blocked the doorway.

And whose fault is that, Rakesh snarked at himself.

To his left was the frosted glass wall. He could shoot out a pane and leap through, but Sandra would probably spike him before he made it. In front of him and to his right were nothing but computer banks and monitors. Looking up, he saw the map. It had stopped spreading when he'd ripped out the wires from the headgear, but it wasn't going down.

Against his back the vibrations stopped.

"It is time to give up, Rakesh." Sandra's voice was raw. "The others will be here soon. After I have them rip the flesh from your bones, I will rebuild what you have broken."

"Yeah?" Rakesh dropped the safety on the pistol. "Rebuild this."

Plastic and metal shrapnel burst from the computer banks as the bullets tore into them. Rakesh fired wildly, blowing holes in computers, monitors, even knocking loose one of the massive power couplings in the wall and exposing the frayed wires behind it.

Across the room, Sandra shrieked as Mary's rage poured into her. She howled madly as Mary tore into her mind and dragged forth every bit of psychic ability. The zip tie around her wrists snapped, wrenched by

228

telekinetic hands. Sandra did not stand, but was hoisted into the air, standing on legs so taut the muscles strained her joints to their limit. With a sweep of her arm, the table slid across the floor and exposed Rakesh as he fell backward. Sandra floated across the floor toward him, her face a twisted menagerie of pain and anger. The gun came up, but Sandra drew faster. Her hand went out, a claw in the air, and Rakesh flew back against the wall. The gun dropped to the floor, and he grasped at his chest. He screamed as telekinetic hands pulled at his ribs from the inside, clawing at the bones and muscles there.

Raising her hand, Sandra lifted Rakesh from the floor to his feet, then from his feet into the air. His face contorted as the hands inside changed to hooks that dug into his flesh, his sinew, his organs, and hauled him up on invisible chains. He couldn't breathe, couldn't exhale, couldn't even open his eyes the pain was so unbearable. Sandra's hand began to close and, from deep in his ribcage, Rakesh felt and heard the distinct crack of bones.

"How dare you?" the words came in spurts and spits from Sandra's lips as she floated toward Rakesh. "Don't you see? I'm just trying to protect them! This is the only way! I will take what I want and use who I need. No one can stop this!"

Rakesh opened his mouth, not to speak but to force air into his lungs. He'd been here before. It was mile twenty-four. His body fought against him. The weight of his own skin was too much. He'd been here before, and he'd pushed through. He'd done it, and he could do it now.

He opened his eyes. Above him, the broken and exposed power coupling hung at the edge of his reach. He stared into Sandra's mangled face. A tear, probably from the pain, ran down his cheek. His hands slowly dropped from his chest to his sides.

Sandra hissed. "Give up and die, Rakesh."

The pain in his chest intensified—something he hadn't thought possible—and the edges of his vision went white. His ears filled with the sounds of an oncoming storm, and with the last bit of consciousness he had, he raised his arm above his head, jamming the arcing stun gun into the power coupling.

There was an electrical crack, like a thousand sheets of paper torn at a thousand miles an hour. The overhead lights exploded. Then the monitors. Then any device that was plugged into the walls. Sandra screamed and pulled away. Rakesh, already falling into unconsciousness, dropped to the ground as the room was destroyed in a series of bursts and bangs that sent chunks of pipe through the frosted glass. In the center of the room, Sandra fell to the ground as ceiling tiles came crashing down all around them.

CHAPTER FIFTY-FIVE

The buildings of Fieldsville's Main Street appeared on the horizon. In the rearview mirror, Colt saw the smoke from the two mangled police cars rising into the air. Somberness had slipped into the vehicle. Colt wanted to tell Vincent that, if anyone were to blame for those deaths, it was Mary. But she'd kept those words to herself. There was no point. Vincent would carry that guilt as long as he lived. And though it made Colt sad to think of that, it also made her proud.

It was a sign of his humanity, of the thing that separated him from people like Mary.

"I'm sorry," Vincent said, suddenly and with a strong voice.

"For what?"

"I saw."

Colt sighed. "Yeah."

Vincent nodded. "And thank you."

Colt's eyes narrowed. "For what?"

"Calling me 'Kiddo'."

Colt sighed, but in the way she would have after a good meal. "Yeah."

"Can I ask you something?"

"Sure."

"Is it the same gun?"

Colt's eyebrows came together. "Yes."

Vincent thought about that a moment, then asked, "Why? You could just shoot the bullets."

Now it was Colt's turn to chew the words over in her mind. "Do you know what a gun is, Vincent?"

"Yeah," he said, as though now he wasn't sure.

"Do you know what it does? What its purpose is?"

"It..." And now he was sure he didn't know. At least, not what Colt was going to tell him.

"It destroys." She let the words sink in. "That's it. Nothing else. It can't show love or compassion, it can't treat wounds or fix what's broken. The only thing it can do is destroy and kill." She shifted in her seat. "Some people, they use them without thought. But I won't do that. Because that's not just a bullet I'm firing, it's a part of me. I have enough power to kill a person."

"The revolver reminds you."

Colt nodded.

"Is that why you point?"

She almost smiled. "If I'm going to shoot someone, I have to make sure I have it in me to at least point at them, to single them out. To tell myself, that's the person I'm choosing to destroy."

Vincent stared down at his hands. They curled, but stopped just shy of fists.

"We're here."

He sat up and looked around. They'd reached the downtown area. His house was on the other side of Fieldsville, and as stupid as cutting through downtown was, it was the most direct route. They watched as the first buildings, the stores and shops that stood on the edge of Main Street, came toward them.

"Colt?"

There was no one. Not a single person. No small line at the coffee place where Colt had talked to Rakesh's psychic projection. No school buses bringing in droves of kids. No morning commuters. No pedestrians.

The stores were dark and empty, their doors wide open. Empty vehicles sat parked neatly against the curb, hoods open, batteries removed along with radios, dash consoles, everything and anything electronic. Each light post had been carefully deconstructed from the back, the heavy-duty cables and power conduits taken. It wasn't a scene of devastation or rioting, but a calm collection of specific items.

Colt expected roadblocks, pickup trucks filled with gun-toting puppets, a melee of controlled commuters dragging their Hyundai into a deadly game of bumper cars. She'd planed on holding down the gas pedal, putting up a telekinetic cow catcher in front of the car, and plowing through until it gave way. She'd told Vincent that was the plan, and they'd prepared for it.

But not for this.

Colt had miscalculated somewhere. She'd figured that Mary's main focus was eliminating her and Vincent. Quickly, she thought back to the chase with the police cars, but she'd spent most of the time pressed against the roof and never got a good look around them.

"Vincent?"

"Yeah?" his voice was laced with anxiety.

"When we came out of the corn, do you remember the houses?"

"Uh... yeah. I guess."

"Do you remember if there were any cars in the driveways?"

"I..." his eyes darted back and forth, accessing memories. Colt saw that he was instinctively using a technique for visual recall that she'd been taught during training. It was like reading your own mind; open the door that leads to your stored optic memories, break them down into a series of

231

photos and short videos, sift through them one at a time. It wasn't the most advanced technique, but it took time to learn how to do it right.

"Not a lot," he said finally. "Here and there, but most cars were gone." He smiled a goofy grin. "Whoa," his eyes were twinkling. "I just—"

Colt nodded once and let out a loud, "Mm-hmm." She had more important things to think about.

The houses were empty. Main Street was empty. No one was trying to stop them from reaching Vincent's house. It was possible that the pyrokinetic and the sheriff's men were genuine attempts on their lives, but they may have also simply been to stall them. Though, that didn't make sense. Mary had control of the town, probably of all those people living out near the farming areas too. If she wanted to stall, she could stall.

So where were all the people?

The population of Fieldsville was about fifteen hundred. What did she need those people for? And all that equipment? Radios? TVs? Power cables?

Colt's face set like quick dry cement in a thousand-degree oven. "Oh no."

"What is it?"

"Where's Mary?"

Vincent, taken aback at Colt's sudden change, flapped his jaw a moment. "I... I though you said she'd be at the house."

"That's what I thought but there's not enough power there, so where is she?"

"I don't—"

"Find her."

"But you said I had to try and keep her from—"

"Do it! Now!"

Vincent pulled back, his eyes growing wide. "But she'll know where we are."

"She already knows where we are."

"Then why hasn't she—"

Main Street zipped by as Colt pushed on the accelerator. "Mary is building a machine, a transmitter. It'll allow her to spread her power and take over hundreds of thousands of people. I need to stop her, now."

"But," Vincent sat up. "But my mom—"

"I'm sorry, Vincent. This is bigger."

Vincent looked out to the road, then back to Colt. Pushing his lips together, he said, "Didn't you tell me that, wherever we found Mary, we'd find my mom?"

Colt opened her mouth but thought twice. Vincent was so sure; Colt wasn't. She hoped that he was right.

"If your mother is still alive."

Vincent's eyes narrowed. "She is. Mary wouldn't do that."

Colt stayed silent.

"She wouldn't," he said firmly. "She... Mom's with Mary, and I'm gonna find them." Sitting back, he closed his eyes, and his whole body tightened. With a gasp, he sat up.

Colt's hardened façade cracked. "What's wrong? Are you—"

"The mall," Vincent said with a shiver. "I felt her at the mall but..."

"What?"

"It's like... like she's huge."

"Huge?"

"Like there's a thousand of her."

Colt's lip pulled up, bulldoggish. "That sounds about right."

CHAPTER FIFTY-SIX

Fire alarms were the first thing Rakesh heard as his mind crept back to him. The second was his own wheezing breath. Sluggishly, his eyes opened and closed. The room was dark, and through the incessant alarm, he heard things falling down, settling, sparking and fizzing. When he moved, it was like a chainsaw was cutting into his chest. His whole body tensed, which was the worst possible thing, and he gasped. His ribs were broken, possibly his sternum too. The world floated in and out of his eyes as the pain overwhelmed him. He slipped back to the floor and pulled his arms underneath him.

It took a minute—or two, or twelve—but he managed to get himself into a fetal position, resting on his forearms and shins. Spreading his hands across the floor and shoving away jagged pieces of broken metal, he pushed himself up.

Sandra's hands clamped onto his throat. She snarled and squeezed, her nails biting into his skin and drawing blood. Rakesh floundered. He heard her breath, rushed and inconsistent. Her face, covered with sweat and blood, knocked against his, and he felt the sting of snapping teeth on his cheek. He tried to pry her off, his own slick fingers sliding away from hers. The world went white, then black, then came back again.

His heart raced in his aching chest. His legs kicked violently. He fell back and dragged her on top of him where she bore down with all of her weight. Drool fell from her lips and splattered his face, and she muttered words that were not words but balls of rage, and Rakesh put his hands against her face and pushed as hard as he could, but she would not relent, would not release him.

His eyes bulged in their sockets, and his skin tore beneath her wringing fingers. He searched the ground with one hand and grabbed the first thing he could. His other hand snatched a mound of Sandra's hair. Desperately, he pulled her back and struck.

There was a dull thunk, but a sharp ping too. Rakesh felt a slicing pain in his hand and a strange, warm wetness. Right away, Sandra's grip loosened.

No, not loosened. It went limp. Her body slumped down on top of him.

Rakesh gasped, re-inflating his crushed throat. His eyes opened wide, and after blinking away the tears, he looked up.

Sandra's face stared down, broken and mangled from Mary's control. Yet, there was no anger, no fury spread across it. Instead, there was nothing. Rakesh stared at the object in his hand. It was a piece of metal from the ceiling. As his fingers unfurled from around it, he saw how it hadn't struck

Sandra, but had pierced her skull. Droplets of red splashed across Rakesh's face, mixing into his sweat and tears.

He let go of the metal bar and slipped his bleeding hand to Sandra's cheek. The skin was still hot, burned by Mary's feverous rage, but it was residual, dissipating. Slowly, he lowered her head and kissed her hairline.

Around him, sparks popped and fell from the walls and ceiling, bright stars that shone for mere seconds before fading into the darkness.

"I'm sorry," he whispered. "I tried. I'm sorry."

They stood, tiny living turrets tracing the very edge of the rooftop. Colt and Vincent had seen them from a distance, lined up and spaced perfectly like fine embellishments upon the crown of a mad queen. They were holding hands, like a human barrier to keep out attackers from whatever was happening atop the roof. But Colt knew that was not what they were doing. Even standing in the parking lot that surrounded the mall, she couldn't count the number of Fieldsville's citizens at the edge of the roof. The building was large, a two level mall, and shaped like an overweight I.

And there were people at every inch of the roof's edge.

They'd parked the Hyundai against the curb, near the entrance. The car idled in sputters and coughs. An odd whining noise came from under the hood, too. Colt turned off the engine. The lot was filled with cars. Every hood was open, every battery removed. The bike racks near the entrances were overwhelmed with bicycles, none of them locked.

"Vincent?"

"Yeah?"

"You ever seen it this full before?"

"Uh..." He crunched his eyebrows. He was having trouble concentrating. His mind was uniquely tuned, set to a near identical frequency as Mary's. Here, her presence was overpowering. It wasn't just a fog or a pressure or a needling, but all of them at the same time. His head was stuck in a pillow, which was being squeezed by a vice, and happened to be filled with bees.

Flexing his fingers, Vincent tried to slow his breathing. "Maybe when we have the barbeque festival, or Christmas."

"The whole town come out for that?"

"Yup."

"Mm-hm."

In the heavy air, they heard sounds from above. An occasional hammer bang, a power drill, heavy things being dragged and moved.

But no talking. Not a word. Not a whisper. They worked as drones, a hive mind, mindlessly and uniformly carrying out individual parts of a greater task. As terrifying as it was to see, Colt couldn't help but be impressed. Mary was simultaneously controlling hundreds of pairs of hands. She wasn't manipulating the flex of each little tendon, but to have that many people working in perfect sync with one another without any type of communication between them, only their final goal in mind, was truly incredible.

It was also one more reminder of why she had to be stopped.

Now.

Colt headed toward the main entrance. Mary would be well aware they were here. She had countless numbers of eyes watching the perimeter. There was no sneaking in, no alternate entry point, no element of surprise.

"Let's go."

"What are they doing?" Vincent stared the people on the roof.

Colt saw the shapes of the people, made out colors and whether people were male or female, but that's where the detail ended. She wasn't sure if it was the exhaustion, the drugs, or the fact that she'd been ignoring how her eyes weren't what they used to be. Still, she glimpsed movement, someone putting what looked like a series of dark strings on the head of a large man with a beer gut and unkempt muttonchops. The strings hung limply behind the man, wavering in the breeze. Colt couldn't keep track of them or count them, not because of her eyes, but because all of the people to the man's left had identical strings hanging down, interlacing with his.

"They're connecting those people so Mary can use them like an antennae," Colt said.

"But they're not psychic."

"Doesn't matter."

"Why not?"

Colt sighed. "That's why." She pointed to the ground.

Vincent followed her finger and scanned the sidewalk, confused at first. Then, he noticed them. Dozens of spots littered the sidewalk right at the edge of the wall. Some were an oxidized brown, rust-like, while others were a more vibrant red. They were liquid, and upon looking at the wall, it could be seen that they'd come from above, some skittering down the mall's side.

"What..." But he didn't need to finish his question. A fresh drop skidded down the mall's façade in front of him. Vincent followed it up to the man on the roof and saw that the blood had come from his ears. And from the person to his left, and the next person, and the next person, and the next.

It was just like the woman at the hospital; Mary was forcing their brains to activate parts that shouldn't even exist, and their bodies were breaking apart because of it.

"Come on," Colt said flatly.

Vincent was already worked up, on edge. He didn't need her encouragement. If it weren't for the connection they'd made earlier, for the fact that she'd passed some professionalism into him, he'd be charging in full steam.

The main entrance opened into the heart of the building. A massive fountain sat in the center, under a huge skylight with panes of glass cut and arranged like a bulging turtle shell. The fountain itself was easily thirty feet wide with a statue in the center like a cubist painter's nightmare about snakes.

Huge rectangular metal columns bent and twisted around one another, lacing in and out in a lazy braid, rising toward the skylight.

On each side of the pool were the escalators and stairs to the upper level. The upper level walkway wrapped around the entire area, plain white columns sticking down to support it.

Throughout the open spaces were sitting areas, huge potted ferns, kiosks and stands with brightly colored signs and the occasional plastic rocket ship, which, for seventy-five cents, would keep your screaming child quiet for two minutes with a gentle ride to the moon.

The fat sides of the building were the department stores with huge, electrically lit signs glaring at one another.

Or, at least, they would normally have been glaring at one another.

Just like the downtown area, every electronic device had been stripped clean. The blue-collar citizens of Fieldsville had built this mall, so they had all the skills necessary to take it apart.

Walking into the courtyard near the fountain, the only sound Colt and Vincent heard were their own footsteps. Through the large skylight, shadows slipped across the walls as Mary's puppets worked overhead.

They stopped, fifteen yards in from the entrance, and as Colt took the place in, she grew increasing aware that Vincent was a covered pot coming to boil. Standing next to him was like being next to a strong campfire.

"Harden up your wall," she said. "I can't feel anyone in here with us, which means theirs are up."

Vincent didn't reply but did obey. A gossamer sheet of rippled glass wavering across his body, his untempered power somewhat contained. She threw up her own wall and was insulated for what felt like the first time in days.

"Do you know how to get to the roof?"

He shook his head. "No."

"What about staircases, ones that aren't out in the open? Maybe one for emergencies only?"

The muscles beneath his eyes flexed as his mind pulled at memories he had no reason to keep. "Yeah," he said softly. "Yeah!" His sneakers bit into the linoleum flooring, and he burst forward.

"Vincent!"

But it was no good; he was on the move. Before Colt could get a decent gait going, Vincent was skirting through the seating area near the fountain and heading for the escalators.

His heart thrashed in his chest. The sweat on his palms squeaked as he snatched the moving rubber grip of the escalator. He hit the wide upper level, sprinting. Colt grunted her way up the escalator, hands gripping the

238

moving railings. She used a telekinetic push to get her to the top, and a flash of light near the floor caught her eye. It was a blink, an instant where the sun slipping through the tortoiseshell skylight shivered across the thread as thin a cobweb, but as strong a piano wire.

A psychic string set up as a trip wire.

Vincent didn't see it and, when his foot caught, was completely off guard. His entire world shifted ninety degrees, and the floor raced to meet the tip of his nose. At his feet, two psychic spikes zoomed down the string from both ends. They missed him, though, as his sneaker popped off the line just in time. The spikes slammed into each other, snapping the trip line.

Years of experience falling off his bike helped Vincent catch himself. He still landed hard, the unforgiving floor biting into his shoulder and arm. A wave of nausea ran through him as his head popped off the tile. Sparks danced behind his eyelids as he slid almost ten feet before coming to a stop.

Colt shot out her arm. Her telekinetic fingers grabbed the waistline of Vincent's jeans and she yanked him toward her. His skin squealed against the floor.

Four sneakered feet shattered the tile floor with a dull thud and a sharp crack.

Colors squirmed to the corners of Vincent's vision as he lifted his head. His little brother and sister kneeled in the spot where he had been just a second before. The floor around their feet was cracked. They'd used telekinesis to make their heels as heavy as sledgehammers.

At the top of the escalator, Colt breathed slow and heavy. She'd only glimpsed the twins before they'd leaped. It wasn't just their feet that had a telekinetic sheathe, it was their whole bodies. Their speed was unnatural, and the control they demonstrated was way beyond what they'd exhibited in the alleyway the other night. However, Colt didn't have to wonder why; she'd seen Mary do it to a puppet before.

Vincent scrambled to his feet. . The twins rose in perfect unison. Colt and Vincent saw the bloodshot streaks and the broken capillaries that mottled the skin around their eyes. Their veins pumped visibly. As bad as it looked, Colt suspected . their brains hadn't been damaged yet, so there wouldn't be any long term effects.

Still, it must have hurt like hell.

Vincent wavered, his mouth opening with questions and concerns that he couldn't speak. Instead, he sent out his tendrils.

There was no trace of anything inside of them. The voices, the itsy bitsy ones that normally called out from the near bottomless pits Mary dug within people, were silent.

They were gone.

Which meant only Mary remained.

239

Snarling, Vincent fired a spike that cracked like baseball bat. The air wavered as it tore across the floor. The twins didn't move, but in front of them there was a shiver.

No, two shivers.

Their walls formed and combined. Vincent's spike landed squarely against them, and though there was some give, the walls remained intact.

Shock crossed Vincent's face. He stepped back, composed himself, buckled down, and prepared to fire again.

"Vincent," said the girl.

"You really should save your energy." finished the boy. They spoke with Mary's inflections. "You still have a long way to go."

Vincent stood straight, his nose wrinkling in anger. "I'm going to the roof, even if I have to go through you."

"Aw," said the girl, her head lilting to the side. The expression on her face was cartoonish, exaggerated and bizarre. She was simply imitating real emotion, real hurt. "Is that any way—"

"—to treat your little brother—"

"—and dear sister?"

Vincent's fists clenched. "Knock it off."

"What's wrong?" said the boy.

"Don't you love us anymore—"

"—big brother?"

Vincent snarled, "Knock it off!"

"Would you really—" said the boy.

"—be so mean—"

"—as to hurt us? After all—"

"—we are family."

Vincent stamped his foot and shouted, "Stop fucking around, Mary!" His words pinged off the walls and echoed throughout the cavernous space. The twin's faces dropped the doll masks. Mary's condescension shone through.

Vincent wiped a droplet of spittle from his mouth. "I'm going to go up there and get Mom, and you're not going to stop me."

The twins sneered, raised their chins, and said in unison, "What makes you think she's on the roof?"

Vincent hesitated for only a second. "Because." His eyes softened. "She means as much to you as she does to me. You won't leave her."

The twins' twisted smiles grew wider. "And what makes you think," they spoke together, "I'm on the roof?"

A tiny tremble rippled across Vincent's body.

"Because I..." Vincent stammered. "I can feel you up there."

The twins shook their heads. "You felt what I wanted you to feel."

Colt's lips pressed together. *Dammit.*

"Why do you think I gathered all those people on the roof?" the twins asked.

Vincent voice shook. "Where is she?" he asked with thin breath. "Where's Mom?"

The twins paused. Their snake-like grins widened farther. "At the house, with me."

Vincent shook his head. "You're lying."

"I'm not."

"You are!"

Colt's voice cut through the air. "She's not." Stepping forward, she reached up and began gathering loose hairs, securing them as best she could. "She wants to separate us. I guess us taking out the sheriff and those other puppets must have made you a little nervous, huh Mary?"

The grins on their faces slithered away.

"So far, the two of us have whipped your ass twice. Three times if you count me smacking you around at the loading docks."

Mary's anger seeped into the twin's faces.

"So you figured the best way to deal with us was a good old-fashioned divide and conquer." Colt walked past Vincent, never taking the twins out of her sight. When she was a good five paces in front of him, she stopped.

"Go on," she said.

Vincent's eyebrows came together. "But—"

"I said, go." Still, she didn't turn back. "Get to the house, save your mom. I'll handle everything here, I promise."

No one moved.

Without a word, Vincent took off. His sneakers squeaked as he headed to the escalator, then thumped as he made his way down. Colt stayed motionless, her eyes glued to the twins. Not because she was afraid they would attack, but because, if she looked back to Vincent, if she watched him go, they would see the expression on her face and know.

Know that she was so scared for him right now.

The mall fell silent as Vincent ran through the front doors. It was just her and the twins.

"Do you think it was smart, letting him go?" the boy asked.

Colt forced a smirk. "I've kicked your asses before, and that was when you had Vincent helping. I think the odds are slightly in my favor."

The twins' mouths twisted into thin, canine grins as the girl said, "Oh Agent Colt, the odds were always against you."

CHAPTER FIFTY-EIGHT

There isn't a sound like it in the world, except for what it is: a thousand pairs of feet all moving in unison. Colt. saw the shadows through the skylight, the twisting mass of bodies moving across the roof.

To the stairs.

Coming for her.

Hands curling into fists, Colt turned back to the twins. They stood, laughter at the tips of their tongues as the sound moved from above to the walls behind them. The stairwell doors, one at each corner, shook in their frames before bursting open and vomiting frantic flailing bodies. Arms and legs and torsos slapping against one another, people erupted out, pushing and shoving each other, clawing their way forward, their eyes burning with hate and bile and their minds brimming over with one simple thought: KILL.

Her hands went up, fingers pointed, revolvers racing to life. She had a chance to take out the twins before the crowd reached her. The boy and girl didn't move; they blurred like wiped chalk on a board and vanished. Colt's eyes went wide, but only for a moment.

Fine. Let them run. She'd deal with them next.

Her hands swung out toward the rushing mobs. Her shots came out hard and fast, shaped like arrowheads and aimed low—at the knees. She hoped to drop the first few and block up the doorways. Unfortunately, it only half worked. The first puppets through fell, men and women and even children among them, and were immediately trampled. To Colt, it looked like a swarm, an ant's nest emptying wildly. There were no voices, no screams or cries or calls, just the pounding of their bodies as they drove toward her.

She kept shooting and took out as many as she could, but the swarm didn't stop. They poured through the doorways, swerving like a flock of birds, and came together in the middle of the floor. Charging forward, they tore at the kiosks and banners and plants that stood in their way.

Colt snarled. Her shirt flared out as she spun and ran. Her legs, already tired, jetted forward. A telekinetic sheath wrapped her lower body, focusing on her left leg. . She needed to get to the lower level. Passing the stairs, she ran toward the upper level's metal railing and slapped her hands down.

Nothing like the direct route.

She sailed over the edge and floated to the level below, rolling when she came down in the middle of a group of tables. She felt a sharp jab in her leg from the fall, but it was worth it. The puppets would bottleneck on the stairs, and by the time they reached the lower level, she would be out the front door.

Grabbing the edge of a table, she lifted herself and started jogging. A gust of air slapped her back as something crashed into the ground behind her. Startled, Colt turned in time to see a second body slam into the ground, blood splattering with a thick, wet slapping noise. Then a third, and a fourth and a fifth and more and more.

The puppets weren't just chasing her, they were following her exactly. Above, hundreds of people pressed against the metal and glass railing, throwing themselves over like fleshy projectiles. Colt's jaw dropped. This wasn't like the police officers at the hotel. This wasn't the twins or the coma patient. These people were no longer thinking, acting beings. They were mindless. They were soulless. They were crazed animals.

No, even animals put their own wellbeing before anything else.

These were goddamn zombies.

Colt scampered back. With a wrenching sound, the railing above bent and cracked under the weight of the swarm. Metal and glass and bodies came tumbling down, a waterfall of flesh and clothing. The first ones landed with dull thunks and the cracks of broken bones, but as they piled up, others pulled themselves from off the dead and surged forward.

From the back of Colt's mind, a strong hand gripped the nail of fear, which held her in place, and yanked it out. She turned and ran. The floor shook from the falling bodies. Cutting through the tables, she headed for the fountain and the swarm followed.

Hopping up, she ran around the narrow concrete edge of the circular pool, using telekinesis to help keep her balance. Behind her, people fell in, splashing wildly, falling atop one another and gumming up the works. Colt didn't look back, didn't want to see people drowning as others used them like stepping stones to get across the pool.

Putting everything she had into her legs, she flew by the escalators and stands. She wove between as many obstacles as she could, heading for the back wall. The puppets followed, crashing into everything along the way. Colt was amazed that they were able to keep up and suspected that many of them were tearing muscles in their mad pursuit. She heard them gasping, panting for air.

Or was that her?

She couldn't think about that. Lungs didn't matter. Sweat running down her face didn't matter. The aching pain in her legs, in her left knee, didn't matter. The dryness of her throat and the stinging in her feet and the hot friction she felt as her denim-covered thighs rubbed together didn't matter. The puppets didn't care about those things, and neither could she. She had to be as focused on escaping from them as they were on capturing her.

243

She zipped by the last kiosk, and the floor space opened. The back wall was a series of advertisements, but to her left and right were the entrances of department stores.

Colt headed in. The walls became a series of soft pink shelves and cubbies. Racks were everywhere, filled with blouses and summer dresses too short for anyone professional to wear. She dashed between the racks, which were arranged like alternating squares on a chessboard, and though it slowed her down, Colt knew it would drag the swarm to a near stop.

Right on cue, there was a tremendous crash behind her of a hundred bodies. And then another hundred behind them. And then another hundred behind them. She peeked over her shoulder, and it looked as though the undulating mass of Mary's puppets was extending a tentacle forward, stretching itself thin to try and snatch her up.

When she passed the last of the clothing racks, she saw exactly what she'd expected—a single up escalator near the back wall of the store, humming softly. Colt gave herself a little extra speed. The swarm, still piling over the falling racks of clothes and crushing one another thoughtlessly, fell even farther behind.

She was up the escalator in five huge bounds. Shoes squealing, her heels planted and she stopped to scan the second level, mapping the most direct route to the exit. Below her, the escalator's metal steps reverberated with the sound of pounding feet. The fastest of the swarm was a teenage girl. She was blonde, athletic build, and had tremendously defined leg muscles that stuck out from beneath track shorts. Her shirt bore the name of the local high school. The girl had kept up with Colt's telekinetic dash and was easily twenty yards ahead of the next person. She was fast enough that she probably had a career ahead of her. Her speed would get her a college scholarship, easily. There may even be medals hanging from the girl's neck in the future.

But right now the only thing swaying back and forth was a thick strand of drool that hung from the girl's open mouth, showing teeth barred like fangs. Though her legs pumped with smooth muscle memory, her arms clawed at the escalator's handrails. Her cheeks puffed as she snarled and spat Mary's hatred that overflowed her mind and filled her with nothing but the desire to kill.

KILL.

KILL.

The girl leaped to the top of the steps, her hand outstretched like a swooping predator's claw.

Colt sighed. "I'm sorry."

The telekinetic energy Colt had wrapped around her legs whipped up like smoke pulled by a vacuum, condensed in her hand, and manifested as her revolver. The shot went off with a deafening thump. It was wide and flat and hit the girl square in the chest, lifting her from the ground and throwing her back. Had the shot not shattered her ribs, the escalator's jagged teeth would have done it anyway.

The girl's body fell down the upward moving stairs like a sewn doll tossed by a tantrum-throwing child. Limbs flailed in directions they were not meant to, and the girl's body bent and twisted under its own weight. She hit the bottom as the next puppet, a fit man in his twenties, reached the first step. His feet tangled with her rolling form, and he collapsed over her. He reached out for purchase, tried to pull himself to a standing position, but feet came down on his back as the next puppet leaped over him, pressing his skull into the escalator's steps so hard that the skin split and blood poured out.

Colt took a slow breath, her finger shaking as she watched the puppets clamor over one another. The tentacle was reaching the bottom of the steps, and they were finally rubbernecking.

But it wasn't enough.

A teenage boy, his hair dyed half black and half green, piercings in his ears, lips and nose, used his skinny legs to get over the heap of people and climbed the stairs on all fours. His eyes, empty and void, stared down Colt's finger with no recognition of fear or concern.

Holding the air in her lungs, Colt's hand stopped shaking. There was a bang and the pierced teen rocked up, arched his back, and tumbled down the stairs; the puppets behind him did not try and arrest his fall, but simply shoved him to the side, smashing him against the railing. Colt gathered her strength and let off two shots that punched holes in the knees of the next puppets and sent blood spraying out behind them across the faces of the swarm trying to climb the stairs.

Beneath her feet, Colt felt the motor of the escalator straining against the weight of the jammed up bodies. The rubber handrails jerked backward as dozens of hands grasped at it, pulling themselves forward. She took that as a sign that it was time to move. The swarm wasn't stopped, but it was slowed.

Her legs pumped, but under their own strength this time. Her gait was lopsided—the brace on her left knee was harder to move without the telekinesis. As she cut around the last of the clothes racks before the wide opening back into the mall's second level, the swarm reached the top of the escalator. They surged forward, their bodies moving together, slipping over and around one another.

Approaching the exit, Colt fired a shot, rolled into a thin cone with a point as sharp as a needle, into a metal faceplate that sat just inside the

245

department store's doorway. From the top of the opening, the rolling security door, which Colt's shot had just unlocked, slipped down an inch.

Racks of clothes toppled as the swarm gushed forward. A table covered in neatly folded neckties was crushed beneath their weight. Colt heard their breathing, their gasping, the squeaking of their sweaty fingers clutching at the ground and pulling them forward.

Putting her telekinesis back into her legs, Colt pumped hard and leaped into the air. The swarm came around the corner of the dress shirts, knocking racks to the ground. Colt's fingers grasped the bottom of the security gate and the wheels inside the walls spun.

The slatted steel gate dropped quickly. The swarm drove for her, their mouths opening and their teeth gnashing. Colt's back hit the floor. The swarm reached out. Slipping her hands away, the gate connected with the floor. They were so close, she felt their breath, their hot writhing tongues.

Reaching up, her psychic fingers stretched out, working their way into the keyhole that locked the gate to the ground. Metal screeched and shivered as the swarm slammed into the gate, bending it and filling the mall with the sound of shuddering steel. Colt pulled back but kept her telekinetic tendrils inside the lock. The gate rose from the ground an inch and Colt, on hands and knees, leaped forward. She grabbed at the gate and pulled down with body and mind. The edge dropped. Fingers like claws reached through the gate. They scratched her face, tore at her eyes. She felt teeth cut through her fingers and the hot saliva of other people splashing across her skin. Opening her mouth to scream, her mind worked into the keyhole and, finding the right angle, snapped it into the locked position. She pulled away from the gate and collapsed to the floor.

The swarm continued to amass, pushing and shoving against the metal barrier. The gate bulged, stretched, and groaned, but Colt felt that it would hold. The swarm wasn't as big as it had been. So many of them had been crushed and drowned, smashed beneath the feet of those whom they had lived with, spent their lives with, grown up and old with. Even now, the ones at the front of the gate were twitching, their eyes rolling up as the others behind them pushed forward, squeezing the air from their lungs and life from their bodies.

On her back, Colt shivered. Adrenaline flooded her veins like boiling water, but her muscles were depleted of strength. Her hands, the fingers torn and bloody, curled up just beneath her chin, squeezing one another in an attempt to hide the pain and staunch the bleeding. It was a good thing too, because had her hands not been there, the psychic thread that whipped down under her jaw would surely have caught her neck.

CHAPTER FIFTY-NINE

She felt it an instant before it tightened. The thread went taut. Pain seared the skin on her hands and the sides of her neck. She kicked out. The thread yanked her backward, away from the gate. She tried to roll, which was the worst possible thing to do. She was being dragged across the floor so fast that she thought a car was pulling her.

Eyes squeezed shut, she couldn't see that ahead, at the ends of the thread, the twins were rocketing forward, their bodies propelled by telekinesis. They leaped, moving as though they were speed skating across the ground, and pulled Colt toward the stairs.

She rolled again, trying to get onto her back, but the ground fell away. She hovered, then crashed. Concrete edges bit into her, and if she'd had the breath, she would have screamed.

The twins stopped at the bottom of the stairs and, as Colt tumbled toward them, drew in the thread like fishermen reeling in a fighting catch. They used the momentum to throw Colt through the air. The thread dissolved. She soared and came down in the reflecting pool. Hitting the icy water, she gasped and choked. . Disoriented, Colt flailed wildly. Her clothes were like a net, dragging her toward the bottom.

When her knees struck, she planted her hands against the pool's rough floor and broke the surface, coughing and seizing for air. She wretched, her stomach and lungs emptying the water they had taken in. Fiery pain flashed through her upper torso. On the inside, her body was on fire. On the outside, she was freezing. Her head was spinning, and the only thing keeping her from collapsing was the knowledge that, if she did, she'd drown.

She rose. Threads sliced into her wrists, jerking her from the water and into the air.

Metal clanged, low and dull, as her body slammed into the modern art statue in the middle of the pool. The threads pulled her arms out to the sides. Her eyes opening into slits, Colt watched as the twins darted around, zipping across the statue like squirrels chasing each other around the trunk of a tree. Another line lashed her leg into place. Another crossed her chest. More and more of the threads wrapped around her limbs and body, squeezing her against the metal statue. Colt grunted and pulled, trying to free herself. Another went around her arm, then two more on the other side. They were seemingly random, connecting in bizarre and asymmetrical places.

She grit her teeth, ready for the psychic spike that would turn her brain into a smoothie. But when the movement around her stopped and the spike never came, she coughed and looked around.

Her feet, tied to the statue at the ankles, were just above the water's surface. At the edge of the pool, statuesque on the skinny concrete lip, the twins stood. Arms hanging loosely, chins held high, they mirrored each other perfectly.

Opening her mouth to say something, to try and get a rise from the twins and their master, Colt could only cough and sputter. Squinting through the pain, she felt that their walls were down. Maybe making the threads had taken too much psychic energy out of them. Maybe Mary had just gotten cocky. It didn't matter. Taking a chance, probably the last chance she would get, Colt summoned a spike and fired it off.

The threads holding her hummed like plucked guitar strings. It was fast, so fast she couldn't completely follow it, but the thread on her chest hummed, then the vibration flew into her arm, carrying her own spike back to her.

She cried out through a ravaged throat as her mind was hammered with its own energies. A rainbow of colors flew into her eyes, dragging behind them tails of black that washed over her vision. Her body shivered and shook, then went limp.

They'd used the threads to reroute her own psychic attacks back at her.

Colt's ears filled with the sound of TV static, and a gentle tingling grew beneath the skin of her nose, spreading across her cheeks and behind her eyes. She was drifting into unconsciousness and didn't have the strength to fight it. The darkness rolled in.

The sound was tiny, a plip of kids' rubber soles slapping tile, but to Colt it was like a slap across the face. Her eyes opened into slits, groaned, and rolled her head. The muscles in her neck creaked like hemp rope as they bent, but the pain was just another call to wake up.

She wasn't done. She wasn't finished. If she could move, if she could breathe, if she could think, she could fight. She'd lived through the desert. She'd lived through her father's madness. She'd lived through hell, and she was going to live through this.

Below, the twins moved away from the pool. They stopped, facing each other. Hands curled into fists, Colt pulled against the threads. They bit into her flesh, but that was okay; the pain reminded her she was still alive. Closing her eyes, she took the tiniest bit of psychic energy she could and sent it zooming away through the thread on her right hand. Her mind followed it, and when it came back to her left leg, she caught it. Colt sent another pulse through the threads, this time coming from her left arm and sending it to her chest.

The twins' shifted their back feet so the toes almost touched. Their knees bent and their hands hovered around each other, as though they were gripping an invisible tennis ball between them.

Colt sent out two pulses—right leg to neck and left shoulder to left hip.

In the space between the twins' hands, the air shimmered. Colt's eyes widened. The twins were combining their spikes, just like they'd done with their walls, and building one massive blast. But there was something else— they were pouring telekinetic energy into it as well. Colt's nostrils flared. They were trying to copy her psychic bullets. It wasn't perfect, but it didn't really matter, did it? With their combined energy, it would be more than enough to both fry her brain and crush her body.

The space between their hands grew to a softball.

Looking up, Colt checked her hands. The right was higher than the left by a few inches. Hopefully, that would be just enough.

She pushed up against the thread with her right hand and pointed her left index finger. There wasn't time to make anything of serious power, so her gun was there and gone, the blink of an eye. The shot went off. Sparks flew from the statue and a cry flew from her lips as the bullet cut both the thread and the back of her hand.

Her weight shifted and her whole body lopped to one side. Colt gasped and pulled her freed arm against her chest, but when she heard the humming, the vibrations in the air of the twins' attack building, she forgot the pain.

They had a basketball between their hands now. The kinetic energy pulsed and rolled like a cloud made of heat. The girl's sandy hair fluttered. Their clothes rippled in the breeze. Their eyes, windows into Mary's twisted soul, came up. Colt took a deep breath and raised her hand.

Finger out.

Right at the twins.

In her palm, the revolver appeared. It was thin and weak, but quickly condensing. At the tip of the barrel, a miniature missile head of kinetic energy built.

She watched them for the moment when they pumped their arms to drive the huge swirling mass of psychic energy forward like a cannonball.

Colt's muscles tightened. She snapped her jaw shut, knowing the pain that was coming. She reached into her mind, tore through all of the locks she'd put up to protect herself from herself, and threw open every door there was. It was like injecting kerosene into her brain. The veins around her eyes bulged against the skin. Her ears roared as blood ran into them, then out of them. The back of her throat was washed with the salty taste of cerebrospinal fluid. Her vision turned psychedelic, colors lighting up and flaring in her eyes. But when she reached in, she came back up with what she needed.

Raw power.

Spikes, half a dozen of them, flew out into the lines. The threads vibrated so fast they cut into the metal statue like bandsaw blades. Just like before, the spikes left and in the milliseconds before they returned, Colt did the craziest thing she could possibly think of.

She dropped her guard. Completely and utterly. Instead of defending herself from the psychic bolts, she opened up every pathway she could, and when the spikes hit, she routed them all to one place.

Her gun.

And there, between the fingers, it became. Every atom of it, every knick in the wooden handle, every ounce of weight, every millimeter of cool steel; she felt it all. It was real. It was the gun that had killed her father but had saved her life. And now, it would save so many more.

The twins' attack split the pool's water. Colt pulled the trigger with a concussive boom.

Outside the mall, the calm air abruptly filled with shattering windows. The white walls shivered. The ground shook. Hundreds of car alarms went off. The mall's front door flew through the air, smashing into Colt's Hyundai hard enough to leave four feet of black rubber scraped across the asphalt. Dust rolled like smoke from the glassless skylight. The machine Mary's drones had constructed atop the building collapsed, large pieces dropping and breaking into dozens of smaller ones. As the shards of the skylight rained down over the parking lot, silence filled the air once again.

From not too far away, down at the edge of the horizon where the highway shrunk into a needle-thin point, sirens wailed. A caravan of SUVs and customized vans, all lined up like a thick, black, metallic centipede, raced toward Fieldsville. Every driver wore a dark flak jacket with the white letters "DSI" sewn across their left front pocket.

CHAPTER SIXTY

He'd expected something; an ambush, a barricade, a local hunter to pick him off from the woods that lined the back roads he raced down, a hundred pickup trucks zigzagging across the asphalt trying to flatten him. Anything.

But there was nothing. No one. Leaving the mall, grabbing the first bike on the rack that fit him, heading across the highway and town, through the alleyways and into the residential areas, Vincent didn't see one person. Fieldsville was empty, devoid of life. It was a shell of a town. Mary had hollowed it out, just like she'd done to their brother and sister. Just like she did to everything.

Vincent peddled harder.

When he turned into the gravel driveway, he felt it; a cloud, a drifting psychic mist which clung to the crumbling house, working its way through the cracks and crags. In Vincent's eyes, the whole house pulsed, beating like a giant's heart. He swore the chipped and peeling walls bent as the house breathed the mist in and out. With a blink, the image left his eyes. He saw the cluttered porch, the stairs sloping one way and the columns tilting the other, the windows so dirty you couldn't see through them, the layer of dust covering the home's siding.

It could fall at any minute.

A numbness crept over him. Not fear or anger or despair, not courage or joy or hope. He didn't know it, didn't have a name for it. His hand hovered over the knob to the house's side door, but he felt like he was a mile away, watching it all through a telescope.

He wondered if this was how Colt felt all the time. Did she see the world from a distance? As a picture? In blacks and whites, rights and wrongs, justice and terror? Would she feel like a stranger, walking into the place she had called home for so many years?

Before he even passed the threshold, he heard it. Humming. Her humming. It came through, pushing past the distance in his heart and pulling him in, pulling him back to where he was. To who he was.

The hesitation was gone so fast it was as though he'd never felt it. His mom was here. She was alive. She was waiting for him.

His feet darted out, and he was sprinting past the stairs, grabbing the railing and swinging into the hallway. He bounded forward, a huge smile spreading across his face. He didn't notice how the hallway, the den, the living room were all dark; shades drawn and lights off. No video games being played. No movement. Just empty.

Hollow.

At the end of the hall, a soft golden glow came from the kitchen doorway. The floorboards cried warnings as he ran forward. Paintings and photos rattled against the walls, telling him to turn around.

But he could not hear them, not over the humming.

"Mom!" he shouted as he rounded the doorway.

A sledgehammer of skin and bone crashed into his chest and folded him like a blanket. His insides felt as though they'd been shoved into all the wrong places. He tried to gasp, to scream or yelp from the pain, but there was no air for it. Tears welled in his eyes as he dropped, landing face down on the worn floorboards. His ears filled with the rushing of his own blood, but he still heard humming across the room. It didn't stop, didn't waver.

Vincent started to push himself up. Hands snatched sharply at the shirt on his back and flung him across the kitchen. The cupboards smacked and cracked when he hit them. Pots and pans rattled inside. Things from the countertop, dishes and spoons and a saltshaker, jumped and fell on top of him. Vincent's legs kicked wildly. He opened his mouth once, twice, again and again desperately seeking to fill his lungs.

Even with all the noise, he could still hear his mom's humming. But if she was there, why wasn't she helping him? What was she doing?

Footsteps came close. He rolled onto his back. His fist tightened. The psychic energy, the hot, cutting power rushed down his arm. He opened his eyes, ready to strike whatever puppet Mary had set against him.

He knew the shape, the outline, instantly. How could he not? He'd seen it every night for as long as he could remember, standing over his bed, bending down and kissing his face and wishing him sweet dreams.

His mom's hands clamped down; one onto the front of his shirt, the other grabbing his hair so tightly that nails dug at his scalp. She grunted and pulled Vincent up, just to throw him again. He crashed against the counter, sending glasses and plates tumbling to the floor in a cacophony of sharp noises.

He started to fall, but his mom pulled him back and launched him through the air. He landed up on the counter, hitting the wall so hard the entire room shook. His back straightened and air rushed into his burning, aching lungs. He gasped and squeezed his eyes, trying to push the tears away.

His mom stood in the middle of the kitchen. In the sunlight that poured through the windows, dust danced in the air around her. It should have looked magical, but his mother's stillness was haunting. Her chest rose and fell slowly, steadily, as though set by a metronome.

Like someone else was telling her when to breathe.

"Mo—" he reached out with a shaking hand, but the movement sent him rolling off the edge of the counter and dropping to the floor.

Panic flooded his brain. He didn't, couldn't understand what was happening.

He dragged his knees beneath him, getting halfway to a sitting position, and gasped a desperate cry.

"Mom!"

She just kept humming. And eventually, it dawned on Vincent.

The humming wasn't coming from her.

Instead, it echoed from the dark doorway of the mudroom. It was his mom's song, her nameless, lilting tune, but it was wrong. It was fake. A copy. It was as cold as the shadows that surrounded it.

Come out. Vincent growled inside. *Come out!*

As Mary stepped into the light of the kitchen, the heat and anger beneath Vincent's skin evaporated. He pulled back, his eyes growing wide.

Thick veins pulsed and slithered beneath Mary's skin, not just on her face, but around her whole head and down her neck. A sheen of sweat glistened on her in the sunlight. The collar of her shirt was stained with the blood that had been running from her ears and eyes. Her expression, usually impassive, was tense. Her lips were drawn thin as knife edges. Her breathing was long and slow, too long and slow. She was trying to maintain control. Over herself or over others, Vincent wasn't sure.

But in spite of all of that, it was her eyes that made Vincent's skin go cold. They were painted with bloodshot so thick that there was no white left to see. In the middle, her irises spun like lazy waterwheels, glowing sickly green.

"Do you see?" Mary spoke softly, her voice teetering on edge. "You made me." She could barely control her own tongue, but she managed to point one trembling finger at their mom. "You did this to her."

Before he could stop himself, before he could even think, Vincent's nails bit into the worn floor, and he launched forward. His arm swung back, the psychic energy racing to his fist, ready for Mary.

Their mom's hand clamped around his throat, arresting his motion entirely. She was strong, stronger than any person her size had the right to be. Inside her body, muscles were ripping and tearing themselves. He grabbed her arm, tried to break her grasp. He may as well of been trying to bend stone.

Gasping and sputtering, he closed his eyes and yanked and pushed and squirmed. Her other hand broke through his flailing and locked around his neck. Together, the hands squeezed.

Vincent swung again and again at her, but half-heartedly. He wanted to call out to her, to beg her to stop, but the air in his lungs couldn't get out. The air outside couldn't get in. She was choking him.

She was killing him.

Panic raced through his mind. His heart pounded. His fingers tingled. The swelling, the power inside of him filled every inch. He pushed it back. She was too close. He couldn't control it yet. Her fingers twisted so tight he thought the skin of his neck was tearing. The power rushed up. He struggled to keep it down, but he couldn't fight both it and her. He needed to breathe. He needed...

Mom! He tried to push the thought into her, tried to reach in with his mind. *Mom, please! Please! I can't... I can't stop it!*

She pulled him closer. Her forehead came down, touching his. For a second, the pain his body felt evaporated. The world went quiet. His eyes opened, and through swimming splotches of color, he saw her face.

She was crying.

Mom...

She blinked, once, slowly, and gazed into his eyes. *It's okay.*

But...

I love you, Vincent.

Her eyes went flat. Her hands wrenched into him. His body kicked, and his arms swung through the air. There was a crack like localized thunder, air being split, the world being torn. The grip on his throat eased just enough that he dropped, folded up on top of limp legs. He fell backward. The cabinet doors were cold as a spring pond against his back. For a second, he simply sat, trying to both breathe out and in at the same time.

"Mom?" Mary's voice didn't just sound far away; it sounded like it was coming through time. It was a voice from long ago, so long that Vincent couldn't even remember ever hearing it. It was the voice of a child, a scared little child.

"Mommy?"

He opened his eyes. The tears had stopped falling from his mom's eyes. Her face was placid, peaceful. Her hands, which had moments before been so tight around his neck, hovered delicately over the deep, gushing wound across her chest.

Through the pain, Vincent sprang up, hands outstretched. But even as he rose, she fell. Not collapsing, not crashing to the floor, but drifting down like an autumn leaf. She fell with nothing more than a whisper.

Everything stopped; the fear, the panic, the thumping of his heart, the ringing in his ears, the shivering world around him, the pain in his throat; it all stopped.

Movement caught his eye. Mary. She was shaking, trembling. The crunched lines of hate and anger were gone from her face. Her eyes were wide, staring at their mother on the floor in disbelief. When she looked up, into Vincent's eyes, he saw a child who had only just realized that there was life beyond their own.

Vincent? Her voice rang in his mind.

It rushed up, lava that had sat dormant for ten thousand years, brewing with pressure building and building into an explosion that could rattle the Earth and shake the sky.

His mouth opened. Even though his lungs ached, he screamed. There was a thunderclap inside the house. Every window cracked, every wall shivered as a psychic blade flew out from his body, slicing through wood, the steel, the drywall and plaster, through wires and pipes and walls and doors and anything else.

He roared, head back and arms out. The walls, the ceiling, the floor all exploded with gashes and cuts. A hurricane rushed about them, the psychic blades slicing through the air, through the house, through every thread that Mary had ever spun.

Screaming, Mary dropped to the floor as, around them, the house finally came crashing down.

CHAPTER SIXTY-ONE

"Agent Colt?"

"Uhhhhgggghhhh."

"Agent Colt, can you hear me?"

"Stop yelling at me, or I will kill you."

The EMT pulled away from Colt's gurney. Her eyes fluttered open. Well, the right one did. Her left eye was swollen shut. She saw the white ceiling and the walls covered with diodes and nozzles and hanging gear. A bag of clear fluids hung above her head, and a tube ran down to what she assumed was her arm. She wasn't sure how much of her clothing had been removed, but she felt the fleece blanket when she wiggled her bare feet. At least she wasn't paralyzed.

Everything around her was rocking back and forth. It took her a moment to realize it was actually her head waving from side to side, which meant the ambulance was already on the move. Beside her, the EMT, a young man, was staring at her, trepidation stretched across his face.

On the front of his jacket, "DSI" was written. Closing her eyes, she smiled as much as her sore face would allow. If the DSI was there, it could only mean one thing.

Good job, Rakesh.

She took a deep breath and immediately realized it was mistake. She coughed and sputtered. Her ribs lit up like someone had poured gasoline on them and dropped a match. She tried to sit up, but that was a much bigger mistake.

"Lie still, please," the EMT said. He reached out to help her down, but hesitated, which was probably the right thing to do.

Colt flopped back down. She growled and groaned and tried to slow her breathing. Whatever drugs they'd given her already, they weren't nearly enough. The EMT adjusted her blanket and fussed with the I.V. When Colt's breathing came under control, she spoke.

"Are we still in Fieldsville?"

The EMT nodded. "What the hell happened in there? It looked like a bomb went off."

Colt closed her eyes. "Which way are we going?"

"Sorry?"

A frown grew on her lips. "Which way?"

"Uh…" The EMT glanced up to the front of the ambulance. "I… West. We're headed west."

"Turn around."

"Excuse me?"

"I said, turn around."

"But—"

Colt's arm came out from under the blanket, finger pointed directly at the EMT's face. "I'm not gonna say it again."

The EMT swallowed once, hard, and nodded. Leaning to the side, he spoke to the driver. There was a moment of debate before the ambulance slowed, swung around, and started back the other way.

Returning to his seat, the EMT gazed at Colt's raised hand.

"Good," she said, relaxing her arm. "Now, what other drugs you got?"

CHAPTER SIXTY-TWO

It took her over a minute just to get out of the ambulance. The EMT had to help her down, and begrudgingly, she let him. They'd fished her wet shoes out of a bag, and as she touched down on the ground, they squished loudly.

Colt curled her lip against the cold, unpleasant sensation. Her left leg was completely locked up in a brace. She couldn't even bend her knee. Thanks to the fact that the only clothing she had on was a hospital gown, she became quickly that a gentle breeze was brushing up against her butt cheeks.

Reaching back, she yanked the blanket down from the gurney and wrapped it around her shoulders. Just the effort of getting to the ground had winded her, so she sat for a second on the edge of the ambulance's opened back doors and looked out over the scene.

DSI cars, black and shining like they'd just been waxed, were everywhere. People were milling about, some taking photos, some carrying guns, others pushing aside or examining the rubble.

The rubble that had been Vincent's house.

The dormer windows, which stuck out on all four sides of the roof, were still intact, but now they leaned up and back, almost touching one another. The house had literally caved in on itself. The second floor was still in big pieces, but the entire first floor had been crushed.

Colt's face grew somber. Pursing her lips, she pulled the blanket firmly around her shoulders and stood. Instantly, she fell forward, her left leg completely unable to take weight. The EMT grabbed at her shoulders.

"Hang on, hang on!" he said.

Colt wanted to turn around and spike him so hard he wouldn't wake up until Christmas, but she decided that he'd be more useful conscious. He jumped back into the ambulance and, reaching down, held out a pair of crutches. She snatched one from his hand, shoved it beneath her left arm, and hobbled off.

The agent who had briefed her when she'd arrived, a heavy-set man who was barely taller than Colt and had a bad comb-over, was coming around the perimeter of the house. Colt flagged him down.

"Where?" she asked between two small huffs. The agent turned and pointed to a large military medical tent that had been set up in the yard.

There were machines lining the walls, all of them just the right height to stand under the edge where the walls turned to ceiling. Each machine had a different set of readouts, which Colt couldn't understand. There was lots of beeping and booping and wires running every which way. Walking inside the tent's white walls, she felt as though she were walking into an operating room.

In the middle, with a group of white-gowned technicians puttering around it, lay a single bed.

Colt stopped in the tent's doorway.

His hair was a mess, pushed aside so they could bandage the cuts on his scalp. Bandages, dozens and dozens of them, covered the tiny nicks and scratches, which went up and down his arms and across his face. His skin was pale, paler than normal, and for a moment, he lay so still that Colt felt a stab of fear in her chest.

His green eyes opened. The fear dissolved, and Colt felt like smiling. But Vincent didn't grin, didn't smile or smirk, so neither did she.

"Out," she said to the room.

The technicians froze what they were doing. They looked at her, then to each other, then back to her.

Colt growled. "Now."

With the tent clear, she pulled a chair up next to Vincent's bed. He watched her, looked at her swollen face and her beaten body, saw how her hands gripped everything around just to keep her from falling, but did not say a word. Instead, they sat in silence a long time. She knew he would have a million what-ifs and why-didn't-I's. He would look back and relive it again and again without it ever changing or growing easier. He could never back.

He could only forward.

"They told me how they found you," Colt said, her voice delicate but still professional. "Your ability saved you, sliced everything that came near you to tiny bits until the house settled. Though, I suspect that was by accident." She paused and stared at Vincent. He did not meet her gaze.

"What happened at the mall?" he asked flatly.

Colt let out a small sigh. "There was an explosion, caused by me and the twins. It trashed the building."

"What about the people?" Vincent asked, still looking away. "The ones on the roof."

"Some... some of them didn't make it."

Vincent's eyes closed, and as he started to turn away, she leaned forward.

"But," she said softly, "some of them did. They're fine now, completely normal."

Vincent looked at her. A tiny smile, one of appreciation, not of happiness, came across his face. It faded quickly. "My brother and sister?"

Colt's lips pulled in. She sat back. Vincent's eyes grew wide. Against the wall, one of the beeping machines quickened in pace. Colt took a deep breath.

"DSI actually saw the explosion from a distance. There were a lot of people running around who were confused and scared, but they managed to wrangle them up and get everyone treated. They found me in the fountain, pulled me out, and got me into this fancy getup you see here." She tried to smile but couldn't even manage a fake one. "They identified all the bodies in the mall, Vincent, as well as the people who'd been inside. Your brother and sister weren't among them."

"So," he said between quick breaths. "They... they could be out there, yeah? And if everyone is... is back to normal than maybe they—"

"Vincent," Colt said, and now it was her turn to look down. She'd felt it, felt the hope rise up inside him, and for as much as her body ached, it hurt her even more to have to say this. "If they're out there, they're not your brother and sister anymore. They're—"

"I know," he said. "But maybe—"

Colt shook her head. "It doesn't mean we won't look. We will. But I don't even know what they would be now. Mary completely hollowed them out, and now that..." She stopped and looked up. "We found them, in the house. I'm so sorry, Vincent."

Vincent stared, her words sinking slowly into him. His mouth, which had been open with excitement, closed. Turning his head, he lay back against the pillow and looked out across the tent, past the fabric, past the night sky.

He looked ahead.

"Colt?"

She glanced up. He turned, his face calm and collected, hard as stone. In that moment, he would have resembled Mary, if not for his eyes. His eyes burned with a purpose stronger than most people could ever understand and a level of humanity, which his sister never reached.

"I'm going to find them," he said.

Colt nodded. What else could she do?

He smiled. "Will you help me?"

She leaned forward and wrapped her fingers over his hand. "Sure, Kiddo."

THE END

260

About the Author:

Everything Nick DeWolf has ever written that's any good came from a dream. Clearly, he doesn't sleep well.

He's a father, a worker, a beer brewer, and cooks a half-decent stir-fry. He waited until the age of 37 to both get a tattoo, and learn to ride a bike. He loves his five kids, hates prejudice, believes in science, and sometimes gets uncomfortably excited about well prepared food.